SNOWFLAKES IN THE WIND

It's Christmas Eve 1920 when nine-year-old Abby Kirby's family is ripped apart by a terrible tragedy. Abby takes her younger brother and runs away to the tough existence of the Border farming community. Years pass. Abby becomes a beautiful young woman and falls in love, but her past haunts her, casting dark shadows. With her heart broken, Abby decides to make a new life as a nurse. When the Second World War breaks out, she volunteers as a QA nurse and is sent overseas, but becomes a prisoner of the Japanese. Abby realizes that whatever has gone before is nothing compared to what lies ahead...

SNOWFLAKES IN THE WIND

SNOWFLAKES IN THE WIND

by

Rita Bradshaw

Magna Large Print Books
Long Preston, North Yorkshire,
BD23 4ND, England.

British Library Cataloguing in Publication Data.

A catalogue record of this book is
available from the British Library

ISBN   978-0-7505-4468-9

First published in Great Britain 2016 by Macmillan

Published in Large Print 2017 by arrangement with
Macmillan Publishers International Ltd.

Magna Large Print is an imprint of Library Magna Books Ltd.

Printed and bound in Great Britain by
T.J. (International) Ltd., Cornwall, PL28 8RW

This book is dedicated to baby Dakota, and to her amazingly brave parents, Jane and Scott, and to Dakota's nanna, my dear friend, Maureen.

There are no answers to such heartache this side of heaven except trust and faith, but Dave's word from God at Dakota's funeral rings in all our hearts.

We believe, Lord.

Author's Note

Until I began my research for this story I had a general if somewhat vague understanding of the part women played in the Second World War, and much of the information concentrated on the European conflict. When I found books and other research data that focused on the women who were captured and interned in the Far East, it literally opened my eyes to a period of history that was stomach turning. Most of it was painful and horrifying to read, but one thing was paramount – through it all, women displayed a courage and resilience that puts paid to the idea that we are the weaker sex.

I decided to take the QAs (Queen Alexandra's Imperial Military Nursing Service) as the main focus, but of course alongside them stood thousands of ordinary women and children who found themselves caught up in the conflict and thrown into the Japanese camps. None of them could have expected the horrors that were to come. Raped, beaten, tortured, humiliated and treated as subhuman, both the women soldiers and civilians were extraordinarily courageous. Starvation and crippling disease were a daily burden, with violence and brutality always just round the corner. The Japanese forced some women to become sex slaves, whilst others were tortured to death by the sadistic Kempeitai, the Japanese military police.

Those who survived the death camps where so many died were scarred mentally, and sometimes physically, for the rest of their lives. This was real life in all its raw savagery and pain, and it is impossible for any story to do them credit.

When we look at white-haired pensioners – few in number now – who survived the conflict, we have no idea of what they went through, or the grit and selfless acts of extreme courage they displayed, because they rarely talk about it. As one veteran said to me, 'We just got on with it, that's all. That's what you do.'

I hope that is what we would do these days, but I wonder. In an age when we are encouraged to put self first because 'we deserve it', and have-a-go heroes are in the minority, would the modern world respond with the amazing qualities of self-reliance, self-sacrifice and sheer guts those people did? We are fortunate to have known only relative peace, after all.

However much our opinions may differ about that, I hope this story shows credit to those who perished and those who survived because I am in awe of their spirit.

Acknowledgements

I drew on research from various sources for this story, encompassing, as it does, both Border farm workers and their past way of life, and also the incredible work of the British Army nurses in the Second World War, particularly the QAs who were taken prisoner by the Japanese in the Far East.

Special help certainly deserves a mention:

A Shepherd Remembers by Andrew Purves
A Nurse in Time by Evelyn Prentis
Sisters in Arms by Nicola Tyrer
All This Hell by Evelyn M. Monahan and
  Rosemary Neidel-Greenlee
Surviving Tenko by Penny Starns
The Real Tenko by Mark Felton

Contents

PART ONE
No Going Back, 1920
17

PART TWO
The New Life, 1921
91

PART THREE
Womanhood, 1929
143

PART FOUR
Bedpans, Sluices and Lavatories, 1930
211

PART FIVE
A Divided World, 1939
295

PART SIX
When All That's Left is Hope, 1944
371

Epilogue, 1949
459

Lullaby

There's snowflakes in the wind, my bonny babby,
Snowflakes in the wind, my little lamb,
But don't you fret, don't you cry,
The sun will come out by and by,
And till then I'll keep you warm, my bonny
  babby.

PART ONE

No Going Back

1920

Chapter One

Where the hell was she? Gone eight o'clock on Christmas Eve and she wasn't home yet. Did she think he was that much of a fool? Did she?

Edgar Kirby ground his teeth, his hands gripping the wooden arms of the old armchair he was sitting in so that his knuckles showed white through the skin. The chair was one of two positioned either side of the fire in the black-leaded range in a kitchen that, although shabby, was spotlessly clean. Some effort to mark the season was evident in the paper chains criss-crossing under the ceiling, and the grate held a good fire of glowing slack and coal that the draught from the chimney kept bright. Two gas mantles on one whitewashed wall hissed and popped now and again as they shed their limited light over the room, and the smell of the pot roast in the oven was mouthwatering.

Anyone entering the kitchen would have been struck by its simple cosiness, from the thick clippy mat the armchairs stood on, to the sunshine-yellow flock cushions positioned on the battered six-foot wooden settle set against the wall opposite the fireplace.

A natural homemaker lives here, they would have thought, as their eyes took in the yellow curtains at the window in the same material as the cushion covers, and the small earthenware pot of

19

white hyacinths in the centre of the scrubbed table. Someone with the touch of making the most wretched surroundings comfortable – and certainly this terraced house, like the ones surrounding it in the tight grid of streets in the heart of Sunderland, was as poor as they come.

Edgar sat immobile for a few minutes more, staring at the fire but without seeing it. Instead his mind was full of moving pictures of Molly and the man she worked for; lewd, explicit images that burned against his eyeballs and caused a rage that brought him to his feet whereupon he started pacing the room, his hands clenched fists.

A creaking of the kitchen door brought his head swinging round to see his nine-year-old daughter standing in the doorway, her younger brother behind her. 'Is Mam home yet?'

It took all his self-control not to shout at them to get back upstairs, and his face must have revealed what he was feeling as he watched both children take an instinctive step backwards. It was this that curbed his tongue. He knew they were frightened of him or, if not exactly frightened, then certainly wary, he thought bitterly. Abby had been barely three years old when he had left in the summer of 1914 for the front, anxious to do his bit in the war 'before it was all over', and Robin a babe in arms. When he had returned from the conflict he was a stranger; to them, to Molly, even to himself. The unspeakable things he had seen and had had to do; how could you go down into the depths of hell and not be changed? And the noise, the incessant screaming shells, the mud, the blood...

Edgar jerked his mind back to the children staring at him as the roaring in his head that accompanied thoughts of the war became louder. As though it was someone else speaking, he heard himself say, 'Why aren't you asleep? Them stockings' – he nodded at the two hand-knitted red stockings hanging limply either side of the range – 'will have nowt in 'em come morning if you don't go to sleep like good bairns.'

'We wanted Mam to tuck us in.'

'Aye, well, doubtless she'll come up once she's back but she won't be best pleased if you two are still awake, now, will she? Now get yourselves to bed and no more coming downstairs, all right? I mean it, mind.'

Abby bit her lip. She wanted to say that her mam wouldn't mind if they were still up, not on Christmas Eve. It was a special night, the night when baby Jesus had been born and laid in a manger with all the animals around Him and the shepherds and wise men worshipping Him, and the star over the stable lighting up the sky. But she didn't. Her mam had told her that their da was poorly. They must always remember that, her mam had warned, and never do or say anything to trouble him. He would get better, her mam had gone on, but it would take time, and they had to be careful never to cheek him or argue, but always to do exactly as they were told and to be quiet when he was in the house. Her mam had added that last bit after one day in the summer when Robin had been jumping on his bed and had fallen off with a crash loud enough to wake the dead, and her da had scrambled under the

21

kitchen table and sat there with his hands over his ears and his eyes shut, his whole body shaking.

Abby now turned, and pushed Robin ahead of her towards the stairs. That had been the day when she had realized that her da wasn't quite … right. In the head. And from that time she had understood why her mam put up with the way he was.

At the foot of the stairs she looked back towards the kitchen door which was now shut. And she'd felt sorry for her da that day, she had, and she still did, except for when he went for her mam. Her mam was the best mam in the whole wide world and she was so kind and good, but sometimes, when she and Robin were in bed, she could hear her da going on at her mam downstairs for what seemed like hours. And once, when her mam was doing the weekly wash in the wash house in the yard with her sleeves rolled up, she'd seen big bruises on her arms. Her mam had quickly covered them up and said she'd had one of the boxes of vegetables at the shop fall on her.

Abby's full-lipped mouth tightened. But she didn't believe it was a box that had done that to her mam. Same as she didn't think her mam had walked into a door and given herself a black eye the very day after Father McKenzie had called by one evening to see her da. The priest had let slip that her mam had confided she thought her da needed help but that the doctor wouldn't have any of it, and her da had all but ordered Father McKenzie out of the house.

Abby slowly followed her brother upstairs. She had been sitting on the bottom of the stairs listening that evening, and after the priest had gone her da had ranted and raved and she had heard scuffling and sounds from inside the kitchen, and then had followed a silence broken by her da's sobs and her mother's voice, soft and soothing.

Her stomach churning, Abby followed Robin into the bedroom they shared in the two-up, two-down terrace. Her brother had already snuggled under the heaped covers on his bed on the opposite side of the room, and when a small voice came, saying, 'Will you tuck me in, Abby, like Mam does?' she walked across and did as she was asked, kissing the top of his head as she murmured, 'Go to sleep and in the morning when you wake up it'll be Christmas Day and we'll have our stockings.'

'And Christmas dinner. Mam said she was going to try an' get a duck or a turkey at the market on her way home.'

'Only if they were cheap at the end of the day, though,' Abby warned, 'so don't go getting your hopes up. It'll be a nice dinner whatever Mam does, and we've the plum pudding after, don't forget.'

'With a sixpence inside.' There was a note of awe in Robin's voice. He had watched his mother make the pudding and add the silver coin, and had said a little prayer that he would be the lucky recipient of such wealth on Christmas Day.

'Aye, with a sixpence for someone so mind you eat your bit carefully cos you don't want to break a tooth on it or swallow it.'

'I wouldn't mind if I broke me tooth if it meant

23

I got the sixpence.'

Abby smiled to herself. 'Go to sleep now,' she said softly, 'and tomorrow will come all the quicker.'

It was another ten minutes or so before Robin's steady regular breathing told her he'd dropped off, and when she was sure he was asleep, Abby sat up in her own bed which was underneath the window and then knelt and opened the curtains.

Outside was a white, cold world. It had snowed on and off since the beginning of December with the temperature rarely rising above freezing even in the day, and the snow was packed hard on the ground. The room she shared with her brother was at the back of the house and overlooked the stone-flagged yard holding their small wash house and the brick-built privy, with the back lane beyond. She breathed on the window and then scraped away at the ice which had formed on the inside of the glass in order to make a little patch where she could see out.

There was a snowflake or two blowing in the wind, and it reminded her of the lullaby her mam had sung to her and then to Robin when they were babies. Even now if they were poorly her mam would sit and sing them to sleep while she stroked their brow. Softly, she began to hum to herself and then to sing the words that always made her feel loved and safe:

'There's snowflakes in the wind, my bonny babby,
Snowflakes in the wind, my little lamb,
But don't you fret, don't you cry,
The sun will come out by and by,

And till then I'll keep you warm, my bonny babby.'

The stark chill of the room caused her to shiver after a while and she burrowed back under the blankets, glad of the thick eiderdowns her mam had bought for the two beds at the beginning of the winter. Her mam was so good, Abby thought again; she never bought anything for herself, and she never complained about the long hours she worked at the shop even although the constant being on her feet had made her varicose veins so bad.

She was still thinking of her mother when she drifted off to sleep after saying her prayers, the gist of them being that God would make her father better so that he could get a job and her mother could stay at home like she'd done when she and Robin were younger. She could remember that time, remember playing out in the back lane with the other bairns secure in the knowledge that her mam was at home and everything was right with the world.

She had been happy then, Abby thought drowsily, and her mam had been happy too, even if some weeks they had all had to sit on the stairs when the rent man had called and pretend they weren't in. She would keep awake until her mam was back so that she could tell her she loved her, she decided, and then promptly fell fast asleep.

Chapter Two

'Ee, lass, I'm sorry I've kept you so late and on Christmas Eve an' all, but it seems like everyone's left their shopping till the last minute this year. We've been rushed off our feet, haven't we?'

'We have, Mr Foster.' Molly Kirby smiled at the shopkeeper, and not for the first time she reflected that she could have worked for a lot worse than William Foster. He was a nice man and a fair and kind employer, and generous too, always slipping her the ends of the bacon or ham to take home for the bairns along with a wedge of cheese or a couple of stale loaves. Not that she could admit to Edgar that Mr Foster had given her the extras; she always made out she had paid for them. Edgar's jealousy didn't take much to fan into a red-hot flame.

William Foster looked fondly at the young woman he liked and respected. Gossip had it that her husband was something of a ne'er-do-well, and that he'd returned from war as whole as the day he had left Sunderland but that he sat on his backside all day and did nowt. Of course you couldn't altogether trust the old wives' tittle-tattle, and what they didn't know they'd make up, but he'd seen Edgar Kirby once and the man looked all right to him – no missing limbs, no scars, no signs of the gas poisoning that some poor devils had to cope with. But Molly wouldn't hear a word against him, bless her, and perhaps that was as it should be.

Reaching behind the counter, he brought out a bag of groceries, saying, 'These are some extra bits for the bairns, lass. There's some nuts and fruit and half a ham, and a box of crystallized jellies. All the bairns like them, don't they. And this' – he drew an envelope out of his white overall – 'is for you, lass, a Christmas box from me an' the wife. Buy yourself something nice, eh? You deserve it.'

Molly couldn't say anything for a moment for the lump in her throat; it wasn't just the gifts that had her fighting back tears but the way Mr Foster had spoken, so kindly and gently as if he understood how bad things were at home.

But not all the time, she corrected quickly in her mind. Sometimes Edgar reached out to her, saying that he needed her, that he didn't know what he would do without her and that he didn't know why she stayed with a mental case like him. But he wasn't mental, he just needed help, help the doctor refused to acknowledge was necessary despite her pleading with him on more than one occasion when she had gone to his surgery without Edgar knowing. Not that she would go again after the last time.

'Your husband ought to be thankful that he survived what so many did not,' Dr Graham had said coldly, when she had told him yet again about the screaming nightmares Edgar suffered most nights, the terror of loud noises, the inability to think or talk clearly at times and the blackness that enveloped him like a dark suffocating blanket. 'I'm

27

sorry to be blunt, Mrs Kirby, but he needs to pull himself together and act like a man. We could all wallow in depression and melancholy at times but we choose not to. It's an act of self-will. He has a home, wife, children – he's a lucky man.'

Molly had stared at the doctor and but for the fact that she knew he had lost his three sons at the beginning of the war in the bloodbath that had been Mons, she would have shouted that this wasn't about self-will or choice, it was about being terribly, desperately ill. But it was useless. As far as Dr Graham was concerned his sons were dead and Edgar was alive so Edgar was the lucky one. And it wasn't just the good doctor who felt this way; so many of her neighbours had lost loved ones, and she had met with closed faces and tight lips when she had tried to explain why Edgar hadn't found work and why he rarely left the house. Mrs Shawe, from three doors up, had even gone so far as to take her aside one day when they had met in the back lane and tell her that everyone thought it was a crying shame that she'd been forced to go out to work to keep a roof over their heads. 'Your man needs a good kick up the backside, lass,' Mrs Shawe had said with a self-righteous sniff. 'There's lads like my Kenneth, shipped home minus his legs and in pain every minute of the day but not a murmur of complaint or feeling sorry for himself, and there's your man as whole as the day he was born and content to sit on his backside and do nowt. I pity you, lass. I do straight.'

She had told Mrs Shawe what she could do with her pity, Molly remembered now, and they hadn't spoken from that day to this, but strangely, rather than discouraging her, the woman's attitude had made her all the more determined they would battle through this harrowing time and Edgar would get better.

'All right, lass?'

Molly came out of her reverie to find Mr Foster staring at her in concern. 'Yes, yes, I'm sorry, it's just that you are so kind and...' She couldn't go on, the tears spilling from her eyes.

'Don't take on, lass. You're tired, that's all.' Mr Foster patted her arm, somewhat embarrassed. 'Now you go home to them bairns of yours and have a grand Christmas. I'll see you Monday morning, seven o'clock sharp.'

After wiping her eyes and putting on her hat and coat, Molly said her goodbyes, thanking the shopkeeper once again and then his wife who had come down from the flat over the shop to wish her a merry Christmas.

It was now nine o'clock and the last-minute shoppers had dwindled somewhat, probably because the snow was coming down thick and heavy and the wind was raw. Stopping in a doorway a short distance from the shop, Molly opened the envelope Mr Foster had pressed into her hand. Her wage packet of ten shillings was in there, along with another ten-shilling note. A week's wages as a Christmas box, she thought gratefully. Oh, they were kind, the pair of them, and she had the bag of groceries too. It would make all the difference this Christmas. It was a constant battle to put food on the table and pay the rent, and she was always weeks behind with the latter no matter how she penny-pinched. What she would do without the extra bits that Mr Foster regularly slipped her way she didn't know. It was a life saver.

She breathed deeply of the icy air, a smile touching her lips. She could get a fine bird for tomorrow's dinner now, and a small toy each for the bairns to add to the orange and sweets and penny whistles she'd already put by for their stockings. And some tobacco for Edgar's pipe. Two ounces. No, three.

Molly set off for the old market in the East End a short distance away, her steps lighter than they had been in months, even though within a minute or two her feet were soaked through and numb with cold from the holes in her boots. She had first been introduced to the old market one Saturday night a few days after she and Edgar had got married. Edgar was a Sunderland lad, born and bred, but she was from the Borders with its hills and wide-open spaces and the old market was like nothing she had experienced before, so full of people and noise and light she'd felt she had stepped into another world. There had been boxing going on, and a stall where you had to throw footballs through holes. Duke's – at the top of the market – was a roundabout, like a fairground, and there were shops of all kinds and a stall where a giant of a man with snow-white hair had sold different kinds of sweets, next to people with barrels of nuts and raisins and hot chestnuts, and a stall that sold tripe. She had been amazed and had stood stock-still, trying to take everything in, until Edgar had laughed at the look on her face and picked her up in his arms, holding her tight as he had kissed her smack on the lips in front of everyone.

As Molly reached one of the entrances to the old market in Coronation Street, she stopped for a moment, lost in memories. That had been a wonderful day. Every day with Edgar had been wonderful until he had gone away to war. He had been thrilled when Abby was born and hadn't minded that their firstborn was a girl, unlike some of the men hereabouts. It had been he who had chosen the name Abigail, after the matron in the orphanage where he had been brought up when his parents had died of the fever when he was just three years old. Matron Riley had been one of the few people to show kindness to him in that place, he'd told Molly, and when he had reached the age of fifteen and been able to leave, she had given him a small Bible with a little card wishing him well, inscribed with her full name. He had read a passage or two from that Bible every day before he had left for the front, but now it dawned on her that he hadn't opened it since he'd returned from overseas.

As she stepped into the noise and bustle of the market Molly shrugged her shoulders, as though throwing off a physical weight. She wasn't going to think about how bad the last months had been or what the future held, not tonight. Tonight it was Christmas Eve and she had money in her pocket and two whole days at home with the bairns, Christmas Day falling on a Saturday as it did this year.

The old market had been built ninety years before as an alternative to the open-air market in

31

the town, and its brick walls and domed roof meant that it was considerably warmer than the bitterly cold night outside. As usual there were a motley collection of snotty-nosed ragamuffins gathered around the hot-potato stall and roasted-chestnut barrels, their pinched faces eyeing the shoppers as they edged as near as they dared to the warmth. Molly's hand tightened on the purse in her pocket. Children as young as five or six were sent out pickpocketing by their dissolute parents, and the East End was a cauldron of petty – and not so petty – crime. In spite of the weather several of the children had no boots on their feet, and such clothing as covered their skinny frames was in tatters.

One forlorn tiny tot caught Molly's attention. The little girl couldn't have been more than four or five and her long unkempt hair was white with nits, but in spite of the dirt and grime she had the sweetest face imaginable. Rickets had bowed her thin little legs so badly it was a wonder she could stand, let alone walk.

Everything in Molly wanted to press a penny or two into the child's hand, but she knew that would bring the rest of the children swarming like a horde of famished hornets, their hunger making them aggressive and persistent, and some of the older lads were already accomplished thieves. Nevertheless, she smiled at the little girl as she passed her, receiving a blank, hopeless stare in return.

Molly continued on, sending up a quick un-spoken prayer of thanks as she walked that her own children were warm and well fed. True, their home wasn't the happy place it had been before Edgar had come back, and Abby and Robin were creeping about like small silent ghosts half the time, but there were worse things than having to tread on eggshells.

When she reached Crawley's butcher's stall there was a crowd gathered round it. It was nearly half-past nine and the butcher always closed at ten. In the last half-an-hour of a working day, old man Crawley was well known for auctioning his remaining lap-ups – parcels of a mixture of different meat items – at knock-down prices, and for those housewives with not a ha'penny in the world who waited until he shut up shop, he always found a few meaty bones dark with congealed blood and sawdust that would make a broth of sorts. It wasn't unusual to see young urchins, bones and ham shanks stuffed up their grubby jerseys or held close in dirt-encrusted hands, making their way out of the market with big grins on their faces. And with ex-servicemen reduced to a life of street hawking by the lack of jobs and the government's Food Controller cutting rations, for some families such windfalls made all the difference between managing and the dreaded workhouse.

But tonight Molly wasn't looking for one of the lap-ups. She could see the butcher had three turkeys hanging up behind him and it was one of those she had set her heart on. Pushing her way through the waiting women with their shawls wrapped tightly round them and hungry faces, she reached the front of the crowd, catching the butcher's attention as she called out, 'How much are the turkeys?'

'The turkeys, lass? All of 'em or just one?' Mr Crawley joked, grinning at her, his rosy-red cheeks like ripe apples.

Molly was used to the stallholders' banter in the old market but she still felt herself blushing. 'Just one,' she said shyly.

'I can do you that big plump fella on the end for half a crown, seein' it's the end of the day, and I'm givin' it away at that price, I tell you, lass.' And then seeing her expression, he added, 'Or one of the smaller ones for a couple of bob.'

Molly gulped. She normally made a ninepenny lap-up feed the family for two or three days. But it *was* Christmas. 'I – I'll take one of the smaller ones, please.'

The butcher stared into the pretty face in front of him. She was a bonny lass, he thought to himself, but clearly, like most of his customers, times were hard if the look of her old boots and threadbare coat was anything to go by. Give it ten years and she'd look as old as a woman twice her age.

He reached for the large turkey. 'Tell you what, seein' it's Christmas, you can have the big beggar for a couple of bob and I'll throw in a tub of dripping for nowt. How about that?'

'Thank you, thank you very much.'

'Aye, well, like I said, it's Christmas, lass.'

By the time Molly left the old market she was carrying the turkey which Mr Crawley had parcelled up for her under one arm and the bag of goodies from William Foster in her other hand, to which had been added some tobacco and Brazilnut toffee for Edgar – his favourite – a football for Robin and a storybook for Abby. And she still

34

had nearly fifteen shillings left.

The snow was coming down thicker than ever but she barely noticed it as she made her way through the warren of streets stretching away from the market, her mind taken up with the pleasure her gifts would bring. On reaching the back lane of Hedworth Street, Molly straightened weary shoulders. It'd been a long and busy day and she was tired to the bone, but doubtless she wouldn't get a lie-in tomorrow. Robin would be up at the crack of dawn to see what was in his stocking. A small smile touched her lips. He was so excited. Abby, on the other hand, was much more subdued and quiet these days, and she knew her daughter worried about how things were at home, even though she tried to keep the worst of Edgar's disturbed behaviour from impacting on the bairns.

The new fall of snow had covered the slides the neighbourhood children had made in the back lane, causing it to become treacherous underfoot. By the time she reached her own backyard, Molly was thankful she'd made it without breaking an arm or a leg, and when she lifted the latch of the back door and stepped into the warmth of the kitchen, she sighed with relief.

It was short-lived. As soon as she took in the glowering expression on Edgar's face she knew one of his rages had him in its grip, and that it was a bad one. At these times – and she wouldn't admit it to a living soul for fear of betraying him – she recognized madness in his eyes. Not a fleeting angry madness, the sort people have when they lose their temper over something or other, but an insanity that took him over and made him into someone she couldn't reach and didn't recognize as her Edgar.

Aiming to hide her fear, she said quietly, 'Hello, love. I'm sorry I'm late but it's been non-stop all day. I'll just put these things away and then I'll dish up, shall I? The bairns asleep?'

'Left him smiling, did you?' It was a low growl.

For a moment Molly genuinely didn't understand. 'Who?'

'Your fancy man.' Edgar didn't move, sitting unnervingly still as he watched her place the shopping on the table. 'Gave him something to tide him over Christmas, did you?'

'Stop it.' She met his eyes, her face white. 'Please, Edgar, don't start on this again, not on Christmas Eve. I've been working, you know that.'

'Oh, aye, I've heard it called that a few times.'

'I work in the shop, that's all. Mr Foster is a good person and so's his wife. They're a nice couple and think the world of each other.'

'So she won't ask him what he's been doing in the shop till' – Edgar glanced at the wooden clock on the mantelpiece – 'till nigh on ten o'clock? Well, that's up to her, isn't it. But I'm asking why this "good" man didn't shut shop at seven like normal and go upstairs to his "good" wife. Like you just pointed out, it's Christmas Eve. But then no doubt he did shut shop and pull down the shutters. He'd want a bit of privacy, wouldn't he? Does he laugh about me, Molly? The man he's making a cuckold of? Told him I can't get it up since I've been back, have you?'

'I have never discussed you with Mr Foster and

I told you why I'm late – we've been rushed off our feet. And once I left the shop I went to the old market to see what I could get cheap. I'd said to the bairns I might be able to pick up a turkey or a duck for tomorrow's dinner.' Her voice had risen despite her telling herself she had to keep calm; it only made things worse when she bit back. Taking a deep breath, she said softly, 'Look at what I've got. We'll have a grand Christmas, just you an' me an' the bairns. That's all that matters to me, us and the bairns. You must know that, deep down.'

Edgar still hadn't moved, his hands gripping the arms of the chair as though he didn't trust himself to let go. 'It might have been that way once.' He raised his tortured gaze to meet her eyes. 'But not now.'

'It is, I swear it is.' Molly didn't know whether to go to him or to stay where she was. She had learned the hard way that when the blackness enveloped him like now he could lash out at the slightest provocation, real or imagined. Other times, like when he awoke shaking and sweating from a nightmare, she would cradle him to her and rock him as one would a child, soothing him with murmured words of love until he could sleep again.

The pot roast was beginning to burn, she could smell it. She hadn't realized she would be so late and it should have come out of the oven a couple of hours ago. Even more softly, she said carefully, 'Why don't I dish up and we can talk as we eat, all right? Come and sit at the table. Please, Edgar. You have to eat.' He had been gaunt and thin when he had returned from the war but over the past months she was sure he had lost even more weight.

For a moment she thought he was going to refuse but then he levered himself out of the armchair like an old, old man and walked over to the table. For the first time he seemed to become aware of the shopping she had placed there, for now his voice came harsh and suspicious as he said, 'How come you could afford all that on what he pays you?'

Molly knew if she told him about the extra ten shillings it would be a red rag to a bull, so thinking quickly, she said, 'I've been putting a penny or two into a Christmas Club each week that one of the regulars who come into the shop runs. You don't miss it that way, but come Christmas there's a bit extra for things.'

Edgar stared at her. Then his shoulders slumped. 'Aw, lass, I'm sorry, I'm sorry.'

Molly slipped off her coat and hat. She didn't ask him what he was sorry for; she'd heard enough of his ranting about her employer to know what he had been thinking. Feeling uncomfortable about the lie she'd told, she walked across to the range and opened the oven door, telling herself it was far better to stretch the truth than have another row. She was unaware that Edgar had come up behind her as she lifted the heavy cast-iron pot from the oven with a folded cloth, until he said wearily, 'I can't go on, lass. I'm losing me mind, I know I am. Half the time I think I'm back there, and the rest of it...' He cleared his throat. 'Let's face it, I'm no good as a husband or a da. I should've died out there with me mates. At least you could have remembered me as I was then.'

Molly turned to face him. 'Don't say that.'

'It's true.' His face was grey now his temper had drained away and it struck her anew just how thin be had become.

'It's not true. We're going to get through this together, I promise you.' She wanted to put the pot down so she could take him in her arms, but as she moved the lid came loose and slid forward. Instinctively she tried to save it from crashing to the floor, jerking the pot towards her, but in so doing the oven cloth slipped and her fingers came into burning contact with the red-hot iron. Her scream of pain accompanied the sound the pot made as it hit the stone flags with a deafening boom, the contents spilling everywhere.

The shells were coming thick and fast, mud and blood and body parts filling the trenches. The Germans were straight in front of them, advancing in waves, and now it was hand-to-hand combat of the most vicious kind.

He had lost his gun, damn it, but his hands were round the neck of the German trying to kill him and he squeezed with all his might, screaming as he did so. Even when they fell to the ground he didn't let go, knowing it was kill or be killed. Mud was pouring into his mouth as he yelled but he couldn't stop, he couldn't stop...

Chapter Three

'And you say the bairns were party to it all? They saw what happened?'

'No. No, I'm not sayin' that, just that when me an' Art came rushing in cos of the commotion, all the screamin' an' that, Abby – she's the eldest – was sittin' holdin' her mam's head in her lap. Pathetic it was, I'll never forget it till me dyin' day. And him, the husband, was sittin' on the floor a little way off, rockin' like a bairn an' just staring like he couldn't see you. The look on his face gave me the willies, I tell you straight.' Betty Hammond, the next-door neighbour, shivered dramatically. 'An' Robin, the little lad, he was standin' crying his heart out in the hall. I think his sister had told him to stay put.'

Constable Walton nodded as he scribbled in his notebook.

'I never want to see anythin' like that again in the whole of me life,' Betty went on. 'Even turned our Art's stomach, it did, and he was at the Somme. But like he said, war is one thing and after a time you prepare yourself for what's likely to be round the corner, but you don't expect goings-on like this on your own doorstep, do you? And young Molly was such a lovely, bonny lass. Worked her fingers to the bone, an' a better wife an' mam you couldn't wish to meet. Not like some of 'em round here who let their bairns run about with their backsides hangin' out, an' scrub their doorsteps once in a blue moon. I could tell you stories that'd make your hair curl about one or two round here.'

The constable raised his head. In his long career he had learned the only way to deal with the Betty Hammonds of the world was to stick religiously to the point. 'And you say you're happy to take the two bairns in for a day or two until we can sort something out? It being Christmas, it makes everything that bit more awkward so I have to say it'd be a great help.'

'Oh, aye, poor little lambs.' Betty nodded. 'We'll, try an' give 'em a Christmas of sorts, although I doubt there'll be much jollity now. What a time for him to do her in. Spoiled Christmas for everyone, he has, the selfish so-an'-so.'

'I doubt he was thinking of anyone else,' the constable said drily, 'and you'd be surprised the number of things we see come Christmas an' the New Year. The whiff of festivities and it seems to bring a madness in the air with some folk.'

Betty shot the policeman a sharp look. 'I don't know about that, but it was temper that caused this an' I'd say the same to anyone who asked. If he tries to pretend he's daft or somethin', don't you fall for it.'

'I'm not saying that.'

'Good.' Betty gave a self-righteous sniff and hitched up her ample bosom with her forearms. 'An' if he comes the old soldier an' tries to make out she gave him cause for what he did, you can knock that on the head an' all. I see some lassies dressed up like the dog's dinner and them with a wedding ring on their finger, but Molly wasn't like that. Her first thought was always for him and the bairns.' She shook her head. 'I can't believe this has happened, to tell you the truth. An' that poor little lass, Abby. Art had the devil of a job to get her to let go of her mam so he could take the bairn through to ours. Speakin' of the bairns, I'll get some clothes for mornin' for 'em before I go back – I don't want to come in here again.' She glanced at the two stockings hanging forlornly either side of the range. 'Never even had a chance to fill the bairns' stockings, did she?' She raised the corner of her apron and dabbed at her eyes. 'Wicked so-an'-so, to attack her like that. What's the world comin' to, I ask you? All that trouble over the water in Ireland with our lads being killed in their beds by the IRA last month – every time you pick up a paper there's more death and destruction. We thought the war was goin' to put a stop to such things but the times are gettin' worse if you ask me.'

Constable Walton didn't have the time or the inclination to discuss the state of the world with Mrs Hammond. Bringing the conversation back to the matter in hand, he said, 'Had he been in the habit of knocking her about?'

'Well, you hear things, don't you, being next door. Mind, I never saw anythin', but men like that are crafty. The lass hasn't been the same since he came back from the war, that's for sure. Frightened she was, you could see it in her face. Aye, I'd say he was handy with his fists all right an' she bore the brunt of it. Never done a day's work since he walked back in the door but he sent her out slavin', bless her.'

'Where did Mrs Kirby work?'

Betty told him, adding, 'Not right that, her workin' all hours while he sits on his backside at home, an' not a mark on him. There's plenty round here whose menfolk came back gassed or blinded or havin' lost their limbs, but Edgar Kirby is as fit as you or me.'

The constable snapped his notebook shut. 'Thank you, Mrs Hammond, that'll be all for now, but doubtless we'll be back after tomorrow.' He glanced at his watch. 'Or should I say today? In the circumstances it doesn't seem quite right to wish you a merry Christmas.'

Betty went upstairs to the children's bedroom and collected some clothes for morning, before she again joined the policeman waiting for her in the kitchen. Looking down at the remains of the pot roast congealed on the stone flags, she murmured, 'Shall I clean this up before I – go?'

'Leave it, lass. It'll be seen to.'

'What will happen to him, Edgar Kirby?' Betty lowered her voice even though it was just the two of them remaining in the house now the constable's colleagues had taken Edgar to the police cells and Molly's body to the morgue. 'It's a cut-and-dried case, isn't it? I mean, he's as guilty as sin.'

'It's not for me to say.' And then the constable lowered his voice too as he added, 'But as you say, it's a cut-and-dried case, all right. He strangled her, so...'

'It'll be a hanging job,' Betty finished for him. 'Oh, them poor bairns, them poor, poor bairns.'

43

Abby heard Mrs Hammond when she returned to the house and then the sound of murmured conversation from the kitchen. She was lying with Robin in a single bed that Shirley, the eldest daughter, had given up for them, having joined her three sisters in the other bed – a double – that the cramped room held. The Hammonds' three sons occupied the second bedroom, with their parents sleeping in the marital bed in the front room.

The doctor whom the police had called to the house had given Abby and Robin a dose of bitter-tasting medicine before he had left – 'To help you sleep, hinny,' he'd said kindly to her when she had objected – and now Robin was fast asleep, curled into her back. The powerful sedative hadn't knocked her out completely, however, but had merely added to the terrible, nightmarish panic that held her in its grip. Her mam wasn't dead, she wasn't, she wasn't, she told herself over and over again. It would all come right, it had to. She would wake up and things would be back to normal. But even through the swirling sick lethargy in her head and the dull heaviness of her body she knew she was crying for the moon.

The urge to scream and keep screaming – as she had done when Mr Hammond had prised her from her mother and carried her into his kitchen where all his children had stared at her and Robin with shocked, wide-eyed faces – was strong, and she had to bite down on her fist to prevent the sound emerging. Her mam hadn't looked like her mam, not with her bulging eyes and her red face and lolling tongue, and when she had shouted at her da to do something, he

44

had raised his head and stared at her as though she was a stranger before putting his hands over his head again like he had when he'd wedged himself under the kitchen table that time.

Mam, Mam, oh, Mam. She whimpered, before biting harder on her fist to quell the sound. She didn't want to wake Shirley and the other girls. They were all older than her – Shirley was grown up and due to get married in the spring – and with the tact of age they'd refrained from questioning her when they'd come to bed, but she had seen the avid curiosity in their faces. And one of the policemen who had come to see her in Mrs Hammond's kitchen had said he would come back to talk to her when she was feeling better, but she didn't want to talk to anyone. And she would never feel better. Tears stung her eyes and slipped down her cheeks. She wanted her mam. More than anything in the world she wanted her mam.

Please God, please let her not be dead. This is the night when Your Son came to earth as a little baby, a time of miracles, so do one now. Bring my mam back to life like You did with Lazarus in the Bible.

On and on Abby prayed, frantic, silent prayers. Outside in the snowy night a dog barked somewhere, and once she heard some late-night revellers, clearly the worse for wear, singing Christmas carols and shouting drunkenly until their voices faded into the distance, but these normal sounds weren't comforting. They only emphasized how her own world had fragmented into a thousand pieces.

At some time during the long night hours she must have fallen asleep, because the room was lighter when she opened her eyes and she could hear whispering from the double bed. Robin was still curled into the small of her back and snoring softly, and she didn't turn to face the room or move a muscle. She could hear what Shirley and her sisters were saying and she knew the terrible nightmares she'd been having were true. Her mam was dead, and her da had been taken away because he had killed her.

'...dunno what'll happen to the bairns,' one of the girls was murmuring. 'Mam said Mr Kirby's got no family and that Mrs Kirby's mam an' da fell out with her because she married him.'

'Well, you can understand why now, can't you?'

'Aye, seems they were right. I still can't believe he's done away with her and at Christmas too.'

There was silence for a moment before another whisper came: 'Reckon it'll be the workhouse for the bairns, then? Nothing else for it cos they can't stay here.'

Abby recognized Shirley's voice when a whisper came sharp and fierce: 'Don't talk about the workhouse, poor little things. It's a living death in that place.'

'I was only saying, that's all. Don't bite me head off.'

'Well, don't talk about the workhouse then, I mean it.'

The whispering went on but Abby had ceased to listen. Her and Robin did have someone, she told herself wretchedly. Their granda. True, he lived a long way away but a little while before the war had ended her mam had received word that her own mother had died and when the funeral was being held. Her mam had sat her down before they had made the journey to what her mam called 'The Borders', and had explained then, for the first time, that she and Robin had a granda and two aunties who were her mam's older sisters. It was one of them who had written, because her mam's parents had fallen out with her when she had wanted to marry someone outside the close-knit Border community.

Her da had been on his annual holiday from the steelworks and had been hiking with a group of pals, her mam had told her, when they had met by chance, and it had been love at first sight. But her parents had planned for her to marry the son of the farm steward who'd had his eye on her for some time, and had been adamant she would do as she was told. There had been a terrible row, her mam had said sadly. Awful, unforgivable things had been said. And the upshot was that when her da left to return home she went with him, and they were married within the month. And she had never regretted it.

Abby had thought it was the most romantic story she had ever heard, and had looked at her mother with new eyes, realizing for the first time just how pretty she was with her beautiful fair hair and big blue eyes. And so the three of them – her mam, her and Robin – had made the journey to the parish of Linton, in the south-east corner of Roxburghshire close to the English border, among the Cheviot foothills, for the funeral of the grandmother she and Robin had never met. It had only

47

been some seventy miles or so as the crow flies, but the trip – travelling first by a slow passenger train and then by horse and cart – had seemed a huge adventure.

Her grandfather, Abby recalled, was a tall man with a stern, weather-beaten face and keen blue eyes below a shock of snow-white hair. He'd barely spoken two words to her mother even though they had stayed two nights in his cottage.

Her grandfather's home had been a disappointment. Whenever she had heard the word cottage, it had conjured up a picture of a pretty thatched dwelling with roses round the door and a bright garden full of hollyhocks and Michaelmas daisies, like she'd seen on the chocolate boxes in the sweet-shop window. Her grandfather's house couldn't have been more different. The slate-roofed, brick-built building was joined to that of the farm steward's home, semi-detached style, and the pair had stood some distance from the farmhouse and farmyard, to the back of which stretched a row of labourers' terraced houses. According to her mother this separateness carried some prestige, but Abby had been disillusioned with the outward ugliness of her mother's old home.

On stepping through the front door, she'd found the downstairs of the cottage to be one big room divided only by the staircase in the middle of it; a big kitchen on one side and a sitting room on the other. Upstairs were three bedrooms. There were no gardens at the front of the building, but at the back each home had a long narrow strip of land about seventy yards long, and divided by a brick wall, for growing vegetables. At the bottom of this each garden had its own privy. She had been horrified that the privy was so far away, but her mother had pointed out that the distance kept away bad smells in the summer months.

The creaking of bed springs and the sound of hushed activity cut into Abby's thoughts. The girls were getting up. She lay tense and still, silently willing her brother not to wake until she was sure they had gone downstairs, and then carefully sat up. The dull half-light of dawn filtered into the room through the thin curtains at the window and it was bitterly cold. She brought her knees up to her chin and sat with her arms round them, her long, silver-blonde hair falling in a curtain as she lowered her head.

What was she going to do? Panic and fear took over again, catching her breath and pressing down on her chest. She couldn't let them take her and Robin to the workhouse. She had heard enough tales about that terrible place to know that if they were transported into its grim confines, she and Robin would be separated and it could be years, if ever, before they saw each other again. And her mam would expect her to look after Robin, she knew that.

Abby bit down on her bottom lip to stop herself crying. Tears would help no one, she told herself desperately. She had to *think*.

If she told the constable or someone in authority about her granda and they contacted him and he wouldn't take them, then that would be that. And she couldn't say with any certainty he would want to give them a home. She pictured his hard face and piercing eyes, and shivered. But it was him or the workhouse.

The more she sat and thought, the more she began to think that she and Robin had to turn up on her grandfather's doorstep to have any hope at all that he would take them in. And even then he might see to it that they were shipped back to Sunderland. But she had to try. It would be too easy for him to refuse them if they weren't standing before him in person. But how would they get to the Borders and the village of Linton? It was impossible. She had no money for a start, and she couldn't remember her grandfather's name or the name of the farm where he worked.

It was another hour before Shirley poked her head round the bedroom door just as Robin was beginning to stir. She dumped some clothes on the bottom of the bed as she said, 'These are your things that Mam got last night. If there's anything else you need she'll get it later after breakfast, all right?'

She smiled at Abby, but for the life of her Abby couldn't dredge up a smile in return.

Robin sat up in bed rubbing his, eyes and her brother's first words told Abby he hadn't understood what had happened the night before. 'Is Mam better now? Are we going back home?'

The two girls exchanged a glance before Shirley said hastily, 'I'll see you downstairs when you've got dressed, all right?' and with that she disappeared, shutting the door behind her.

Abby turned to her brother. She had been nearly two and a half years old when he had been born on an icy December day and from the moment she had seen his red, screwed-up little face she had loved him. With the war and then her mam working long hours, she had taken on the role of a second mother rather than a sister and now she took him in her arms, cradling him as a mother might do when she said softly, 'We can't go back home, Robin. Not ever.'

'Why?'

'Mam isn't coming back. She's in heaven.'

He struggled away from her, his face crumpling. 'No, she's not. She's not. You're lying. An' what about Da?'

She knew she had no choice but to tell him everything.

Robin listened without interrupting, biting down on the fist he'd got to his mouth as he tried to stem his tears. It was only when Abby tried to take the small taut body in her arms that he exploded in a storm of tears and screaming, but then after a few moments he collapsed against her, holding her so tightly it hurt.

It took a while to calm him down, but then after persuading him to get dressed, Abby caught his arm before they went downstairs and brought him to face her. 'Da's not a bad man,' she whispered, 'whatever people might say. He's ill, Mam said so now, didn't she? The war did things to his mind, things you can't see on the outside but they are there, sure enough. Look at how he was when you fell off your bed that time.'

Robin stared at her. 'He didn't have to do that to Mam, though, did he. She never did anything wrong. I hate him.'

'Don't say that.'

'It's true, I hate him. I wish he was dead and

51

Mam was alive. We were all right before he came home and everything changed.'

For once Abby didn't know how to help him, partly because she was fighting feeling the same way. And yet the pain of her turmoil and grief was tempered by the terrible lost look on her father's face when she had walked into the horrific scene in the kitchen. At first he hadn't seemed to know where he was or what he had done. He *was* ill, she told herself for the umpteenth time. This wasn't his fault.

'If you really loved Mam you would hate him too.' Robin's voice was fierce but choked with the tears he was holding at bay.

Abby stared at her brother sadly. It was no use talking about this now, she could see that. She opened the bedroom door. 'Come on, we'd better go down,' she said quietly, wondering how she was going to get through the day.

Chapter Four

The murder was the talk of the town and the newspapers made the most of it, happy to concentrate on something other than the state of the country which was becoming less and less 'A Land Fit for Heroes' as unemployment began to rise and rationing restricted food supplies. Folk wanted to hear about poor souls who were in a worse position than they were, taking comfort from it even as they expressed their shock and horror at such goings-on.

Constable Walton, along with his inspector, returned to talk to Abby on Boxing Day, writing down everything she said whilst keeping a studiously blank face and refusing her request that she be allowed to see her father. She pleaded his case, saying that he was ill and had been since he had returned from the war, but even as she spoke she could see her words were falling on deaf ears.

'We have to deal in facts, hinny,' Constable Walton said quietly, 'and according to Dr Graham your father is fit and well.' He paused. 'Did he often lose his temper with your mam, Abigail?'

She stared at the two policemen. They were trying to catch her out and make her say things, about her father. 'No.'

'Or with you and your brother?'

'My da never lost his temper, not in the way you mean.'

'And what way is that?'

She couldn't find the words to express herself. After a few moments, she murmured, 'He's ill, I told you. My mam knew he was ill and she tried to get help for him but no one would listen to her. What ... what happened isn't my da's fault.'

The questioning had gone on for a little while, and afterwards Abby felt tired, and sick in the pit of her stomach. No one was listening to her. They'd all made up their minds that her da was bad, even Mr and Mrs Hammond. She could read it in their faces.

Two days later Constable Walton returned, this time to talk privately to Betty Hammond. Mr

Hammond and his sons and the three older girls were at work, leaving at home only the youngest daughter who was due to leave school in the summer, and Abby and Robin. After shooing the three of them out into the back lane, Betty remained ensconced in the kitchen with the constable for some time.

Hannah joined a couple of the older girls who were her cronies. They were looking after younger brothers and sisters who were playing on a long slide they'd made in the lane, much to the annoyance of the neighbourhood grown-ups who'd come to grief on it more than once. Within moments Hannah and her pals were whispering avidly, glancing over their shoulders now and again to where Abby and Robin were standing by the backyard gate. Abby knew they were talking about them and what had happened, and it added to her misery and despair.

The air was raw, cutting her throat like a knife, and her feet in her old boots were blocks of ice within minutes. She made no effort to keep warm as some of the children were doing, however, by jumping up and down or stamping their feet. She noticed Robin glancing at the group playing on the slide, and said quietly, 'Go and have a play for a bit. Ivor's over there, look. And Tim. Go on, Robin.'

He shook his head. He'd remained so close to her since Christmas Eve he could have been attached by a piece of rope. Abby didn't press him, her mind chewing over the problem of finding her grandfather. She was in no doubt whatsoever that the constable's visit meant time was running out

54

and the spectre of the workhouse was looming ever closer. And this feeling was strengthened when, on being allowed back into the house after Constable Walton had left, she asked Mrs Hammond point blank what he had wanted.

'Nothin' for you to worry about, hinny,' had been her answer. But Mrs Hammond hadn't met her gaze.

And later that evening, once everyone was home and the kitchen was a hubbub of chatter, she had seen Mrs Hammond murmur something to Shirley. Abby had been blessed with particularly keen hearing, and she had heard Shirley's response of, 'Poor little devils! Oh, Mam, can't somewhere else be found?' before Mrs Hammond had shushed her daughter.

Now it was past midnight and the house was in darkness. Abby had lain awake for hours, but for the first time since Christmas Eve her mind was clear and she knew exactly what she was going to do. And the first step was terrifying. She had to go back into the house she'd always known as home, back into the kitchen where she had found her mother, and everything in her recoiled from the prospect.

Only the knowledge that there was no other option had her sliding silently out of bed and dressing in the icy darkness. If she and Robin had any chance at all of escape, they would need enough money to see them on their way. She had no idea what train tickets cost, but if there were any coins in the little pot where her mother had kept the rent money, it would be a start.

Carrying her boots in one hand she tiptoed out

of the room and down the stairs, mindful of Mr and Mrs Hammond asleep in the front room as she reached the hall. Once in the kitchen, she pulled on her boots and then her coat, her heart thudding fit to burst. Slipping the bolt on the back door she opened it slowly, hoping it wouldn't creak.

It was snowing heavily, the big fat flakes being whirled in a frenzied dance by the raw north-east wind. Picking her way carefully and mindful of the ice the new fall of snow was covering, Abby made her way out of the Hammonds' yard and into her own. As she approached the house in the dark silent night a fear settled on her, the memory of how her mother had looked in death causing her mouth to become dry with terror. She wanted to remember her mam as she had been before that night, but try as she might, she couldn't.

After standing for some moments outside the back door, she nerved herself to lift the latch only to find the door was locked.

Of course it would be, she chided herself. The constable would have made sure the house was secure – that was what the police did. Retracing her steps she opened the door of the privy and felt in the darkness for the spare key, praying with all her might it would still be in its hiding-place. When her fingers closed over it she felt weak at the knees, whether from relief or the knowledge that there was now nothing stopping her from entering the house she wasn't sure.

It took all her willpower to insert the key into the lock and open the door, and when it swung open she stood for long moments before she could force her legs to carry her into the kitchen.

The white world outside the window provided the faintest of illumination inside the house, but it was enough for her to grope her way to where her mother had kept a small stock of candles for emergencies. After she'd lit one, the flickering flame proved to be even more frightening than the darkness, sending grotesque moving shadows into every corner of the room.

Telling herself she didn't believe in ghosts and goblins, she found her eyes drawn to the spot where her mother had fallen. Someone had cleared up the remains of the pot roast and the pan was nowhere to be seen; everything was clean and orderly.

Abby's gaze moved to the pot of white hyacinths in the middle of the table. They were drooping, their sweetly scented blooms dying and their stems bent over for lack of water. On one of the rare occasions when her da left the house he had bought the hyacinths, then just bulbs in the pot, for her mam with his tobacco money. Her mam had been so thrilled when she had come in from work that day. That had been a nice evening, a lovely one.

Swallowing hard against the lump in her throat, Abby made herself walk over to the range. Apart from every Sunday morning when she and her mother raked out the warm ashes and black-leaded the range from top to bottom, she couldn't ever remember it without a fire burning in the open grate. But the range was cold and dead. She looked round the kitchen. It was familiar and yet not familiar; without her mam it was no longer home.

On her tiptoes, she reached up to the wooden mantelpiece above the range where the pot holding the rent money stood, beside the big kitchen clock. There was a chink of coins as she lifted it down and inside were a sixpence and two shillings. Momentarily her heavy heart lifted. It was something.

Putting the coins into her pocket, she replaced the pot exactly where it had been and then lifted the candle in its metal holder which she'd placed in the middle of the table. She had to go upstairs and fetch the remainder of her and Robin's clothes; they would need them. So scared that her stomach was swirling and making her feel in dire need of the privy, Abby crept into the hall. Once upstairs in the room she and her brother had shared, she stripped the pillowcase off her pillow and filled it with the few clothes she and Robin possessed. Her breath coming in jerky gasps, she left the room, only to stand hesitating on the landing as she looked towards the closed door of her parents' bedroom. For a moment she could believe that they were in there, sleeping, and that this was all a nightmare she'd had. But it wasn't.

Tears streaming down her cheeks, she retraced her steps to the kitchen, but just as she was about to blow out the candle she caught sight of her mother's hat and coat lying across one of the kitchen chairs. Putting the pillowcase and the candle on the table, she walked across and lifted the coat to her, burying her face in its folds as she tried to smother her sobs. She would never see her mam again, never be able to touch her and be held by her, never have her mam's arms keeping her safe. It was too much to bear...

How long the storm of grief lasted she didn't know, but at the end of it she found herself sitting in a huddle on the floor with the coat held against her heart. Wearily she lifted her head and forced herself to get to her feet, so spent she felt that if she were to die right at that moment she wouldn't care.

It was as she tenderly folded the coat back on the chair that an image of the kitchen table strewn with groceries and other bits and pieces came into her mind. The table was devoid of them now and presumably they'd been disposed of, but it reminded her that Christmas Eve had been a pay day for her mother.

It felt wrong to feel in the pockets of her mother's coat for her purse, and when her fingers closed over it, even more wrong to take it out and open it. Telling herself not to be so silly and that her mam would approve of what she was doing, Abby tipped the contents of the worn leather purse onto the kitchen table: A number of coins rolled out but it was the folded ten-shilling note that brought her eyes opening wide.

Her hands trembling, Abby added the two shillings and sixpence from her pocket to the money on the table and counted up. Seventeen and six. She breathed out slowly. *Seventeen shillings and sixpence!* It was a small fortune. They could go and find their grandfather now.

She gathered up the coins and note and returned them to the purse, stuffing it in the pocket of her white pinafore. A sudden feeling of panic that someone would find her here and demand to know what she was doing and confiscate the purse had her heart racing. Quickly blowing out the candle, she returned it to its box at the bottom of a cupboard and let herself out of the back door, locking it and replacing the key in the privy.

It was still snowing heavily, her earlier footsteps already obscured which was all to the good. Entering the Hammonds' backyard, she was vitally conscious of the purse in the pocket of her pinafore, and when she stealthily opened the back door she bent and took off her boots so as not to make a sound. On straightening up, she found herself staring straight into the eyes of Shirley Hammond.

Shock brought her hands over her mouth to stifle the scream she'd almost let out, and it was Shirley who whispered, 'Where on earth have you been? And don't say the privy cos I just went there myself. I woke up a little while ago and realized you weren't in bed and thought you'd been took bad, so I came to check. What have you been doing?'

Abby stared at her, unable to think of a thing to say.

'Why are you dressed?' Shirley went on. 'It's snowing a blizzard out there and it's not the night for a little walk. Come on, spit it out else I'll call Mam.'

'No, don't.' The threat brought Abby back to life. 'I – I went next door, that's all.'

'To your house?'

Abby nodded.

'Why?' Shirley stared at her in amazement. It

was the last place she would have expected Abby to venture in view of what had happened, and she, for one, wouldn't have wanted to go in broad daylight let alone in the middle of the night.

'I – I wanted to see...'

'What? What did you want to see?' Shirley pressed.

Abby's shoulders slumped. 'I know they want to put us in the workhouse, me and Robin. They do, don't they?' Without waiting for confirmation, she went on, 'And I can't let that happen. I went to see if there was any rent money I could use to go and see my grandfather.'

'Your grandfather?' Shirley took Abby's arm, leading her to one of the kitchen chairs and pushing her down on it before she pulled one out for herself and sat facing her. 'All right,' she said softly. 'Start from the beginning and tell me.'

Abby started from the beginning as she knew it, explaining about the trip she and her mother and Robin had taken when her grandmother had died, and finishing with the fact that she felt she and Robin had to present themselves in front of her mother's father to have any chance of him agreeing that they could stay. 'He was still angry with my mam,' she murmured miserably, 'but I know if I can see him and explain what's happened, he'll take us in.' She didn't know, but felt it appropriate to say in the circumstances.

'And you don't think he'd do that if he was notified by the authorities properly?' Shirley whispered.

'I don't know.' Abby's bottom lip trembled. 'My mam said him still being angry with her was a

61

matter of pride. She said my grandfather's people are a law unto themselves and unless you're one of them you wouldn't understand. Even the way they name their bairns is handed down. My mam's eldest sister was named after her mam's mother, the second girl after her father's mother and my mam after her mother and so on. Same with the lads 'cept the eldest son is named after the father's father, but my grandparents didn't have any boys, just girls. My mam said you can trace a person's place in the family by his or her name and antecedents. Family is everything to them so when my mam ran off with my da...'

'She committed the unforgivable sin,' Shirley finished thoughtfully. 'Aye, I see. And he wouldn't want to lose face. Whereas if you and Robin are standing there in front of him pleading your case... But what would you do if he won't give you a home?'

'I suppose that wouldn't be up to us. He'd see to it the authorities were notified. But I know he'll take us in if I talk to him, Shirley. I know he will.'

Shirley didn't know what to think. 'I'll say one thing,' she murmured, 'you're a plucky little lass. How did you think you were going to travel to... Where is it? Linton, you say?'

Abby nodded. 'It's near Kelso. I remember my mam saying that. Kelso's a town but Linton is tiny. I can only remember a school and smithy and the mill house and the farms.' She took a deep breath. 'Please, Shirley, don't say anythin' to your mam.'

Shirley looked into the young face. Abby was

62

lovely, she had always thought it. The child's skin was as smooth as satin and her eyes were unlike any Shirley had seen. Large and heavily lashed, their colour was a mercurial blue-grey, seeming to change with the child's emotions, but it was Abby's hair that picked her out from the other bairns. The silver-blonde fairness was unusual in itself, but when added to the fact that it was thick and gleamed like raw silk it made the child unique in these parts. Abby's mother had been pretty but Abby was beautiful, and she was a nice little lass, that was the thing. How would she fare in the workhouse? She'd carry the stigma all her life and you heard such awful stories about the place; Shirley found she couldn't bear the thought of such innocent loveliness being crushed and trampled underfoot. There was more to being alive than being housed and fed.

Impulsively, Shirley said, 'You know my Len works for the railway?'

Abby shook her head. She had no idea how Shirley's fiancé earned his living.

'Well, he does.' Shirley took one of Abby's small cold hands between her warm ones as she leaned forward. 'If I ask him, he'll help us.'

Abby's heart gave a great leap. Shirley would never know how much the 'us' meant when she had been feeling so lost and alone. 'You ... you won't tell your mam about us getting away?'

'Only after the two of you are on your way. I'll have to tell her then as she'd be worried.' Shirley didn't dwell on what her mother would say; there would be an almighty row, that was for sure. 'And even then I won't let on exactly where you're going, but if it all works out will you write and let Mam know you're safe?'

Abby nodded eagerly, 'Thank you, thank you so much.'

'I'll talk to Len tomorrow.' Shirley paused. Her mother had told her that the police had arranged with the Board of Guardians that Abby and Robin were to be admitted into the workhouse the following week, before the schools opened again after the Christmas holiday. The police would have taken them earlier but for her mam saying there was no rush and that the children could stay to see the New Year in with the family. Shirley knew her mother felt bad about Abby and Robin ending up in the workhouse and she hoped that would temper her mother's reaction when she admitted her part in getting the bairns away. 'Have you got everything you need to leave now?'

Again Abby nodded. 'I've got our clothes in there,' she said, pointing to the pillowcase at her feet. 'Will seventeen shillings and sixpence be enough money for the train tickets?'

'Don't worry about that.' The cost of the tickets was the least of it, Shirley thought soberly, as the enormity of what she was going to do swept over her. If this went wrong there'd be the devil to pay. 'Now let's get to bed and we'll see what Len says, all right? And don't say anything to Robin, not yet.'

'No, no, I won't, he's only a bairn,' Abby said, as though she was an adult herself.

Shirley smiled but Abby's words added to her misgivings. The lass was only nine years old and here she was, aiding and abetting Abby's harebrained scheme to travel upcountry to find a grandfather who'd expressed no desire to have anything to do with his grandchildren. Whatever was Len going to say?

Len said plenty, and by the time he had finished Shirley was near to tears. It was only then that Len took her in his arms and murmured, 'Come on, come on, I'm just thinking of the trouble you are liable to find yourself in if this goes belly-up.'

Shirley sniffed, nestling her head under Len's chin as she put her arms round his waist. 'Imagine if it was your Elsie facing the workhouse,' she said softly. Len's baby sister was the same age as Abby and Len doted on her, the rest of his siblings being brothers. 'Wouldn't you want someone to help her?'

Above her head, Len smiled wryly. Shirley knew which buttons to press, he thought ruefully. 'Aye, I would.' He moved her to arm's length, keeping hold of her. 'And I tell you now I want me head testing for agreeing to this.'

Shirley grinned, throwing her arms round his neck. 'I love you, Leonard Bell.'

'Aye, an' you can cut out the soft soap an' all.'

Shirley's smile widened. She had lain awake the rest of the night after she had talked to Abby, worrying that Len would come down on the side of law and reason and refuse to be part of what was a risky venture at best. But with Len on board suddenly it was doable.

Shirley was telling herself this selfsame thing three days later as she stood with Abby and Robin on the platform of Sunderland's Central station. It was the last day of December, New Year's Eve, and all over the town housewives were baking for the evening's festivities when they invited neighbours and friends in for some jollification. Then, on the last stroke of midnight, one of their number would hammer on the door of the house holding a piece of coal in one hand and a bottle in the other, giving it their blessing as 'first foot' as they entered. Betty Hammond always made a big thing of New Year's Eve, and Shirley was hoping her mother's busyness would delay her noticing Abby and Robin's absence.

She sighed silently as she glanced down at the two children, one on either side of her. At this moment they were supposed to be playing in the back lane with some of the other bairns, but Abby and Robin had slipped away once no one was looking to meet her at the end of the street before the three of them had made their way to the train station. For her part she was going to plead a stomach upset as her excuse for being late into work that morning, but she didn't doubt that Miss Vickers, the supervisor at the laundry where she was employed, would be less than pleased. Tongue on her like cheese wire, had Miss Vickers.

Shirley passed the cloth bag she was holding, which contained the children's spare clothes, to Abby, saying, 'Here's your things.' She often took a few bits and pieces to the laundry to wash and press in her lunch hour – it was one of the perks of the job – so no one at home had passed comment when she'd left that morning with the bulging bag. Delving into her handbag, she then brought out the two tickets that Len had bought for the children. 'And here's your tickets. Now Len's had a word with the conductor, Mr Irvin, and asked him to keep an eye on you, all right? You're travelling up the coast till you get to Tweedmouth and then you change trains, but Mr Irvin will see to all that. And here's some sandwiches and a bottle of pop for the journey. Make them last, won't you,' she added to Robin who had eyed the sandwiches appreciatively.

'Thank you.' Abby's voice was small; standing here in the busy station she felt overwhelmed by the size of it and what she had embarked on. Over the last days she had asked several times to see her father but to no avail; now she felt she would never see him again. And she had wanted to tell him she didn't believe he had meant to hurt her mam. She kept remembering that day when he had sat huddled under the kitchen table after Robin had fallen off his bed upstairs. Her da hadn't known where he was or what he was doing, and he'd had the same look on his face when she had found him and her mam on Christmas Eve. She shuddered at the memory.

'Cold?' Shirley had noticed her shiver.

Abby shook her head, reaching into her pocket and bringing out her mother's purse. 'How much do I owe Len for the tickets?'

'Don't worry about that, it's all seen to.' Shirley didn't add here that if things went wrong Abby would need every penny she had. Instead she said gently, 'When you change trains at Tweedmouth, Mr Irvin won't be with you any more. Len says you have to count seven stations before

Kelso, and then it's the station after Kelso that's the nearest to Linton. All right? Can you remember that? Ask the stationmaster to direct you to the farm where your grandfather works. There might be a horse and cart or something going that way.'

They could hear the rumbling of the train now as it approached and then there it was, in a great belch of steam and noise. The last time Abby had stood in this station with her mother and Robin when they had been setting off for her grandmother's funeral it had seemed an exciting adventure. Now it was just terrifying, the more so because she didn't know the name of the farm where her grandfather was shepherd, or even his surname. But she hadn't admitted that to Shirley.

Aware that Shirley was staring at her anxiously, Abby made herself smile. 'We'll be fine,' she said with a confidence she was far from feeling. 'Please don't worry. I'll write as soon as I can and let you know how things are.'

The goodbye between the two girls was tearful, although Robin was all agog at the gleaming steaming monster of a train and seemed unaware he was leaving everything that was familiar.

And then Mr Irvin, a fussy, bespectacled, bald gentleman, appeared at their side and bundled Abby and Robin unceremoniously into a third-class carriage that was already half full. They perched on the hard wooden seats nearest the window to wave to Shirley as the whistle blew and a cloud of steam wafted down the platform. Then they were moving, the great metal beast trundling slowly at first and then quickly gathering pace, its belly sending billows of smoke that obscured Shirley from view and brought a panic into Abby's chest that made her feel sick.

'All right, hinny?'

She must have looked as frantic as she felt because a motherly matron opposite her – who had produced a knitting bag even before the train had left the station and was now busily clacking away on her wooden needles – was smiling kindly at her. Abby nodded; she couldn't reply just at that moment.

'You two bairns travelling by yourselves?' It was said with an element of disapproval.

Again Abby nodded, and it was Robin who said, 'We're going to see our granda.'

'Oh, aye? Where's he live then?'

Abby pulled herself together. 'On a farm in the Borders.'

The woman's bushy eyebrows rose. 'Quite a journey in front of you. Where's your mam an' da?'

Abby stared at the woman. She was just like old Mrs Tollett at the end of their street, she thought. Her mam had always said Mrs Tollett wanted to know the ins and outs of old Maggie's backside and not to talk to her. A stiffness in her voice now, she said shortly, 'Our mam's passed away – that's why we're going to our granda's.' Turning her head she pretended an interest in the view outside the window, breathing a sigh of relief when the woman left the train at the next station. Despite her anxiety, Abby found the interest became a reality as the train chugged laboriously on in its journey up the coast.

The snow-covered landscape dotted with towns

and villages and tiny hamlets was enthralling, and Robin remained glued to his window the whole time. Abby had never heard of the names on most of the painted station signs they encountered after leaving Sunderland and then the Tynemouth area. Pretty little stationmaster houses with picket fences marked some of the stops, whilst others were more utilitarian. Names like Widdrington, Chevington, Warkworth and Little Mill passed by, passengers alighting and others climbing aboard.

After some time, Robin declared he was *starving,* and so they ate half the sandwiches Shirley had thoughtfully packed for them. Abby decided to leave the rest in the bag – just 'in case'. In case of what, she didn't let herself dwell on.

At the next station, a place called Goswick, Mr Irvin came to their carriage window and told them Tweedmouth was the next station but one and to prepare themselves to leave the train. He would direct them to the right platform and buy their tickets with money Len had given him, he said quietly, and then the train would take them inland to their eventual destination.

Abby thanked him with more aplomb than she was feeling. She had to give the appearance of being in control, she told herself once the train was moving again. For Robin's sake as much as anything. He needed her to be strong.

Once they reached Tweedmouth, Mr Irvin was as good as his word. After handing Abby the tickets and telling them the train would arrive shortly, he left them sitting on a wooden bench. This station was busier than most of the ones they had seen en route, and as the hustle and bustle ebbed and flowed around their little bench, Abby racked her brains, trying to dredge up from the depths of her memory anything that might help them in the hours ahead. She thought back to the previous journey with her mother. When the three of them had left the train station, her mother had told them they had to put their best foot forward to walk to the farm, but what had she called it? She shut her eyes, picturing the scene.

Suddenly the name Crab Apple popped into her mind. Crab Apple Farm. She frowned to herself; had she actually remembered it or had she made it up? She couldn't be sure but, nevertheless, a glimmer of hope lifted her spirits.

Boarding the next train was more of an ordeal without the kindly Mr Irvin smoothing their way, and when an enormously fat, red-cheeked man carrying a sack of flour almost knocked Robin off his feet, Abby said very loudly, 'Excuse *me!*', grabbing hold of her brother's arm to right him.

After looking surprised, the man grinned and then bowed slightly, waving his hand for the pair of them to climb on board ahead of him. Maintaining her air of dignity, Abby ushered her brother in front of her and they sat together in a corner of the carriage, the cloth bag on Abby's lap. Within a few minutes they were on their way once more.

It was now early afternoon, and as the train chugged onwards the view outside the windows showed the emptiness of barren fields and bare trees, crows gliding like shadowed ghouls above the snowy countryside. Mindful of Shirley's instructions, Abby counted each station with one part of her mind; the other part was thinking how bleak and desolate everything was. It had been spring when they had made the previous journey and Nature, with the artistry of a great conductor, had been orchestrating the magic of new life. Swathes of blossom and unfolding green leaves had adorned the trees and hedgerows, and wild flowers had painted the landscape. Abby recalled that the sky had been a bright cornflower blue with cotton-wool clouds; today it was hanging sullen and heavy, carrying the promise of more snow before long, only fleeting wisps of silver, tingeing the greyness now and again. In Sunderland the only view of the sky was mostly confined to the narrow strips above the terraced streets, and now the great wide expanse seemed menacing and unfriendly.

Abby checked her thoughts. She was being silly, she told herself firmly. The sky was just the sky, that's all. She had more than enough problems to contend with without inventing more.

Kelso turned out to be a large station but the next one, Roxburgh, where Abby and Robin alighted onto an almost deserted platform, was considerably smaller. There was no sign of the stationmaster and Abby found herself praying that Len had known what he was talking about and that they were in the right area. Two other passengers, a man and a woman, had got off the train in front of them, and now Abby took Robin's hand as she tried to give the impression that she knew what she was doing as the two of them followed the couple out of the station. The pair in front were clearly being met by a youth who was sitting waiting for them on a horse and cart; otherwise the country lane outside the train station was empty. To make matters worse, big fat flakes of snow were beginning to fall.

Abby waited for the couple to climb up into the cart and seat themselves beside the young man before she approached them, Robin at her side. She had to ask directions; she had no idea if they should even turn left or right.

'Yes, lass?' It was the woman who spoke as she eyed them up and down, but not unkindly.

'I ... I'm sorry to bother you but I wondered if you could direct us to Linton?' Abby hoped she looked more confident than she felt.

'Linton, is it?' The woman turned her head and glanced at the man. 'The bairns are going to Linton.'

The man's eyes narrowed as he surveyed the two-bit bairns, as he had termed Abby and Robin in his mind. There was nothing much at Linton; it was a parish without a village, the original hamlet having disappeared during the agricultural improvements long before he was born. All that remained was the kirk, the mill house, the school and the smith and joiner's shop, and they were in three separate clusters about half a mile apart. There were farms, of course, and common to the locality they all had steep fields and stony ground, but there was a treacherous bog that formed part of an ancient lake and was dangerous to the unwary. He wouldn't like to see these two little 'uns venturing near that. He bent slightly forward as he said, 'Where exactly in Linton are you bound, lass? A farm, is it?'

73

Abby nodded. Hoping she had remembered correctly, she said, 'Crab Apple Farm. Our granda is the shepherd there.'

'Is he, by gum? Wilbert Craggs is your granda?' Unbeknown to Abby, the shepherds wielded a great deal of power on Border farms and commanded respect. This was reflected in the man's voice. The sheep were the linchpin of the farming practice, and the farm work and crop rotation revolved around them. A good shepherd was worth his weight in gold, and Wilbert Craggs was a very good shepherd. 'I own the farm adjoining the boundary of Crab Apple,' the man said. 'Farmer Dodds's the name.'

Craggs. That name was familiar now that Farmer Dodds had said it. Abby's knees went weak with relief. She remembered her grandfather being referred to as Mr Craggs at her grandmother's funeral. Crab Apple Farm *was* the right place.

Farmer Dodds was frowning. 'Frankly, lass, it surprises me that your granda's not here to meet you. It's nigh on four miles as the crow flies to Crab Apple.'

'He didn't know we were coming today,' Abby said hastily, stretching the truth when she added, 'We ... we had to come earlier than planned. Our mam' – she took a deep breath, it was still hard to say out loud – 'our mam died suddenly.' And to pre-empt the inevitable, she said quietly, 'And our da's been took bad too and he can't look after us.'

'Oh, dear.' Farmer Dodds's wife looked horrified. 'You're Molly's bairns, aren't you? And she's died? Oh, the poor, poor lass.'

Abby wasn't surprised the farmer and his wife knew her mother, and had put two and two together when she said that Wilbert Craggs was her granda. Her mother had told her that the Border community was such a tightly knit one that if someone sneezed ten miles away, everyone knew about it. All the folk hereabouts would have known about her mam running off with her da.

'Well, hinny, we can't have the pair of you standing here, can we,' Mrs Dodds said briskly. 'You nip up on the back of the cart and sit on them sacks there, and we'll drop you off at the bottom of the track leading to Crab Apple. This is not the weather for gallivanting about the countryside.'

Abby drew in a shuddering breath. They'd done it. They'd found the farm and her granda. Now all she had to do was to convince him to let them stay.

Chapter Five

Wilbert Craggs sat staring into the crackling flames of the fire, his big gnarled hands resting on the worn knees of his old tweed trousers as he puffed on his pipe, a steaming mug of black strong tea at his side. An observer might have been forgiven for thinking that his stance was one of contentment, but they would have been wrong. His temper was simmering.

After a moment Wilbert's gaze shifted to the picture above the mahogany mantelpiece. The beautifully embroidered scene of poppies and cornflowers and other wild blooms in a meadow had a Bible verse in a heart in the centre: 'The grass withereth, the flower fadeth, but the word of our God shall stand for ever. Isaiah 40, verse 8.'

His Moll had sewn that in the first years of their marriage, he thought painfully. After the day's work was done, she had sat opposite him across the hearth and worked on the picture, each small flower a work of art. Their Bertha had come along after ten months of being wed, and for a while Moll hadn't had a minute to herself, but then once the babby was going through the night and she had her evenings free, out had come her embroidery. It had taken her nigh on three years to complete the picture, just before their second daughter had been born, and he had framed it himself, hanging it with pride over the mantelpiece. His Moll had been the best of women. The very best.

Wilbert stood up abruptly, beginning to pace the sitting room for a minute or two before coming to stand with his back to the fireplace, his legs slightly apart. What would Moll say to this latest confrontation with Andrew McHaffie? But then why ask the road you know? Moll had always shied away from any kind of conflict. He shook his shaggy head. But at the bottom of her, Moll must have known that once their Molly had slighted Andrew's lad by running off and marrying someone else things would never be the same between them and the farm steward and his family. The McHaffies weren't ones for forgiving and forgetting at the best of times.

He shifted slightly, warming his buttocks in the heat from the fire as he glanced towards the window. The worsening weather meant he'd be lighting the lamps earlier than usual, but at least the hardware van had delivered the paraffin oil for the farm and cottages the day before so there was no chance of running out if they got snowed in again. Two of the farmhands had had to walk into town the last time that had happened.

Wilbert reached for his tea, sipping the scalding-hot liquid as he continued to brood about the McHaffies.

He blamed Joe McHaffie for the tension that existed between Andrew and himself. Joe had been eighteen or thereabouts when Molly had run off, and the lad hadn't attempted to hide his bitterness at what he saw as her betrayal. Joe must be getting on for thirty now, and he was as sour as a barrel of vinegar. Worse, his resentment had spread like a canker through the whole family. It certainly didn't make the working day any easier.

In the general run of things he knew shepherds and stewards could be at odds on any farm, sheep being so central to the business they were all engaged in, and because the steward and shepherd maintained a degree of independence from each other and their positions meant they both had direct access to the master, niggles could arise. Especially if one felt the other was being favoured. But he and Andrew had been all right before Molly had scarpered, in fact they'd been friends. Now Andrew dragged his feet in meeting any request he made, be it getting handling gear shifted or turnips laid out or feeding stuff taken out of the bins in the fields. And this last episode, when Andrew had 'forgotten' to let him know that he had had the farm boar, a bad-tempered animal, moved into one of the hay barns could have been downright dangerous. Stupid so-an'-so.

Wilbert straightened, his bruised backside making itself felt. He had gone into the barn earlier to collect an armful of straw for bedding for an ailing sheep that he was keeping separate from the rest of the flock for a few days. He'd got the animal into a small pen he'd constructed in one of the outbuildings, and his mind had been on the matter in hand when he'd entered the barn. The next thing he'd known was a terrific roar and he'd found himself flat on his back. He'd got the fright of his life before he realized he'd been bowled over by the boar as it had started up from where it had been sleeping amongst the straw. To add insult to injury, Andrew had been passing the entrance to the barn and had stood laughing his head off.

Wilbert's jaw clenched. Andrew had soon stopped his guffawing when he'd given him a few home truths, though, the idiot.

Draining the mug of tea, Wilbert set it down but continued to stand brooding about the incident as he gazed across the darkening room. Their Molly had caused more trouble than she'd ever know when she had done the dirty on Joe McHaffie, but it wasn't that which stuck in his craw when he thought of his youngest daughter. No, it was the fact that Molly had broken her mother's heart when she had upped and disappeared out of their lives.

Wilbert turned and looked up at the picture again, his rugged face set in lines of deep sadness.

After their second daughter, Ruth, had been born, he and Moll had waited for more bairns to come along, but the years had gone by without a sign of a babby, despite them both being as fit as fiddles. Then Moll had fallen for Molly and she had been beside herself with happiness, and when the baby was a girl and could take her mam's Christian name, Moll had been tickled pink that tradition at last allowed it. And in truth, despite the fact that he'd been hoping for a little lad to follow him into shepherding, he wouldn't have swapped Molly for ten sons once she'd arrived. And the sun had shone out of the bairn's backside as far as her mam was concerned.

He paused in his reflections. Perhaps, it was judgement on him and Moll that things had turned out the way they had, because you shouldn't have favourites among your bairns. The others would always sense it. But if Bertha and Ruth had resented their sister, and he didn't know if that was the case, when Molly had thrown his and Moll's adoration back in their faces they'd certainly had the last laugh. And when Molly had come back for her mam's funeral and acted as though butter wouldn't melt in her mouth, he hadn't known which way was up. And her with two little bairns in tow from that fella she'd cleared off with. To be fair, that must have been hard for Joe to take.

Wilbert sighed deeply, the gnawing ache that had been with him ever since his wife's death and which took every ounce of pleasure out of his days, making itself felt more strongly. He prided himself that he was tough, resilient and hard-bitten, only Moll had known he had a soft centre, and he missed her more than words could express.

Knowing that he'd be black and blue come the morning after his fall in the barn, Wilbert pulled on the heavy tweed jacket he wore over his shirt and indoor dungaree jerkin. An 'inbye' shepherd, his flock of sheep were confined to fields rather than living on the open hills all the year round, and during the winter when the snow could reach the tops of the hedgerows and the drifts were treacherous, the animals were brought into big sheds until they could go back into the fields again once he was sure they wouldn't perish. Like most Border shepherds, he knew every individual sheep in his flock. For Wilbert, no two sheep any more than any two human beings looked exactly alike. Their faces, the shapes of their bodies, their gait and even their characters set them all apart. The one that was presently ailing he had reared by hand after its mother had died and he hadn't had a foster mother available within the flock. He didn't get emotionally attached to the sheep – although he was fond of his two Border collie working dogs, Meg and Jessie – but when the lambs had been sent away to St Boswells Auction Mart last year he had kept this particular one back and bought it off the farmer to add to his own shepherd's 'pack'. He had settled the animal in its individual pen on the straw after his altercation with Andrew, but now he needed to check it again.

Wilbert had a few sheep of his own, as was the custom on Border farms, and with the one in the summer his pack now numbered thirteen animals. They ran along with the farmer's flock and were kept in regular ages, older ones being sold off at some point, the same as those of the farm flock, whereupon lambs would replace them. Besides this benefit, he had the keep of a cow – at a charge of four shillings a week deducted from his wage by the farmer – paid no rent for his cottage, and was given forty stone of oatmeal for use as dog feed. He also had licence to plant several hundred yards of potatoes in one of the farmer's fields, and these, added to the vegetables from his strip of garden, provided the bulk of his diet. When Moll had been alive she had milked the cow and made cream and cheese and butter, selling any excess to the grocer who called weekly at the farm in his van, or bartering it for other supplies. Now he paid one of the farm labourers' wives to do the job. The vegetable garden, along with planting the potatoes and then digging them up – which had also been one of Moll's many jobs – he attempted himself when time permitted. Which was not often.

He knew full well Moll would be aghast at the state of the cottage which she had kept as neat as a new pin, and even more horrified that since she had been gone he tended to live on bread and cheese and cold meats. Mrs Burns, whom he paid to see to the cow, had offered to clean the house and provide a hot meal once a day for a charge, but it wasn't the money that prevented him taking the woman up on her offer. He didn't want anyone poking about in what had been Moll's domain, that was the long and short of it.

Wilbert had his hand on the latch of the door when a knock sounded from outside. He paused for a moment, knowing who it was. In his temper with Andrew he had said more than he should have, and some of his tirade had featured Joe who was often more awkward than his father on a day-to-day basis. He was sick to death with the pair of them, that was the truth of it, and if Joe thought to take him to task, then he would give him what for. Joe wasn't the first lad to be jilted by a long chalk and he should have got over it years ago rather than bearing a grudge that affected the whole farm community. Miserable so-an'-so.

Scowling ferociously he flung open the door, only to freeze with his mouth open as he stared down at the two snow-covered children on the doorstep whom he recognized as Molly's bairns. It was the girl, who had her arm round her brother, who spoke first. 'We ... we've come to ask you if we can stay,' she said, her voice shaking so much he could barely make her out. 'There was nowhere else to go and they wanted to put us in the workhouse.'

'*What?* What did you say?' Even to himself his voice sounded over-loud.

She repeated, 'We've come to ask if we can stay here with you. We won't be any trouble and I've got seventeen an' six you can have, an' we'll work for our keep. I promise.'

Hardly able to believe his eyes, Wilbert stared into the swirling snowflakes. 'Where's your mam?' he muttered, his voice lower, expecting Molly to step out of the snowstorm behind her children. 'Sent you ahead, has she?'

Abby was cold and wet and terrified by this man who was their grandfather, this man with the loud angry voice and whose face was as black as thunder as he glared down at them. A convulsive shiver went through Robin, and her arm tightened round her brother. 'Our mam's dead.' It came out more baldly than she had intended.

'*Dead?*' And then, as if he had only just realized the state of them, he said, 'You're wet through. Come into the house.'

As he stood aside for them to enter, Abby was aware that Robin was crying. She felt like crying herself. Farmer Dodds had dropped them at the end of the farm track with instructions to follow it until they came to the pair of semi-detached cottages which were some distance in front of the farm, but the snow had been so deep and the blizzard so fierce it had been hard going. And now they were here and their grandfather was even more fierce than she remembered.

He didn't immediately follow them into the house, standing at the door as he said, 'Who brought you here if not your mam? Your da?' as he peered once again into the murky afternoon.

'We came by ourselves.' There was a good fire burning in the fireplace in the sitting-room half of the big room, and Abby pushed Robin towards the warmth, saying, 'Go and get thawed out,' whilst remaining where she was.

At last their grandfather seemed to understand there was no one with them. He shut the door and stared at her, his gaze moving briefly to

Robin crouched in front of the fire before returning once more to her pinched white face. 'We had to come,' she said, her voice small. 'They were going to put us in the workhouse.'

For probably the first time in his life Wilbert was completely out of his depth. If he had been confronted by two of the goblins that were said to roam the countryside he couldn't have been more taken aback. 'Your mam?'

Again she said, 'She's dead.'

So he had heard it right. Molly was gone. A pain equal to when Moll had breathed her last seared his chest. Pulling himself together with some effort, he saw the child was shivering uncontrollably and the little lad by the fire had steam rising off his clothes. Wilbert was nothing if not a practical man. 'I'll bring you some blankets and you two get them wet things off,' he said gruffly. 'Sit by the fire along with your brother, lass, an' we'll get a hot drink inside you. Now, now, no blubbering,' he added as his words brought tears pouring down her face. 'We'll get you warm and comfortable, and then you'd better tell me it all. All right?'

Abby nodded. From the look of her grandfather when he had opened the front door, she wouldn't have been surprised if he had ordered the pair of them out into the snow, but now he seemed different. Hope rising in her had brought tears. The one thought that had tortured her during the journey was what she would do if their grandfather refused to help them. But now, perhaps, it wouldn't come to that?

It was two hours later. After getting the children settled in front of the fire wrapped in blankets and with a plateful of bread and cheese and cold bacon each, and a mug of tea, Wilbert had gone out to do his rounds checking the sheep in the outbuildings and seeing to his two dogs. His tasks completed, he had retraced his steps, relieved to find Molly's bairns had colour in their cheeks and looked much better than they had done, when he entered the house. After making himself and them another hot drink, he had sat down by the fire and told Abby to start at the beginning and to tell him everything that had happened in the last weeks.

Abby had just finished her story and she had kept nothing back. She had expected her grandfather to start ranting and raving when she had explained what her father had done, but surprisingly he had said not a word although his eyes had narrowed and he'd looked really scary again, causing her to falter. Nervously, her stomach trembling, she waited for him to say something. After several long moments he spoke.

'So these neighbours, the ones who took you in at Christmas, didn't know you were going to come here?' Wilbert was struggling to grasp the enormity of what the bairn had told him. Molly murdered by her husband; it seemed too incredible to be true. It made him feel physically sick.

'Shirley knows and she was going to tell her mam once we were gone.'

'But I'll still need to get word to them to say you're safe,' he murmured dazedly, one part of his mind chewing over what he would do to

Edgar Kirby if he could get his hands on him.

Abby stared at her grandfather. She could see he was shocked and upset so perhaps he had still loved her mam after all, but she had no idea if he was going to let them live here with him. She and Robin were sitting in what had been her grandmother's chair, Robin snuggled into her side and half asleep, and although she didn't want to make her grandfather cross or irritate him, she had to know what he was thinking. Tentatively, her voice little more than a whisper, she said, 'If we go back home they'll take us to the workhouse. I heard them talking.'

Wilbert came out of the maelstrom of his thoughts and his voice was firm when he said, in what was a gentle tone for him, 'There'll be no workhouse, lass. Your place is here with me. Mind you, it'll be different to what you've known before, and with your grandma gone things don't run like they used to.'

Abby's face lit up. Eagerly, she said, 'I can keep house an' cook an' that. Mam taught me when she had to go out to work.' When she had first come into the house she had noticed a number of smells and none of them pleasant. The kitchen was in a state, the range clearly hadn't been black-leaded in months, thick dust lay everywhere and the floor was covered in bits. 'And Robin will do his share. I'll see to it.'

For the first time since she had set eyes on her grandfather his mouth moved in the semblance of a smile. 'Is that so?' he said gruffly. 'Then no doubt we'll rub along just fine. Your grandma liked everything spick an' span and never had idle hands, in the house or out of it.'

Abby nodded. 'My mam said idle hands make work for the devil. She told me her mam always said that.'

'Aye, she did.' He looked into the small heart-shaped face that was so like her mother's, although the bairn's hair was more silver than golden like Molly's, and his daughter's eyes had been a clear vivid blue whereas the little lass's were blue-grey. But Molly's lass was a beauty, all right. His Moll would have loved her. The lump in his throat threatening to choke him, Wilbert took control of himself. The bairns had been through enough; he couldn't break down in front of them. Rubbing his hand over his face, he said gruffly, 'We'll have to see about getting you along to the schoolhouse in the next week or two. Can't have the pair of you falling behind with your lessons, can we?'

'No, although...'

'What?'

'Robin would like that. He hates school, except for the playtimes.'

'Is that so? Never was over-fond of it meself. How about you? Do you like doing your lessons?'

Abby nodded.

Aye, he could see she'd do all right at school, her eyes were bright with intelligence. She was a canny little lass all round. Just like her mam. And the little lad seemed all there whatever his sister said about him not liking school.

Wilbert sighed inwardly. You never knew what a day was going to bring, sure enough. He'd got up this morning thinking the weeks and months ahead were going to stick to the pattern of the last years, but here he was suddenly in charge of two bairns, his grandchildren. If anyone had told him that was going to happen he'd have run a mile, but now that it had, to his great surprise he found he wasn't displeased. He just wished it hadn't taken Molly dying to bring about the change of circumstances. He was a stubborn old beggar, he admitted it, and in the past had even been slightly proud of the fact, but he never would be so again.

Aware of a pair of intent blue-grey eyes on him, he smiled. The lass had been scared of him at first, he'd seen that, and he wanted to reassure her. 'I think the best thing is to make up a bed tonight for you both down here in front of the fire. I've got an old put-you-up somewhere. Tomorrow we'll light a fire in the two spare bedrooms and air the beds with hot-water bottles because the rooms are damp. They haven't been used for a while.'

He didn't mention that the last time the rooms had been occupied was when Molly and the bairns had arrived for Moll's funeral.

'That bag, lass' – he pointed to the big cloth bag Abby had brought – 'is that all your things?' There didn't seem much.

Sensing criticism, Abby nodded, her voice defensive when she said, 'Mam needed to watch the pennies.'

'Aye. I dare say she did.' Wilbert felt as though hot coals were being poured over his head. What sort of a life had his daughter had since that wicked devil had come back from the war? And it was clear Molly hadn't felt she could ask him for help. Why hadn't he taken the olive branch she'd offered when she had come for her mam's funeral? And now he had no chance to tell her that he and her mam had never stopped loving her, not for a minute.

'What ... what are we to call you?'

The small voice again brought him out of the darkness of his thoughts. He swallowed hard before he could speak. 'I'm your granda, hinny, so I think that'll do, don't you?'

Abby stared at her grandfather in the dimness of the room lit only by the fire and the oil lamp hanging from the ceiling in the centre of the sitting-room area. Strangely, especially in view of the fact that she was still a little frightened of him, she wanted to comfort him. Robin was fast asleep beside her now, and she carefully slid out of the chair and walked across to her granda. Kneeling down by his chair, she put one small hand on the bony gnarled one resting on the arm of the chair and pretended not to notice the tears rolling down his leathery cheeks.

PART TWO

The New Life

1921

Chapter Six

During the next few weeks Abby and Robin were plunged into a new life, a life that proved to be bewildering and perplexing most of the time as they grappled to learn the unspoken rules of their new existence. But they learned fast; Abby, because the spectre of the workhouse hung over her head in spite of her grandfather's assurances that their home was now with him, and Robin, simply because he took to Border life in general, and shepherding in particular, like a duck to water.

In Sunderland, Abby had had her work cut out to make Robin do the jobs allotted to him before and after school. Now he couldn't get home from school quick enough to join his grandfather, even doing chores first thing in the morning like feeding the ewes housed in the barns their corn and turnips. Once lambing time came he was up at the crack of dawn, inspecting the parricks – the small separate pens built into the perimeter of the lambing shed, in which a ewe and her lambs were put after she lambed at night – with Wilbert, and bottle-feeding hungry or motherless lambs before he went to school. In the evenings and at weekends he was stuck to his grandfather's side like a limpet no matter what the weather. He was like a small sponge as he learned shepherd lore and Wilbert couldn't hide his delight in his grandson's interest.

'It's in his blood,' Wilbert was heard to remark on more than one occasion, and in truth it seemed so. Within a short time Robin was able to pick out his grandfather's pack sheep from the rest of the flock, and know how to check the newly born lambs to ascertain if they were full enough if a dam was short of milk. He watched his grandfather skin a dead lamb to put the skin on a live one and set it onto the mother of the dead one so that the ewe would adopt the orphan as her own and feed it, without flinching, and was already well on his way to reading the lugmarks – the snips taken out of the sheep's ear – that were used as a stockmark signifying what farm it belonged to, to distinguish the various ages of the ewes, and for a variety of other purposes. A shepherd needed to understand the significance of the lugmarks on any sheep at a glance, and Robin soaked up this information along with many other facts seemingly instinctively.

It was a weight off Abby's mind that Robin had settled into life at Crab Apple Farm so naturally, confirming as it did that her decision to find her grandfather had been the right one. Her first task had been setting the cottage to rights and it had taken some days, but at the end of the first week the house was as clean and tidy as her grandmother would have wished it, according to Wilbert. But housekeeping, along with cooking and seeing to the laundry, was only part of the new life. At Crab Apple Farm the workers' cows, including her grandfather's, a gentle animal called Lotty, were housed from autumn till early summer in a byre of their own, having a few hours out in a field by day. They were fed and tended by the workers' wives in the main, although the byre lad, who had charge of the farmer's milk cows and the pigs in the row of pigsties, would step in and help if an emergency arose. The workers' cows, being milk cows, were fed on a diet of hay, straw and turnips, plus a small ration of cattle cake as they came up for calving.

Now she was living with her grandfather, Abby had taken over the care of Lotty, at first under the supervision of the labourers' wives who had been generous in their support and help to the 'poor motherless bairns' as they privately called Abby and Robin. They taught her how to milk the cow, separate the cream and use some to churn butter, which was exhausting work. Nevertheless, the evening milking was Abby's favourite time of the day once she got used to the routine. By the light of a hurricane lamp hung up on the byre wall, she would give Lotty a pailful of bran mash she had prepared and after wiping the udder clean sit down on a stool against the animal's flank.

Once jets of milk were pinging into the bucket, Abby relaxed and let her tired mind – which during the day was often tormented by thoughts of her mother and father – be soothed by the peace of the byre. The smell of straw, cows and paraffin; the flickering shadows cast upon the wall by the lantern; the rattling of cow chains and other movements of the animals in their stalls, and the occasional rustling of mice in the straw, was a step out of her busy and gruelling existence. The fact that Lotty was such a placid and obliging cow that never kicked out or tried to upset the milk bucket the way some of the workers' cows did, made the time pleasant, and sometimes one of the farm cats would appear from nowhere, purring as it rubbed against her hoping for a sup of milk.

The women had also promised to show her how to plant and tend her grandfather's vegetable garden at the back of the house in the spring, and see to the potato planting and lifting in due course. They were kind, all of them, but none of the women or any of the farm workers knew the truth about what had caused Abby and Robin to turn up at the farm. Not the whole truth. Wilbert had told the children to say only that their parents had died, and if questioned further, to say it was the fever that had taken them and nothing more. The farm was far enough away from Sunderland, and the Border community sufficiently remote, for this to go unchallenged, and for news of the murder not to reach them. Wilbert had written to Betty Hammond to tell her the children were safe and well and would make their home with him, but he would appreciate them being left alone to readjust to their new life. If she could let him know the outcome regarding their father in due course it would be greatly appreciated. Betty had replied saying she would do that, and so the matter had been left.

Wilbert had forbidden Abby to enter into communication with anyone from the time before she and Robin had come to the farm. The past was the past, he had declared firmly when she had objected to this, saying she would like to write to Mrs Hammond and Shirley. It was best forgotten. She had more than enough to do in the present without keeping in touch with folk she would never see again.

Abby disagreed. The Hammonds had been wonderful at a time when she and Robin had never needed help more, but as her grandfather had made it clear that he would not be swayed over the issue, she had to admit defeat. And in truth, he was right about her having enough to cope with on a day-to-day level. Besides her jobs at home, she and Robin had to adapt to their new school at Linton which was half-an-hour's walk from the farm. There were just under forty pupils who attended from neighbouring farms and a tiny hamlet to the south of Linton.

The school consisted of two rooms and a tiny annexe of a cloakroom with a small paved yard outside holding the one privy. The infant class took children up to the age of eight, and Miss Crawford was in charge, an elderly spinster with a soft voice and fluffy-grey hair.

Mr Newton, the headmaster, taught the older children of whom Abby was one. He was a different kettle of fish from the gentle Miss Crawford. A strict disciplinarian, he ruled his pupils with a rod of iron and could strike dread into the most wayward child with one look. He had no compunction about using the tawse on the older boys if he considered they deserved it, and was universally feared and respected. A great believer in education for the working class, he made sure each boy and girl in his school received a good grounding in the three R's, history and geography, whether said child wanted it or not.

Abby had always possessed a keen desire to learn

and had enjoyed school in Sunderland as much as Robin had hated it so the lessons were no problem for her; the playtimes and lunch break were a different matter. Robin had made a couple of friends of his own age within the first week of attending the school, and as the boys and girls always seemed to play separately in the school playground she didn't see much of him during the day, which wouldn't have been a problem if she had had a friend of her own. As it was, with sixteen boys in the class and only five other girls – two of whom were due to leave school in the summer and the other three being over two years older than her – the first few weeks were a lonely time.

She wasn't aware that Mr Newton had noticed her predicament until one lunchtime, some weeks after she had started at the school. Everyone had finished eating the food they brought from home and the class was ready to file out into the fresh air despite the bitter wind that carried the occasional snowflake in its icy blast, when he asked her to stay behind as the others left.

Quaking in her boots she had gazed into his be-whiskered face wondering what she had done wrong, but instead of the reprimand she'd expected, he had said quietly, 'I intend to set up a small library here at the school, Abigail.' He always called each child by their full name, having a bee in his bonnet about nicknames being an affront to God, not being the name they were christened with in church. 'Pupils from both Miss Crawford's class and mine will be allowed to borrow books, once they have mastered the art of reading, and the library will be arranged in order of appropriate age and so on.'

Abby stared at him. As one who loved to read she thought the notion a wonderful idea, but she wasn't so sure some of the boys would feel the same. At home in Sunderland a couple of her friends had had a storybook or two and she had envied them; there had never been any spare money for her to receive such a gift. On arriving at her grandfather's she had found he possessed an old and revered family Bible which she and Robin were not allowed to touch, but he didn't read books as such. He didn't take a daily paper but got the *Scotsman* handed down from the farmhouse now and again when it was a few days old, along with the *Southern Reporter* which was sent to the farmer every week by post from the Selkirk office. Whenever she had a spare moment, which wasn't often, she devoured the contents of these although they weren't the kind of reading to take her into another world the way storybooks did.

'Well?' Mr Newton surveyed her from under bushy eyebrows. 'What do you think about helping me with it?'

'Me?' It was all she could manage, she was so taken aback.

'Yes, you.' Stanley Newton allowed himself a small smile. He liked this child. She was as bright as a button and old for her years, but then having lost her parents recently he could understand the air of sadness and aloneness that set her apart from her contemporaries. 'I have many books at home – my children have long since flown the nest and their section of my bookcase merely sits gathering dust. There are books on various subjects as well as novels and so on, even adventure stories to tempt the most unlettered of the boys. It would have to be done properly, of course. I wouldn't like to think of them being taken home and never returned so each withdrawal would be noted down along with the child's name and a date given when the book must be brought back. Are you acquainted with how a library runs?'

Abby shook her head.

'No matter, I'll show you. First I'll arrange for Mr Lee from the joiner's shop to come and construct some shelves in the alcoves over there' – he pointed to the back of the room where either side of the stone fireplace containing the paraffin stove two recesses holding some old stacked chairs and other bits and pieces reposed – 'and then I'll start bringing some books in and you can begin an inventory. That's if you have no objection to working through playtime and part of your lunch break some days?'

'No, not at all,' she said eagerly. It would be heaven to stay in the warm classroom rather than wandering round in the freezing cold with no one to talk to. 'I'd like that, sir.'

'Once the library is set up you will be in charge of recording the books in and out along with inspecting them for damage when they are returned, among other things. It is a very responsible job, Abigail, so think carefully before you agree to do it.'

'I don't need to think about it, Mr Newton.' Her face, if she had but known it, had already told the teacher how thrilled she was by the prospect. 'I would love to do it. Thank you, thank you so much.' She would be able to read books, to handle them and learn different things as well as enjoy stories and adventures through the eyes of the writer. Suddenly this new life which had seemed so hard and lonely and strange just minutes before was transformed. And Mr Newton had entrusted *her* with this important role.

The teacher's smile widened. He wished all his pupils were as thirsty for knowledge as this child. She stood out among the children presently at the school. He would hate to see her go into service or work in the fields when she was older, but private service or farm work were about the only choices for farm girls. Maybe he could see to it that this child got into Kelso High School when she was old enough? Of course her grandfather wouldn't be able to pay the fees, or at least he doubted it, but there was always the bursary available for such pupils who were able to pass the entry examination and he was sure Abigail would do so. Places were strictly limited, and her grandfather might not be willing to see her remain at school longer than the age of fourteen? But there, he was crossing a number of bridges before he came to them. The girl was nine years old, there was plenty of time before she reached the age of twelve and they took them at the High School. She might lose her desire to learn and better herself; he had seen it happen before when puberty hit. But – he looked into the grey-blue eyes with their thick lashes a few shades darker than her silvery hair – he rather thought that wouldn't happen with Abigail...

'Stay in at playtime to sort out a load of old

books?' Robin's voice was full of disgust. 'You're barmy, Abby.'

They were walking home from school in the thick twilight in the company of several other children who walked their way, and she had just related Mr Newton's idea to her brother, fully expecting him to react the way he had. Robin begrudged every minute he was stuck in the classroom and lived only for the playtimes and lunch break when he could be with his new pals.

One of them, a small but sturdy lad called Humphrey, now joined them, along with his two older brothers who were in Abby's class. The oldest boy was hauling a sledge behind him on the hard-packed snow, a home-made affair of wood nailed together with two stout sideboards to which were fixed iron runners obtained from the smith. Lots of the country children had sledges their fathers had cobbled together, some single seaters and others long enough to hold two or three children seated one behind the other.

Abby and Robin had discovered the other great winter pastime among the country bairns was sliding on the ice, and they had their own name for it called slying. At one of the farms in the district there was a curling pond, used now and again by the farmer and his friends and family. This made an ideal playground in hard frozen weather for the locals, and Humphrey and his brothers had taken Robin along with them the week before although Abby had refused the invitation. Robin had come home, red cheeked and sore bottomed, reporting that he'd had a rare old time and that a number of the young men and lassies round about had come to join in the fun once evening had drawn in, it being a moonlit night. None of them had possessed the luxury of skates, he'd said – they were an extravagance enjoyed only by the well-to-do – but some of the lassies in particular had been amazing to watch, pirouetting and gliding round the pond like birds.

Now Frank, Humphrey's oldest brother, ruffled Robin's hair as he said, 'Fancy a bit of sledging on the way home? There's a grand hill a hundred yards on.'

'Can we?' Robin looked at Abby. *'Please?'*

'Just for a bit then. There's jobs to do when we get home and I need to get the dinner on for Granda.' She always prepared whatever they were having before she left in the morning; that way she was ready to pop the food in the range as soon as they got in, unless it was a pot roast or a stew she could leave slowly cooking all day.

A couple more of their companions had sledges, and when they reached the allotted place – an extremely steep hill with a mass of old bramble bushes at the bottom of it – Abby stood holding the hands of two little five- and six-year-old sisters from Robin's class who had no wish to sledge. All the lads, on the other hand, were fired up by the excitement, more than one coming to grief in the bramble bushes when their sledge went too far.

The sun was setting in a blaze of glory as they stood watching the spills and thrills below them, the bitterly cold icy air carrying the shouts and laughter for some distance. Somewhere in the fields on the other side of the lane Abby heard the haunting 'tu-whit, tu-whoo' of a tawny owl, the plaintive sound making her shiver. Her grand-father had told them that to some country folk the owl was a symbol of death and was feared, being credited with supernatural powers. He hadn't said whether he believed this to be so, but Abby thought the bird's nocturnal habits and eerie cries enhanced the creature's supposed magical quali-ties. She turned and then, just for a few moments, she saw the owl silhouetted against the dying sky before it swooped down, presumably to catch its prey in its powerful talons.

She shut her eyes for an instant, her hands in-stinctively tightening round those of her two small charges, and when she opened them again her head turned to see a horse and rider galloping up the lane towards them. She just had time to pull the two little girls closer to her, the three of them stepping perilously near to the edge of the slope in the process, before the big black stallion and its rider was upon them in a flash of lethal hooves. She was still getting her breath when the horse cantered to a halt, and then the rider turned the animal and glanced towards them. He looked to be a youth of eighteen or thereabouts, dressed as the gentry dressed, and both his attitude and voice confirmed this when he said, 'What the *hell* were you doing standing in the middle of the lane like that?'

Normally Abby might have felt a little intimi-dated by the young man's obvious wealth and the cultured voice that held no evidence of a nor-thern accent, but the fact that but for her quick thinking he could easily have charged into them with disastrous consequences, and clearly was unrepentant of his actions, brought her temper to the surface. 'What was *I* doing?' She glared at him, angry colour in her cheeks. 'More to the point what were *you* doing, riding like a madman? If you want to kill yourself that's up to you, but this is a public road and people walk down it. You ought to be ashamed of yourself.'

The youth sat up straighter on the horse that was prancing slightly, clearly eager to be off. His eyes narrowing, he said somewhat imperiously, 'And who are you?'

Abby's chin rose a notch. He wasn't going to browbeat her with his highfalutin voice and fine clothes. 'My name is Abigail Kirby, not that it's any of your business.'

'Well, Abigail Kirby, do you know to whom you are speaking?'

She didn't know where her fury was coming from; maybe it wasn't just this situation but the events of the last weeks that made her want to scream and shout into the good-looking, haughty face viewing her with such disdain. Her voice quivering with rage, she said loudly and distinctly, 'No gentleman, that's for sure, in spite of your clothes and the fancy saddle on your horse.'

'Why you little...'

He moved the restless stallion a few paces towards them, and as he did so Abby felt the two little girls either side of her shrink back which made her even more angry. He was a bully, that's what he was, for all his grand appearance. When she next spoke it was how she would have addressed any bully in the playground. 'You don't frighten me, you and your horse.'

105

'What's going on, Abby?'

She hadn't been aware that the confrontation had caught the attention of the other children, but now she found that Robin and most of the other boys had scrambled up the hill and had come to stand behind her. It was Humphrey's brother, Frank, who had spoken and he moved slightly in front of her as he did so, eyeing the youth on the horse bravely but with caution.

'He nearly ran us down and then he blamed me.' She was so angry she was shaking. 'He's a bully boy.'

The young man surveyed them all from the vantage point of the horse. Then, his lip curling, he turned the powerful animal in one movement and dug his heels into its sides. Within moments he was lost to view in a turn in the road.

Abby heard Frank breathe out loudly. 'Phew.' He faced her, shaking his head. 'Do you know who that was?'

'He asked me the same thing and I told him he was no gentleman however he looks.'

'You didn't!' Frank's voice held a note of awe. He looked at the others clustered behind them. 'She told Nicholas Jefferson-Price what for – what do you think about that?'

Robin had come to stand with Abby and it was he who said, 'Who is he then, this Jefferson-Price?'

'The laird's son, that's who.'

'The laird?'

'Aye, the laird.' And then seeing their puzzled faces, Frank said, 'They own most of the land hereabouts, didn't you know that? Aye, well they do, and even the farmers have to mind their Ps and Qs.'

Abby and Robin's eyes widened. They knew that scarcely any of the farmers sent their children to the village schools; instead they were packed off to boarding school at an early age for a better education which generated the 'them and us' attitude between farmers and their employees. Abby had supposed the farmers were at the top of the pecking order in the community, but apparently not.

'Most of the farmers are tenant farmers and the laird makes sure they remember that,' Frank went on. 'He's an evil so-an'-so, the laird – that's what me da says anyway. They live in a great big house called Brookwell and the estate is run like a military establishment because the laird's an ex-army man and can't forget it. Me da knows the head gamekeeper quite well an' he says, the gamekeeper I mean, that the laird's a devil. Set about one of the little lads belonging to one of the estate workers with his riding crop one day because he found the bairn rifling a pheasant's nest. Anyway, him, Nicholas Jefferson-Price, is the only son. He's usually away at his private school this time of the year so you wouldn't see him about.' Frank paused. 'And you gave him a mouthful, lass.' The note of awe was back. 'Bet that's the first time he's been spoken to like that by the likes of us.'

Abby stared at Frank, her voice small when she said, 'What do you think he will do?' She had told him her name and she didn't want to cause trouble for her grandfather.

Frank shrugged. 'Dunno.' Looking at the other children who were standing silently now, clearly subdued by the episode, he said, 'Come on, tim to get home,' and as one they began to move, the previous chatter and laughter gone.

It was almost dark now, the faintest glow left in the wide expanse of sky above them as the night drew on and the twittering birds settled down for the cold night in the hedgerows. Abby glanced at her brother as they walked. 'Do you think I ought to tell Granda what happened with the laird's son?'

'No.' It was immediate.

'What if he tells his father and they take it further and find out that Granda's our granda?'

'He might not, and if he does you can put your side then,' said Robin with the inescapable logic of a seven-year-old who sees no sense in owning up to a misdemeanour unnecessarily.

Abby nodded. She might worry her grandfather for nothing if she said anything now, but she was going to be on tenterhooks for the next weeks, that was for sure. Any delight in her new position at school had drained away and the whole day was spoiled. She hated the laird's son and if she never saw him again in the whole of her life she'd be happy.

Chapter Seven

Nicholas Jefferson-Price – Nick to his friends – was frowning as he cantered home in the encroaching darkness. That little slip of a thing to talk to him like that, and to call him a bully! *Him.*

If there was one thing he detested it was bullies, having lived with one all his life. His earliest memory was of his father ranting and raving and throwing his weight about; he didn't know how his mother stood it.

And then he corrected himself in the next breath. Of course he knew how she stood it; his mother was a lady born and bred and anything she didn't like she distanced herself from, including her husband. She had her elite circle of friends, and privileged lifestyle, and spent most of her time reading, playing the harpsichord, titivating herself up with the latest fashions and arranging select dinner parties when they were in the country. And when in London, she fully embraced the glittering social scene in the capital. He had been brought up witnessing the occasional ball and fancy-dress party at Brookwell, as well as shoots when game rained down from the skies, and the hunting, fishing, boating and gambling. His father's wealth provided his mother with the means to live as she had always been accustomed to, and so she was satisfied. He had long been aware of the separate bedrooms they occupied; it was only in the last year he had found out his father had a long-standing mistress whom he kept hidden away in a house in the countryside some distance from the estate.

Shrugging his shoulders as though throwing off a weight, he rode on, his mind returning to the young girl in the lane. Now that his temper was cooling, he felt ashamed of the way he had behaved and he didn't like the feeling. But for the row with his father before he had left the house he wouldn't have reacted as he had done with the child, he told himself. He had been in a rage since he had left the house, that's why he had ridden Jet so hard. He bent and patted the animal's sleek neck in silent apology for working the horse up into a lather. But the chit still shouldn't have spoken to him the way she had, damn it. She had shown him no respect whatsoever.

However, within a minute or two Nicholas's innate sense of fair play had him admitting to himself that the girl had been fully entitled to take him to task. He'd been a prat, as his school friends would say, he acknowledged ruefully. And she'd been a fiery little thing, for all her fragile appearance with that unusual silver-blonde hair and great eyes. Eyes that had blazed her contempt of him, he remembered with a wince. Not his finest hour.

By the time he rode through the open wrought-iron gates leading onto the drive of the house, he had put the incident on the road behind him, preparing instead for the battle he knew was in store with his father. In the summer he was due to leave the public school he had attended since preparatory school. He was more than ready for this and a university life. What he wasn't ready for was this university life to be conducted at Oxford or Cambridge as his father demanded. They might be the two senior universities in the land, but the fact that sport was practised with even greater intensity than at his public school, and a good number of undergraduates chose these two establishments to have a good time rather than to read or work hard, did not make them places he wished to be.

Since the start of the century the growth of new universities had flourished but it was London University, which comprised not just University, King's and Bedford Colleges, but in addition ten medical schools, six theological colleges, the London School of Economics and more besides, that was his choice. This, along with the fact that he wanted to become a doctor rather than follow his father into an army career, had caused his father to become apoplectic earlier. Their row had rocked the household and his mother had taken to her bed with a fit of the vapours, whereupon he had stormed out of the house and taken Jet for a wild gallop in the countryside to let off some of the steam that had him wanting to commit murder.

Nicholas paused on the drive as the house came into view. Even the sure prospect of what awaited him inside couldn't dim the rush of emotion the beauty of Brookwell always afforded him.

The imposing neoclassical country house set in thirty-five acres of formal gardens and parkland was perfectly framed by the tall ancestral trees either side of it, and he had always loved his home. His grandfather, a rich and influential man who had added to his considerable inherited wealth by making more money in the Baltic trade in hemp and herrings, had bought the estate in 1850 as a marital home for his then fiancée. Almost immediately his grandfather had begun to enlarge the Georgian house, adding a Doric porte-cochère to the existing Ionic pillared entrance porch, a French Renaissance-style mansard roof and additional bedrooms for the servants. Apparently his grandfather had been the perfect country land-owner of the 'new money' variety, being an excellent shot, good at sport, a fine horseman and possessed of considerable charm. He had also been a keen businessman and had seen to it that he bought up most of the surrounding farms and land in the district, covertly increasing his power and dominion decade by decade.

Nicholas sighed heavily. He wished some of his grandfather's charm could have been passed on to his firstborn, because if ever there was a surly individual it was his father. He might look the personification of the landed gentry, being tall and well-built and handsome, but there it ended. Taciturn and without conversation unless it embodied his money-making activities, it was simply his father's wealth and influence that had always guaranteed him a place in the social scene.

Digging his heels gently into the horse's side they trotted up the drive, a couple of his father's gardeners doffing their caps to him as he passed.

When he had first realized as a youngster that physically he was the image of his father he had been mortified, so even then he must have disliked the man who had sired him, Nicholas reflected as he led Jet round to the back of the house where the stable boy was waiting to take charge of the horse. But it had been in the last year or two that his dislike had turned to something stronger, when he had come to understand that his father considered it his absolute right to control every aspect of his son's future. And it seemed that in this, if nothing else, his mother was one hundred per cent in agreement with her husband.

Nicholas pictured the shock and horror on his mother's pretty face when he had announced that he intended to take up medicine as a career. 'But you'll be dealing with illness and disease,' she had said, as though he didn't know that. 'And all manner of unpleasant things. Really, darling, that's quite impossible, you must see that?'

No, he had replied. He didn't see that at all and it was what he wanted. More than that, he intended to make it happen.

His father had cut in then, shouting and swearing as his countenance had grown purple with rage at what he labelled his son's ingratitude. On and on he had gone, using the brow-beating tactics that usually terrorized an opponent into submission, but not on this day and not with him, Nicholas thought with a degree of satisfaction. And he intended to stand his ground. Medicine was a noble pursuit, whatever his parents thought to the contrary, and he had no interest in business, he had told them.

At this he had genuinely thought his father was going to have a seizure. No *interest?* he'd yelled back. No interest? What did he think paid for his fancy schooling and the rest of it? Not some 'noble pursuit', that was for sure. He'd been mollycoddled all his life, that was the trouble, spoon-fed and pampered and indulged. But no more. Damn it, no more. He'd do as he was told and that was the end of it. And then his father had turned on his mother, shouting that if she'd had to provide him with only one son instead of the quiverful that should have been his right, why had she presented him with this ungrateful so-

113

an'-so? That had been the point at which his mother had taken to her bed saying she was unwell, but he and his father had continued their yelling match for some time.

On reaching the stable block he left Jet in the care of the stable boy, with instructions that he rub the animal down thoroughly and make sure he was comfortable for the night. Entering the house through the beautifully furnished conservatory off the breakfast room – his father had always flatly refused to countenance any of the family using the kitchen door although that was the more direct route from the stable block – he made for the stairs and his suite of rooms on the first floor, but he only had one foot on the bottom step when the door to the drawing room sprang open and his father's voice said, 'Don't think you can skulk off upstairs, m'lad. We've got things to settle. Get your backside in here.'

Nicholas closed his eyes for a moment and then turned to face the man in the doorway.

Gerald Jefferson-Price was tall – taller by some three inches than his son who was six foot – and his height was further enhanced by his broad shoulders and straight military bearing. His contemporaries would label him a fine figure of a man and they would be right, but the undisputed good looks and athletic body hid a nature that was cold and harsh and insensitive. He was not an unintelligent man but had recognized years ago that his son possessed a brain that was vastly superior to his own, and although outwardly he professed scorn at Nicholas's scholarly achievements, secretly – and he would never have admitted it to a living soul – he was proud to have sired a son who was an intellectual. Gerald's own father had been a clever man, but his aptitude had shown itself in a business acumen that had allowed Gerald to inherit great wealth and social influence which he used to ruthless advantage.

Now, as he surveyed his son, Gerald was well aware of the tight obstinate set of Nicholas's mouth and the anger still burning in the dark brown eyes, and such was his strange character, his son's mulishness afforded him some satisfaction. The boy was such a highbrow he had been worried at one point that Nicholas was all wind and water, given to poetry and other such effeminate goings-on. No, although he hadn't let him see, he was glad Nicholas had it in him to behave like a man. His mother had spoiled the boy from infancy, that was the trouble, giving in to his whims and fancies. But this last notion of Nicholas's, this idea of becoming a doctor, hadn't gone down well with Camilla.

Gerald pictured his wife's horrified face and inwardly smiled to himself. If for nothing else he might just let the boy have his way in this. It would be good to see Camilla squirm.

Once Nicholas had entered the drawing room Gerald shut the door and turned to face his son who was standing in front of the ornate fireplace, legs slightly apart, shoulders back and head up. It was a fighting stance, and again Gerald felt a dart of pleasure. Nicholas would be eighteen in the summer and although his son looked like a full-grown man, Gerald had been doubtful he had the backbone to act like one.

His father's next words took Nicholas by surprise. Instead of the tirade he had expected, Gerald's voice was quiet, even propitiatory, when he said, 'Brandy?' as he gestured at the bottle and two glasses on the small table next to the armchair where he had been sitting. 'It's devilishly cold out there and a brandy will warm you up.'

Nicholas's dark eyes narrowed but he could read nothing in Gerald's bland countenance. After a moment he nodded.

'Sit down then.' Gerald seated himself in his armchair and poured two brandies, and once Nicholas had sat down opposite him, handed him a glass. Draining his own glass in two gulps, he poured himself another which he set on the table. Then he said with no preamble, 'How serious are you about this doctor idea? And be truthful. Is it just a way of getting out of a military career or something more?'

'I'm deadly serious.'

'And how long have you been thinking this way? Again, be truthful.'

'For a long time, some three or four years, I suppose. I want...'

'What?' As Nicholas hesitated, Gerald leaned forward slightly. 'Come on, spit it out.'

'I want to be a surgeon eventually. It's that branch of medicine I find fascinating.'

Gerald sat back in his chair. At least the boy wasn't intending to be a common general practitioner. One of their circle in London was a surgeon and held in some esteem. This might not be as bad as he had first thought. His voice still mild, he said, 'And what if I don't agree to this,

116

Nicholas? What will you do then?'

Nicholas stiffened. 'With or without your help and blessing I shall pursue a medical career, Father. It will be harder if you don't back me, financially and in every other way, I'm aware of that, but I shall do it. I'm sorry, but my mind's made up.'

'In that case it will be easier all round if I agree.'

Nicholas blinked. 'You agree? To my becoming a doctor?'

'Like you said, your mind is made up. Of course you will have to work damn hard compared to your peers, but if that is what you want...'

'It is. It is what I want.' Nicholas was still grappling with his father's capitulation; he couldn't believe Gerald meant what he said. There had to be a catch.

'All right then, it's settled. And you're set on London rather than Oxford or Cambridge? I know the dean at Oxford, and Major Mallard's twin boys are going to Cambridge this year.'

'I want London.' Nicholas knew Vernon and Vivian Mallard and considered them Hooray Henrys of the worst kind without a brain cell between them.

'So be it.' Gerald was quite aware of his son's amazement at his stance – Nicholas had always had a transparent face – and was thoroughly enjoying the boy's bewilderment. 'I'll talk to your mother and tell her what we have decided.'

'She won't like it.'

'That is of no consequence.' Gerald downed his second brandy. All things considered, it was far better to keep Nicholas on side for the present.

This doctor notion might die a death anyway, and even if it didn't, the boy's ultimate destiny was to take over the estate and everything that entailed. As his heir, Nicholas would marry well and take his place in society. He could afford to indulge the boy for the time being. And the added bonus, and one he hadn't foreseen before today, was that this would drive a wedge between Nicholas and his mother, whilst making his son beholden to him. Something he would remind him of if necessary.

Gerald poured them both another drink and then stretched out his legs, settling back comfortably in his chair and half-shutting his eyes. And when Nicholas did the same and what could be termed a companionable silence ensued – something that would have been an anomaly before this day – Gerald's sense of well-being increased, especially when he contemplated his wife's distress at the turn of events.

He had been as annoyed and perturbed as Camilla when Nicholas had arrived home in the middle of term saying he had to talk to them because he had decided neither Oxford nor Cambridge was for him. But now – Gerald took another good swallow of brandy – now this might turn out very well, even though this desire of Nicholas's to become a surgeon was surprising in view of the fact that the boy had no stomach for shooting or hunting or any of the blood sports. He remembered the first time Nicholas had seen a fox torn apart by the hounds and had vomited all down his coat. He'd had a job to keep his hands off his son that day, embarrassing him in front of their friends and acquaintances. And Nicholas had further compounded his crime by refusing to join the hunt again. But no matter, no matter.

Gerald took a deep breath to diffuse his temper which could rise to the boil suddenly at the slightest provocation.

Their friends had accepted on the whole that Nicholas was an academic and, as such, allowed certain peculiarities, and as his intelligence went hand in hand with a quick wit and keen sense of humour, his son held his own in company. The ladies certainly seemed to like him.

Gerald nodded mentally at the thought. He had noticed how the young ladies simpered and fluttered in Nicholas's company, and some not so young too. Nicholas had the credentials to make an excellent marriage, and as his father he would see to it that any alliance would benefit the family both socially and financially.

Gerald settled further in his chair, the only sound in the room the crackling and occasional spitting from the logs burning in the great fireplace. The warmth, good brandy in his stomach and the knowledge that he had made the right decision regarding his son settled on him satisfyingly, and after some minutes more he was gently snoring.

Chapter Eight

The following Sunday, when she and Robin joined Humphrey and his brothers for a walk in the countryside, Abby was still thinking about the laird's son and the trouble he could cause for her grandfather if he complained about her behaviour to the farmer. On arriving at her grandfather's, she had discovered that within the Border community all games were frowned upon on a Sunday and even whistling was forbidden by the grownups. This left little to do on a Sunday afternoon for the children who, weather permitting, usually congregated together away from the adults on Linton or Primrose Hill after Sunday lunch.

According to Frank, the far glen was a favourite spot from spring to autumn. It was a great place for wild flowers, he told Abby, and some of the girls collected specimens and pressed them in books, whilst the lads looked for birds' nests among the whin bushes. A place with sinister associations which the adults forbade them to frequent was the Bog, a marshy tract divided between the farms hereabout and Morebattle Tofts. It contained several pools of water, surrounded by bulrushes, which were reputed to be bottomless; Frank had regaled Abby and Robin with stories of such pools having been measured for depths with a weight tied to a cart rope that had never reached the bottom. It looked innocent enough, he told them, especially in summer when the marsh flowers were in bloom, but one wrong step and you'd be sinking in the ooze and then that was the end of you.

Normally Robin went on his own with Humphrey and the others on a Sunday afternoon, Abby preferring to stay in the cottage rather than tramp through the snow and ice – something she had to do every weekday for school. The Sunday before, however, Robin had arrived home covered in blood after cutting his head badly on a stone when he had fallen off a rope swing some of the lads had made, and Abby still hadn't got over the shock of seeing her brother in such a state. Consequently she felt she needed to keep an eye on him, and as Robin flatly refused to stay indoors, she had little option but to join him and the others for an afternoon ramble.

Her grandfather had been reading the paper he had been given by the farmer that morning, tut-tutting over the trouble across the water in Ireland where Sinn Féin supporters had had a gun battle with the army resulting in several deaths, and then relating that the first flight in a helicopter – as opposed to merely hovering a few inches off the ground – had taken place in France. Abby would have much preferred to stay in the cottage and read the new paper once her grandfather was finished with it, but instead had pulled on her outdoor clothes, resigned to tramping through inches of snow yet again.

Once outside with the others, however, the high silver-blue February sky and crisp snow underfoot proved exhilarating. At the beginning of February

121

Mr Newton had told them that the month, named after the old Roman festival 'Februa', was called the 'Gateway to the Year', and that although it was often a cold and cruel period, despite its snow and frosts the frail promise of spring could be sensed in the air on certain days.

Today, Abby decided, as she followed the others, was one of those days. 'Lamb's tails' hung daintily from the hazel's bare twigs, and the occasional icicle was falling to the ground as the pale sun weakened their hold. Winter sunbeams lit the snow in places and as they reached the lane leading from the farm track, a yellowhammer sang from within a gorse bush, and in parts of the hedgerow that were protected from the snow the flushed red stems of coltsfoot were pushing their way through the damp soil.

Her mam had loved the spring, Abby thought sadly. Her mam hadn't known about Mr Newton's 'Gateway to the Year', but she'd always said that the worst of the winter was over once February came, and, even if it wasn't, that it wouldn't be long before it was.

Tears stung at the backs of her eyes and Abby willed them away. Crying was for when she was in her bed at night. Then she often cried herself to sleep, but in the day she had to be strong for Robin. It worried her that her brother was so full of bitterness and anger towards their father, and in this respect she knew her grandfather was no help at all. He had made it clear how he felt, and in front of Robin too, and when she had tried to argue that her da was poorly and not in his right mind because of what the war had done to him, she had received short shrift from both of them. But her da *had* been sick, she told herself again. And her mam had known that. Hadn't she tried to get help for him? And because the doctor and everyone else had ignored her mam's pleas, it had ended as it had. And her da couldn't have been the only one to be so badly affected by the horrors he'd seen and the noise of the shells and everything – her mam had told her that there were other poor men like him. Her mam had understood.

She breathed hard against the pain in her chest which was emotional and not physical, and always accompanied thoughts of her parents. She hated Dr Graham, she thought fiercely, using the anger to fight the inclination to cry. If he had tried to help her da, everything would be different now.

Frank had told them that they'd arranged to meet some of their friends from Morebattle village that afternoon for a snowball fight, well away from grown-up eyes, and as they reached the agreed spot some time later, several snotty-nosed, red-cheeked children were waiting for them, stamping about to keep warm.

Within minutes the snowball fight was under way amid much laughing and shrieking and carrying-on, but after Abby had twice had a fistful of snow slide down the inside of her coat and melt in an icy trickle down her back, she decided enough was enough. Wandering away slightly from the others and the risk of a snowball in the face, she walked down the side of the hedgerow before stopping to look at a family of finches busy pecking at the scarlet wild haws on some hawthorn bushes.

A high, gentle tinkle, reminiscent of small wind-bells, drew her further on, the sweet liquid melody, wafting on the February air. As quietly as she could she followed the sound and then stood entranced watching dozens of goldfinches flitting from one thistle-head to another, clinging delicately to the weed stem or dried flower as they darted their heads among the soft down extracting seed after seed in quick succession. Coming from the town she had never seen goldfinches before, and to see such a large flock of the dazzlingly beautiful birds was intoxicating, their golden-yellow wing-bars lighting up the afternoon.

As they moved further and further on so did Abby, captivated and mesmerized by the tiny birds which appeared exotic compared to the thrushes and sparrows and blackbirds. They didn't seem to mind her presence, if they noticed it, and she hardly dared to breathe as she tiptoed after them, time seeming to stand still.

It was some time later and only when the flock suddenly took flight high into the sky in a whirl of brilliant gold and yellow brighter than any sunshine, that Abby realized she had strayed too far. The snow and ice underfoot had hidden the fact that the ground had become more marshy, but now, as she spied bulrushes in places, it reminded her of what Frank had told them. So intent had she been in watching the birds that she hadn't noticed the rush-like plants, but as she turned and looked back whence she had come she saw others. Just up ahead must be one of the pools Frank had spoken of, because although the surface was hidden by snow on top of ice and looked fairly innocuous, a big circle of the bulrushes stood out as warning.

Carefully, her heart beating fit to burst, she began to retrace her steps, angry with herself for being so stupid. She must have wandered into what Frank had called the Cut, a vast long ditch running between banks of ground where the tract naturally drained and caused the fearsome pools. Now she realized that either side of what she had assumed to be a lane or farm track were great bramble bushes and gorse bushes and other vegetation that would make it impossible for her to try and scramble onto higher ground.

A few yards in front of her was another big circle of bulrushes, and to her horror Abby realized she must have walked over one of the pools as she had followed the birds. When she came to it she stood for a moment, looking at her footsteps in the snow. Her mouth had gone dry with terror. It was all very well for reason to tell her that if she had walked over the ice covering the pool once and it had held, the chances were it would do so again. What if it didn't? No one knew where she was for a start. She could sink without trace and be lost for ever. Suddenly the day that had seemed so magical just minutes before was nightmarish.

When a movement high above her accompanied by a rustling and breaking of twigs caught her senses, she thought at first it must be an animal, a fox perhaps or a deer. And then she felt weak with relief when she saw Joe McHaffie from the farm gazing down at her, his hands stuffed in the pockets of his breeches. She had never really spoken to Joe – he was a dour kind of man – but she knew he was the beau who her mother had thrown over for her father, and she could understand why her mam hadn't wanted to marry him. It wasn't just that he was surly and morose but it was the way he looked at folk, or at her anyway. She always felt afraid when he stared at her with his hooded eyes, afraid and exposed to whatever it was that emanated from him. But just at this minute she would have welcomed the devil himself if it meant she could get out of the Cut. Her voice high with relief, she called, 'Mr McHaffie, it's me, Abby. Abby Kirby.'

'Aye, I know who you are.'

'I need to get out of here. I didn't realize where I was going.'

'The Cut's treacherous.'

'Yes, I know. I know that but I was looking at the birds–' She stopped abruptly; it wasn't the time to go into details. 'Can you help me?'

'Help you? How?'

She stared at him. He must understand the position she was in. He'd said himself that the Cut was treacherous. 'I need to get out of here,' she said again, her voice uncertain now.

'Then walk out the same as you walked in.' His voice was flat but there was something, just the merest inflexion, that frightened her.

Swallowing hard, she said, 'The – the ice might break over one of the pools.'

'Aye, it might.'

What was the matter with him? He wasn't simple so why was he talking like this? Gathering her composure, she said firmly, 'If you could tell them back at the farm where I am, my granda

126

can bring a rope or something. Or tell my brother to run to the farm. Robin's playing with some other bairns back there and–'

'I know where your brother is.' Joe shifted slightly, pulling his cap further down over his eyes. 'I watched the pair of you leave earlier with Frank Armstrong and the rest of them. Already getting the lads calling for you, aren't you. Like mother, like daughter. Got in a mood when Frank didn't pay you enough attention, was that it? Is that why you stalked off on your own?'

'I didn't stalk off,' Abby said indignantly. And then, as his words registered, she added, 'Did you follow us from the farm?'

'Free country. I can walk where I like.'

Twilight was beginning to fall, and the icy air was sharper with the smell of frost but it wasn't that which made Abby shiver. 'If you saw me heading this way why didn't you call to warn me about where I was going?'

'Like I said, it's a free country and folk can walk where they like. Besides, I'm not your keeper.'

He wasn't going to help her. Not only that but he actually wished her ill – she could read it in his face. Her chin drooped before she raised it defiantly, glaring up at him now as she said, 'When I first heard what my mam did to you I felt sorry for you but I don't now. I can see why she acted as she did and I don't blame her.'

'Is that so?' His voice had risen and she could see she had caught him on the raw. 'Well, let me tell you your mother was a loose piece and once I found out what she was I wouldn't have touched her with a bargepole. And you'll be the same, it's written all over you.' He was talking to her as though she was an adult rather than a child, and in this moment that was how Joe was seeing her. Every time his eyes had fastened on Molly's daughter since the children had arrived at the farm, he had seen the mother, and the hate that had replaced the love he'd once felt had burned stronger and stronger. Molly had made him a laughing stock and worse, someone to be pitied. Oh aye, he knew how others had seen him, how they saw him still. Poor old Joe, not man enough to hold on to the lass of his choice. He knew what was said behind closed doors. And it was a constant thorn in his flesh. And now this chit who was the image of her trollop of a mother had come to flaunt herself, with her long blonde hair and bonny face. But beauty was only skin deep, as he had learned the hard way.

Abby wasn't quite sure what a 'loose piece' was, but she could tell it was something not very nice. Her glare deepening, she said, 'Everyone loved my mother but no one likes you.'

Even in the gathering shadows she could see his face had turned a deep puce with temper and his voice, when it came, could have been dredged up from the deepest of the pools. 'Is that so, missy? Well, be that as it may, you're the one down there and I'm up here. And I tell you one thing for nowt, it was a miracle you came as far as you did without the ice cracking over one of them pools and I wouldn't want to push my luck in trying it again, but then if you stay where you are you'll freeze to death for sure come nightfall. Tricky, eh? But then you having all the answers, it won't bother you.'

'You're going to leave me here.'

It wasn't a question but he answered as though it was.

'Aye, that's exactly what I'm going to do and we'll see what fate decides. You might be lucky, you might make it back, but it'll be dark soon and the temperature will fall like a stone so I wouldn't wait too long before making up your mind.'

'If I get out of here I shall tell my granda what you've done.'

'And I shall say you're a liar, like your mam, and we'll see who folk believe. Either way it'll cause trouble at the farm and is that what you want for your grandfather? I'll take him on any day but he's getting an old man now. Not that my fight is with him, not really. He couldn't help breeding something that went bad, now could he?' He waited a moment and when she didn't speak, he went on, 'It's a pity you came here, up-setting everyone. A great pity. But perhaps that might be taken care of today.'

She wanted to come back at him again but terror was making her shake so much she knew her voice would tremble and she didn't want him to see her fear. Her eyes wide, like those of a trapped animal, she stared at him and he watched her for a moment more.

'I'm going now, Abby,' he said very softly. 'I know a couple of short cuts so it won't take me long and I shall make sure the first sight of me anyone has at the farm is my working in one of the barns, and who knows how long I've been there? Most of the afternoon, I shall say.'

Despite herself, she found she was pleading

with him as he turned to walk away. 'Don't do this, don't leave me.'

He looked at her for a moment over his shoulder. 'Funny, but that's exactly what I said to Molly the day she said she was going. Begged her, I did. Course, it made not a scrap of difference. And I told her then I'd see me day with her, her and her fancy man. Well, I can't give them their just deserts, can I, the fever did that for me, but you... You're here. A little mini Molly if ever I saw one. An' really you could say I'm doing the lads round here a favour because ten to one you'd cause a whole heap of trouble among 'em in a year or two. You've got the taint of her about you, do you know that? But the lads'll think it's a sweet, enticing thing, like I did with your mam. From when we was bairns I wanted her, never so much as looked at another lass. No, I never did.'

As Abby watched him he seemed to shake himself, as though throwing something off, and then in the next moment he had stepped out of sight at the top of the bank.

She called after him until she was hoarse, but the steep sides of the Cut heavily covered with vicious brambles and thorns muffled her cries. Only someone passing very close would hear her, she knew that. For some time, in spite of all he had said, she couldn't believe he wouldn't come back after giving her a fright, but the only sound beyond her grave-like prison was the twittering of birds as they settled down for the night and the occasional harsh call of the carrion crow in the field beyond the Cut.

As she looked back the way she had wandered

she knew she wouldn't dare retrace her steps. The image of the ice breaking and dank black water covering her head as it drew her down into the bowels of the earth wasn't to be borne. So that left attempting to climb up the sides of the embankment. The barren tangle of briar and hawthorn festooned with thick masses of old man's beard and bark fungi stretched above her on both sides like the walls of a stockade, gorse intermingled here and there and snow and ice clinging to parts of the jungle of vegetation.

What if she got part of the way up and then slipped and fell and hit one of the pools with enough force to break the ice? Trying to edge carefully over it would be better than that.

No. She shuddered. She couldn't walk back along the Cut, she just couldn't. And doing nothing wasn't an option. Like Joe McHaffie had said, she wouldn't survive the night in the open. So that left nothing for it but to try and climb.

She looked down at her knitted gloves. They would offer no protection against the vicious thorns and brambles she'd encounter but that couldn't be helped. Taking a deep breath, she said out loud, 'Help me do this, Mam,' as tears ran down her cheeks. She had never felt so frightened and alone.

It took her several attempts before she could even begin to climb because each time she grasped the web of brambles and thorny shrubs the pain instinctively caused her hands to spring back. But somehow, after a few minutes, she was several feet from the bottom of the embankment, scratched and bleeding and still with a long way to go. The winter sun had set now and the charcoal sky only had a few fleeting wisps of silver tingeing it; soon it would be completely dark. A thin crescent moon gave little light and all was desolate and still; even the birds were quiet.

It was when she reached a large and cruel gorse bush that had been partly hidden by briars that Abby gave a sob of despair. Her lacerated hands were agonizingly painful as were her legs, and her face was raw and smarting. Her feet had formed some sort of precarious hold in the midst of the thick brambles but she was virtually hanging like a starfish, as much by the thorns piercing her clothes as anything else. She knew she had reached the end of herself.

Somewhere in the distance an owl hooted and she briefly remembered the time before when she'd heard the bird, and then caught a glimpse of the ghostly brown-and-white predator as it had dropped onto its prey. She shivered convulsively. Were the old stories about the bird true, about it being a symbol of death? Had the last time been a warning? And then, faintly in the distance, she heard the sound of a horse's hooves.

For a moment she thought she had imagined it borne out of desperation and the memory of the laird's son galloping towards them as she had turned from watching the owl, but no, the sound was nearer now. She didn't have to think about what she did next, and it was as well her hands tightened on the savage briars because her whole body lifted as she screamed again and again at the top of her voice, terrified that whoever was beyond the tract of the Cut would ride by without hearing her. How long she screamed she didn't know – it could have been minutes or hours so lost was she in dread and panic – but it was only when a voice bellowed above her, 'All right, all right, I see you,' that she became silent. There was a pause, and then, 'Good grief, it's the child from the road.'

The laird's son was standing above her, legs apart and bending slightly forward, and then his stance changed when he dropped to his knees, saying, 'Shush, shush, don't cry. Don't cry. We'll soon have you out of there.'

'I...' Abby took a great gulp through her tears. 'I can't climb any further.'

'You just hang on, all right? I'll come down to you.'

'*No!*' She had lost her woolly pom-pom hat during the climb when it had become entangled on a bramble, and now her silver hair poured down her back, catching the faint shreds of moonlight filtering down from the black sky. 'No, the pools. You could drown in them.'

'The pools? Is that why you're trying to climb up here like a monkey? They're pretty sound this time of the year and the ice doesn't usually begin to give until April when the weather lets up. Not that I'd want to run a horse and carriage over them.'

He smiled, but for the life of her Abby couldn't respond in like manner. 'But the ice *could* crack, couldn't it?'

'Technically, I suppose.' His voice became brisk. 'Anyway, as you're halfway up the bank we might as well get you the rest of the way. Stay where you are for a minute' – and then, as if realizing the

133

stupidity of his words, he added – 'not that you intend to do anything else, of course.'

When he moved back out of sight she wanted to scream again but forced herself to remain quiet. Now that rescue was within reach a weakness was filling her small spent body and she was frightened her hands and feet would lose their precarious grip.

A few moments later, amid grunting and breaking of twigs and the like, he reappeared, thrusting a great branch of a tree, that must have sheared off the main trunk in the winter storms, down the bank to the side of her so that when it reached the ground it stood on its end. After twisting and pushing the branch which was as thick as half a young tree to make sure it was firmly jammed in position, he panted, 'Look, we're going to use this to get you up, all right? It'll give us the anchor we need. I'm going to shimmy down a bit and then reach out to you and hoist you up. Pity we haven't got a rope handy but I guess you don't want to wait for me to go and get one? No, I thought not. All right, we'll do this now but nice and easy.'

She could see he had on stout riding boots that reached to just below his knees and thick leather gloves, but the air was still filled with curses as he edged towards her and the thorns and briars pierced his flesh. Abby had been so petrified she hadn't felt the cold before, but now her teeth began to chatter.

He was at arm's length from her when he said, 'Are you here by yourself or is there anyone else down there?'

'No, just me. I left my brother and his friends

134

playing somewhere. They ... they'll be worried by now.'

'Let's not concern ourselves with them for the moment. Can you edge a little to your left? I think I can reach you then. What's your name again?'

'Abigail Kirby.'

'Come on then, Abigail, be brave. I promise you I won't let you fall. Just try for me, all right?'

It was only when she attempted to do as he asked that she found the brief delay in climbing meant the briars had penetrated her clothing even more deeply. She didn't dare let go with one of her hands to prise them loose, however, but as she wriggled and arched to work herself free she put herself in more danger. Exhausted and frozen to the marrow, she made one last supreme effort to tear herself free, and in the split second that she felt herself lurch outwards as the momentum of her body jerked her fingers from their hold, a strong male hand grasped her arm.

'I've got you, Abigail, I've got you. Now just take a second and steady yourself.' Nicholas's voice was soothing and calm, and Abby wasn't to know that it had been a nasty moment for him too when he had thought she was going to plunge downwards. 'Feel with your feet and get your balance on the smaller branches coming off the main one, that's right. See, you won't fall, this bough will hold you safe. It weighed a ton to move, believe me. We'll do this bit by bit, there's no rush. Just take your time.'

Abby was less aware of his actual words than their steady reassuring tone and his hand on her arm. Her next movement enabled him to grab both her arms and bring her in line with his chest where he held her for a moment, before continuing to direct her hands and feet in their upward climb as he stayed a foot or so below her, supporting her as she slowly and painfully ascended.

When she reached the top of the bank she scrambled on all fours away from the edge before coming to sit in a small huddled ball, watching him as he emerged. Standing up, he walked over to her holding out his hand as he said, 'Come on, Abigail, let's get you home. A hot drink and something to eat will work wonders and by morning you'll be thinking of this as an adventure.'

Even in the shadowed darkness there must have been enough moonlight for him to correctly read what she thought of that as she looked up into his face, because in the next moment he had laughed, hoisting her to her feet as he said, 'All right, perhaps not an adventure then, but a hot bath and some ointment on those scratches will make you feel more yourself. Where do you live?'

'With my granda. He's the shepherd at Crab Apple Farm.'

'Crab Apple Farm? Yes, I know it.' He was relieved the child was speaking normally; for a while there he had been worried she'd been scared senseless. He was leading her by the hand as he spoke, and as they walked he kept up a stream of what he would call small talk in the hope it would begin to calm her.

After emerging from the dense thicket and hedgerow Abby found herself in pastureland, and some distance away, his reins looped round the low bough of an ancient tree, she saw the silhouette of the laird's son's great stallion pawing the ground in the moonlight. She stopped instinctively. Even from thirty or so yards away the huge beast terrified her.

'What's the matter?' Nicholas stared down at the child he described to himself as fairylike. If she had been one of the will-o'-the-wisp sprites that were said to roam the marshes he wouldn't have been surprised. Although, he reasoned in the next moment, beneath the seemingly fragile exterior the girl must be a tough little thing to try to climb out of the Cut unaided. 'Don't you like horses?' he asked gently.

Abby hesitated. She could hardly say that his stallion looked less like a horse to her and more like a beast from the underworld with his gleaming body and sharp hooves. The laird's son's horse was as different from the placid ones on the farm as chalk from cheese. 'I've never had anything to do with them,' she managed nervously after a moment or two. 'My brother and I only came to the country from the town a little while ago.'

'Is that so? Well, there's nothing for you to worry about with Jet, believe me. He's a well-trained animal and he likes people on the whole.' Admittedly the folk he didn't favour Jet often took a sly nip at, Nicholas thought to himself, praying the animal would behave himself in this instance.

The stallion narrowed his eyes and flared his nostrils as they got closer, catching the scent of blood. Whether the horse sensed that Abby was a child and no threat, Nicholas wasn't sure, but instead of becoming skittish, Jet lowered his magnificent head and allowed his master to lift the little stranger onto his back, remaining perfectly still as Nicholas climbed up behind her.

At first Abby was as rigid as a board as Nicholas dug his heels into the horse's side and it began to trot forward, but again the animal seemed to sense what was required of it, making no attempt to break into a canter when it would normally have done.

'I suggest we try and find your brother and the others before I take you home,' Nicholas said softly after a moment or two. 'As you say, I'm sure they'll be worried. Where did you leave them?'

'Near the crossroads to Morebattle village.' She paused before she added, 'But they might be gone by now.' One thing was for sure, no one would have thought of looking for her in the Cut of all places. 'We were supposed to be back before dark, so my brother might have decided it was best to go and tell my granda if it got late.'

Once again he was pleased she was talking normally after her fright and the small body that had been so stiff a few moments before was more relaxed now.

When they reached the crossroads Abby was proved right – it was deserted – and so after skirting round for a minute or two and calling Robin's name, Nicholas turned in the direction of Crab Apple Farm and they set off at a brisk trot once he was sure she was no longer nervous of riding on Jet.

In fact, and to Abby's amazement, she found all fear had left her. Nicholas had one arm tightly round her waist and with the other he was holding the reins, but although the ground seemed a long way away she trusted him that he would not let her fall. He was different from how she thought he was, she told herself, correcting this in the next instant with: no, not exactly different, but he had another side to him than the one she had seen that day on the road. A nicer side. Her mam had always said that everyone had two sides to them, and that the loveliest person could be nasty and vice versa, and the laird's son certainly bore this out. Not so Joe McHaffie, though. She screwed up her eyes, as much at the thought of him as at the pain from the scratches – some of them deep and still oozing blood – that were throbbing unbearably. Joe McHaffie was all bad.

The laird's son had seemed to think that the ice covering the pools would be thick enough to safely walk on at this time of the year; had Joe McHaffie known that? Had he merely been trying to frighten her, or had he hoped the worst would happen? Either way, he'd abandoned her to the cold and dark and her fate without compunction, simply because her mother had refused to marry him all those years ago.

She shivered, causing Nicholas to say, 'Nearly home now. Look, here's the turn to the farm and if I'm not mistaken that's a search party coming down the track.'

He wasn't mistaken. Her grandfather led the group of men with lanterns walking down the lane, and as Nicholas called out, 'If you're looking for a certain little lady by the name of Abigail Kirby you need look no further,' his tone jovial, Abby heard her grandfather say, 'Praise to God,' which she thought was strange as he wasn't a religious man.

She was aware of the laird's son handing her down to her grandfather's arms and explaining the circumstances in which he had found her, and of her grandfather thanking him over and over again and the goodbyes that followed, but she found she couldn't say a word. She was feeling very strange – sick and dizzy – and the voices seemed a long way off. Her head was on her grandfather's shoulder, and as she tried to lift it to add her thanks to the laird's son a whirling darkness took her over, taking her down, down into oblivion.

Abby spent the next twenty-four hours in bed being tended to by Mrs Gibson, one of the farm labourers' wives. This good lady was a great believer in her special home-made embrocation, the ingredients of which, she told Abby, were a family secret that had been passed down by her grandmother and mother, and which served the family well for all manner of ills. This might have been true, but the rancid oily mixture stank to high heaven and stung like a swarm of angry bees when it was applied to Abby's lacerated hands and legs and face.

Nevertheless, Abby endured the woman's ministrations three times a day without complaint, aware that she had given her grandfather, and Robin too, a bad fright, which she felt terrible about.

The morning following the night the laird's son had brought her home, she had told her grandfather about the goldfinches and how she had come to wander away from the others, explaining that once she had realized the danger she'd inadvertently put herself in, she hadn't dared to retrace her footsteps over the frozen pools. She made no mention of Joe McHaffie. She had lain awake most of the night wondering whether to relate her mother's old beau's part in the proceedings, her wounds smarting and throbbing and her head aching. Eventually she'd come to the conclusion that it would only cause more bad feeling between her grandfather and the McHaffie clan. Joe would deny everything, that was for sure, and she had no proof the farm steward's son had been at the Cut. It would be his word against hers, something that would inevitably cause folk to take sides.

Once she had made her decision she fell into a deep sleep, and when her grandfather awakened her with a hot drink and a plateful of buttered toast before he went out to tend to the sheep, she had her story clear in her mind. But the incident had both frightened her and put her on her guard, and the latter, she decided, as the long day progressed, was perhaps no bad thing. Joe McHaffie wished her ill, and all because her mother had refused to marry him when they had both been young years ago.

It seemed incredible to Abby that someone would hold a grudge that long, not only hold it but transfer it to someone else, because that's what Joe McHaffie had done. And the things he had said about her mam – he had to be a bit unbalanced, that was the only answer.

She was still mulling it over in her mind when she fell asleep and she dozed on and off until

141

evening, only getting up when her grandfather agreed she could go downstairs to eat the meal the kindly Mrs Gibson had prepared for them. By the time she went back to bed she was feeling more herself and determined to go to school the following day. She wanted everything to return to normal, or as normal as it could be now Joe McHaffie had shown his true colours.

Eight weeks later Wilbert received a letter from Betty Hammond. It was a short missive and to the point. She had thought it only right and proper to let him know that Edgar Kirby had been found guilty of the murder of his wife, and was sentenced to be hanged shortly. She had been to visit him in the prison, and he had told her that he neither wanted nor expected a reprieve, especially now he knew the children were being cared for by their grandfather, to whom he sent his thanks.

Wilbert brooded on the letter for a while before informing his grandchildren of its contents, and then only when he was sure enough time had elapsed for the death sentence to have been carried out. He knew how his granddaughter thought about her father. He didn't understand it – in his eyes it had been a cold-blooded murder and deserved the ultimate penalty – but he knew her father's execution would hit Abby hard.

It did.

PART THREE

Womanhood

1929

Chapter Nine

Now eighteen years of age, to anyone meeting Abby for the first time she would appear like a woman in her early twenties. Her face was beautiful and her skin perfect, and she carried her five foot six inches very straight, making her seem taller. Outwardly composed though she was, it was her eyes that gave the impression of someone older than her years. The mercurial blue-grey colour was arresting and could change with her emotions, but it was the underlying sadness in the depths of her eyes that held the onlooker and made them want to know more about the lovely woman in front of them.

Abby and Robin had lived with Wilbert for almost nine years, and the neighbours who had known them as children in Sunderland would have had a hard time recognizing them now. Robin, too, appeared considerably older than his actual age. Having just passed his sixteenth birthday, the last years of helping his grandfather in the fields and around the farm with the sheep had developed muscles in his upper torso and arms that a man of twenty-one would be proud of.

As soon as he had been able to leave school at the age of fourteen, he had joined Wilbert as under-shepherd, having found in his grandfather a mentor and kindred spirit. And on Wilbert's side, this beloved grandson who he might so easily not have had any contact with, was the longed-for son he had never had. He now had Robin to follow in his footsteps and it was more than he could ever have hoped for. The two were so one in mind and spirit they could have been identical twins rather than grandfather and grandson.

Both Abby and Robin had adapted so well to the hard Border life that it was rare anyone remembered their beginnings; anyone, that is, but Joe McHaffie and also Wilbert himself to some extent. Much as the old man loved his granddaughter, her likeness to her dead mother was bittersweet. Every day Wilbert was reminded that he had not been reconciled to Molly before her untimely and violent death at the hands of her husband. And he tortured himself with the fact that if he had been, if he had forgotten his pride and taken the olive branch that Molly had proffered in attending her mother's funeral, he might have been able to prevent what had happened to his daughter.

Thus it was, when Abby had reached her twelfth birthday and Mr Newton had approached Wilbert about Abby trying for a place at Kelso High School, Wilbert's guilt and remorse concerning the mother had persuaded him he had to do his very best for the daughter. When he had questioned his granddaughter and Abby had confirmed she wanted to attend the high school, he had promised not to stand in her way.

Abby had sailed through the entry examination and had been one of the few children to obtain a bursary. The school ran courses for three- or six-year periods of higher education, and it had been decided that Abby would take a six-year course owing to her aptitude. Wilbert had duly bought his granddaughter a stout second-hand bicycle on which Abby had cycled the seven or so miles to school each day, although in the worst of the northern winters the school had arranged for her to board with another pupil's family in the town, the country roads being impassable at times.

Wilbert would rather have cut out his tongue than admit to a living soul that during the periods when Abby was boarding in the town, he experienced a different, happier state of mind than when his granddaughter was there in front of him pricking his conscience about Molly. He and his grandson managed perfectly well, he felt, even though Abby inevitably lamented the state of the cottage on her return to the farm.

Like most men of his generation, Wilbert would rather be hanged, drawn and quartered than so demean his masculinity by doing 'women's work', and once he had reached a certain age Robin was more than happy to follow in his grandfather's footsteps. In one particularly bad winter, when Abby had been gone for over six weeks on the trot, she had come back to a filthy house with dirty dishes piled high on every available surface and mice droppings competing with thick dust and grime.

Having had no joy about the mess with her grandfather, Abby had tackled Robin about it when they had five minutes alone. 'You can't live like this if I'm not here.' She'd sniffed at his clothes, wrinkling her nose. 'You smell, the house smells, it's disgusting. If you just do a little bit each night it won't get so bad.'

Robin had glared at her. 'Real men don't do housework.'

'Well, when you're a man we'll have this conversation again, but as you're a boy when I'm away there'll be extra things for you to do.'

His glare had deepened. 'Granda and me are too busy to bother about menial stuff.'

'I'll give you menial stuff!' Abby had narrowed her eyes at him which Robin knew meant trouble. 'If you don't pull your weight when I'm not here I swear I'll never cook you a meal again or wash your clothes or darn your socks. You'll soon find out how much "menial" work matters, my lad. I'll just look after Granda and me, and you can starve in your own muck.'

'Huh!' Knowing she meant every word, Robin turned his back on her. 'All mouth and no drawers, she is,' he muttered under his breath, an insult he'd heard used by his cronies at school.

Content she had put her point across, Abby pretended not to hear, and from that point on the house had never got in such a state again.

But now it was the middle of December, and this particular winter was different from the ones that had gone before. Abby had completed her studies at the high school in the summer, and to Wilbert's surprise and her teachers' disappointment had resisted all attempts to persuade her to follow a career in the academic world.

Abby could fly high, the teachers had stated, perhaps ending up as a headmistress in a select private school somewhere. Times were changing; the female sex was coming to the fore in a way that would have been impossible before the

Great War and the suffragette movement. Abby was so bright that it was her duty, one impassioned lady teacher had declared earnestly to Wilbert when he had answered a summons to the school, that she strive for greatness.

Wilbert had been polite but non-committal. He had had a long talk with his granddaughter before attending the appointment, and like her mother before her, Abby knew her own mind.

'I want to train as a nurse, Granda,' she'd told him. 'And this isn't a whim. I've got my secondary education certificate so I know I'll be accepted somewhere. I'd hate to be a teacher, to be stuck in a classroom every day. Please, Granda, please.'

Privately Wilbert was in agreement with Abby's teachers when they'd said she was wasting her scholastic achievements by taking up nursing as a profession, but he didn't voice it. What had been the point of her six years at the high school, something that was still rare for country girls, he had asked himself. Especially when she could have gone into the respected and highly thought-of world of education. Certainly among his kind, nursing was still tainted by the old days when it was felt that nurses worked for love or gin – never both – and that girls who followed Florence Nightingale's ideals (admittedly an extraordinary woman but one of a kind, virtually a winged and haloed angel who could never be tempted by anything as filthy as mere money) were more to be pitied than the latter, who inevitably turned into old soaks. There was something 'not quite nice' about a young woman working among the diseased and ill, especially if the unfortunate patients were male, and to do so for the pittance nurses received as salary meant they were further suspect. Who would choose to do that if they weren't barmy or a bit odd?

Wilbert was well aware that he was already held up as something of a fool by allowing his granddaughter to continue at school long after she could have left, rather than putting her into private service or farm work where she could earn a wage. Now to further compound this error of judgement by permitting her to take up nursing was seen as sheer weakness. The hardy and tough Border community didn't believe in illness for a start; such feebleness vanished if you were firm enough with it or ignored it completely like a naughty bairn. Any small complaints were always arrested before they got bigger with tried and tested remedies handed down from mother to daughter – brimstone for bowel trouble; plenty of cold water from the well to drink if a cold was brewing; butter and sugar worked together with a drop or two of vinegar for a cough; and home-made embrocation slapped on any ache in any part of the body. For more serious complaints, like accidents with scythes or turnip cutters or other farm equipment, there was always a slice of mouldy cheese to coat the wound, tied down firmly with a large clean handkerchief or a piece of old boiled linen cloth.

Abby knew how the farming community would view her decision, but just in case she didn't, Joe McHaffie had taken great pleasure in informing her that she was being held up as daft and dizzy. 'You're a disgrace to the Craggs name,' he'd growled over the garden wall, where he'd appeared as she was working on the vegetable patch one autumn day. 'Your grandma'd turn in her grave for sure, you know that, don't you?'

She had learned years before how to deal with Joe McHaffie. Straightening, she had looked at him steadily. 'I'm not a Craggs, I'm a Kirby,' she said coolly, 'and what my grandmother might or might not think is none of your business.' She'd left him cursing and muttering under his breath as she had marched away, but in truth she had to admit to herself that Joe McHaffie was perhaps the main reason she would be glad to leave the farm when she began her training at the Hemingway hospital in Galashiels in January. His hate of her had not lessened as she had got older, but now there was another, more sinister aspect to it that turned her stomach. She had caught him on more than one occasion running his hand up and down the inside of his thigh when he had stared at her, working at the obscene bulge in his trousers as he had watched her with hot eyes.

Although she would rather die than have him know, Joe McHaffie frightened her more and more as time had gone on. Since she had finished her schooling in the summer, she had been helping with the farm work besides her normal chores and she had been very careful not to be put in a position where she was alone with the steward's son, especially at harvest time. Every minute she had worked building the neat round stacks of oats and barley she had kept one eye on where Joe was, and she had made sure she walked home from the fields with one of the other women when the day's toil was done.

The worst time of the day was when she took her grandfather and Robin their lunch of cans of cold tea and fried ham sandwiches and found them in the fields or wherever they were working. There were too many lonely spots, too many quiet and secluded hedgerows where a man with evil intent on his mind could wait unnoticed. When she milked Lotty she made sure it was in the company of the other women, and as much as possible any work in the garden vegetable plot was undertaken when she knew that Joe would be occupied else-where. She was constantly on edge, only really relaxing when she was in bed at night. It hadn't seemed so bad when she was still at school. Once she'd arrived home in the evening the cooking, cleaning and other numerous jobs had kept her too busy to worry, and after she'd finished them there had always been homework to complete. She'd mostly fallen into bed about midnight and then had risen at five to get the three of them breakfast, pack up lunches, and prepare the even-ing meal. She'd left on her trusty bicycle only after she'd milked Lotty, fed the hens and collected any eggs from the enclosure at the bottom of the garden.

Her grandfather and Robin had built the en-closure shortly after she and Robin had arrived at the farm, after Wilbert had bought some hens from the farmer along with a fine cockerel. This acquisition was a mixed blessing as far as Abby was concerned. The hens kept them well sup-plied with fresh eggs, it was true, but as they were allowed to roam during the day, rounding them up at night took valuable time. The cockerel in particular was an awkward bird.

But today, the snow being thick on the ground and the low sky threatening more, the hens were safely tucked up in their pen and Abby was busy baking. Christmas was just days away. Sliding a tray of mince pies into the range oven, Abby dusted her floury hands on her hessian apron and then walked across the room to stand staring out of the window.

This time of the year was always painful with its dark memories, but she was careful to give no hint of how she felt to her menfolk. She didn't know if her grandfather and Robin thought about the terrible events of that Christmas Eve that had changed their lives. It wasn't the Border folks' way to indulge in what they would term as sentiment. 'Least said, soonest mended' was their attitude to life regarding matters both great and small. If anyone saw her now, blinking away the sudden rush of hot tears, they'd simply ignore her until she was 'herself' again. But she missed her mother as much as the day she had died, Abby admitted silently, and the ache in her heart was just as fierce in spite of what people said about time being a great healer. And her poor father, he was as much a victim as her mother. She couldn't bear to think about how he must have felt, knowing he had killed the woman he loved and just waiting for the hangman's noose to release him from his torment.

Thanks to Mr Newton and then the library at the high school, she had read in depth about the after-effects of the Great War. Its deadly new weaponry – bombs, land-mines, torpedoes, tanks, flame-throwers, machine guns and poison gas –

had brought an era of mass killing never seen before. One post-war psychologist had written that it was patently obvious the hitherto unknown horrors would affect men's minds as well as their bodies, but whereas wheelchair-bound amputees were given every sympathy, those men without obvious physical injuries were at best ignored and at worst branded malingerers and cowards, even sometimes by their nearest and dearest once the war was over.

Abby had devoured books on the subject and had come to the inescapable conclusion that if her father had received help and understanding from the medical fraternity, he and her mother would still be alive. And with this certainty had come the passion to take up nursing.

The same psychologist had gone on to say that it was the ordinary doctors and nurses, the ones dealing with these damaged war veterans, who would bring about change in the medical system, once they themselves accepted and understood it and in turn convinced their colleagues of the reality.

That one sentence in a book had determined the course of her life, Abby thought now. It had been like a light going on in her mind and she had known what she wanted for her future. Her grandfather and Robin and the rest of them at the farm wouldn't understand, but that didn't matter.

She had been gazing unseeing out of the window, lost in her thoughts, but suddenly she became aware of a dark figure standing motionless in the whiteness, the fine hairs on the back of her neck prickling. As her eyes focused, she saw that

Joe McHaffie was watching her over the brick wall that separated the two long narrow strips of garden.

She had to force herself not to spring out of sight as instinct dictated, but she wouldn't give him the satisfaction of knowing he had intimidated her. Instead she stared back at him for a moment, her chin up and her expression calm and composed, before turning slowly away into the room. Once out of sight of him, however, she leaned against the table, her heart pounding.

It was always the same, she thought wearily as she gathered herself together. Some sixth sense kicked in even before she physically saw Joe Mc-Haffie, alerting her to his presence and warning her of danger. There had been hundreds of such instances over the years and she was tired of always looking over her shoulder. But soon that would finish.

She straightened, her shoulders going back. Much as she'd miss her grandfather and Robin, she longed for Christmas to be over and the start of the new year when *her* new life would begin.

Making her way upstairs to her bedroom, she walked over to the pile of clothes folded neatly on top of the battered old trunk that would transport her belongings to the hospital. Besides underwear – including navy-blue knickers, black woollen stockings and other 'unmentionables' that had caused her grandfather to blush when he had read the list the hospital had sent to them with the contract to start her training in January – the inventory had included two pairs of house shoes, winceyette nightdresses, a dressing gown, wristwatch, fountain pen, propelling pencil and other items that they could buy in any town. On top of this formidable expenditure, the matron had included a separate list of clothes to be obtained from a firm specializing in nurses' uniform, and also the name of a publisher for books on anatomy, physiology and hygiene, and a nurses' dictionary. All had been sent for and subsequently delivered.

Abby was determined she would pay her grandfather back every penny he had taken from the biscuit tin on top of his wardrobe that contained his old-age nest egg, even though he had insisted he wouldn't hear of it, and now she brushed her hand along the top of the pile of clothes before picking up, for the umpteenth time, the neat little wristwatch with a second hand – the matron had been very specific the watch had to have a second hand – that reposed on the books she read through every night. All the new things had filled her with wonder, but the watch most of all. No one at the farm possessed the luxury of a watch, except perhaps the farmer although she wasn't sure about that, and this more than anything spoke about how different her life was going to be. Galashiels was only twenty or so miles away as the crow flies, but it could have been hundreds to Abby and the farm folk. The furthest most of them had travelled was to Kelso on market days. It had dawned on Abby over the last years just how much her mother must have loved her father to leave everything she'd ever known in the close-knit Border community, and run off with a man she'd only just met.

'You were so brave, Mam,' she whispered softly, stroking the small glass face of the watch. 'I'll try and make you proud of me, I promise.' There was a lump in her throat and her eyes were smarting, and she clasped the watch tightly, bringing her hands against her chest. She would give up all thought of this new life with its escape from the farm and Joe McHaffie, for one day with her mother. One day of seeing her, touching her, hearing her voice...

And then she wiped the tears from her face with a swift rub of her hand, replacing the watch beside the pile of clothes.

It was no good crying for the moon, moreover it was weakening, bringing with it, as it did, a whole host of regrets. If only she had asserted herself with her father that Christmas Eve and brooked no refusal about waiting up for her mother; if only she hadn't gone to sleep and had heard her mother return and had gone down to the kitchen; if only she hadn't been too late in running downstairs when the screaming and shouting had begun, but it had been her father's voice and she had thought he was having one of his turns and so it was best to leave him to her mam...

'Stop it.' She whispered the words out loud. She knew from experience this train of thought took her into a downward spiral of bitter anguish and remorse, and then the whole world became a grey place. Squaring her slim shoulders, she told herself to go downstairs and take the mince pies out of the oven and get on with the rest of her housewifely duties. Life had to be faced looking forward – it was the only way.

Chapter Ten

It was Christmas Eve, and it had started to snow again in earnest the day before, adding to the mounds piled up from the previous weeks. The fresh fall swiftly covered the ground around the farm that had been cleared previously to make daily life a little easier, piling itself on windowsills and forming drifts against the barn doors and outbuildings.

When Abby had awoken that morning the farm had become white and hushed, and when she'd peered out of her bedroom window she'd groaned softly. Beautiful as the clean new world was, the snow meant the walk to the parish church at Morebattle where the bairns' Sunday school Christmas party was being held at midday would be heavy going. The party took place in the church hall and the ladies of the congregation organized the annual treat. She had promised to help on the day, along with Tessa, one of the labourers' wives who had two young children who attended Sunday school.

At least she was now too old to be expected to go to the farmhouse on Christmas Day though, she thought, as she pulled on her clothes in the icy room. Every year the farmer's womenfolk entertained the workers' bairns to a fine tea, but before they were fed they were expected to recite poetry or sing the songs learned at school, and she had hated that. When, after her first Christmas at the farm, she had told her grandfather she didn't want to go again, he had replied that all the bairns on the farm went to the farmhouse on Christmas Day, and that was that.

Each child had left the farmhouse with a bag of sweets, and the farmer would present a gift of a cut of beef or mutton and a bag of shortbread to each householder, which was generous enough, she supposed. It was the singing for her supper that caught her on the raw.

It was the same rigidity about maintaining tradition on Hogmanay morning too. The bairns of the parish were always invited to the minister's house to take part in a short service, singing the second paraphrase and a prayer of thanksgiving and kneeling as they were blessed for the coming year. Then each child was presented with an apple and orange and a picture postcard of the church. Some of their friends used to go on from the manse to the surrounding farmhouses and even the Brookwell estate to seek their 'Hogmanay cakes' in time-honoured style, receiving sweets and cakes and fruit. Robin had always entered into this wholeheartedly but she had gone straight home. To her, arriving at the door of the houses had seemed like begging, and she would rather have walked barefoot on hot coals than meet the laird's son in such circumstances.

Not that she had really come across Nicholas Jefferson-Price since the day he had rescued her from the Cut. She had seen him in the distance once or twice, galloping across the fields on his horse, but that had been in the early days after the

159

incident and she had always made sure she remained out of sight until the coast was clear. He had called at the cottage a short while after that day – causing a great stir among the farm folk in the process – asking how she was, but she had been at school for which she was thankful. She was grateful to him, very grateful, but the whole episode had become infinitely more embarrassing in hindsight, besides which the laird was universally loathed and she didn't want anyone to think she was friendly with the enemy. Then in the last years she hadn't seen him at all; common gossip had it that since he'd gone away to university he rarely came home, no doubt making the most of the high life that all young bloods with wealth and influence indulged in to a greater or lesser extent.

Slipping her cold feet into her boots, she buttoned them up and put all thoughts of the laird's son out of her mind as she went downstairs to prepare breakfast. Her grandfather liked his porridge thick and creamy rather than stiff with salt and water as was common with Border folk, and once in the kitchen she set about stoking up the range fire that she had dampened down with tea leaves and slack the night before, before warming the pan of porridge she had left soaking in milk overnight.

They had finished the porridge and started on the eggs and bacon and crusty loaf that followed, when Robin dropped a bombshell that had caused Abby to choke on a piece of bacon and her grandfather's mouth to gape.

Smiling happily, steam wafting round his pleasant square face from the mug of tea he was holding, Robin announced, 'There's somethin' I want to ask you, Granda. I'm going to ask Rachel to marry me and once we're wed I wondered if you'd be happy for us to live here with you. She's a good cook and she knows what hard work is, sure enough.'

This last sentence carried a trace of bitterness. Robin had been walking out with Rachel Mc-Arthur for twelve months and had often come home with tales of the ill-treatment she received at the hands of her parents. Jack McArthur was the innkeeper of a public house situated in a small hamlet set between Frogden and Linton, and anyone meeting him for the first time would think him a genial enough fellow. He had a big blowsy wife and eleven children, and Rachel was the eldest girl. According to Robin she was worked to death by her father and regularly beaten by her mother who was handy with her fists when she was drunk, which was fairly often. From as young as seven or eight Rachel had been set to work in the inn kitchen and had received virtually no schooling, the excuse given to any-one who enquired as to her absence being that she was 'weakly and suffered with her stomach'.

A shy, timid young woman, Rachel was slight in build and looked much younger than her eighteen years, and although Robin was two years her junior he appeared much older, both in his phy-sical appearance and his manner. The courtship had been difficult, not least because Rachel was used like a workhorse by her parents and the occasional minutes when they managed to meet always had to be stolen. But in spite of the rarity of the secret meetings, Robin's regard for his sweetheart had never wavered. All this Wilbert and Abby had learned from Robin in the past year; they had never met Rachel, although they knew of the family.

It was Wilbert who now brought this fact to the fore when he said quietly, 'How can I answer that when I've never met the lass, Rob? And what do you think Jack McArthur and his missus are going to say? If what you've told us is right, they're not going to want to lose their chief cook and bottle washer, are they?'

'I know, I know.' The brightness in Robin's face dimmed. 'We won't have their blessing, that's for sure, but that won't matter if we have yours. You'll like her, Granda, I know you will. She's...'

He was unable to express what she was, waving his hands helplessly.

Abby couldn't contain herself any longer. Her baby brother talking about getting *wed?* 'Robin, you're sixteen years old,' she said hotly. 'Far too young to think about marriage. And what if you find out you don't love her in a year or two? I know you want to rescue her from life at home but she has to do that herself. She could leave, couldn't she? She's eighteen, she's not a bairn.'

Robin looked at the sister he adored. But for Abby, they would both have been incarcerated in the workhouse, that terrible place of no hope, but by the sheer force of her will she had transported them here to a place he privately called heaven on earth. He had been born to be a shepherd, he knew that now, and it was all thanks to his sister that he'd found the life he loved. But it was her strength that made her impatient with the short-comings in others at times, like now. 'Rachel is not like you, she hasn't got it in her to stand up to them but that's all right because I love her just the way she is. And aye, I want to rescue her, more than anything else I want that, I won't deny it. As for me being sixteen, I don't feel sixteen inside, Abby, and I sure as hell know my own mind. She's the one for me and she says I'm the one for her. That's enough for me.'

'She might say that to anyone who was pre-pared to take her out of the inn and her life there. Have you considered that?'

Robin took a deep breath. 'If you met her you wouldn't think that.'

'But that's the rub, isn't it? I *haven't* met her. Granda hasn't met her, because when you see her it's for half-an-hour here and ten minutes there. I bet if you add up the amount of time you've spent together it wouldn't be more than a few hours in the whole of the year you've known her. You can't know someone like that, it's … it's artificial.'

'You know nowt about it, about how we feel.'

'I know this whole thing is ridiculous.'

'Shut up, Abby.' Robin's fists were clenched by his sides. 'Just shut up.'

'No, I won't, because this doesn't just concern you, it concerns me and Granda too.'

'Oh, and you're really bothered about Granda, aren't you? So bothered you're going to disappear off to Galashiels without a by-your-leave.'

'That's so unfair.' Abby was cut to the quick. 'You take that back, Robin Kirby.'

'No, I won't, an' I'll tell you somethin' else

while I'm about it. I'd have thought if you were really bothered about Granda you'd have been pleased someone is willing to come and take your place here and see to the house and the rest of it. Or are you jealous about another lass coming in?'

She couldn't come back at him the way she wanted to because he had hit her on the raw. It was only as he had spoken that Abby realized that *was* part of it. She didn't want another woman in what was her home, taking over where she had left off. Which was horrible and petty and mean-minded, but it was how she felt. And hurt – she felt hurt that she could be replaced so easily. She had taken care of Robin all his life, worried about him, protected him, defended him. Even when their mother was alive her affection for him had been more maternal than sisterly, and now it felt as though her love had been thrown back in her face.

She must have looked as stricken as she felt, because her grandfather stepped into the fray, his voice still quiet but holding authority when he said, 'That's enough from both of you. Robin, you do a man's job and you do it well and have done for the last two years since you left school. I'm proud of you, but I can understand your sister's concerns and I echo them to some extent. Bring Rachel to meet us, all right? First things first. Then we'll talk again, the three of us, because this involves Abby just as much as you or me. Regardless of where she is, this will be her home for as long as she wants it to be and she has a say in who lives here. Do you understand me?'

Grandfather and grandson stared at each other for a moment before Robin turned his gaze on

Abby's white face, and such was the fury in his eyes that she bit hard on her lower lip to stop the moan deep inside from escaping. He looked as though he hated her, she thought painfully. Never in her life would she have dreamed Robin could look at her like this.

He stood up, thrusting his chair away with such force that it skidded across the, floor and crashed over. And then he stamped out of the cottage, pulling on his jacket and cap as he went and ignoring her anguished, 'Robin, wait.'

'Let him go, lass.' Wilbert stood to his feet. 'He'll calm down when he's had time to think.'

'He hates me.'

'Don't be daft. He should have expected we'd want time to take it in.' Wilbert was pulling on his coat and cap as he spoke. 'I'll have a word with him later, don't fret.'

'But he *didn't* expect it.' She recalled Robin's face, so bright and joyous when he'd told them he was going to ask Rachel to marry him, and felt worse than ever.

Wilbert looked at his granddaughter. He sensed something of what she was feeling and the reasons for it, but he was a man of few words and had no way of expressing himself. Instead he walked over to her and gently patted her shoulder before following his grandson out of the cottage, thinking as he did so, *What a to-do, and at Christmas an' all. Why* was it that things always seemed to happen at Christmas with these two grandchildren of his?

Chapter Eleven

Abby was still thinking about the altercation with Robin when she left the church hall later that afternoon. The party had gone well, but once the children had been dispatched home – grubby-faced and sticky-fingered – it had taken some time to clear up the resulting mess, and it was after three o'clock when she said goodbye to the group of Morebattle women who had also stayed behind. When she had called on Tessa earlier that day, she'd found both Tessa's bairns had been up all night with sickness and diarrhoea, and so she had walked to the church by herself. She had been glad of this; her mind was so occupied with Robin it had been a relief not to have to make conversation with anyone.

All the way to the church she had berated herself for her part in the row that had erupted so suddenly. She should have voiced her misgivings differently; Robin could be as stubborn as a mule at times and she had gone about it all wrong, simply because he had wounded her with his breezy manner when he'd spoken so happily about someone taking her place. Now, whatever happened, this would cause a wedge between her and her brother.

Stepping out of the building into the winter afternoon, Abby looked up into the low white sky from which the occasional snowflake floated gently down in the freezing, still air. Mr Newton

166

had once described December as a dead, naked month of long nights and brief days, a grizzled, grey month, dreary and barren. Most of the other children had looked at him as though he was mad but she had understood exactly what he had meant. But it could be beautiful too, she told herself as she began the walk back to the farm. Like today. The hedgerows either side of the lane she was following were thick with snow, icicles hanging from the laden trees and bushes and glittering in the winter light like delicate crystals, but far more exquisite than anything manmade.

Abby smiled ruefully. She would never dare express such a fanciful thought to anyone at the farm. To them, the winter was an enemy that made their already hard life just that bit harder. She had discovered at the high school she had a flair for poetry, but when she had read a couple of pieces of her work that her English teacher had been particularly pleased with to her grandfather and Robin, their faces had expressed surprise and bewilderment. Her grandfather had tried to be supportive in his way once he had collected himself, but not Robin. Her brother had stared at her before shaking his head and saying, 'I'm sorry, Abby, but I can't be doing with airy-fairy stuff, and what are them teachers encouraging it for anyway? Waste of time, I call it. Poetry and books won't help a lass keep house, now, will they? You're a working-class lass, and marrying and settling down with a good man who'll provide for you and any bairns is what you should be aiming for. The gentry might have time for such things but not us.'

She had told him in reply that it was up to he

what she aimed for, and that her future was her own business too and she didn't thank him for mapping it out for her. But the whole episode had emphasized what she had already known at heart – Robin was very much a product of his environment and saw the roles of a man and a woman very differently from her.

But then she and Robin *were* different. Abby paused, biting her lip. They might have been born of the same parents but apart from that they had little in common now they had got older. Robin was a Border lad through and through and she accepted him as he was. Why couldn't he return the compliment? But he made no secret of despising her education and then her decision to go into nursing.

A snowflake landing on Abby's nose brought her out of her reverie, reminding her she needed to get home before the forecast snow began in earnest. She began to walk on, but the feeling of aloneness that had begun with her mother's death and had deepened with the years was strong.

She couldn't live the rest of her life as the wife of a man from within the farming community, she told herself for the umpteenth time. Just the thought of it produced a panicky claustrophobia that made her heart pound. Robin and the rest of them would never understand that, though. Even if she hadn't determined to take up nursing as a career, she would have left the area sooner or later. It wasn't that she was afraid of the hard life the women led; she had already been warned over and over again that nursing was a tough, exhausting and often thankless task, and that it could be grim and distressing some of the time. But she would be *alive* in a way she never would here, and making her own way in the world outside the tight constrictions of what was expected of her as her grandfather's granddaughter. She wanted to *live* and see more of the world than the Border neck of the woods before she thought about marrying and settling down – if she ever did decide to marry. And she might not; it wasn't obligatory, whatever Robin might have her believe.

The last thought brought her mind back to that morning and the frosty state of affairs that existed between Robin and herself. She would have to apologize for the way she had spoken, she decided. Not the content of what she had said because she *absolutely* believed Robin was too young to think of marriage, but the way she had couched her comments. However, whether Robin would accept her apology was another kettle of fish, of course.

She had been so deep in thought that she couldn't have said when she first became aware that she was not alone. There had been no sound as far as she knew, but suddenly she was certain that she was being followed, and with the realization came the knowledge that she had inadvertently put herself in just the position she had guarded against for so long. Her anxiety about the falling-out between Robin and herself had made her careless.

The familiar sickly feeling that assailed her when Joe McHaffie was anywhere close was strong, but added to it was a dread that quickened her footsteps. She wanted to turn round and face him and tell him she wasn't frightened of him or his intimidation, but the truth of it was that she *was* frightened, and confronting him on a deserted road with no one within earshot would be stupid.

Frequent falls of snow over the last weeks that had briefly partially melted in places and become slushy, only to freeze again once night fell and then had been covered by more snow, had made the lane treacherous in places. Twice she nearly went headlong as she tried to hurry, and she was forced to slow down to a steady pace once more in spite of her fear.

She knew he was gaining on her. She could hear the crunch of snow under his feet now, and then a cough, as though he wanted to announce his presence, which of course he would, she thought, as a dart of anger replaced the panic. He would love to think he was scaring her, that was Joe McHaffie all over. The anger helped, putting iron in her backbone.

She wasn't going to scurry along like a mouse. Casually, as though she was straightening her hat, she withdrew her hatpin and held it tight in her hand, before stopping and swinging round to face the man she had come to loathe. And then her eyes widened with surprise.

For his part, Nicholas Jefferson-Price was equally taken aback. When he had first noticed the figure of a young woman in front of him he had checked his long strides for a moment before telling himself he was being silly. He had no wish to alarm her, of course, but he needed to get home for a dinner he was attending with his parents and he was already late. He shouldn't have gone for so long a walk, perhaps, but as usual the stifling atmosphere at the house had driven him out. He'd taken Jet for a gallop the day before and sprained the animal's foreleg in the process, which he felt bad about.

He had coughed to alert the woman in front of him as to his proximity, and he had expected her to turn whereupon he could have passed the time of day and then quickly hurried on. As it was, she had spun round with such ferocity it had stopped him in his tracks. That and the look of her. She was beautiful, lovely, and for some reason he felt he had seen her before. But no, he would remember such a stunning face if he had met her in the past.

Recovering, he said quietly, 'I'm so sorry. Did I startle you?'

'No. Yes. I mean–' Abby was floundering. She couldn't very well admit the truth and so she prevaricated. 'It's a lonely road.'

'Yes, it is rather, but please be assured I mean you no harm.' He paused. 'Would you allow me to accompany you? For protection, I mean, if you are a little nervous? I have no intention of– What I mean to say is that you are perfectly safe with me.' He could hear himself stumbling for the right words and knew he'd gone red in the face but he felt all at sea. It was the first time in his life a young woman had affected him thus and he felt acutely embarrassed. Normally he was totally at ease with the opposite sex. And the feeling that he knew her was stronger. Her clothes were those of a working-class woman and yet her voice didn't carry much of an accent; it was mellow and pleasing to the ear, as if she had had elocution lessons.

Nicholas was right here. Part of the high-school

171

curriculum to prepare their young ladies for the outside world had included the art of distinct pronunciation and articulation, and the twice-weekly lessons had gradually transformed the way Abby and her classmates spoke, mostly without them being particularly aware of it.

Pulling himself together, he said formally, 'Nicholas Jefferson-Price, at your service.'

His discomposure had given Abby time to collect herself. 'I know who you are,' she said, a slight smile touching her lips. 'We have met before. Twice before, actually. The first time you almost ran me down with your horse, and the second you made amends by rescuing me from what I perceived as certain death but was certainly a perilous situation.'

Her voice had a soft huskiness to it; he could listen to her all day. 'The child caught in the brambles at the Cut,' he said, his voice high with surprise. 'Of course. I'm sorry, I didn't recognize you. You've grown.' As soon as the words left his mouth he thought how stupid they sounded. 'What I mean is, you're not a child any longer.' That was worse.

Abby laughed, she couldn't help it. He didn't seem like the man she remembered who had been so in control. This Nicholas Jefferson-Price was much more human, nicer. 'I know what you mean and it *was* nine years ago. I'm eighteen now. I wouldn't have expected you to recognize me.'

She was being kind but she must think him an absolute fool; he *was* an absolute fool.

His obvious embarrassment was doing Abby's poise the world of good. The laughter in her face reflected in her voice, she said, 'I think I can safely put this back in my hat now,' as she stuck the hatpin back whence it had come.

'Good grief.' He stared at her. 'Would you have used it?'

'Most certainly. If I'd had to.'

'Thank goodness *you* at least recognized *me!*'

He was smiling now and it struck her he was really very good-looking with his jet-black hair and deep-brown eyes, but there was something else, a kind of maleness was the only way she could describe it, that made her heart beat faster. Glad he couldn't read her thoughts, she said, 'I should be getting home,' as she began to walk once more, and it seemed natural he should fall into step beside her. 'You're not riding today,' she said after a moment or two.

'No.' He looked down at her as they walked. A wisp of her glorious hair had escaped from under the hat and he had the almost overpowering desire to feel it beneath his fingers. 'To be honest I shouldn't have ridden yesterday either, the snow is too deep in places. I took Jet out and he ended up with a sprained foreleg. I should have known but I'm only back from the hospital for a few days so I wanted to make the most of it, I suppose.'

'The hospital?' She turned her head up to him. 'Are you ill?'

'No, no, I'm a doctor. Well, a junior doctor, as our esteemed consultant reminds his minions of all too often. He's the autocratic type.'

Her face lit up, causing him to catch his breath 'I'm going to be a nurse.'

'You are?'

173

'I leave for the Hemingway hospital in Galashiels in the New Year to start my training.'

'That's great.' He sounded as though he meant it which was wonderful after all the negativity she had encountered. 'What made you decide on nursing?'

She had been asked this question more than once since she had made her decision known, and always there had been a note of censure in the asker's voice. But not this time, and it checked her from giving the short, non-committal reply of the past. But if she told the truth, if she revealed the real reason, it would open up a whole can of worms. Her grandfather had sworn Robin and her to secrecy about the circumstances in which they had arrived at the farm, and she had never talked about it to anyone. And, much as she didn't want to lay bare what the laird's son might well regard as a shameful heritage, she found she didn't want to prevaricate either. Which was strange, odd, she told herself. He was nothing to her so it shouldn't matter one way or the other, should it? Quietly, her head down now, she said, 'It's a long story.'

'I've got nothing but time,' he said just as quietly, ignoring the fact that he was already late and his mother would raise merry hell when he got in. The dinner party they were dragging him to tonight was at the home of his mother's closest friend, and he knew full well both women were angling for a match between him and the daughter of the family. Felicity Hutton's three brothers had been his childhood playmates, and when Felicity had been born ten years after the youngest brother much had been made of her by her doting mother. In spite of this Felicity had grown into an agreeable young woman with a quick wit and a pretty face, but he had no more wish to marry her than she him. At his mother's insistence he had come home for a day or two in the summer to attend Felicity's eighteenth birthday ball, and on that occasion she had laughed with him at their mothers' match-making designs and confided she had her eye on someone else who would be deemed unsuitable by her parents if they discovered her intentions. Her beau was abroad making his fortune, she'd whis-pered, and he would come back and claim her for his own once he could afford to keep her in the manner that her family would expect. Apparently she had offered to elope with him but the young man wouldn't hear of it, which Nicholas thought was in his favour.

Abby didn't speak for some moments, and when she did he had to lower his head so soft was her voice. 'It started with my father– No, that's wrong. It started with my mother running away with my father, I suppose, and then him going off to war. We lived in Sunderland then...'

As she went on with her story, Nicholas found himself listening with bated breath. She had been a brave, gutsy little thing as a child, but he hadn't realized *how* gutsy all those years ago although even then there had been something different about her. He had thought about the beautiful little blonde girl he had hauled out of the Cut a few times in the months after the event but then university had taken him away from the area. And he had been glad to go, often making ex-cuses in the holidays to disappear off somewhere with one or another of his chums rather than return home.

'And you say your family and the folk round here think nursing is a somewhat disreputable occupation?' he said when she finished speaking. He had been touched to the heart of him about her father and mother but sensed she would not wish to talk further about that. 'I could tell them it is not.'

'I think my grandfather feels I am wasting my education.'

He was surprised she had attended the high school until she was eighteen years of age. Not that he didn't think she was bright enough, she certainly was. Even as a small child there had been something quite exceptional about Miss Abigail Kirby. But even among his own class education for daughters was considered far less important than for sons.

'And the tutors at the high school didn't help in that regard either. They wanted me to become a schoolmistress like them. One teacher even said to my grandfather that she was very disappointed I was choosing not to use my mind in the future.' She glanced at him. 'I put her right about that after he told me what she'd said.'

From the tone of her voice Nicholas felt sorry for the hapless schoolmistress.

'And you? What made you go into the medical profession when–' Abby stopped abruptly. She had been about to say, 'When you are the laird's son,' but was worried that might sound rude.

It seemed Nicholas had read her mind, though. 'When I don't need to work but could spend my time hunting, fishing and shooting, and in other

176

gentlemanly pursuits?' he said wryly.

'I'm sorry.' She felt awful. He had been so nice when she had told him about her father and mother; if he had been shocked and scandalized he hadn't shown it and his manner to her had not altered. And now she had offended him.

'Don't be.' He smiled. 'It's a valid question and one my mother among others has asked more than once.' His tone had hardened when he spoke of his mother. 'The truth of it is I would go stark, staring mad living the life expected of the laird's son and heir. My father was hoping I'd follow him and make the army my career for a few years until I took over the estate. Go in as an officer, of course, and lord it over the common throng.' He paused. 'Now it's me who's sorry. I don't mean to sound sour but I have no intention of following in my father's footsteps in any regard.'

'Do they know that? Your parents?'

'They're beginning to.' Hence the reason for his walk this afternoon. The atmosphere in the house was unbearable. His mother flitted about with trembling lips and a wan face, and his father was even more unpleasant than usual. 'Ungrateful little cur,' his father had called him in their last row the night before, and when he reminded his father that he was a man of twenty-seven and had his own life to live, his father had been scathing. If he insisted on playing at doctors for a while he had no objection, his father had said scornfully, but the estate must always come first. At some point he would inherit and he needed to be fully conversant with what was entailed in running the estate and the myriad business dealings connected with it.

'But don't you want to become the laird eventually?'

'No, I sure as hell don't,' Nicholas said emphatically before immediately apologizing. 'Forgive me. But no, no, I don't want that. I'm well aware my father is deeply resented and disliked and with good reason. I am not a fool – I know how people are treated by him. He's a thoroughly objectionable man.'

'You don't like him?' Abby couldn't hide the fact that she found this shocking. Whatever the laird was like, Nicholas was his son after all. 'Your own father?'

The sun was beginning to set and a dusky pink glow was colouring the silver-white winter sky, bathing their path in a softer, more mellow light. They had been walking slowly, Nicholas measuring his pace to hers, but now he stopped and drew her to face him before letting go of her arms. He found he wanted her to understand how it was. He didn't want her to think badly of him, which was crazy, ridiculous in fact, because until this afternoon he hadn't known she existed. Oh, he had known about the child, of course, and he remembered her as a brave and unusually beautiful little thing, but this woman in front of him...

Swallowing hard, he said, 'You think me harsh, don't you, and I don't blame you. From infancy we are taught to respect and love our parents, but what if that is impossible? My father is incapable of normal human affection, you see. Once in a while every generation throws up an individual such as him. Some are merely oddities, men or

178

women who choose to live solitary lives or become recluses. Others have a more sinister bent and become monsters, committing the sort of crimes that are beyond ordinary people's comprehension. And then there is my father's kind.'

Abby stared at him. She was conscious of thinking that this Christmas Eve had taken the strangest turn. Never in her wildest dreams would she have imagined she and the laird's son would be talking like this, or that she would have told him what had brought her and Robin to the Borders.

'My father is totally self-centred,' Nicholas went on. 'He believes absolutely in his God-given right to rule his subjects as he sees fit – he has no compassion, no tenderness, none of the human virtues that one would expect of a husband and father. Living with such an individual is ... soul-destroying. When I was growing up the slightest resistance on my part to his decrees brought forth a rage that was terrifying to a small boy. Mistakes were treated in the same way as disobedience. I was his son and heir – he expected a mirror image of himself in every way. I'm afraid I was, and am, a severe disappointment.'

He smiled, but there was no humour in his eyes.

'I suppose, in a way, the desire to become a doctor and help people was a direct result of my rebellion against everything my father stands for. Certainly the psychiatrists would say so. But it's not only that. I'm good at it.'

His smile this time was real.

'That sounds arrogant, doesn't it, but it's true. I intend to become the best surgeon it is possible for me to be and I won't let anything or anyone

179

stand in the way of that.'

So there was a little of his father in him. And then Abby checked herself. No, that was unkind. It wasn't the same at all.

They started walking again by unspoken mutual consent and now Nicholas began to tell her stories about hospital life: funny, self-deprecating stories on the whole that made her laugh out loud. By the time they came to the beginning of the track that led to the farm she was aware she didn't want the interlude to end. She hadn't enjoyed herself so much since– Well, there was no since, she admitted silently. She had never enjoyed being with someone so much. He wasn't at all like she'd imagined and there was something about him, something that made her stomach flutter and her heart race and brought the blood singing through her veins.

It was this last thought that brought her to a halt as he turned with her into the track. 'I ... I'd better go on alone,' she said awkwardly, suddenly remembering who he was. He had been so natural and unaffected that she'd forgotten he was the gentry. If she was seen talking and laughing with the laird's son there would be gossip of the worst kind.

Nicholas looked at her, his deep-brown eyes narrowing. He had a fair idea of what she was thinking but he couldn't let her go without asking to see her again. He knew there were a whole host of reasons why he shouldn't, not least this wretched business of class and what his father would say if he discovered he was walking out with a farm girl. But then he wasn't walking out with her, he reasoned in the next moment. They were simply friends. No, not even that. Acquaintances, who had their interest in medicine and hospital life between them. And after Christmas he would be returning to the hospital and she was off to start her training in Galashiels. Without thinking further, he said, 'Could ... could we meet again and talk some more before I go back to London?'

'Your hospital is in London?' Abby was both disappointed and relieved it was so far away; disappointed because there would be no chance of running into him again once she left for Galashiels, and relieved for the same reason.

Nicholas nodded. 'I leave the day after Boxing Day.'

It would be stupid to risk her reputation and she would have to meet him secretly which would mean lying to her grandfather and Robin as to where she was going. It was impossible.

She nodded. 'All right.'

'You will?' His face lit up.

And it was in that moment that Abby knew she had fallen in love. As quickly and as irrevocably as that.

Chapter Twelve

When Abby turned the corner of the track and the farm cottages came into view, she saw her grandfather in the doorway of their house and he waved to her. As she got nearer, he called, 'You're late, lass. I was beginning to think you wouldn't get home before the snow started again.'

'I stayed to help with the clearing up.' That wasn't a lie, Abby reassured herself.

'Where's Tessa and the bairns?'

'The bairns are poorly so she couldn't help as planned.'

'That's a shame. A trek like that never seems so long if you've got someone to talk to.'

'No, I suppose not.' That wasn't a lie either, not really.

As she reached her grandfather he looked at her keenly. 'You look bright-eyed and bushy-tailed. Anything happened?'

'No, of course not.' That *was* a lie. Guilt prompted her to continue, 'It's a bracing walk. It puts colour in your cheeks, I suppose.'

'Aye. Well, maybe your brother should have gone into Morebattle then. He's as miserable as sin.'

The guilt she was feeling was further compounded by the knowledge that in the last little while she hadn't given a thought to Robin. 'I'll talk to him. Is he in the house?'

'He's in the far barn with that ewe that's been ailing.'

As she walked to the barn the snow began in earnest, big fat flakes that fell on the frozen ground and immediately settled, hiding any icy patches beneath it. Pushing open the door she saw Robin had already lit a paraffin lantern above the pen where the sick sheep lay deep in straw, and although he glanced up as she entered he immediately turned away again.

She didn't prevaricate as she joined him where

he was sitting on a straw bale, plumping down beside him as she said, 'I'm sorry for going for you earlier and I don't want to fall out about this.' When he didn't respond she put her hand on one of his. 'Really, Robin. I'm sorry.'

She thought he was still going to ignore her, but after a moment or two he said thickly, 'I know you think you know what's best for me, Abby, but you don't. Not over this. Rachel is the one for me and she feels the same, and not just because she wants to leave home.'

'I shouldn't have said that.'

He shook his head before looking at her. 'I love her, Abby. I'll always love her. And aye, I want her out of that place where she's part punchbag and part unpaid help. The life they lead her you wouldn't believe. I wouldn't treat a dog that way.'

'But you're both so *young*.'

He sighed, but then he said, 'Abby, I don't feel young, not inside. I think what happened with Mam made us both grow up quick. From when I came here I've known exactly what I want in life and it's to work as a shepherd an' marry an' have a family of my own. I know you don't want the same and we're different. Chalk an' cheese, I suppose. But ... but you're my sister and it's important you understand. I love everything to do with being here. Like at clipping time when the air's full of the smell of hot tar and sawdust and the sheep, and the swallows twittering round the farm buildings blends in with the clank of the shears and the voices of the men and sheep.'

Abby stared at him. It sounded almost poetic. 'I know, and you're good at what you do, Granda's

183

always said that, but *marriage*, Robin. It's a big thing.'

'It's the natural thing, for me an' Rachel.' He covered her hand that was on his with his other hand, turning to face her. 'I've asked her to come to the cottage tomorrow morning to meet you and Granda. Christmas Day is the only time the inn shuts, but she'll still be cooking for them all later in the day, Christmas or no Christmas.'

'Oh, Robin.' He sounded so bitter about Rachel's family.

'Will you give her a chance? Make her welcome?'

'Of course I will. You shouldn't have to ask that.'

'And I'm sorry an' all, lass. About saying what I said about Galashiels and the nursing and all of it. I … I suppose at the back of me I've felt once you go from here you'll never come back. I've been sitting here thinking and I know I've always gone on about your learning an' the high school being a waste of time, but it's because I don't want you to leave. But you've got to do what you want, same as I have. I see that now. And it'd be selfish to try and keep you here when your heart's not in it.'

Abby didn't know what to say. This was a side of her baby brother that was new to her, and if it was Rachel who had brought it out then she was grateful for that, if nothing else.

Robin's voice softened still further when he murmured, 'Don't cry, lass. Come on, come on.'

'I … I thought you weren't bothered about me going when you said about Rachel coming to live here.'

'Don't be daft. Course I don't want you to go. You're my sister and' – his voice became gruff with embarrassment – 'I love you.'

The following morning when Abby awoke she lay for a while cocooned under the blankets in the freezing room, thinking back to the evening before. Christmas Eve had always been a difficult time but this one had almost been joyous. She and Robin had been back to normal, something she would have thought impossible earlier in the day, and her grandfather's relief had been palpable. After their evening meal her grandfather had brought out a box of sugared almonds he had bought specially for the occasion, and they had sat round the fire together drinking home-made blackcurrant wine and chatting. It had been a special time and each one of them had been aware of it and the changes that would soon take place.

Sliding out of bed she went to the window and peered out into the still-black morning, although the snow brought its own luminescence to the scene. It had piled itself on the deep windowsill outside, forming a drift halfway up the panes which meant it would be lying thickly on the ground. Abby frowned to herself. She had arranged to meet Nicholas that afternoon some way down the lane so no one from the farm would see them, but it was going to take some explaining if she said she was going walking in such conditions.

She would think of something. She nodded to the thought, her shoulders hunched against the cold. It wasn't snowing at the moment but if it started again, the farm would soon be cut off from the outside world, though Border folk were used to that. Sometimes in the worst of winter the farms and hamlets were isolated for weeks in a frozen world of their own.

Would he come if the weather worsened? And then she remembered the look on his face when she had agreed to meet him. He would come.

Lighting the lamp at the side of her bed, Abby dressed and made her way downstairs. Once in the kitchen she stoked up the range and added more wood and coal to the flickering flames, before doing the same to the glowing embers in the grate in the sitting room.

By the time her grandfather and Robin came downstairs a few minutes later, the black kettle was on the hob and boiling, and within a moment or two the tea was mashing in the teapot. It was six o'clock. Once the menfolk had drunk their tea scalding hot they went out to see to the sheep that had been brought into the lower fields because of the weather, and as they opened the door of the cottage a feathery drift of snow fell inwards across the cork matting.

'We're goin' to have to bring 'em all into the barns if this keeps up,' Wilbert said to his grandson as they trudged out into the bitterly cold morning, leaving Abby to sweep the snow out through the door before getting on with the breakfast she'd have ready and waiting for them when they returned. It was the same routine she had done a thousand times and more, but today for some reason it seemed poignant. Whether it was the fact she would soon be leaving the farm for Galashiels, or meeting Nicholas the day before, she didn't know, but she felt even more emotional than ever this particular Christmas.

She was clearing a path with the shovel from the cottage door ten minutes later when she thought she caught sight of someone in the distance down the farm track that led to the lane. The sky was still dark but the small figure showed up clearly against the white snow. Abby squinted, trying to see clearer, and as she did so the person stumbled and then fell.

Throwing down the shovel, Abby hurried as best she could towards the sprawled shape that was making no effort to rise, thinking as she did so, *Who on earth is it at this time of the morning and on Christmas Day too?*

She became more perturbed the nearer she got because she realized the person was a young woman with no hat or coat and furthermore she was lying face down in the snow as though she was dead. As Abby got within arm's length the girl moved and struggled to sit up and it was then her long hair fell away from round her face. Abby gasped with shock – she couldn't help it. There was no way of knowing whether the girl was normally pretty or plain because her face was a swollen, bloody mass of bruised flesh. Her eyes were narrow slits in the blackening puffiness and her lips were drawn back slightly, showing a gap where one of the front teeth was missing.

Falling on her knees, Abby put her arms round the girl who was shivering violently. 'It's all right, it's all right,' she found herself murmuring, trying to lift her up. 'Come on, we need to get you in the warm. Lean on me, I'll help you.'

Somehow she managed to get the girl on her feet but only because she was taking most of the weight of her body, and they began to stumble towards the cottage, both nearly going headlong more than once before they reached the narrow stretch of path Abby had cleared. As they reached the doorstep of the house Andrew McHaffie stepped out of his, only to stand transfixed as he looked at them. 'Get my granda.' Abby was gasping for breath as she was virtually carrying the girl, but when Andrew didn't at first respond she practically screamed at him, *Get my granda.*

As the farm steward hurried off Abby managed to haul the limp figure across the threshold, heaving her over to the old sofa in front of the sitting-room fire and dropping her down onto the big soft cushions. Kneeling beside her Abby touched the girl's hand which was icy cold and caked with dried blood. 'Who's done this to you?' But she already feared she knew the answer. This had to be Rachel, and if her parents had beaten her this badly Robin would go and see them and there would be hell to pay.

When she saw the girl's distorted lips try to move, Abby said, 'No, don't try to talk. I'm sorry, don't try to talk. Lie still and I'll get some blankets.'

She flew upstairs to her bedroom and gathered the blankets and eiderdown off it before dashing downstairs and covering the still figure on the sofa with them. Hurrying across to the range, she lifted the kettle off its steel shelf at the side of it and poured some hot water into one of the stone hot-water bottles that were kept as spares in the cupboard. After she had pulled off the girl's sodden boots she chaffed her icy-cold feet for a few moments, trying to instil some warmth into the blue flesh, and then placed the hot-water bottle at her feet before tucking the blankets more tightly around her.

It was at this juncture that Robin came bursting into the house closely followed by Wilbert.

'Oh, Rachel.' The words were a groan as he fell on his knees beside the sofa, putting his arms round her as gently as one would handle a new-born babe. 'Rachel, Rachel...'

'Who did it?' Wilbert looked at Abby who shook her head indicating that she didn't know. 'Well, whoever it was they want stringing up,' he added grimly.

Abby motioned with her hand for her grand-father to say no more. They needed to calm Robin down. Her brother was quite capable of taking Rachel's father on and in a physical fight between the two, Robin might come off worse. Quickly mashing a pot of tea, she half-filled a cup and added two heaped spoonfuls of sugar before pour-ing in enough milk to make the tea lukewarm. It would be all Rachel's swollen bloody lips would be able to stand. Taking it to Robin who was still kneeling at the side of the sofa, tears in his eyes, she whispered, 'Get her to drink this, there's plenty of sugar in it for the shock. She needs to get warm inside and out, poor thing.'

'I'll kill them.' Robin took the cup from her and the look on her brother's face frightened Abby. She didn't care about harm coming to Rachel's parents – they deserved beating to within an inch of their lives too – but if Robin attacked them who knew where this would end? Her brother was angry enough for murder.

Rachel stirred for the first time since Abby had got her onto the sofa. 'It wasn't my da, Rob.' They could only just make out her words. 'Ma did it. She ... she found out about us.'

'But I bet your da stood by and did nowt as usual.' To Robin the guilt was equal, and Abby and Wilbert agreed with him.

'He ... he pulled her off me in the end. And ... and it was my fault. I knew she was drunk but I wouldn't agree to stopping seeing you.' Tears were seeping out of the swollen slits of Rachel's eyes and trickling down her cheeks. 'That's what made her so mad. She went barmy, even da couldn't hold on to her and she kept fighting him to get back to me.'

She had said Rachel needed to stand up to her parents, Abby thought guiltily; for once in her life the girl had and look at the result. Her mother was a monster. It was hard to imagine any woman could do this to her own child.

Any misgivings Abby had about her brother's relationship with this girl were swept away in a wave of compassion and sorrow. Rachel needed Robin. It was as simple as that, and it was clear her brother loved Rachel to distraction. She watched him as he held the cup to Rachel's poor lips and helped her to drink. It made Abby want to cry.

It was a few hours later. The smell of the Christmas dinner cooking in the range pervaded the house but the peace of the night before was absent. Rachel was warmly tucked up in Abby's bed, hot-water bottles at her feet and sides, and

190

had been fast asleep for an hour or so after the doctor Wilbert had fetched from Morebattle had come to the farm in his horse and trap. He had stitched the inside of Rachel's lip and given her a powerful sedative before coming downstairs with Abby to the sitting room where Robin and Wilbert were waiting, their faces grim.

'She's lost a tooth and two more are loose but hopefully they'll settle,' he told them. 'It will be some time before we know whether the injuries she's received will leave permanent marks, but apply the ointment I'm giving you every three hours for the next week or so. Her face is a mess at present but she's young and nature heals. She's in shock, and no wonder. That woman wants locking up.'

'Do you know Mrs McArthur?' Wilbert asked.

'Everyone knows Mrs McArthur,' said the doctor, shaking his head. 'Or at least of her. She's drunk more than she's sober, and her husband makes no effort to keep her under control despite the fact that he's a great hulking brute of a man. I've heard rumours before of how she is with the children but this is beyond the pale. I shall be calling in to see her within the next twenty-four hours, make no mistake about that. If the girl names her mother to the police as I have advised her to do, Mrs McArthur will find herself enjoying the luxury of His Majesty's prison in the forseeable future.'

'She won't do that, Rachel, I mean,' said Robin quietly. 'She's loyal.'

'Misplaced loyalty can do as much harm as deception.' The doctor's gaze held Robin's. 'Tell

191

her that from me, would you? I take it you care for the girl?'

Robin nodded. 'Very much.'

'And she won't be returning to her parents?'

'Not while I have breath in my body,' said Robin grimly.

'Then it might be worth threatening Mrs McArthur that you will see to it Rachel goes to the police if she touches one of the other girls. Apparently it's only her daughters she goes for and up to now Rachel has always tried to protect them, but with her gone...' He shrugged. 'Dreadful woman.' He met Wilbert's eyes. 'Perfectly dreadful woman.'

Wilbert nodded. 'That about sums it up, Doctor.'

'I shall read Mrs McArthur the riot act. If you follow up with threatening to set the law on her, it might afford some protection for the other girls in the future.' The doctor's voice became brisk. 'I must be going. My wife is doing a grand Christmas lunch for her parents and mine, and it would be a brave man who was late for it.'

That had been over an hour ago. Since the doctor had left, Abby, Robin and their grandfather had been sitting downstairs discussing how to handle Mrs McArthur. Robin was adamant Rachel wouldn't go to the police, but they agreed that if Wilbert and Robin went to see Mrs McArthur and convinced her otherwise, it might help Rachel's sisters. Robin was all for going straight over to the inn this minute, but Wilbert and Abby had persuaded him to leave it to the next day when he had calmed down a little. They were both worried he would lose his temper and make things even worse, which wouldn't help Rachel in the long run.

Abby found her hands were trembling as she dished up the Christmas Day fare at midday. Only another couple of hours and she would meet Nicholas. Rachel was fast asleep and so the three of them ate together downstairs but without much appetite after the events of the morning.

Once the meal was over, the men disappeared outside to do certain jobs that were necessary, Christmas Day or no Christmas Day, and Abby saw to the dishes and tidied round after checking on Rachel, who was sleeping soundly. The doctor had said the sedative would probably knock her out for around twenty-four hours and that was all to the good. Sleep was better than any medicine he could give her, he'd added, because in a case such as this the mind needed rest as well as the body.

It was just after two o'clock when the men returned to the house and it had started to snow again, which was the last thing Abby wanted. Nevertheless she was determined to keep the rendezvous with Nicholas. She let her grandfather and Robin take off their coats and caps and boots, and slip their feet into their slippers which she'd put to warm by the fire. After making them a cup of tea and cutting a large slice of Christmas cake each for them, she said casually, 'I need a spot of fresh air, I've got a headache coming. I'll just have a short walk outside for a while.'

Two heads turned as one from the armchairs positioned in front of the crackling fire. 'A walk?' Robin stared at her. 'It's snowing.'

'So?'

'And the wind's getting up.'

'Better I go now then before it gets too bad. Rachel is asleep and won't wake up for hours, probably not until tomorrow morning according to the doctor.'

Wilbert shook his head. 'It's not the day for a stroll, lass. Come and sit yourself down with us.'

'I will when I come back. I won't be long.' She was already pulling on her hat and coat

'I'll come with you.'

As Robin went to heave himself out of the armchair, Abby forced a light laugh. 'Don't be silly. Sit yourself in front of the fire for a bit. You ought to be here just in case the doctor's wrong and Rachel does wake up. I won't be long.'

She left her brother muttering something about, 'As daft as a fruitcake,' and walked outside still buttoning her coat.

The wind was beginning to whirl the big fat flakes in a frenzied dance and the cold made her gasp as she took her first breath. Already the path from the cottage she had cleared earlier was half an inch thick with snow, and as she pulled on her woollen mittens she again asked herself if Nicholas would come on such a day, and it being Christmas Day too. He had said they had a houseful and that he could slip away without anyone noticing, but it was a good walk from the laird's house to the farm and with the weather worsening...

She plodded down the farm track with her shoulders hunched and her head bent against the swirling snow, thinking Robin was right – she must be daft. He wouldn't come, and he probably wouldn't expect her to venture out either.

When she turned into the lane the drifts either side of the road were at least six foot deep, and once more she told herself she was daft, acknowledging at the same time that she could no more have sat in the cottage all afternoon than fly to the moon. If he wasn't at their agreed meeting place so be it, but at least she would know. Quite what she would know she didn't pursue in her mind.

Pushing as she was against the snow-filled wind she didn't notice Nicholas until he reached out and took her arm, and then she gave a little shriek of surprise.

'I'm sorry, I'm sorry, but you nearly walked past me.' He smiled at her and it wasn't the effort of having battled through the snow that made her feel weak at the knees. 'I didn't know if you would come,' he said softly. 'I've been standing here cursing the snow.'

'I said I would meet you.'

'So you did.' His smile widened. 'And I should have known you would keep your word.'

'How?' Now she smiled too. 'You hardly know me.'

'I feel I've always known you.'

It wasn't so much the words as the intensity with which he spoke them that made her feel trembly inside. And then he broke the moment which had seemed to lengthen by taking her hand and saying, 'Come on, there's a spot further on that's more sheltered.'

He led her to a small curve in the lane where the hedgerow combined with the direction of the wind had left the ground almost clear. The snow was coming down thickly but few flakes reached their spot, and Abby had the strange feeling they were enclosed in an enchanted circle cut off from the outside world. He had let go of her hand but was standing close enough so she could see the tiny bristles on his chin coming through where he had shaved that morning, and again her knees weakened.

Nicholas looked down at the girl who had filled his every waking moment since yesterday. He hadn't been able to sleep for thinking of her but had sat at his bedroom window all night staring out into the darkness. He couldn't have put a name to the feeling that had enveloped him; it was part excitement, part turmoil, part hunger for another sight of her and above all a physical and mental longing that was so strong he could taste it. Now that she was here in front of him she was even more beautiful than he remembered. 'Happy Christmas,' he said softly. 'Have you had an enjoyable day thus far?'

'I would say more of a memorable one.' There had been a touch of wryness in her voice, and when Nicholas said, 'Oh, yes?' she went on to tell him about Rachel and what had happened, finishing with, 'You're probably shocked but I can assure you not all working-class families are like Rachel's.'

'I'm well aware of that but believe me, in many fine houses up and down the land the same sort of disturbing scenario is played out behind closed doors. One of my mother's aunts has been separated from her husband since I was a little boy because he was violent towards her and their children. It is never talked about, of course, not socially, but everyone knows.'

Her eyes had widened and his tone was rueful when he continued: 'You think wealth and influence protect against violence and unhappiness in the home? Not so. Human beings are the same the world over and the outward trappings are merely a veneer.'

'A veneer that can make life very comfortable nonetheless.' She wasn't quite sure why she was emphasizing the difference in class between them except that it was to combat what was in his eyes. They couldn't have a relationship, they couldn't even be friends, and he must know that as well as she did. She shouldn't have come today; it had been foolish.

'True enough, but...' He paused. 'I think I would rather live in a hovel where happiness reigned than a mansion where it didn't, and before you remind me that I am speaking as one who has been privileged all his life, let me say in my defence that since I have been working as a doctor I have seen more of life than I could have imagined when I was growing up in my ivory tower.' He paused again. 'And that was bad enough.'

Abby said nothing because she didn't know what to say; the conversation was not going as she had expected. And then he began to talk. He talked about his boyhood, the loneliness, the feeling of being a square peg in a round hole, of not belonging to anyone. She had heard a little of this the day before but she hadn't realized how deep the scars were. 'I was eleven years old when my father insisted I accompanied him on my first hunt, and when I saw what happened and was violently ill he took pleasure in humiliating me in front of the assembled company. Not that that was a shock – he had always made it plain I was a disappointment – but from that point on there were a hundred and one things he did to point out I was girlish in my thinking. Weak. An embarrassment to the family name. And I believed it then, he was my father after all.'

'But you don't now.'

The deep-brown eyes smiled at her. 'No, I don't now. I finally know myself. Does that sound strange?'

It didn't. She knew exactly what he meant because since she had made her decision about nursing she'd felt she was growing into her own skin at last.

She said as much, and Nicholas nodded. 'I look at my patients sometimes, and wonder what has gone on in their lives and how they are feeling inside. They might have come to me with broken bones or a disease or goodness knows what, but that's just the part that is obvious.'

The snow continued to fall as they talked on, and it was with a little shock some time later that Abby realized the winter twilight was beginning to take hold. Suddenly panic-stricken, Abby said quickly, 'I have to get back. It's getting late.'

'Don't go.' He heard the note in his voice and cursed himself for it. He didn't want to frighten her by coming on too strong, damn it. They'd talked so freely; certainly he had told her things he had never admitted to anyone else, and he got the impression it was the same for her.

'I must.'

'Can I see you tomorrow morning? Before I have to leave?'

'I don't think so.'

'Why not?'

She was silent for a moment, her head averted, and then she looked straight at him. 'You know why not.'

'I don't.'

'Yes, you do.' She turned from him, stepping out into the driving snow that was fast becoming a blizzard so he was forced to accompany her. 'People wouldn't understand us being friends,' she said so quietly he had to bend his head to hear her. 'They would put two and two together and make ten – that's the way of it round here – and it would be my grandfather and brother who would bear the brunt of their gossip with me being away.'

'Then can I see you when you are in Gala-shiels?' he said eagerly. 'I could come and visit when I have leave and no one from here need know. Not that I would mind,' he added quickly, in case she had thought that, 'but if you wish to keep it a secret for now that is fine.'

The beating of her heart was threatening to suffocate her. He couldn't be suggesting... But he was, he was talking as though they could start seeing each other as a couple. Didn't he realize how impossible that was? And it wasn't just the furore it would cause at the farm and in her own family which would be great. Robin and her grandfather had nothing but disgust and hatred for the laird and all his kind who made their lives so hard. But Nicholas's father, the laird, he would be quite capable of throwing her grandfather out of his cottage and seeing to it that her granda and Robin got no work anywhere else. The laird's power was absolute, everyone knew that. And besides all that, a relationship between them could never be. They came from different backgrounds, a different class; he would wed a society woman whose family was as wealthy and influential as his, that's how things were done with the upper class. And she would be left with nothing, not even her good name.

Summoning all her strength, she said quietly, 'I can't see you – you must know that at heart?'

'I don't, I don't know that. Why not? Tell me why not?' Even as he said the words Nicholas knew he was lying. He knew exactly why a relationship between the two of them would be verging on madness, but he didn't care. He wanted her.

She didn't answer him; she merely stared into his eyes as she stopped walking. The snow was covering both of them and coming down so thickly you couldn't see a hand in front of your face, but as she remained silent he shook his head as though she had spoken. They stood tense and still, their gaze holding, and it was then that Abby heard her name being called.

'It's my brother.' She turned to the direction of his voice. 'He's come looking for me.'

'Don't sound so distraught – you haven't done anything wrong.'

'He won't see it like that.' Nicholas didn't understand, but then how could he? His father was the man who held all their lives in his capricious, cruel grip, the man who expected his pound of flesh from his tenants and then much more. 'Please, he can't see you.'

But it was too late. Even as she spoke, Robin called again and before she could explain further, she saw him come out of the snow. 'Abby?' There was a wealth of relief in Robin's voice but then he saw who it was who was with her. Stiffly now, he said, 'Granda's worried to death. Where have you been? You said you would only be a few minutes.'

'I'm sorry, it was my fault.' Nicholas spoke, his tone easy as though he couldn't see the hostility and suspicion on the face of the young man in front of him. 'I happened to meet your sister in the lane and I'm afraid I detained her too long. I recognized her as the child I came across at the Cut years ago and was just asking how things were. She tells me she is off to start her training as a nurse in the New Year and I was wishing her well. As I am a doctor myself we got talking about hospital life and so on.'

Robin stared at the laird's son. It sounded plausible enough; but for Abby insisting she walk out this afternoon in such weather and her manner now, he would have believed Nicholas Jefferson-Price, but he felt in his bones there was more to this meeting than they were letting on. Abby had never been able to lie convincingly – her face always gave her away – and it was telling him she was more than a little flustered. But then he supposed meeting the laird's son like this, especially after what had happened when she was a child, would make her feel that way. Nevertheless... His voice as wintry as the weather, he repeated, 'She said she'd only be a few minutes,' as his eyes took in the expensive thick coat Nicholas was wearing.

201

his hat, his polished leather boots. If this man was up to no good, if he thought he could turn Abby's head and use her like the gentry always used women who were beneath them, then he'd got another think coming.

'Oh for goodness' sake, Robin. I haven't been that long.' Abby had recovered herself and now her voice held nothing more than the irritation of an older sister to an unreasonable younger brother. 'Mr Jefferson-Price has been telling me what to expect when I start my training.'

'Aye,' he said. Nodding curtly to Nicholas, Robin took Abby's arm. 'Granda is waiting.' Shaking off her brother's hand, Abby turned to Nicholas. 'Goodbye, Mr Jefferson-Price,' she said quietly, 'and thank you for our talk. It was most interesting.'

'Goodbye.' Nicholas was inwardly cursing Robin up hill and down dale. 'May I wish you all the best for the future?'

'Thank you.'

This time when Robin took her arm his grip made it plain he meant business. Abby thought about defying him, but a scene, in front of Nicholas was not how she wanted their meeting to finish, and so she let Robin lead her away. She had never felt in such turmoil.

Nicholas watched them go, drawing his hand around the back of his neck in frustration at his powerlessness. But this wasn't the end. Long after Abby and Robin had disappeared into what was fast becoming a blizzard, he stood quite motionless. No, by all that was holy, this wasn't the end, he told himself. He would write to her at the hospital in Galashiels and demand that she see him. She had to understand how he felt. He didn't care about class or his family or what people would say, none of that mattered. He would make her see that, and together they could face her family and the rest of them. He had decided long ago that he would make his own life away from the ancestral home, and there was no reason why she couldn't be part of it. Somehow he would convince her. Somehow. He had to...

Joe McHaffie waited for a full five minutes after Nicholas had walked away before he moved from his spot deep in the hedgerow on the other side of the lane. He had caught sight of Abby leaving the cottage earlier when he had been standing gazing morosely out of the window, his parents snoring softly in front of the fire after the huge Christmas dinner his mother had cooked. He hated Christmas with its forced gaiety; the only bright spot in the day had been when his father had nearly choked on the silver sixpence his mother had put in the plum pudding. There hadn't been too much of the Christmas spirit after that.

Pulling on his cap and jacket, he had followed Abby down the track away from the farm, making sure he was far enough behind her not to be seen, the dark excitement he always felt when he was close to her knotting his stomach. He couldn't imagine what she was doing out in such conditions but she was walking with purpose and his curiosity was aroused. The thick snow muffling any footsteps and making visibility difficult, he almost walked up on them before he heard a man's voice a little way in front where Abby had gone. He stopped abruptly. She was talking to someone up ahead. A man. And it was no chance encounter from the way she had been walking; neither did she want to be seen.

He stood for some moments hesitating, unsure whether to continue walking and give her a fright when she realized she'd been rumbled, or to backtrack to where a farm gate would give him access into the field beyond the hedgerow. He decided on the latter. He wanted to hear what they were saying and determine who this bloke was.

Retracing his steps he found he was grinding his teeth in fury. Like mother, like daughter, meeting this man on the sly. He'd bet his last penny the bloke was someone old Wilbert wouldn't approve of and she knew it. Perhaps he was married? He wouldn't put anything past Molly's daughter; blood was thicker than water. There were some lassies who didn't want good reliable men but hankered after the bad 'uns or other women's blokes; more exciting, he supposed. Molly had wanted excitement. She hadn't known her fella more than a few days when she had scarpered with him; wanton through and through she'd been, but with an angelic face that would have fooled the devil himself. And her daughter was the same.

Once he was in the field he waded through snow that was waist deep in places, keeping to the hedge line where he could but treading slowly and warily to avoid any ditches. When he came to the place where Abby was standing on the other side of the hedgerow he couldn't see through the dense vegetation blanketed in snow, but he could hear the odd word or two that was being said. After a while when it dawned on him who the man talking to her was, his eyes opened wide in surprise before narrowing into slits. He'd gathered pretty quickly the bloke was a toff from the way he spoke, but it wasn't until he heard Abby call him Nicholas that the penny dropped. She was aiming high, the laird's son no less.

He pictured the scene on the other side of the hedgerow, his stomach muscles tightening in rage as he imagined Abby smiling up into Nicholas Jefferson-Price's face.

What did she think the man would do once he'd had his fun with her? The gentry used such as her for one thing only. But perhaps she didn't mind? From the moment he'd heard from his father that Wilbert's granddaughter was leaving in the New Year to train as a nurse, he had known it was with a view to nabbing some rich old man under her care, or a younger one maybe. Men were vulnerable when they were ill; they let their defences down and everyone knew nurses were easy and got up to mischief. All those blokes they handled, it was obvious, wasn't it. No nice girl would want to do that. And you heard about wealthy old blokes marrying their nurse and then dying; there had been a case in the paper not so long back. Disgusting, he called it.

By the time Joe heard Robin calling Abby he couldn't feel his feet and was shivering from head to toe, but he hadn't contemplated moving from where he was. He heard the exchange between brother and sister quite clearly; they spoke louder than Abby and Nicholas had done, and then after a while he heard the laird's son leave, his footsteps crunching in the snow.

He continued to stand where he was for a minute or two more, his face dark with brooding temper. She was a little trollop through and through, even worse than her mam.

He stirred, only to find that his frozen feet refused to obey him, and it wasn't until he had stamped about a bit and massaged his legs that he started for home, his thoughts as bitter as the air around him. She'd give it away to anyone, would Abby. Anyone but him, that was, but he'd fix her. Oh, aye, if it was the last thing he did, he'd fix her all right. She had it coming...

'What are you talking to the likes of him for?' They were barely out of earshot when Robin rounded on her. 'He's the laird's son, woman. Have you gone mad?'

'Don't "woman" me.' Abby glared at the brother she adored. 'I can talk to whoever I like, thank you very much.'

'Not him.'

'Oh, for goodness' sake, we were just talking. He was telling me about hospital life like I said. Where's the harm in that?'

Robin's 'Huh!' spoke volumes. They walked in silence for a few moments before he said, 'It's a good job you're off to Galashiels soon, that's all I can say.' And the silence lengthened.

Abby was glad when Boxing Day was over. Despite all she had said to Nicholas, she was worried he would take it into his head to call at the farm and ask to see her. It had been the look in his eyes as she had walked away with Robin.

But he hadn't come. And she was glad, she *was*, she told herself over and over again. It would have caused problems she could well do without. However much he liked her – and he *did* like her, she believed that – whatever he felt, any affair between them was doomed. He was a man of standing and wealth and he would marry a woman who was his equal, that was how things were done. He might tarry with her for a while but it could be no more than that, and she wasn't prepared to be any man's plaything, even Nicholas's. Just saying his name in her mind made her heart leap and race, and if that wasn't a warning that she would be playing with fire, she didn't know what was. No, she had to forget their brief encounter and get on with her life.

Brave words, and in the time before she left for Galashiels she could cope with her decision in the day as she showed Rachel what her duties would be, getting to know the girl better in the process and finding she liked what she found. But at night in the pallet bed her grandfather had brought up to her bedroom because she'd insisted Rachel have her more comfortable bed, she had tossed and turned until dawn as she fought the longing to see Nicholas again.

But now it was the first week of January, the old battered trunk was packed with her things and it was the morning of her departure. The night before, her grandfather and Robin had surprised her with the gift of a new hat and coat they had bought and kept for the occasion of her leaving.

'Can't have you turning up in Galashiels like the poor relation, now, can we?' Wilbert had said gruffly as she and Rachel had oohed and aahed over the lovely deep-plum wool coat and matching hat, Abby with tears streaming down her face.

'But it's too expensive,' she had murmured, touched to the heart of her at their thoughtfulness. It was true her old coat and hat had seen better days and the sleeves of the coat were halfway up her arms, but she had been content to make do. Once she started earning a wage she was determined to begin paying her grandfather a monthly sum of money for the uniform, books and everything else he had so cheerfully bought her; buying a new hat and coat had been something way in the future.

'Nonsense.' Wilbert had touched his granddaughter's face in one of his rare gestures of affection. 'You'll look as pretty as a picture, lass, so let's hear no more about it.'

Abby thought about this now as she pulled on the coat and hat before walking downstairs where the others were waiting for her. Her grandfather had ordered the carrier's cart to come to the farm that morning to take her to Kelso station where she would catch the train for Galashiels at midday. She and Rachel and the menfolk had had breakfast together earlier and it had been a subdued meal, and Abby had found she had no appetite whatsoever. Her stomach was doing cartwheels and she was already homesick. Surprisingly, in view of how she had felt about Rachel initially, it was the fact that the other girl would be here to look after the men and keep things running smoothly that comforted her. They had already begun to forge a strong friendship, and Abby could see that Rachel genuinely adored Robin which was all that mattered. She and Rachel didn't know exactly what had occurred when her grandfather and Robin had gone to see Rachel's parents the day after Boxing Day, but they had returned with grim faces, saying only that Rachel's previous life was finished with for good.

The carrier's cart was already outside with her trunk loaded in the back, and as Abby looked at her grandfather and brother a wealth of memories flooded her mind and brought a lump to her throat. The little picnics the three of them had enjoyed when she had taken their lunch to them in the fields on the days she wasn't at school; she and Robin feeding the motherless lambs with pap bottles in the warmth of the big barn; the comforting smell of her granda's pipe in the evenings when they'd sat before the fire after the day's work was finally done... So many things.

Hugs and kisses had never been part of their family life but now Abby flung her arms round her grandfather first, then Robin, and lastly Rachel. 'I'll write,' she choked out through her tears. 'As often as I can.'

'Aye, you do that, lass.' Wilbert's voice was thick.

She was halfway out of the front door when Robin suddenly gave her another hug, a bear hug this time as he lifted her off her feet and held her close for some moments. He didn't say anything, but he didn't have to.

Abby climbed blindly onto the seat next to the carrier, feeling utterly desolate. And then the horse was plodding down the track and the shouted goodbyes were fading and she was actually leaving the farm. For a moment she considered jumping down from the cart and running back and saying she had changed her mind, but then they reached the lane and the horse's amble became a trot. They were some distance along the lane and she had dried her eyes and composed herself, when she saw a dark figure standing half-concealed by the hedgerow. For a moment she thought it might be Nicholas but of course that was silly; he had left to return to his hospital days ago. And then, as the cart passed, the man stepped forward and she saw who it was. They'd gone by in the twinkling of an eye, but for some minutes afterwards Abby's heart continued to pound sickeningly. Joe McHaffie had doffed his cap to her but not in a nice way; his eyes had been narrowed like hard bullets and his teeth drawn back from his lips in a sneer and his whole persona had been one of dark menace...

PART FOUR

Bedpans, Sluices and Lavatories

1930

Chapter Thirteen

Abby arrived at the hospital at three o'clock as the matron had instructed in her letter. She was shown to a small waiting room that smelt overpoweringly of disinfectant and was spotlessly clean. The young taxi driver who had brought her from the train station dumped her trunk at her side, accepting his fare and the tip she gave him with a cheery, 'Ta, lass,' and as he left she felt that her last friend in the world had gone.

She sat down on one of the hard-backed chairs lining the walls and looked around her. The room was painted in a dull shade of green – vomit green, Robin would have called it – and there were no pictures on the wall to relieve the gloom.

Abby swallowed hard. She felt very small and very alone. The girl who had shown her to the waiting room hadn't said two words beyond, 'Wait here.' And so she waited.

It was a full ten minutes later, which had seemed like ten hours, when a brisk personage in an immaculate blue-and-white uniform, her hair hidden under a white butterfly cap, peered in at the open door. 'Are you the new nurse?'

Was she? It was the first time she had been called a nurse and for a moment Abby thought the girl must be looking for someone else.

'Abigail Kirby?'

This time Abby nodded.

213

'Come on and don't look so scared – you'll soon get used to everything. I started in the summer and for the first few weeks I didn't know my backside from my elbow but now it feels like home.' The girl wrinkled her small snub nose. 'Albeit one that runs like the army. I'm Florence Kane but my friends call me Flo, by the way.'

'I'm Abby.'

Lifting the handle on one side of the trunk, Flo gestured for Abby to take the other and together they left the room to stagger down corridors and up stairs where the same sickly green of the waiting room dominated the colour scheme. Abby was completely lost by the time Flo stopped outside a door.

'Here we are, your home from home.' Again the snub nose wrinkled. 'But don't worry, you are going to be so tired it won't matter there's not enough room to swing a cat.' Pushing open the door, Flo led her inside to where four iron beds, four chests of drawers and one wardrobe were crammed into such a tiny space that Abby couldn't imagine how four occupants could live in the room as well. Pointing to one of the beds, Flo said, 'That's yours next to mine.'

Abby gulped, Flo's remark about the army coming back to her. The beds were made with such neat precision and tightness it didn't look possible to sleep in them, and as though Flo had read her mind, she said, 'Like everything else here, our beds have to be just so. Sister inspects them every day and if they're not up to scratch you'll come off duty dead on your feet to find them stripped to the springs and the bedding on the floor. She's a tartar, Sister Duffy. Everyone hates her. She can make your life a misery.' Flo smiled cheerfully. 'Let's put your things away.'

Feeling more unnerved every moment, Abby helped Flo unpack the trunk, most of her belongings being deposited in the chest of drawers and the hangables in the section of the wardrobe allotted to her. While they worked, Flo filled her in on a few of the rules. 'Keep your drawers tidy, don't let Sister catch you sitting on your bed and no smoking in the room, and definitely no alcohol.' Flo grinned. 'No one keeps the last two but woe betide you if Sister finds out. We're not supposed to leave the nurses' home unless our uniform is perfect and our hair tidy, and ten o'clock is the deadline for being in if you have an evening off. The great thing is there's a very convenient beech tree just outside our window and if anyone's going out we leave the window open so if they're late back they can climb up and come in that way.'

Abby looked at Flo aghast. They were two floors up.

Flo giggled. 'No one's broken their neck yet, although Pam – you'll meet her later, along with Kitty – Pam got stuck the other night when she was the worse for wear after too many gins with her boyfriend. Somehow she found herself hanging by her knicker elastic, poor thing. We got her in eventually but in the morning there was this strip of white lace still hooked on the branch and blowing like a flag in the breeze. Pam had to climb out and get it before Sister noticed. Eyes like a hawk, she's got.'

Abby was overwhelmed. Smoking, drinking, climbing through windows, boyfriends. It wasn't how she had pictured hospital life and if her grandfather or Robin caught an inkling of it they'd throw a blue fit. She suddenly realized that she had led a very sheltered life thus far.

'Right, that's done.' Flo straightened her apron. 'The bathroom's at the end of the corridor and dinner's at six. Do you want me to come for you then? You don't need to wear your uniform today but from tomorrow you will. Do you know how to put in the studs and rubber buttons and fold your cap?'

Abby shook her head. The uniform seemed horribly complicated, especially the cap. How she was going to convert the large square of white material into a small, neat, wearable butterfly cap like Flo's, she couldn't imagine.

'I'll show you tonight before we go to bed. Now, I've got to get back to the ward before Sister has my guts for garters for being too long.' Flo was halfway out of the door when she turned, saying, 'Make the most of the next few hours, Abby. From tomorrow morning every minute will be accounted for and you won't know what's hit you at first.' And on that cheery note she left.

True to her word, Flo returned at six o'clock and took Abby down to the dining room. The room was large and bleak, but at least the walls were whitewashed rather than being painted in the sickly green colour that seemed to be everywhere. When they walked through the door the noise of chatter and laughter hit Abby after the hushed quiet of the corridors, along with the very distinct smell of boiled cabbage.

Flo led her across to a far table. 'The nurses all sit in order of seniority. Sisters are on that table over there, then the staff nurses on the one next to it, and so on. We're on the juniors' table, of course, and I hate to tell you, but you are the lowest of us all until another poor dogsbody comes. Starting from tomorrow, you'll have to pass the cruets and man the water jugs and teapots, and cut bread for everyone on our table, besides going to the kitchen hatch for fresh supplies if we run out which we always do frequently. Sorry, Abby, but that's the way it is. I was so glad when Kitty came after me, and she'll be pleased you've started. Sometimes you hardly get anything to eat you're dashing about so much, and I can tell you once I'm a senior I'll never slice another piece of bread in my life.'

Pulling out a chair on the table furthest from the kitchen hatch, Flo said, 'Sit here.' She introduced Abby to the girls nearest them and Abby looked at what the nurses were eating. The brownish substance on their plates was clearly meant to be a stew, but it had the consistency of water, and a few nondescript pieces of vegetables floated on the surface as though looking for a final resting place. The girls had great slabs of bread at the side of their plates that were being used for soaking up the insipid-looking mixture. Sinking down onto her chair, Abby swallowed uncomfortably. She had been feeling quite hungry, having been unable to eat any breakfast, but not any more.

A girl at the far end of the table called to Flo. 'Flo, do you and the new lass want any bread?' She was hovering over an enormous loaf, a wicked-looking bread knife in her hand, so Abby assumed this had to be Kitty whom she was scheduled to take over table duties from. This was confirmed a moment later when the girl came to their side and deposited hunks of bread on the plates of food one of the dining-room maids had placed in front of Flo and Abby. 'I'm *so* glad to see you,' she said to Abby. 'Perhaps I can sit down and actually eat my meal in peace tomorrow, without cramming food into my mouth whilst looking after this lot. I'm Kitty, by the way.'

Kitty was the antithesis of the neat, slim Flo, being tall and heavily built with bright red cheeks and matching wisps of red hair escaping her cap. Her face was covered in freckles and she exuded an air of friendliness that was very comforting in the circumstances. Abby liked her immediately. 'Call me Abby,' she said quietly. 'Pleased to meet you.'

'And I'm Pam,' another nurse further down the table called to Abby. This girl was a willowy blonde with a peaches-and-cream complexion, and huge blue eyes. She was what Robin would have labelled 'a looker'.

'Pam's our Mae West,' Kitty announced in a stage whisper. 'Don't let her lead you astray, Abby.'

Pam smiled serenely, apparently unconcerned. 'Life's too short,' she drawled, 'and just for that insult to my good name I'll have another slice of bread, Kitty, if you please.'

Abby was beginning to relax. Her room-mates seemed a nice lot. She had missed the camaraderie of her bunch of friends at the high school since the summer more than she had realized, she thought, dipping her bread in the stew the way everyone else was doing. It tasted as it looked but she cleared her plate anyway; she was going to have to adapt to hospital food which clearly wasn't like anything she had been used to. When she had made a stew at home she had left it slowly cooking for hours so the result was a thick, delicious meal that was mouthwateringly good.

A stodgy pudding that masqueraded as a lemon sponge followed. The heavy, indigestible square of glutinous dough tasted of nothing and certainly didn't have a discernible trace of lemon in it, and the custard was a thick congealing mass of lumps, but the nurses at the table fell on the food as though it was the best cuisine.

'Wait till you've been here a day or two,' Flo said, noticing that Abby had left her pudding. 'You'd eat the table you'll be so hungry after working on the wards.'

'Is that pudding going begging?' Kitty appeared at Abby's side again. 'I'm faint with hunger.'

Abby passed her the dish and Kitty returned to her seat where she made short work of her second helping. Abby noticed no one else had refused their pudding, and when enormous jugs of cocoa were plonked on the table by one of the maids for Kitty to serve, again each girl drained her mug dry in moments. The brown, watery concoction was nothing like the thick milky drink of home, and Abby was beginning to realize that living on a farm had had definite benefits regarding food. Her grandfather and the rest of the farmer's workers might be as poor as church mice on the wages they received for their hard labour, and there were no niceties like electricity or inside lavatories at the farm, but food and milk and cream had always been plentiful and mealtimes had been something to look forward to.

She found her way back to the room alone; Flo and the others had dashed off to their wards as soon as dinner was over. Plumping down on the hard bed, she let the feelings of homesickness swamp her and had a good cry. Then she blew her nose, squared her shoulders and found she felt a whole lot better for letting the emotion out.

She was sitting reading through one of her textbooks just after ten o'clock when the others came back to the room.

'Phew, what a day!' After grinning at her, Pam flung herself prostrate on the bed and lay dramatically still for a moment or two before leaping to her feet again and opening the window, ignoring Kitty and Flo's protests as icy-cold air swirled into the room. 'I've got to have a ciggy else I'll die. I wish I hadn't finished that bottle of gin I brought back from home, my mouth's as dry as Deuteronomy.'

'I'm glad it's gone,' said Flo grimly. 'If Sister Duffy had found it under the floorboard where you hid it, we'd all have been in hot water.'

Pam had already lit her cigarette and taken a deep drag, short bursts of smoke shooting out of each nostril. 'She's a fiend, put on earth to torment us all and me in particular. I don't know why but she seems to think it's her personal mission to catch me out. I swear the woman's obsessed.'

'Not that you ever give her any reason to doubt

you,' said Kitty drily, and then took one of the cigarettes Pam offered round. 'You're such a bad influence,' she said gloomily. 'I'd given up smoking at Christmas.'

Over the next half-an-hour Abby discovered Flo was a Newcastle lass born and bred and the only girl in a family of ten; Kitty was the oldest among them being twenty-two and hailing from Peebles some twenty miles away, and Pam was a farmer's daughter from a village on the outskirts of Galashiels. Once they'd had a chat they started getting undressed, totally unconcerned with stripping off in front of each other. Abby decided, 'In for a penny, in for a pound,' and did the same, although not without some embarrassment. She had been brought up to think getting undressed was a private thing but was beginning to realize that this notion, along with many others, wasn't going to work here.

Once they were in their winceyette nightdresses and dressing gowns, visits to the bathroom followed, and then Pam had one more cigarette before shutting the window and turning the light off. A chorus of 'Goodnight's followed and within moments, or so it seemed to Abby, all three girls were gently snoring. She lay awake for some time, her head whirling with the events of the day and thoughts of Nicholas filling her mind, but the friendliness of her room-mates had soothed something inside her and she drifted off to sleep without more tears.

It was in the middle of the night when she awoke from a nightmare with a violent start, her heart pounding fit to burst. She had been back at the farm but it hadn't looked the same, and she had been wading through thick mud in a panic, unable to run but knowing something terrible was behind her.

Up in front of her she knew Nicholas was trying to reach her – she could hear his voice shouting her name over and over again – but she could make no progress through the bog that was hampering every step. Desperately afraid, she fought with all her strength to move forward but the sounds behind her told her she was losing the battle. At the last moment she found the strength to turn and face the dark entity at her heels ... and then she woke up.

She sat up in bed, oblivious to the icy chill of the room. She hadn't seen who or what it was behind her, but she didn't have to. Joe McHaffie had followed her here...

Chapter Fourteen

Abby woke up in the morning to someone shaking her shoulder. For a moment she didn't have a clue where she was, and then she stared up into Kitty's round bright face, her red hair drawn back in two long plaits which hung over her shoulders and made her plump face look even plumper. 'Wakey wakey, rise and shine. It's six o'clock and breakfast's at six-thirty. No one is ever late. Old Duffy makes sure of that. Flo's laid out your uniform for you so nip to the bathroom first.'

Abby nipped, returning to wrestle with the uniform and in particular the dreaded cap. After three attempts to master it which had resulted in the cap first slipping over one eye, then sliding straight down the back of her neck, and finally unfolding itself gracefully as she turned her head, Flo folded it and fixed it on Abby's thick hair with long grips. Once Flo pronounced her ready to face Sister Duffy, Abby looked at herself in the wardrobe-door mirror. A smart unruffled nurse stared back at her which wasn't at all how she felt inside.

She felt even less like it by the time breakfast was over. Now she was in uniform she was expected to take Kitty's place as the table skivvy, and as no one – apart from her three room-mates – made any allowances for her newness, she was soon as red-faced as Kitty and more flustered than she had ever been in her life. If she wasn't sawing off wedges of bread or pouring out mugs of tea, she was rushing backwards and forwards to the kitchen hatch for more supplies. By the time breakfast was over she had managed to gulp down a sausage and a fried egg and one slice of bread and marmalade on the go, swallowing the occasional sip of tea in the brief moments she returned to her seat.

The sisters' and the staff nurses' tables were the only ones served exclusively by the kitchen maids, and the calm order of these emphasized just how exalted these seniors were. Matron Blackett ate in her own private sitting room, apparently, which was considered the Holy of Holies by every member of staff. Abby had been told she was due to present herself outside the matron's office at seven o'clock once breakfast was over and before she was taken to her ward, and she was already filled with trepidation.

At five to seven the dreaded Sister Duffy materialized at her elbow. 'Nurse Kirby?' A pair of gimlet eyes in a face that could have been set in stone surveyed her with withering contempt from the top of her bead to the bottom of her feet. 'You don't seriously think you are going to insult Matron's sensibilities by appearing in front of her like that? Tidy yourself.'

Abby smoothed her apron and straightened her cap, wondering how on earth the sister expected her to remain pristine when she had been rushing around like a cat with its tail on fire.

'Come with me.' In a rustle of starch the sister marched off without bothering to see if she was being followed, and Abby scurried along behind her. When they arrived at an imposing-looking door at the end of one of the many corridors, the sister stopped, turning to look at Abby again. 'Listen carefully to what I am about to say. You do not speak until you are spoken to and only then to answer any questions Matron might ask you. You do not proffer opinions' – here the sister's eyes narrowed to black slits as she contemplated such a heinous crime – 'and you stand straight with your hands behind your back. Do you understand?'

'Yes, Sister.'

'You do not fidget, you do not look Matron in the eye but keep your gaze respectfully lowered unless you are answering something Matron has asked you. Then, and only then, you may raise your eyes to hers.'

'Yes, Sister.'

'Hmm.' Sister Duffy wasn't convinced, if her glare was anything to go by, but nevertheless she turned and knocked on the door before opening it a crack and putting her head in as she announced, 'The new nurse is here, Matron.'

Abby sidled past the sister who shut the door after her. Alone with the matron, Abby felt her heart thumping as she tried to remember everything Sister Duffy had hissed at her, but it was the welcome warmth of the room that struck her most. Overall the hospital was a chilly place and there had been ice on the inside of their bedroom window that morning, but here in Matron's office the fire burning in the fireplace lent the room a homely, cheerful air.

Not so the matron when, after what seemed an age, she spoke, enabling Abby to raise her head. 'I hope you are aware that academic ability does not necessarily qualify you to become a good nurse?' she said coldly.

Not knowing if a reply was expected, Abby stared into the thin, beak-nosed face for a moment before managing, 'Yes, Matron.'

'Strict obedience, hard work and dedication are what are required, and I will accept nothing less than perfection from my nurses.' The matron waited a moment for her words to sink in. 'You obey orders from a superior without question and adhere to the rules of the hospital at all times, whether you are in its confines or not. By that I mean I expect the highest standards from my nurses even when they are off duty – you carry the reputation of Hemingway's with you. Is that clear?'

'Yes, Matron.'

'Punctuality, respect and unwavering devotion to duty need to run through your core like a stick of Blackpool rock.' Abby's eyes widened; was the matron making a joke? She looked into the steely-blue eyes. Apparently not. 'And integrity, attention to detail and compliance are a must. I will tolerate no excuses, Nurse Kirby.'

Now the steely gaze was piercing, and for a terrible moment Abby felt that the matron was looking into her mind and seeing the activities of Pam and the others the night before and blaming her for them.

'Nursing never has been, and never will be, a soft option for a woman. It requires physical endurance and stamina that many men would find difficult, and a mental acceptance of the unacceptable at times.' Now the matron leaned forward slightly, and although her face did not soften there was a difference to it when she added, 'But in my opinion, one day as a nurse is more worthwhile than a lifetime in a different occupation. Nursing is a vocation, Nurse Kirby. Do you have what is necessary?'

Here Abby could answer from the heart, her voice full of emotion when she said, 'Yes, Matron. I do.'

The matron surveyed her for a few moments before nodding. 'We'll see.' Reaching to the side of her, she pulled on a cord that was presumably connected to a bell somewhere. 'I don't want to see you here for any misdemeanours, Nurse Kirby,' she said grimly, adding, 'I understand you are sharing a room with Nurse Lyndon?'

Abby stared at the matron blankly.

'Nurse Pamela Lyndon?'

The penny dropped. She hadn't known Pam's surname. 'Yes, Matron.'

'Then I repeat, I do not wish to see you in here for any misconduct.' The eagle eyes left Abby in no doubt that the matron was aware of every transgression that went on under her roof. Abby could almost smell the smoke from Pam's cigarettes.

A quiet knock at the door sounded in answer to the matron's summons for which Abby was extremely thankful; she had gone red to the roots of her hair.

'My secretary will take you to the ward where you will be working until the next changeover day. On that morning a change list will be on the noticeboard informing you where you will go. I'm sure the other girls will explain the procedure fully to you. Work hard, Nurse Kirby. Work brings its own reward.' The matron looked down at the papers on her desk.

Assuming the interview was over, Abby murmured, 'Yes, Matron. Thank you, Matron,' and escaped into the corridor outside, where the matron's secretary – only a little less formidable than the lady herself – was waiting to escort her. Her head reeling, Abby followed the secretary down yet more corridors, wondering if by mistake she had joined the army rather than enrolled as a nurse.

By dinnertime that evening, Abby was asking herself how she could ever have thought life on the farm was hard, and also at what point in her nursing career she would actually get to *nurse* any patients. On her arrival at the ward, the secretary had left her with the staff nurse, the sister being busy with more important matters than talking to a junior nurse. The staff nurse had the face of an angel and the voice of a sergeant major which she used to good effect most of the day.

'I expected you before this,' was her greeting, to which Abby wisely made no response. Thanks to Flo and the others she was learning that with any person more senior than herself – which was everyone – it was best to say nothing and observe much. Explanations were always looked on as impertinent excuses.

'Well, you're here now,' the staff nurse continued irritably. 'I hope you're not one of those who turn green at the sight of blood and faeces. Come with me.'

Abby followed the imperious figure down the ward which had beds either side of it and a nurses' station in the middle, and out into the sluice. The smell nearly knocked her backwards but the staff nurse seemed oblivious as she instructed another junior nurse who was already working there to show Abby the ropes.

Once the staff nurse had swept out again, the junior grinned at Abby. 'Welcome to Florence Nightingale land,' she said cheerfully. 'Except it's not. I've been here two months and it's all scrubbing and polishing, not to mention sluices, bedpans and lavatories. They seem to think they've got to immerse us in muck and vomit and blood and the rest of it before we're safe to be let loose on the patients. Still, at least I'm not the most junior nurse on the ward any more.'

Abby smiled weakly. She didn't need reminding.

There followed a detailed list of her duties. 'I'll collect the bedpans and bring them here to you,' the nurse said importantly, obviously full of the fact that at last she was senior to someone. 'Then you empty them, wash them well and warm them up under the tap ready for me to take out. And make sure they're clean else Sister will go barmy. Bits of nasty get stuck down the handles sometimes.'

Abby gulped.

'Then we clean the floor and wash down the walls before going on the ward, but we're not allowed to speak to the patients. We sweep and polish the floor first, under the beds, everywhere. Not a speck can be left. Then we wash down the walls and windowsills and everything with disinfectant, before starting on the bed springs.'

Abby stared at her. *'Bed springs?'*

The nurse giggled. 'They all have to be polished so there's not a spot of dust on them for when Matron does her rounds. She sometimes picks up the edge of a mattress to inspect the springs and if she's not satisfied there's hell to pay. Then we do the frames of the beds and so on, then the nurses' station, then...' She stopped, noticing the glazed expression on Abby's face. 'I'll show you as we go, all right? I'm Kath, by the way.'

They had slaved all morning, then had lunch which had consisted of bread and cheese and pickles, before returning to the ward and the sluice room where dirty linen had to be counted and bagged for the laundry, more bedpans emptied and washed, and vomit bowls cleaned and scalded. Abby's hands were red and sore, her back was aching and every muscle in her legs and feet was screaming, when Kath said brightly, 'Right, the two bathrooms next. You can clean the lavatories.'

From Kath's tone, Abby suspected – rightly – that the lavatories had hitherto been Kath's job as most junior nurse, and that she was thrilled to be passing the task on to someone else. She soon found out why. They were in the men's ward for infectious diseases, and the state of the lavatories showed all too clearly that the patients weren't too particular in their habits.

Kath grimaced sympathetically as Abby stood surveying the condition of the first lavatory. 'I know,' she said, in answer to Abby's unspoken thoughts that were nevertheless clearly visible in her horrified countenance. 'Dirty beggars, aren't they, but that's men for you. Here's the bleach and disinfectant, and you have to be careful to clean right round the U-bend as far as you can reach. Matron has a tour of inspection most days and she always pays a visit in here.'

Kath giggled as she realized what she'd said and Abby had to smile. The thought of the imperious matron seated on one of the men's lavatories was unthinkable.

'Not in *that* way, of course,' Kath said between giggles. 'If all the rumours are true, our beloved Matron has never and will never indulge in bodily functions like the rest of us mere mortals.'

They worked hard for the rest of the day, and by the time the staff nurse instructed Abby to go and get her dinner she felt light-headed with a mixture of hunger and exhaustion. She had quite forgotten she was the drudge for the table until she entered the noisy dining room. Wearily she took her place and began the endless chore of slicing wedges of bread to go with the two spoonfuls of wet, over-cooked cabbage, stringy mutton and round hard objects that professed to be boiled potatoes. Gazing at her plate, Abby wondered how on earth the hospital cooks could ruin good wholesome food so spectacularly well. Even the gravy in the tin gravy boat was more like dishwater.

'Absolutely disgusting, isn't it,' said Kitty, who was sitting opposite her. 'I can't believe they expect us to eat this stuff.' She paused for a moment. 'Do you want all your potatoes?' she added hopefully, beaming her thanks when Abby silently passed her plate over the table.

The meal over, it was back to the wards until ten o'clock, by which time Abby staggered off duty wanting nothing more than to fall into bed and sleep for ever. When she reached the bedroom, it was to find Flo standing looking at their beds. The four of them had been stripped to the springs, the mattresses lying higgledy-piggledy on top of each other.

'Sister Duffy.' Flo sounded as weary as Abby felt. 'Everything Pam says about that woman is true. I could strangle her right at this moment. Help me get the mattresses back on the beds, would you?'

Between them they lugged the mattresses on the four beds and then threw Pam and Kitty's sheets, blankets and pillows on top of their beds. 'They can make them up when they come back,' Flo panted. 'We're not doing theirs as well.'

Abby heartily agreed. It was all she could do to pull her bedclothes roughly into place and climb between them, still in her uniform minus her cap.

Flo came and stood by Abby's bed for a moment on her way to the bathroom, toothbrush in hand. 'I was like that for the first couple of weeks,' she said sympathetically, 'but you will get used to it although you don't think so now. I'll tell Pam and Kitty to be quiet when they come back.'

The other two girls had gone to the nurses' sitting room to listen to a wireless programme they were interested in and have a smoke. The sitting room was the only place where officialdom allowed the nurses to have cigarettes; consequently the air was always thick and hazy with smoke, and on the rare occasion it began to clear, the fire in the small fireplace at the far end of the long narrow room sent more smoke billowing back over the girls than it ever managed to expel up the chimney. Old sofas and chairs lined two of the other three walls, and a coffee table was piled high with blankets that parents and grandparents and aunties and uncles had donated to keep the nurses warm in the winter months. The tiny fireplace was woefully inadequate and the two windows let in such a draught that the curtains constantly fluttered in the breeze. But at least it was a meeting place, a room to air grievances imagined and otherwise, to laugh, chatter and occasionally cry in each other's company, and without exception to rail against sisters and staff nurses who could –

and usually did – make all their lives a misery.

The third wall consisted of shelves from floor to ceiling holding a number of books and magazines, all of which were carefully vetted by the matron before being allowed on the hospital premises. Anything slightly racy or in any way suspect never made it to the sitting room. Flo had told Abby that there had been a huge rumpus just before Christmas when a copy of D. H. Lawrence's scandalous book *Lady Chatterley's Lover* was found in the sitting room, obviously having been smuggled in. When Abby had confessed she had never heard of it, Flo had told her the book dealt with a love affair between a woman whose husband was impotent from war disablement, and the gamekeeper on their estate. There were passages of unprecedented frankness, Flo had whispered, using swear words and everything.

Abby had gazed at Flo wide-eyed. 'Did you read it then?' she'd whispered back.

Flo had giggled. 'Of course, and I shouldn't say this, because she would never admit to it, but I wouldn't be surprised if it was Pam who brought it in. She's quite a free spirit, is our Pam.'

As Flo disappeared off to the bathroom, Abby shut her eyes. She would just have a little nap until the bathroom was clear – there was always a queue when everyone came off duty – and then she would go along and have a wash and brush her teeth and change into her nightdress.

It was her last conscious thought before the faithful Kitty woke her at six o'clock the next morning.

Chapter Fifteen

Over the next weeks Abby began to slot into the hospital life at Hemingway's. She discovered the half-day a week and day off a month that every nurse was supposed to have as off-duty time depended very much on the sister in charge of the ward where she was working. Some bitterly resented their probationers having any free time at all, and always seemed to say that the ward was far too busy and they couldn't be spared. Others allowed the nurses their small amount of freedom, but always with a disappointed air that their dedication to duty was not what it should be.

It was the same with mealtimes. It seemed there were no laws against the nurses missing meals, which happened on some wards more than others, but plenty against said nurses asking if they could be excused to eat. As Flo had warned Abby, it would be more than her life was worth to remind Sister it was lunch or dinnertime. Some nurses got round this problem by surreptitiously eating what was left of the patients' food before it was collected by one of the kitchen maids, but it was a procedure fraught with danger. The penalty for being caught eating on the wards was a visit to Matron's office and was universally dreaded. Nevertheless, hunger is a powerful motive, and with one nurse standing guard another would often gobble down cold boiled cod or the remains of a pork chop followed by congealed baked jam roll. Abby had been horrified when Flo had first told her of the practice, but within a little while her fastidiousness was a thing of the past; neither did the ever hopeful Kitty receive more offerings. Abby ate every single thing on her plate in the dining room.

She learned that Matron was the be-all and end-all in every situation, and although the consultants and doctors were demigods and to be exalted at all times, even they trod carefully around Matron Blackett. Under her jurisdiction the hospital ran like a well-oiled machine; her word was law, her power absolute.

This didn't mean that some of the more daring nurses weren't above taking chances by breaking the rules; Pam being a case in point. Abby had been at the hospital for six weeks and had just come off duty at night exhausted after scrubbing out all the lockers and cupboards in the ward, and then scraping the fluff and other adhesions from the wheels and castors of anything movable before washing the whole floor in a mixture of disinfectant and water so hot she was surprised her hands had any skin left on them. She was now on Gynae Ward which she much preferred to the men's ward, most of the women being clean and particular in their habits, and she was beginning to work with the patients, albeit in a minor way. That morning she had helped a second-year nurse wash several old women who were incapable of washing themselves, one of her regular jobs now, and then settle them back in bed, brushing their hair and tying it back from their faces with the blue ribbons the hospital provided. The day before she had been given her first independent task by Sister, that of getting a tray ready holding a small-toothed comb and swabs of sassafras oil and then going through the patients' heads looking for lice and nits. Each patient was checked before being admitted but often the nits were missed, added to which, with visitors who were infected themselves coming in to see loved ones, the patients often got reinfected.

Opening the door to the room she shared with the others, Abby saw that Flo and Kitty were already in bed and that the window was open a crack. Knowing it had been Pam's half-day, she guessed the reason for the arctic breeze blowing into the room, even before Flo whispered sleepily, 'Leave the window open – she's not back.'

Tired though she was, Abby knew she would find difficulty falling asleep tonight so the fact that it was always better for one of them to remain awake and help Pam in the window, after the affair with the knicker elastic, wasn't the problem it might have been. Much as she preferred Gynae Ward, some of the women's stories were harrowing, especially the ones who had been admitted as the result of botched abortions. One such patient was a truly beautiful young woman of eighteen called Cecilia, and she had whispered her story to Abby earlier in the day when Abby had been given the task of feeding her, Cecilia being too weak to even lift a spoon. It appeared that the son of the big house where she was housemaid had noticed the lovely Cecilia and had waylaid her one morning when she had been making his bed, the result of which had resulted in a pregnancy. When she had claimed she had been raped he had denied it and she was packed off the same day, returning home to parents who had been adamant she had to get rid of the baby. A visit to a filthy old woman with dirty hands and an even dirtier crochet hook had resulted in Cecilia being admitted to hospital, but in spite of the surgeon's best efforts, sepsis was taking Cecilia's young life. It was a word that kept many a surgeon awake at night. Abby had looked down into Cecilia's white face in which her huge amber-brown eyes with their thick lashes had pleaded with Abby to help her, and had felt bereft. She still felt bereft, knowing that if Cecilia made it through the night it would be a miracle.

After visiting the bathroom she changed into her nightie and lay down in bed, curling herself into a ball against the chill of the icy room and trying to block Cecilia's delicate heart-shaped face out of her mind. Why was it some men, especially those with money or influence or both, thought they could treat women so badly? she asked herself, and it wasn't just the sons of rich men or the rich men themselves sometimes who behaved in such a manner. A number of the doctors at the hospital thought they were God's gift to women; she had been warned by Flo and the others on her first day about one or two who thought nothing of having their way with a new nurse and then moving on when they'd had their fun.

Such conjecture brought Nicholas to the forefront of her mind, much as she had tried to block all thoughts of him for the last weeks. Was he like that? she wondered miserably, before sharply refuting the idea. But she didn't *know*, that was the thing, she admitted. Not that it mattered one way or the other because she couldn't see him again, much as she ached to. She thought of the letter hidden in the hidey-hole where Pam kept any bottles of gin she smuggled in; she hadn't wanted Sister Duffy reading it when she did one of her room inspections. Nicholas had sent her the letter a week ago, asking how she had settled in to Hemingway's, and wondering if he could come and see her on her next day off.

Abby twisted under the covers; just picturing the strong black scrawl and the way he had simply signed himself Nicholas, doing away with formality, made butterflies dance in her stomach.

She had dithered for a day or so about whether she should just ignore the letter, but deciding Nicholas was quite capable of writing more or simply turning up at the hospital one day, she had written a reply couched in the formality he had avoided, making it plain any friendship between them was impossible. It would place her in an untenable position, she had declared. Her reputation in the community where her grandfather and brother still lived would be torn to shreds which would be humiliating and embarrassing for them, and their faith in her would be destroyed. They came from different worlds, and, more than that – and she was sorry to have to be so blunt – the laird, his father, was hated and feared, and with good cause. No good came of different classes attempting to mix, everyone knew that. She had finished by saying that while she appreciated his offer of friendship (here she hoped he would read

238

between the lines that she didn't expect anything more from him – it would be too awful if he thought that she thought he might be wanting an affair, especially if he didn't), other people would not understand. She had addressed him as Mr Jefferson-Price, and signed herself Miss Abigail Kirby. Then she had gone out and posted the letter and cried herself to sleep that night.

'Stop thinking,' she muttered to herself out loud, but it was easier said than done, and at one o'clock in the morning, when a stone hit the window, she was still wide awake. Padding barefoot across the floorboards, she peered down into the snowy, frosty, still night, gasping as the icy-cold air washed over her. The moon was sailing high in the star-studded sky and the snow and heavy frost illuminated the grounds of the hospital, but for a moment she could see no one. Then as she continued to hang out of the window there was a rustle at the base of the huge tree that regularly provided Pam with her entrances. Pam had made it her business to make a friend of Matron's spy, the lodgekeeper whose small cottage was situated at the end of the pebbled drive, regularly bribing him with packets of Park Drives or Woodbines and flirting with him until the poor man didn't know if he was coming or going. The fact that he was sixty-odd, bald, with a belly on him that resembled a nine-month pregnancy, didn't seem to deter him from thinking he had a chance with the lovely Pam, and she used this to her advantage quite shamelessly. Most nurses who sneaked into the hospital late and got away with it were left with feelings of guilt, but not Pam. Brazen, Kitty called her, and she was probably right.

Now, as Abby called in a loud whisper, 'Pam, is that you?' a muted giggle reached her as Pam staggered into view from where she had presumably been sitting at the base of the tree before promptly falling over again. Abby gazed at her in dismay. Pam was far too drunk to attempt to climb the tree, but just in case the idea occurred to her in her inebriated state, Abby hissed, 'Stay there, don't move.'

Ducking back into the room, she woke Flo and Kitty, which wasn't easy – they both slept like logs – and after she had explained the predicament they joined her at the window. Pam was now lying full length in the snow from where she responded to their questions with helpless giggles.

'Can you stand up?' Giggles.

'Sit up then?' More giggles.

'If one of us climbs down and helps you, do you think you could make it up the tree and through the window?' A guffaw, which they took to mean no as the three of them shushed her.

They stood looking at each other. If Matron caught Pam the worse for drink at one o'clock in the morning, it could mean dismissal. 'She can't climb the tree,' said Kitty, stating the obvious. 'We're going to have to get her in some other way.'

'Any suggestions?' said Flo caustically.

'We could make a rope with the bed sheets and haul her in that way.'

'And what if she lets go and breaks her neck?'

'She could tie it round her.'

'The state she's in she's likely to hang herself if it moves.'

Kitty stared at Flo. It took a lot to offend Kitty, but her tone was distinctly prickly when she said, 'All right then, Miss Know-it-all, how do we get her back in?'

'I think the bed-sheet idea is a good one,' said Abby, aiming to pour oil on troubled waters, 'but how about if I go down first and tie it round her? I could help push her up from underneath and then when she's in, I'll climb back up the tree.'

Flo looked at Abby doubtfully. 'You don't like heights.'

'Neither do you.'

'I don't mind heights. I'll do it,' said Kitty. 'And let's face it, you two aren't built for lifting her up from the ground but between you you could pull her if I'm pushing from below.'

Now she had made the suggestion Abby was worried. 'The tree's slippy with ice and snow, Kitty. What if you fall?' She would feel responsible. 'I'll do it.'

'Oh, for goodness' sake, I'm going.' Kitty began to lug the bedclothes off her bed and the others followed suit, making a thick swathe of linen from the combined sheets that they wound into a rope. Pam had begun to sing gently to herself and the strains of one of the hits from the year before – 'Tiptoe Through the Tulips' – wafted up to them on the icy air.

'I'll "Tiptoe Through the Tulips" her in the morning when she's sober,' said Flo grimly, and then, as Abby and Kitty began to chuckle, Flo gave a reluctant smile. 'Well, honestly, she is the limit.'

They soon realized it was a lot easier climbing

in the window from the tree than it was climbing out, especially as the bare branches were coated in snow and ice and then a thick layer of frost that twinkled and glittered in the moonlight and looked enchanting, but was in fact lethal. Somehow, with Abby and Flo leaning out as far as they could stretch and helping Kitty, she made it onto the branch of the tree just outside the window, clinging hold for dear life for a few moments before she began a cautious descent. Pam was quite oblivious to the drama being enacted above her, having added to her repertoire a somewhat risqué version of 'I Can't Give You Anything but Love, Baby' which had Flo shaking her head and pursing her lips in disapproval.

The next ten minutes or so were filled with anxiety, not least because when the able Kitty hauled Pam to her feet she stood swaying for a moment before falling flat on her face. They heard Kitty muttering words they had no idea she knew as she hoisted Pam into her arms and supported her weight, before tying the knotted sheets securely round Pam's waist and then crisscrossing them across her chest, securing them again round her waist for good measure, Flo's dire warnings in everyone's minds.

It was clear Pam was in no condition to help herself; how she had made it down the drive after her boyfriend had dropped her at the lodge gates was a mystery, and so once Kitty had got her ready to be winched up by Abby and Flo, she bodily lifted Pam to shoulder height to give them a chance. One of Pam's shoes was already missing and the other one fell off and cracked Kitty on the head as she stood beneath the gently swinging figure being hauled inch by inch towards the window. Careful though they were, a number of times Pam's head made contact with the wall of the building but Pam was well into 'Show Me the Way to Go Home' now and didn't falter in her rendition.

Abby and Flo were sweating by the time they grasped Pam's wrists and dragged her into the room, dropping her unceremoniously on the floorboards before they turned to watch Kitty's careful progress up the tree. It wasn't until Kitty was safely in the room that they saw to Pam, untying the bed sheets and attempting to smooth them out before, making their beds once again. Pam they simply dumped fully clothed on her bed, flinging the blankets on top of her.

It was the virtuous and upright Flo, panting heavily and still red in the face from her exertions, who lifted the floorboard and extracted Pam's latest bottle of gin from its hiding place, much to Abby and Kitty's amusement. Pouring a good measure into each of the beakers that they took along to the bathroom when they brushed their teeth, she drank hers in one swallow before refilling it once more. 'Bottoms up,' she said to the others, grinning widely. 'We've earned this.'

By the time she slid under the covers again, Abby's melancholy was quite gone. It could have been the neat gin coursing through her system that immediately sent her into a deep sleep, but the fact that her heart was lighter was due entirely to the three girls with whom she shared a room. They were more than room-mates – they were friends and comrades-in-arms and for the first time since she had arrived at Hemingway's she felt settled in spirit and mind.

Chapter Sixteen

It was the middle of May, and the old rhyme, 'March winds, April showers, bring forth May flowers', had proved to be abundantly true. Everywhere, even in the confines of the hospital, the scent of hyacinths and bluebells and other spring blooms filled the air, combating the smell of disinfectant and antiseptic and diseased bodies as vases and jam jars filled with flowers from visitors appeared on bedside tables. Outside in the hospital grounds, pink and white blossoms loaded the boughs of trees, and the horse chestnuts on the perimeter of the land close to the dry-stone walls that surrounded the building were lush with foliage, displaying their pyramids of bloom. After the long harsh northern winter, the deep-blue skies and milder air provided a tonic that was welcome to patients and nurses alike.

Abby's days off had been stopped three months running because the sister in charge of the ward had insisted she couldn't spare any of her nursing staff, but Abby wouldn't have contested this even if she had had the nerve – which she hadn't, knowing her life wouldn't have been worth living. A day off would have meant she was duty bound to go home, and much as she longed to see her grandfather and Robin, it was the possibility that she might – she just might – run into Nicholas that made her glad she had a viable excuse. He had written twice more, asking her to reconsider her decision and requesting that he be allowed to come and visit her, and finally after she had replied so forcefully that it had taken every ounce of her courage to post the letter, he had written saying he would never forget their talk on that cold winter's day and she would be for ever in his heart. The letters had stopped after that.

But now she had to go home. Abby paused outside Matron's office and took a deep breath before knocking on the door. She had made an appointment to request a sleeping-out pass, and she knew, as did every nurse in the hospital, that such passes were a special privilege and only slightly less rare than hen's teeth.

Matron Blackett looked up as Abby entered the room, her gimlet eyes raking Abby from top to bottom. Satisfied that this particular junior nurse didn't have a hair out of place, she raised her thin eyebrows. 'Yes?'

Abby had had to state the reason for the appointment to Matron's secretary so she knew the matron would be fully aware of why she had asked to see her, but her superior liked her full pound of flesh. 'Please, Matron, I would like to ask for a sleeping-out pass this weekend. My brother is getting married.'

'I see.' The long nose quivered with disapproval. Matron clearly didn't approve of such frivolity. 'So I take it you will be sleeping under your parents' roof?'

'My grandfather's roof, yes. My parents are dead, Matron.'

'Ah, yes, I remember, Nurse Kirby. Your grandfather sent you to Kelso High School until you were eighteen years of age. Is that correct?'

Remembering the matron's less-than-effusive comment about academic prowess in her first interview, Abby's voice was expressionless when she said, 'Yes, Matron.'

'He must be very fond of you.'

She didn't know how to reply to that so she said the truth. 'Yes, he is, Matron, as I am of him.'

'Quite.' There was a pause while the matron continued to survey her. 'Well, I suppose you would not wish to miss your brother's wedding.' This was said with some reluctance and the tone stated quite plainly that as far as the matron was concerned it was scant reason to leave the sanctity of the hospital and her duties. Nevertheless, she wrote out the pass and handed it to Abby. 'You will return to the hospital the following day by twelve noon ready to come on duty at two in the afternoon. I will accept no excuses about missed trains or anything else if you are late. Do you understand?'

'Yes, Matron. Thank you, Matron.'

'And you carry the reputation and prestige of Hemingway's with you, Nurse Kirby, whether you are in uniform or out of it. I trust you remember that at all times.'

'Yes, Matron.' Abby was unable to keep the elation out of her voice. She was going home to see Robin and Rachel married, and until this very moment she hadn't realized just how much she needed to see the farm and everyone on it again – or almost everyone.

A twist to her lips that was the nearest thing anyone would ever see to a smile touched the matron's mouth for a moment. 'That is all, Nurse Kirby. Please give your family the hospital's regards.'

'Thank you, Matron.'

Abby left with the precious piece of paper. Now she just had to inform the sister on her ward that Matron had authorized her leave which would go down like a lead balloon, but that was a small price to pay for seeing her grandfather and Robin again.

It felt strange to be wearing ordinary clothes once more rather than the hospital uniform, but by the time Abby walked down the farm track after the journey home, it felt as though she had never been away. Sweet vernal grass filled the air with the scent of new-mown hay, and the hedgerow floors and grass verges were covered with the countless blooms of bluebells reflecting the deep-blue sky. Cow parsley and buttercups and daisies clothed the rough pastureland either side of the lane she'd just walked down, and high above her the skylarks were soaring in the heavens, their sweet, exuberant and familiar song warming her heart.

The smells and sights of the country were so at odds with those of the hospital that it hadn't dawned on her how much she had missed them, she thought now with a feeling of guilt. But then you didn't have time to think about anything but the job in hand, she excused herself in the next moment. And if, by some good fortune, you did actually manage to have your half-day off, which wasn't by any means a certainty, all you wanted to do was to catch up on that wonderful thing called sleep.

The lambing of March and April was over now, which was why Robin and Rachel had chosen to get married in May when things were a little calmer for a few weeks for a shepherd before shearing time in June and the summer dipping of the sheep in early July. The sheep were dipped in the summer to protect them from the maggot fly, and again in late September to rid them of wool parasites before winter. Although the farmer detailed men to help her grandfather and Robin, Abby knew the operation was hard work from dawn to dusk for a few days. But then every day was hard work, which was why Robin wasn't having so much as a day's honeymoon after the wedding.

Abby stood for a moment, drinking in the scented air and the warmth of the sun on her face, and on a whim she took off her hat and shut her eyes, lifting her head to the blue sky. It was a beautiful day and warm for mid-May by northern standards; Robin and Rachel were going to have a lovely wedding. She had left the hospital straight after breakfast that morning and it was now nearing lunchtime; the wedding was at three o'clock, and for a few blissful moments all felt right with the world. Then she opened her eyes and saw Joe McHaffie walking down the track towards her.

She watched him as he approached, his hands in the pockets of his thick cord trousers, his jacket open showing the flannel shirt beneath, and his cap pulled low over his eyes. He was now in his late forties, and his thickening girth bore evidence to this. For a fleeting moment she wondered if he had ever had a lass or whether her mother's rejection of him had soured him in that regard, and then she pushed the thought away. It wasn't her mam's fault she had preferred someone else; you couldn't make yourself love another person if the feeling wasn't there.

He stopped a few yards away, and his voice was low and guttural when he said, 'So you are gracing us with your presence for the big occasion? Took your brother getting wed to get you home, did it?'

'You really are the most nasty of individuals, aren't you.'

For a moment, he was slightly taken aback at the direct verbal attack but he recovered almost immediately, forcing a 'Huh' of a laugh before saying, 'Can't take the truth? Well, unlike the rest of the poor sops, I see you clearly, Abigail Kirby. Oh, aye, I know exactly what you are. None of the farm lads round here are good enough for you, are they? Not when there are doctors sniffing around, and not just ordinary doctors either. No, you go for the toffs, don't you.'

Now it was Abby who was taken aback. She stared into the face that had grown coarser as he had got older, her mind racing. He couldn't know about Nicholas – could he? It was impossible. But that was a strange thing to say.

'I have no idea what you are talking about, nor do I wish to,' she said, taking care no part of her touched him as she stepped to the edge of the track and passed by.

He said no more, but she was aware of his eyes burning into her back as she continued along the track. He had ruined her homecoming. For a moment she felt angry enough to turn round and call him every name under the sun, but only for a moment. She wouldn't give him the satisfaction of knowing he had riled her.

Joe watched her progress along the track until she opened the door of Wilbert's cottage and disappeared inside. What would she say if she knew he had come to the hospital a few times now, casually skirting the high stone wall that surrounded the grounds and taking care to avoid the gate man in the lodge? He couldn't have explained to anyone, even himself, why he felt the need to be in the vicinity where she was, and he was aware of the futility of catching a glimpse of her. Nevertheless, on market days when he had seen to any farm business and had enough time left, the lure of Galashiels had proved too strong to resist. Now that he was gradually taking over more and more of the steward duties from his father with the farmer's blessing he had more independence to come and go as he wished, and a good number of stewards from other farms finished their market days by getting together in the local inn, some of them drinking themselves senseless. That had never appealed to him, but he always made sure he had one tankard of beer before he started for home so his father and mother could smell it on his breath and assume he had been drinking with the others.

The rush of excitement he'd felt when he had

seen her standing there on the track was subsiding now, and he wiped his damp hands down the sides of his trousers before walking on. She could always make him sweat, same as her mother, but whereas he had wanted Molly as his wife, had loved her before she had done the dirty on him, his feeling for the daughter was quite different. He nodded to the thought. Oh, aye, quite different.

The wedding at Morebattle parish church that afternoon was a happy one in spite of the fact that not one of the bride's family attended – or maybe because of it, as Robin muttered in an aside to Abby once the wedding party was back at the farm. One of the hay barns had been cleared and decked out by the women with garlands of wild flowers and ivy, and long trestle tables brought in and set down the middle of it.

Rachel looked pretty in a simple white dress, her short veil held in place by a wreath of fresh daisies, and Robin positively glowed with pride the whole day.

The labourers' wives and the farmer's womenfolk had been baking for days to provide the wedding feast, and the farmer had graciously provided a barrel of beer and several bottles of wine and spirits for the occasion. By the time the meal was over and the tables had been dismantled to make room for the dancing that would follow – one table left at the side of the barn holding liquid refreshments – quite a few of the guests were a little tipsy.

The farmer and his household left just before

the dancing began, as was the custom, and once they had disappeared the melodeon player struck up 'Ain't She Sweet' as a tribute to the bride amid clapping and cheering. A waltz followed, and soon the dusty barn floor was covered by dancing feet as most of the guests followed the bride and groom in the first dance.

Abby was content to sit with her grandfather and watch the others, and when Wilbert murmured, 'She's the right one for him, lass. No doubt about that,' she nodded her agreement. Rachel had kept the cottage spick and span while she had been gone, and according to her grandfather, Robin's bride was a good cook too and not afraid of hard work, but the main thing was that the girl clearly loved Robin as much as he loved her. It was a marriage made in heaven, as the minister at the church had said in his address to the congregation. Then why did she feel so heavy-hearted, at the same time as being glad for her brother and Rachel? As with many of her other emotions these days, she could not dissect this one, or perhaps it was that she didn't want to? she thought in the next moment.

Suddenly she had a feeling swamp her for the hospital that was akin to homesickness. Every minute of every day was accounted for there; the routine was rigid and – as the sisters and staff nurses reminded them constantly – they weren't required to think for themselves but to follow orders and do their duty. Hospital life was like a bubble – an exhausting and harrowing bubble admittedly, but the outside world seemed a million miles away at Hemingway's. She had been mistaken earlier when she had thought it felt as though she had never been away, she realized with a little shock of awareness. The farm, the cottage, everything here was no longer home, and she felt she would never come back to her grandfather's cottage to stay for any length of time. Rachel was the woman of the house now, and once Robin and his wife started a family even the bedroom she had called her own since she and Robin had arrived at the farm all those years ago would no longer be hers.

As though her grandfather had picked up on her train of thought, he said softly, his eyes on his grandson who was whirling his bride round the floor, 'I'm glad you're happy about Rachel being here, lass. The farming depression is beginning to bite but according to what Andrew McHaffie's been told by a couple of the farmers, the laird still wants his rent on time and has even put it up the last two years. He's a swine, that man. Anyway, you being settled about Rachel means they can live here and not have the expense of a place of their own now that wages are falling. It'll make all the difference when the bairns come along.'

'I know, Granda.' She patted his arm. 'And I am happy for them, truly. To be honest, I think it's the best thing that could have happened because if we're facing facts, it's unlikely I'll ever come back here to live, isn't it?'

She had expected him to object to that, or at least make a token protest, so when he put his gnarled hand over hers and murmured, 'Aye, I suppose so, lass,' she felt a moment of deep hurt before telling herself she was being silly. She had chosen her road and she was walking down it; more than that, her granda had supported her decision when others wouldn't have.

Nevertheless, the old feelings of aloneness and isolation that were quite different from loneliness and which had first reared their heads after her mother's death welled up inside, and for the rest of the evening she acted a part, laughing and chatting and dancing as though she hadn't a care in the world. She was aware of Joe McHaffie at one end of the barn where he stood drinking with some of the other men who weren't dancing, but avoided looking his way, and she also tried to ignore the whispers behind cupped hands and pointed looks her way from the more gossipy of the women who clearly didn't approve of her decision to become a nurse and leave the farming community. All in all, it was a relief when, come ten o'clock, her grandfather took her aside in a brief break from the dancing, when the small band consisting of the melodeon player and a couple of his pals who played the flute and the banjo, took a well-deserved break at the refreshment table to wet their whistles.

'I'm for bed, lass.' Wilbert downed the last of his beer, smacking his lips. 'I can't keep the hours these young 'uns do, and they'll go on for a while yet.'

Abby nodded. 'I'm dead on my feet too. I'll say goodnight to Tessa and some of the others because I'll be leaving straight after breakfast and I won't see them again. I can't risk being late back at the hospital. I'll follow you across shortly.'

Abby had made her goodbyes and given Robin

and Rachel a hug, and was halfway between the farm and the cottage walking along the track, when she heard the distinct sound of footsteps behind her. Swinging round, she came face to face with Joe McHaffie. Even in the dim light she could see he had had a skinful.

He stood, swaying slightly and his eyes bleary, and when he spoke his beer-laden breath was strong enough to make her nostrils quiver in distaste. 'Leaving early? But then I suppose the entertainment's not sophisticated enough for you?'

She'd known this confrontation would happen sooner or later today. She had been expecting it. And over the last hours she had made the subconscious decision that when it did, she would be ready for him. All her life Joe McHaffie had tried, and often succeeded in, intimidating her, and she was sick of it. And him. Her shoulders back and her head held high, she stared at him, and her voice would have done credit to Matron Blackett's when she said icily, 'Stop following me.'

'Following you? Huh! Taking a lot on yourself, aren't you? I live here an' all. Who's to say I wasn't going home?'

'Then go home.' Abby stood to one side, gesturing with her hand towards the pair of cottages a little way down the track. 'And leave me alone.'

Now his voice was venomous when he hissed, 'Don't tell me what to do.' He took a step towards her as he spoke, but she held her ground. 'You, with your airs and graces, but it don't cut no ice with me. I know what you are, like your mam afore you, but at least she had the sense to keep to her own class.'

255

There it was again. He had to be talking about Nicholas.

Abby wasn't aware her face had given her away until he said, 'Oh, aye, I saw you that day, missy. Heard you an' all, all lovey-dovey with the laird's son and heir. At the same hospital as him, are you? Is that why this nonsense about being a nurse came about? So you could carry on away from here?'

So he didn't know everything. But he must have been spying on them that day at Christmas, hiding somewhere. What was the matter with him? He had to be unbalanced at the very least. This was more than the grievance he held against her mother; he wasn't right in the head. Disdainfully she said, 'I have no intention of discussing my private life with you, McHaffie.'

She turned to walk away but he caught her wrist, jerking her round so violently that muscles screamed in her back as she twisted and almost fell over. She didn't think about what she did next – it was instinctive – but later she realized it had come about by listening to some of the women on Gynae Ward. To them, the nurses were sexless and ageless and certainly their contemporaries, and they told dirty stories, revealed fascinating insights into their married lives with a crudity that had had Abby red to the roots of her hair at first, and not least many tips on how to repel a man's unwanted advances. It was this last that now rose to the fore. Abby's knee came up into his groin with all the force she could muster. It was enough to send him crumpling to the ground as a high-pitched squeal left his lips.

Abby didn't wait to see how badly she had hurt him, turning and running towards the cottage and only stopping for a moment on the doorstep to straighten her hair and gain her composure. Then she opened the door without looking back down the track and went inside the house.

'All right, hinny?' Wilbert was making two cups of milky cocoa in the kitchen. 'Sit yourself down and we'll have a chat for a minute or two afore we turn in. By, it's been a day and a half, hasn't it. One to remember, all right.'

Chapter Seventeen

Contrary to what she had expected, Abby didn't see hide nor hair of Joe McHaffie the following morning, and the journey to Galashiels was uneventful. Going home had been a mixed blessing for many reasons, and although she wouldn't have admitted it to a living soul because it would have felt like disloyalty, Abby knew the umbilical cord had been well and truly cut for good.

If she'd had the time; she might have grieved about the end of an era. As it was, what with a ward change and lectures three times a week, it was all she could do to keep her head above water in the day, and at night she was asleep within moments of snuggling under the covers. Within a few days it was as though she had never gone home as the hospital routine took over so completely.

To Abby's delight, she found Pam was one of the nurses on her new ward, Male Medical. This was doubly comforting in view of the fact that the sister in charge was a terrifying creature with the reputation of a fearsome temper. Sister Woodrow was also a born nurse, from the top of her immaculate cap to her pristine shiny shoes, and she expected nothing less than perfection from every single one of her nurses, even the trainees. The patients on the ward were as frightened of her as were the nurses, and to see forty men, some twice the sister's age, grovelling in obedience to her orders, was not unusual. Needless to say, Male Medical ran like clockwork.

Now bottles were added to the bedpans, sluices and lavatory duties. The first time Pam had explained what the bottles were for, Abby stared at her in horror, especially when Pam added that in certain cases the men were either too old or too ill to insert the offending organ into the bottle themselves and it was the nurses' job to do it for them. 'But be careful,' the worldly-wise Pam whispered. 'Some of them make out they can't do it just to get a cheap thrill. You know what I mean?'

Abby hadn't known, and when her friend had elucidated further, she'd been doubly aghast. It hadn't helped that Pam had had a fit of the giggles at the shock on Abby's face. 'I keep forgetting what an innocent you, are,' she said when she could control herself. And then, as the staff nurse called down the ward, 'Could you break the habit of a lifetime, Nurse Lyndon, and actually get on with some work?' Pam muttered under her breath, 'She's got a mouth on her like a bee's backside, that woman,' in response to the stinging remark.

Abby smiled. She'd thought reading the nursing text-books had broadened her horizons, but she found she could still be surprised, like today. She might be an innocent in Pam's eyes, but she felt that Male Medical and her friend were definitely completing the education that the women in Gynae Ward had begun.

By the month of August, when unemployment had broken the two million barrier bringing more and more destitutes who'd grown too ill or frail into the hospitals from the streets and workhouses, the medical staff at Hemingway's and other hospitals were working seven days a week. Where once there had been an empty bed or two on most wards, this was no longer the case.

Economists were saying that the government needed to reverse the current trend by introducing new policies to boost the economy but all Abby and her colleagues knew was that whole families were starving to death, and by the time such folk were admitted to the hospitals, it was often too late to save them, especially the very old and the very young.

A killer heatwave towards the end of the month brought more problems for medical staff, and by the time the September crops were ready to be gathered in Britain's countryside and the first gentle days of autumn had slipped by, Abby and most of her nursing friends hadn't had even a half-day off in weeks. This made the planning of a social life impossible and had Pam and a few others champing at the bit, but it was Flo, who had found herself a boyfriend in the spring, who was suffering the most. Fortunately her beloved seemed as besotted with Flo as she was with him and took any crumbs she could offer; even an hour or two between shifts standing outside the hospital gates, or a clandestine late-night meeting when Pam charmed the lodgekeeper to look the other way for her friend. It said a lot for the strength of Flo's feeling for her young man that she was prepared to shimmy up the tree outside their bedroom window, but by the time its leaves were changing to bronze and gold and copper, she had become quite adept at midnight ascents.

The worst thing was when leave was cancelled at the last moment, something which one or two of the more sadistic sisters seemed to take great pleasure in doing, and it was this that had Abby bewailing her lot one Saturday morning at the end of September. She hadn't placed a foot outside the hospital grounds in weeks, and while they were pleasant enough to walk and sit in and were something of a relief from the smell and endless corridors of the building itself, she longed to go into Galashiels town centre or take a brisk walk somewhere – anywhere. She and Flo had planned to go into the town that afternoon, both having a half-day off – Flo to see her boyfriend and Abby to wander round the shops and perhaps visit the cinema – before they returned together by the ten o'clock deadline. Abby had actually been walking out of Male Medical on her way to lunch when Sister Woodrow had caught her, demanding that she return to the ward once she had eaten.

Bitterly disappointed, Abby had broken the

cardinal rule that was above all others and had argued her case, as she was telling Flo who had been waiting for her in the dining room before they went to get changed out of their uniforms.

'You didn't!' Flo's eyes were like saucers. 'Not with Woody.' All the sisters and staff nurses were to be feared but Sister Woodrow was in a class of her own.

'I just said I'd missed all my time off since I had been on her ward, that's all.'

'And what did she say?'

Abby swallowed hard. 'She wasn't pleased.' It was the understatement of the year. Abby had thought the sister was going to burst, she'd worked herself up into such a fury.

'So you're not coming?'

Abby shook her head. The way Sister Woodrow had carried on she'd be lucky if she ever got so much as an hour's leave the rest of the time she was at the hospital. 'This will go on my report,' she had hissed at Abby, her face red with fury and her eyes popping out of her head, 'and believe me I will inform the sisters on other wards about it. I can hardly believe one of my nurses would put her own gallivanting before the welfare of the patients.' There had been more, much more, and by the time Abby had slunk off Sister Woodrow had looked like a boiling kettle ready to blow its lid.

Flo patted Abby's arm. 'She's a spiteful old cat,' she whispered comfortingly, 'but only another couple of days to go before you change wards.' They were due to change on Monday and it couldn't come quick enough for Abby.

'I know.' Abby took a deep breath. It wasn't the end of the world. 'And you have a nice time with Simon.' Flo was due to meet Simon's family for the first time for afternoon tea, and she'd been in a tizzy about it for days. On an impulse, she said, 'Why don't you wear my hat and coat as I won't be using them?' Flo's coat was an old thing. Like Abby, Flo sent most of her wages back home, but in Flo's case it was to help support her siblings, all of whom were still at school.

'Really?' Flo's face lit up.

'Of course. They'll fit you perfectly – we're the same build and height. I don't know why I didn't think of it before.' At least some good would come out of her misfortune. 'And the colour will suit you so. You'll look the bee's knees.' It would give Flo the confidence she needed to face the Hogarth clan.

As Flo whirled off to get changed, Abby finished her bread and cheese and pickles but without any appetite. She could imagine what her afternoon was going to be like and she wouldn't have wished it on her worst enemy.

It was twenty to ten that night when Flo got off the bus opposite the long side road which led to the hospital. Simon was working a night shift at the steelworks where he was employed, so they had had to make do with a furtive kiss and cuddle at the bus stop in the town before the bus came and she went one way and Simon another. But it had been a lovely afternoon and evening.

Flo smiled to herself as she set off down the dark lane, her mind full of the meeting with

Simon's family and how well it had gone. His mother especially had been nice, so nice that when she had been getting ready to leave and Mrs Hogarth had commented how bonny she looked in Abby's hat and coat, she had been able to confide that she had borrowed them from a friend for the afternoon because her coat had seen better days. 'Ee, lass,' Simon's mother had said, her plump face rosy and smiling, 'you'd look as pretty as a picture to our Simon whatever you wore, you know that, don't you? Fair gone on you, he is, and having met you I can see why.'

Yes, it had been a lovely afternoon.

Flo was halfway down the road, walking on the pavement that stretched on the hospital side of the unlit lane, when she thought she heard the snap of a twig behind her. The pavement was littered with twigs and leaves from the trees on the perimeter of the hospital grounds on the other side of the high stone wall, and in the darkness she'd had to be careful not to trip, especially with her mind occupied with the events of the previous few hours. Now she turned, looking back, and she could just make out someone a little way behind her, but the night was cloudy and moonless and in the darkness she couldn't see whether it was a man or a woman. But surely if it was another nurse, she would have called out before this, and there had been no one getting off the bus besides her.

Suddenly the darkness that was almost pitch black became frightening and her footsteps quickened, her stomach turning over.

Joe McHaffie swore softly to himself as he realized Abby had become aware of him and he broke into a run. She wasn't going to get away from him; this was the chance he had been waiting for all the times he had patrolled the area, countless times lately since she had humiliated him at the wedding. He had been leaving Galashiels to catch the last train home and had been at the end of the side road about to step into the main thoroughfare when he had noticed a girl getting off the bus that had just pulled up; a girl in a deep-plum coat and hat. He had known instantly it was Abby, even though her head had been down and the hat and the dim light had obscured her features. The reddish-purple hat and coat had been unmistakable.

He had slunk into the shadows, his heart beating fit to burst and his hands instantly clammy, unable to believe his good luck. Not a sight of her in months and now here she was, bold as brass. No doubt she was all dressed up because she'd been meeting Jefferson-Price on the quiet, or perhaps she'd moved on to someone else now?

He reached her just as she tried to run, grabbing her from behind with one arm round her neck and the other round her waist. Her scream panicked him, and he pulled her harder against him, his arms tightening as he muttered, 'Shut up, shut up, shut up,' as she struggled, her hat tipping forwards as he got both hands round her neck and fell on top of her so that she was face downwards on the ground.

He couldn't have said afterwards when he first realized it wasn't Abby; perhaps it was when her hat fell off and her hair was revealed, although the night was black and perhaps it hadn't dawned on him then? He wasn't sure, but his overwhelming feeling was that he had gone too far and he couldn't stop now, he had to stop her screaming before someone heard her. And then she was still. He continued to sit astride her back with his hands round her throat for some moments before he moved, a sickening fear replacing the panic. When he rolled her over and saw the face with its tongue protruding and eyeballs bulging he crawled to the edge of the pavement and was violently sick, retching and retching until there was nothing left in his stomach.

It wasn't Abby. He didn't know this girl. He had killed her and he didn't know her.

He crawled back to the body, praying that there would be something, some flicker of life, the slightest breath, but knowing she was dead. Whimpering to himself, he smoothed down her clothes and then put the hat over her face.

He hadn't meant to kill her. He sat swaying back and forth, an owl hooting somewhere in the blackness beyond the lane. Not this stranger. Had he had murder on his mind with Abby? He shook his head; perhaps, he didn't know. He had wanted to talk to her, to warn her to stay away from the farm or else... He had wanted to frighten Abby, aye – to get some sort of reaction from her and prove himself a man. She had treated him with such contempt from when she had come to the farm; even Molly had been kinder. This was Abby's fault. Molly's daughter had done nothing but goad him since the first day he had set eyes on her.

A sob caught in his throat. And why was this

girl wearing the same hat and coat Abby had? What were the chances of that? This wasn't his fault, it wasn't. He hadn't *known*.

Eventually he stood up, stumbling down the lane in the opposite direction to the main road and heading towards the open countryside. The hospital was built on the edge of Galashiels and he had patrolled the area enough recently to know that there was a dense forest area a few miles up ahead. It was there he made for, falling over several times in the black darkness but picking himself up and continuing on. He didn't think as he walked, his mind blank now, just the occasional night sound penetrating the stupor like a fox barking or the sudden startled cry of a bird disturbed from its roosting.

He passed through a small hamlet at one point, the cottage windows dark and shuttered against the night and only one small black cat that was sitting on a doorstep watching him with un-interested eyes.

When he reached the edge of the forest he turned off the road, climbing over the dry-stone wall and jumping down into the dense bracken and undergrowth on the other side, before making his way into the trees. Great ferns and tangles of brambles hampered his progress the deeper he went; it was clear few people ever ventured this way, and the further he walked, the more difficult it was to fight his way through. Eventually after some time he came to a kind of clearing under a massive ancient oak tree and here he stopped, sitting down with his back against the great trunk

He was bleeding from numerous scratches and

lacerations but he didn't feel the pain; he didn't feel anything.

And hours later, when the beauty of first light touched the dawn sky, the morning dew gleaming on the trees like pearls and the pine-scented air as clean as crystal, the body hanging by its neck from a leather belt swung gently on one of the boughs of the oak and a pair of crows with hungry nestlings to feed, attracted by the scent of dried blood, edged near and nearer...

Chapter Eighteen

The horror of Flo's murder reverberated around the inhabitants of the hospital, patients and staff alike, as though a bomb had been thrown into their midst. It proved useless for Matron Blackett to insist that she didn't want any of the patients informed of the situation for fear of what the shock would do to their recovery; the hospital grapevine had whispered the news into every ward by noon the next day.

Flo's body had been discovered shortly after eleven o'clock by two nurses who had missed their ten o'clock deadline after attending a party in the town where they'd had too much to drink. Needless to say, they sobered up very quickly when one of them fell over Flo in the darkness. The screams of both girls and their shaking of the locked gate of the hospital brought the lodge-keeper running to their aid, but nothing could be

267

done for Flo.

On being roused, Matron Blackett – for the first time in living memory less than immaculate, being in her night attire with her hair in pin curls and papers – sent the lodge man off on his motorcycle to notify the police, and called Abby, Pam and Kitty to her sitting room. The three girls broke down and Kitty, who had been particularly close to Flo, all but fainted. And if they had needed proof that they were really awake and not in the middle of a horrific nightmare, it came when Matron Blackett gave each of them a glass containing neat brandy and told them to drink it straight down. 'For the shock,' she added in a voice quite unlike her own, her face as white as a sheet under its halo of pin curls.

The next few days were grim for everyone, and even Sister Duffy was subdued and unusually gentle. For Abby, the way her friend had died was almost unbearable, bringing to the surface all the feelings about her mother's death she kept buried most of the time, feelings that were made worse because she couldn't tell anyone what had happened when she was a child. She slept little and ate even less, going about her duties in a fog of misery.

At first the police suspected that Flo had had a row with her boyfriend and he'd had some kind of brainstorm and killed her in a fit of rage. Apparently, according to the constable who took statements from Abby, Pam and Kitty, it was often someone close to the victim who committed what the police called a crime of passion.

None of the girls believed for a moment that Flo's boyfriend was capable of murder, and after

Simon's story that he had seen Flo onto the bus and then gone straight off to work was corroborated by the bus conductor and also his employer, the police were forced to think again.

The fact that Flo hadn't been interfered with tended to rule out a sexual assault, but as she didn't have any disgruntled former boyfriends lurking in the background, or anyone else who might wish her harm, the police, along with her family and friends and work colleagues, were at a loss. It was when Abby received her next letter from home, three weeks after the murder, that the first inkling of a terrible possibility reared its head. Her grandfather and Robin were no letter writers and Rachel had volunteered to correspond with Abby while she was at the hospital. Rachel's letters were always chatty and informative, full of the smallest events that happened at the farm so that often Abby glossed over whole paragraphs at a time about the hens not laying or a quarrel between two of the labourers' wives, but this time a couple of lines made her stiffen. Maybe if the police hadn't returned her hat and coat to her that very day, freshly laundered, she might not have linked Joe's disappearance with the murder of her friend.

'The strangest thing,' Rachel wrote in her big childish script, 'is that Joe McHaffie seems to have vanished off the face of the earth. No one's seen him for weeks now, but Robin says he's big enough and ugly enough to look after himself and he'll turn up when he's ready. His mam's worried though – well, you'd expect her to be wouldn't you.'

Abby's blood froze, the letter dropping from her fingers onto her lap. She had picked up the letter from the nurses' cubbyhole in the big hall during her lunch break and as she had to change her apron before the afternoon shift, she had run up to her room to read it. She sat on the bed, her mind racing, and looked across at the wardrobe where she had hung her hat and coat that morning after the constable had arrived with it first thing. Flo's funeral had taken place the week before and Flo's mother's grief had been harrowing to see and was still fresh in Abby's mind.

Flo had been wearing *her* hat and coat when she had been murdered. Could someone – no, not someone, could *Joe McHaffie* – have mistaken Flo for her in the darkness? In lending Flo her things, had she been the cause of her friend's death?

No, no, she was putting two and two together here and making ten, she told herself as she began to tremble. Joe McHaffie disliked and resented her because of her mam, but he wouldn't plan to kill her would he? Especially now she had left the farm? He was rid of her, that was the way he would think about it, surely? But then look at how he had behaved the night of Robin's wedding. He hated her.

It was five minutes later when Sister Duffy, on one of her room inspections, poked her head round the bedroom door. The words she had been about to say about one of her nurses sitting on her bed in the middle of the day died on her lips when she saw Abby's face. Instead, her voice uncharacteristically soft, she said, 'What's the matter, child?'

'Oh, I'm sorry, Sister.' Abby jumped up from the bed. 'I only came to change my apron and then I read a letter from home and ... and...' To her consternation she couldn't go on, and when she burst into tears Abby surprised herself as much as Sister Duffy.

It said a lot for Sister Duffy's genuine concern for the well-being of her nurses – an attribute normally zealously concealed lest it be taken as a sign of weakness – when she sat down beside Abby, regardless of the crumpled counterpane. Again she said, 'What is it, child?' before waiting as Abby pulled herself together.

When she could speak amid the occasional hiccuping breath, Abby said, 'It's to do with Flo's death, Sister.'

The sister's eyes narrowed. 'You know something about Nurse Kane's murder?'

'No. Yes. I don't know...' Abby took a deep gulp of air. She wasn't making sense. Blowing her nose, she tried again. 'There's a man at the farm where I lived after my parents died who bore me a grudge because of my mother – she had been expected to marry him but she ran off with my father instead. And Flo was wearing my hat and coat.'

The sister held up her hand. 'Collect your thoughts,' she said in her old, imperious way, 'and then begin again from the beginning.'

This time Abby was able to do just that, explaining how Joe McHaffie had treated her from the first day she had gone to live with her grandfather until the night of Robin's wedding. She told the sister about Rachel's letter, her fear that Joe McHaffie had come to Galashiels on the night of Flo's murder, and the fact that Flo had been wearing her clothes. When she had finished speaking, the sister sat quiet for a moment. Then she said, 'I think because of the distress regarding Nurse Kane's death you have got this out of all proportion, Nurse Kirby. Quite understandable of course, but nevertheless, I fear you are letting your imagination run away with you.'

'So you don't think I ought to inform the police about Joe McHaffie?'

The sister looked at her. 'And say what exactly? Did this man ever threaten to kill you?'

'Well, no, not exactly, Sister.'

'Has he done you physical harm in the past? Assaulted you in any way?'

'Only when he tried to grab me at the wedding.'

'Since you have been residing at Hemingway's, have you seen him in the area?'

'No, Sister.'

'And could he have known you were due to have leave that particular day?'

Abby shook her head.

'And why, if he did commit this terrible deed, would he disappear thus bringing attention to himself? Surely he would have simply gone home and acted as normal? You say he has lived with his parents all his life? Then perhaps he just wanted to get away for a time. People do, you know. But with his work commitments it would perhaps have been difficult for him to do so and therefore he took the easy way out. I am sure he will turn up at the farm sooner or later or write to tell his parents all is well.'

When Abby continued to look doubtful, Sister

Duffy patted her hand. 'I did the same kind of thing when I left home to take up nursing, Nurse Kirby. My parents would never have agreed to it. With my sister and two brothers having left home and married, it was generally assumed I would be the one to remain a spinster and take care of my parents in their dotage. I'm afraid, for my own sanity, that wasn't an option, and neither was marriage.'

'My grandfather did say that Joe is taking on more and more of the steward's duties now his father is getting older.'

'There you are then. Presumably he's lived on the farm all his life? Then perhaps he wanted to see a little of the world before he stepped into his father's shoes. If you point the finger at this man now, with no proof and nothing to substantiate such an accusation, save that Nurse Kane happened to be wearing a borrowed hat and coat, I fear the police would laugh at you. But if they did take it seriously and investigated further, surely that would cause an immense amount of bad feeling with the family which could rebound on your grandfather and brother? Which, according to what you have told me, is the very thing that has kept you concealing this man's animosity towards you all these years?'

Abby nodded. 'Yes, Sister.'

'An animosity which, I might add, never resulted in more than unkind comments and taking your arm at a wedding. In hindsight, even the incident when you were a child, although upsetting, was something and nothing. He must have known, as you discovered later, that the pools would be

273

frozen well into the spring and that you were in no danger, save for being frightened. As I say, unkind, but one could hardly take the great leap to the man committing murder on such flimsy supposition.'

Put like this, her fears did seem ridiculous. And yet... Abby looked into the sister's well-meaning face. Sister Duffy didn't know Joe McHaffie. She hadn't seen the look in his eyes when he stared at her. But was he capable of murder?

Sister Duffy patted Abby's hand and then stood up. 'We are all still feeling the effects of the terrible tragedy of Nurse Kane's death, the more so because the police have not apprehended the person or persons responsible, but the police inspector has told Matron he is leaning towards the possibility that a passing vagrant, intent on robbery, committed the crime. He probably had no intention of killing Nurse Kane, but if she cried out and he panicked...' Sister Duffy shrugged. 'That is a far, far more likely explanation than the one you speak of. The farm is umpteen miles away, he would hardly have picked the very night that someone wearing your hat and coat walked along the lane after dark, Nurse. You must see that?'

Again, put like that her suspicions did seem far-fetched. 'Yes, Sister.' Abby rose to her feet, smoothing her apron.

'And if he had had evil intentions towards you, wouldn't he have carried them out while you were still living within the farm community? There must have been numerous times when he could have acted on them.'

That was true, but... 'I suppose so, Sister.'

'You have to look at this logically, my dear. And at the moment that is difficult, I understand that.'

'I'm sorry to harp on about it, Sister, but he did follow me on the night of my brother's wedding.'

'But after you'd repulsed him, he made no attempt to come after you or attack you.'

She'd left him rolling on the ground clutching his private parts, Abby thought. He'd been in no position to come after her.

'And the next morning he did not threaten you or attempt to detain you? Is that right?'

'Yes, Sister.'

'I am not being difficult, Nurse Kirby. I am merely putting the case the police would, if you spoke to them. You do see?'

Yes, she saw. 'Yes, Sister.'

'Nurse' – Sister Duffy hesitated for a moment – 'don't let your friend's death, shocking and up-setting as it has been, impinge on your own mental health and peace of mind. Of course such a ghastly thing is bound to impact you and the other girls and disturb you, but life has to go on. You have the makings of a good nurse, a very good nurse, but something like this could cause you to lose focus and I wouldn't want to see that happen. Hard though this may sound, you need to put it behind you and concentrate on your work here. Now, time has gone and you need to return to your ward but first' – Sister Duffy glanced at Abby's bed – 'I expect you to leave this room as I would wish to find it.'

'Yes, Sister.' Strangely it was comforting. What-ever disasters befell and however terrifying h

275

thoughts, Sister Duffy remained the same.

Time has a habit of dulling even the most chilling of eras. For a long time after her talk with Sister Duffy, Abby went over and over it in her mind, especially during the night hours when she was so tired her head and body ached but sleep didn't come.

Sister Duffy had been logical and reasonable and – most importantly – neutral in her summing-up of the facts. The sister hadn't been influenced by guilt and fear, and her conclusion that Joe Mc-Haffie had nothing to do with Flo's murder and that to implicate him would be harmful to everyone concerned, was a valid and plausible one.

Abby had written to Rachel, asking Robin's wife to let her know when news was heard about Joe, and, despite the cost, had thrown the beautiful hat and coat into the hospital rubbish. The first deed had been in recognition of Sister Duffy's deduction of the facts. The second had been based purely on emotion, and despite the irrational and probably absurd aspect, Abby had been overwhelmingly glad to see the clothes destroyed. The bulk of her wages went to her grandfather to repay him for the cost of her books and uniform and other expenditure, and she couldn't afford to replace the hat and coat, but that didn't matter. Kitty and Pam, although not knowing about Joe McHaffie because Abby had shared that with no one but Sister Duffy, could totally empathize with her decision, and offered their own hats and coats or when she needed to borrow them.

Flo's passing left a deep sense of loss and injustice in each of the three girls' lives, but at the same time drew them together as nothing else could have done. Flo had been the mother hen in their quartet, and when the matron had decided not to introduce another nurse into their room and had had Flo's bed removed, they had gone together to thank her.

Matron Blackett had looked at the young faces in front of her, and had grieved for their innocence, fearing they would soon have more than their friend's death to face. The environment of the hospital, the nursing exams, inspections and the constant demands for perfection created a small world within the world, and she, wise in years, knew this. Her junior nurses had no time or inclination to think about civil wars in distant lands, and fascism and communism were only words to them. She doubted if there were a handful of her nurses who could even name the prime minister of the day. But she, like others born before the Great War, was watching the rise of Adolf Hitler's National Socialists with some trepidation. In a stunning German election the Nazis had come second, and the meeting of the new Reichstag, in which the Nazis had 107 deputies, had been marked by rowdy scenes in the chamber and violent anti-Jewish demonstrations in the streets of Berlin. The newspapers had reported that mobs of Nazi supporters had chanted, 'Down with the Jews,' and smashed windows of Jewish-owned stores.

But she could be wrong, she thought, as she accepted her nurses' thanks and sent them about their business. Certainly the government didn't seem unduly concerned about the Nazis, or the fact that this Hitler – a small, nondescript little man in the matron's opinion – had publicly denounced previous peace treaties, saying he wanted to build a huge conscript German army.

But then her father had been a small, nondescript little man, and he had made her life hell on earth, as well as her mother's and brothers' and sisters'. Men were a different species. The matron nodded to the thought. A species she neither liked nor respected apart from a few exceptions among the consultants and doctors at the hospital. Men thought differently from women; it was all about power and prestige and domination with them, and the Nazis seemed to epitomize this from what she had read.

No, there were dark days ahead. She shook her head sadly. And how many of her girls, as she privately thought of her nurses, would be put in danger if the worst happened and war reared its head once again? The last war had been called the war to end all wars, but men never learned the lessons of history.

But for now she had a hospital to run. Clearing her mind of everything but the day ahead, she picked up the first paper from the pile on her desk and began to read it.

Chapter Nineteen

By the third week of December, when the snow lay thick in the hospital grounds and the nurses' sitting room was so cold that the ice on the inside of the window was half-an-inch thick, the shock of Flo's death had begun to fade. Abby thought about her friend often and she knew that Kitty and Pam did the same. Sometimes the three of them talked about the good times they had shared, and what Flo would have said about such and such a thing. But as Sister Duffy had declared, life went on, and life at the hospital meant one was on the go from morning to night.

And now, on the approach to Christmas, Abby was finding that the festive season at Hemingway's was different from anything she had experienced before. There was a gaiety in the air, an anticipation, and it kindled forgotten memories of how things had been at Christmas when her mother had been alive, especially before her father had returned from the war and joy and merriment had left the house.

Since her mother had died, Christmas had simply been a time to get through as best she could, a dark time, stirring nightmares that haunted her in the day as well as at night. But this year was different. She even found herself humming the old song that had been one of her mother's favourites – 'Snowflakes in the Wind' – a she went about her nursing duties.

Kitty and Pam did nothing but grumble about being on duty over Christmas, but Abby had no wish to go home. She felt guilty about this if she thought about it, and so she didn't let herself think about it. The farm was linked in her mind with Joe McHaffie, and although there had been no word from him according to Rachel's letters, and the probability of him having anything to do with Flo's death was remote, she still didn't want to go where she would be reminded of him all the time. Rachel had taken her place as woman of the house, and Robin's wife's letters radiated a quiet happiness and contentment that reassured Abby all was well. With that she was satisfied.

The second week of December Abby and the rest of the nurses had put up streamers and holly and blobs of cotton-wool snow in the wards, hanging bits of mistletoe in strategic places where the more forward of the nurses hoped the junior doctors would see it and take advantage of the none-too-subtle invitation. Pam had given her boyfriend his marching orders some weeks before and had her eye on one of the more senior doctors, a dashing, slightly greying forty-year-old with film-star good looks. Declaring he would notice her even if she had to dance stark naked in front of him, Pam had secured a piece of mistletoe which she carried about in the pocket of her dress in the hopes she would bump into him at a time when there were no sisters or staff nurses about. Abby and Kitty felt sorry for the poor man – as Kitty said, he was hooked and he didn't even know it yet.

The boy scouts had delivered a large tree for the entrance vestibule and the nurses who were off duty that afternoon, of whom Abby was one, had decorated it with glass baubles and tinsel and yet more cotton-wool snow. It was the first tree Abby had ever dressed and she felt inordinately proud of the result.

To the junior nurses' delight, they found the strict rules and regulations they had to abide by all year were relaxed a little as Christmas Eve dawned. Amid much giggling and carrying-on, they had formed a choir and had been having singing practices when time permitted. Once it was dark on Christmas Eve, Abby and a number of the other nurses went from ward to ward, singing carols while holding candles flickering in jam jars, wreaths of tinsel sitting on their hair instead of the regulation caps. In the children's ward, they distributed cuddly toys wrapped in bright paper that had been donated by shops in Galashiels, along with small bags of sweets and a picture book for each child that Matron Blackett had bought.

Most of the children who'd had to stay in hospital over Christmas were long-term patients, and several of them had never had a cuddly toy or any other toy to call their own. Some of the little ones had regular visitors; others had been more or less abandoned by their families who were either too busy, lived too far away or just didn't care enough to make the journey to see their offspring. One such little tot, a tiny fair-haired boy with eyes like saucers, had clutched his teddy bear as though he would never let it go. 'He's mine?' He looked up at Abby, his blue eyes shining. 'For ever?'

'For ever.'

He smiled at her, a sweet wondering smile, made all the more poignant by his ravaged, emaciated body. 'I'll look after him,' he promised.

'I know you will.' She stroked the fair curls, her heart breaking. It was doubtful he would see another spring. 'What are you going to call him?'

He thought for a moment. 'My bear.' He held the teddy close to his face for a moment. 'My brown bear.'

'Brown Bear. That's a lovely name.' The other children were already gobbling their sweets, but Archie only had eyes for his bear.

After singing 'Away in a Manger' to the children the choir left the ward, but Abby had had a job to join in for the lump in her throat. She was still thinking about the little boy when she reached her room later. Kitty was already in bed, the blankets pulled up to her chin and her coat spread over the counterpane to combat the icy chill in the freezing room. Each of the girls went to bed with a jumper or two over their nightdress and bed-socks, but they were rarely warm enough since winter had taken hold. It was as well that exhaustion usually claimed them in sleep before the cold penetrated their bones, but each morning when they awoke, instinct having turned them into little curled-up balls under the covers, they ached all over.

'Where's Pam?' Abby asked, swiftly divesting herself of her dress but keeping her underclothes on, over which she pulled her nightdress and then a thick jumper before scrambling into bed. In the last changeover Pam and Kitty had been placed on the same ward.

Kitty chuckled. 'Probably in seventh heaven as we speak. We were leaving the ward and walking down the corridor when Dr Ferry came towards us and quick as a flash Pam pulls out her mistletoe. He didn't stand a chance. Honestly, Abby, she practically ate the poor man. What could he do after that but ask her if she wanted a coffee? He included me in the invitation too, to be fair, but it would have been more than my life was worth to take him up on it! I think Santa is going to bring Dr Ferry a lot more than he expected for Christmas if the gleam in Pam's eyes when she walked off with him is anything to go by. She's shameless, she really is.'

Kitty spoke a little wistfully. She had never had a boyfriend, and while she was regularly shocked by Pam's antics and complete disregard for propriety, she rather admired the other girl's confidence.

'Well, we never doubted she would get her man,' said Abby drily, her feet so cold they felt like blocks of ice.

'He is gorgeous, though, isn't he,' murmured Kitty dreamily. 'And there's something about doctors. Do you know what I mean?'

'No, not really, and I'm going to sleep.' Abby had been thinking about Nicholas all day and she couldn't face a discussion about the merits of doctors. 'We probably won't see Pam for hours, so I'd advise you to do the same. Tomorrow is going to be even more rushed than usual what with the mayor and his dignitaries coming.'

Kitty pulled a face. 'All that work and I bet they don't even want to set foot in the place.'

Abby didn't doubt that. Every year the civic

party arrived just before lunch, and the mayor was given the honour of carving the turkey for the top table where he, his hangers-on – as Pam irreverently called them – and the matron and consultants sat.

The amount of work to get the hospital's patients ready for this visit was immense, especially for the poor junior nurses who happened to be on duty on the male and female chronic wards. Most of these inmates didn't know what day it was or where they were, existing in a world known only to them and having conversations on a regular basis with folk long since departed.

The civic party would dutifully tour every ward of the hospital after lunch, distributing smiles and nods and stopping for a chat with a patient now and again. That was fine on the other wards; but on the chronic wards they often encountered a wizened granny who would whip off her nightdress and lie there as naked as the day she was born before the nurses could get to her or an elderly gentleman with a glazed smile on his face doing something unmentionable to himself under the covers.

This tour used to take place before lunch, but an incident some years before had put paid to that. A sweet-faced, white-haired little old lady who had, unbeknown to the nursing staff, done her business in her bed, then decided to give her gift offering to the nice visitors by throwing it at them with a deadly aim when they stopped to talk to her. The resulting screams and stampede for the door had resulted in the mayor's wife slipping on the foul-smelling mess and ending up sliding down the ward on the carefully polished floor, to the accompaniment of clapping and garbled calls from the patients who genuinely thought it was a show put on for their benefit.

'Night then.' Kitty's voice was already drowsy, and within a minute regular snores from her bed told Abby her friend was out for the count, but tonight Abby found sleep eluded her. All day, no matter what she had been doing, memories of Christmas Eve the year before had darted into her mind. Perhaps it was because an air of sentiment and festive mawkishness pervaded the usually austere confines of the hospital? she thought, trying to harden her heart. But it was no good. Tonight Nicholas wouldn't be denied access. She lay picturing his tall strong body and handsome face, his shock of black hair and deep-brown eyes, and fought the tears that pricked at the backs of her own eyes.

It had been right to send him away, she reassured herself, and she knew that. Any liaison between them was doomed from the start, what with his father and Nicholas's position in life, and her own family. Her grandfather and Robin would never understand. Only last week Rachel had written that a deputation of farmers had gone to see the laird to ask for a reduction in the rent on their farms now the depression was worsening so rapidly, but he wouldn't give them the time of day. Wilbert was predicting dire times ahead, Rachel had written, and she and Robin were so grateful to him that he had already agreed with the farmer that Robin would take over as shepherd in the next few years and continue to live in the cottage. Every so often now they saw whole families tramping the roads, and the men would offer to work for nothing more than a roof over their heads and food to eat. And there was the laird, in his big house and with more money than he knew what to do with, refusing to lower the rent by so much as a penny. He was a fiend, a devil, that's what Wilbert said.

She had read the letter and she had agreed with it. Nicholas's father *was* a monster, but his son wasn't like that. She knew he wasn't. But she also knew her grandfather and Robin wouldn't accept that in a million years.

She fell to sleep eventually through exhaustion, and woke just before six to Kitty shaking her shoulder and thrusting a small present into her hands. 'Come on, wake up, it's Christmas Day,' said Kitty, for all the world as though she was a small toddler rather than a grown woman.

Pam was sitting on her bed, amazingly bright-eyed and bushy-tailed considering she still hadn't been back when Abby had fallen asleep in the early hours. The three of them exchanged gifts – small bottles of Californian Poppy from Kitty, scented soaps from Pam and boxes of chocolates from Abby – while Pam regaled them with tales of her lurid night of love with her Dr Ferry who apparently was 'the one'. The fact that each of Pam's boyfriends was 'the one' until she decided otherwise when she got bored was neither here nor there, and Abby and Kitty wouldn't have dreamed of reminding Pam of this, not on Christmas Day.

Then Pam produced a small bottle of brandy from her hidey-hole and poured a measure into each of their toothbrush glasses. 'To Flo,' she said, a catch in her voice. 'The best of friends.'

'To Flo,' Abby and Kitty echoed.

'And may the swine who killed her burn in hell,' Pam added.

It wasn't quite in the spirit of Christmas but they were all in agreement nonetheless. Abby had never tasted brandy before and she thought it was horrible, but the warm glow it produced in her stomach was welcome in view of the freezing-cold room and lack of sleep. It provided the boost of adrenaline needed to start what was bound to be an exceptionally busy day, especially considering that in the matron's eyes the visit of the mayor was considerably more important than the birth of the Saviour of the world.

After a hasty breakfast the morning flew by. An hour before the mayor was due, each sister in charge of a ward called her nurses into her office to give them a pep talk on how smoothly she expected her respective ward to run when the mayor and his party arrived. To the junior nurses' amazement, this was followed by a cup of coffee from a big urn the kitchen staff had brought to each ward minutes before, along with the offer of a cigarette by the sister and dates and chocolates from a tray on her desk. Abby drank her coffee quickly, as did everyone else, feeling acutely uncomfortable. All year the sisters and staff nurses ranted and raved at them and it seemed the strangest of things to be standing in the sister's office, hitherto only a place of sharp rebukes, drinking coffee and watching some of the nurses smoke.

Christmas dinner was equally uncomfortable. It was the only time in the year the matron ate with them, and what with the mayor being present and everyone on edge lest something went wrong, the meal was far from relaxed.

Then the visit to the wards began, each sister listening with bated breath for the spy she had positioned at the end of her particular corridor to come running to say the mayor's party was approaching. Patients were warned on pain of no Christmas dinner later that day not to say a word out of place; the chronics – heavily sedated for the occasion after the disaster of a few years before – had their bedcovers straightened for the umpteenth time as they snored loudly showing ancient toothless gums, and on the children's wards – bodily functions taken care of well before time – washed and scrubbed little angels sat or lay meekly in their beds, the promise of a chocolate and a cup of milky cocoa for everyone who behaved enough to ensure perfect calm.

The sigh of relief when the mayor and his party drove away from the hospital could be heard throughout the building, and once they had gone, there was a couple of hours to feed the patients their Christmas dinners and do necessary jobs before the Christmas festivities began in the concert room. Skeleton staff were left on each ward during the entertainment as the main bulk of the patients were taken to enjoy the sight of their medical staff 'doing turns' as one granny described it. Everyone, even the sisters and staff nurses, entered into the spirit of it, singing songs, acting short sketches – often with a risqué element attached to them – telling jokes and even doing a spot of conjuring.

It was in this interlude after the mayor had left

and before the concert began, that the staff nurse on Abby's ward came into the bathroom where Abby was helping a young woman who had been beaten to within an inch of her life some weeks before to take a bath. Everyone knew the husband had been responsible for the woman's appalling injuries, but the woman – who was really little more than a girl – feared him more than death itself, and had insisted it was a stranger who had broken into the house and hurt her.

The staff nurse eyed Abby balefully. 'You've got a visitor and Sister says it's a good job it's Christmas Day or you'd be for it, encouraging a young man to come to the hospital.'

'What?' Abby stared at the staff nurse in surprise. 'I don't understand?

'I don't understand, *Staff Nurse.*'

Abby stared into the thin, pinched face. This particular staff nurse was universally loathed. 'I don't understand, Staff Nurse.'

'There's someone in the waiting room off the front lobby to see you so Sister says to cut along and she wants you back in time to help take the patients to the concert room.'

Utterly bemused, Abby cut along. A young man? Was it Robin? Was something wrong at home? And then reason kicked in. Robin would have said he was her brother. That left... No, no he wouldn't. He wouldn't come to the hospital. He of all people would know the protocol, the rules, the code of behaviour that was expected.

When she reached the front lobby Abby took a moment to compose herself before she opened the door of the waiting room. Nicholas was standing with his back to the door, looking out of the window.

She had forgotten how broad-shouldered and tall he was. It was a silly thought to have at such a time, and even more silly that her heart seemed to be trying to thump its way out of her chest.

He turned, and his first words were disarming. 'I'm sorry, I know I shouldn't have come, but I had to. It's different when I'm in London, but coming home and being so close... Well, I had to come. I ... I said I was your cousin, by the way, and that I had some family news I needed to impart regarding the death of a great-aunt.'

She stared at him. What a ridiculous lie. It wouldn't fool anyone.

'I know,' he said, as though she had spoken out loud. 'But I played my trump card and showed my credentials to prove that I'm a doctor. The family thought in view of the fact that you were close to this great-aunt and were bound to be upset, a doctor was probably the best person to come and tell you the news.'

She didn't want to smile; it was outrageous. *He* was outrageous. Nevertheless her lips twitched in spite of herself.

Nicholas's eyes narrowed as he tried to gauge her mood. 'Say something,' he said after a few moments had slipped by.

'Do you always lie to get what you want?'

'When I said, "Say something," I was thinking of, "Hello, Nicholas," or, "It's nice to see you, Nicholas."'

She tried, she really tried not to smile, but then they were both laughing. When he came and took her hands, though, her face became straight. Carefully she removed her fingers from his, sitting down on one of the hard-backed chairs lining the waiting-room walls as she said, 'You shouldn't have come here. I thought we had agreed it was best we didn't see each other again.'

'Did you?' He sat down himself, not next to her but with a chair between them. 'That is not my recollection. If I remember rightly, you gave me a list of reasons why you thought a relationship between us was impossible, but I certainly did not agree with them.'

He looked wonderful. Worried that the deep pain in her heart, the longing, the feeling that was coursing through her and making her feel heady and dizzy, would reveal itself in her eyes, Abby lowered her gaze to her hands. They were red and sore; they were always red and sore with the incessant scrubbing and cleaning and scouring and polishing that took up a large part of her day, but it was worse in winter when it was so cold. A woman of his own class would never have hands like hers. Without raising her eyes, she said flatly, 'A gentleman would not press his attentions where they weren't wanted.'

'I agree so let's take it I am not a gentleman and that's one of your reasons null and void. I am simply a man, Abigail, and you are a woman. All this talk of class that seems to preoccupy you is so much hogwash.'

'It's not and you know it.'

'Well, it damn well should be.' He made an exasperated sound in his throat and stood up, and in the next moment he pulled her up and into his

291

arms. The kiss was not the sweet and tender thing she had always imagined her first kiss from a man to be; it was something so far above that it took her breath away. It spoke of hunger and desire and frustration; it made the blood course through her veins like fire and brought every nerve singing.

When he at last raised his mouth from hers he drew in a long shuddering breath but didn't let her go, his brown eyes raking her flushed face. 'I had to come,' he said for the third time. 'I think of you all the time. You can't let my father and your grandfather and brother stand in the way of what we feel, you can't.'

The mention of her grandfather and Robin acted like cold water on the fire of her emotions; she jerked out of his hold, taking a step backwards. 'I haven't changed my mind and I can't see you again. You'll meet someone else, someone more suitable for you–'

'Don't say that.' His voice was angry now, harsh. 'At least give me the credit that my feelings for you are genuine if nothing else.'

'Then if you do feel the way you say you do, you'll go.'

'Do you care for me, Abigail?'

It wasn't the words, it was the look on his face as he spoke that undid her. She wanted to deny it but she couldn't. After an endless moment, she whispered, 'I do, but...'

'Not enough,' he finished for her. And when she said nothing, he murmured, as though to himself, 'Yes, I see that now. Not enough. If you cared for me as I care for you, nothing else would matter. You would let nothing and no one stand in our way.'

She wanted to scream at him that that was unfair. He was the laird's son; if he took up with her and his father disapproved, the most that would happen to him was that he might be thrown onto purely his career as a doctor for earning his living, but even that was doubtful. As the son and heir, his parents would probably forgive him anything in time. Whereas for her it was so different. Nicholas's father had the power to turn her grandfather and Robin and Rachel out of their home and take away their livelihood if he wanted to punish her for enticing his son. And even if the laird was reasonable, which verged on the laughable, her grandfather and Robin would look on her as a traitor; worse, they would face suspicion and resentment from everyone because of her. They would be ostracized and cold-shouldered and their lives made unbearable. She couldn't be responsible for that. Her granda had taken them in and given them all he had; she couldn't make his twilight days ones of misery and heartache. She *wouldn't*. Nicholas had no idea of how it would be and that alone spoke of the huge gulf between their two worlds.

'If I go now, I won't come back.' He looked at her standing white and still in front of him. 'I won't trouble you again. Is that what you want? Think before you answer.'

She could talk until she was blue in the face and he would never understand. How could he? He had been born with a silver spoon in his mouth. He had never been hungry; never lived in dread of the rent man; never shuddered at the thought of the workhouse. But for her granda, that's where she and Robin would have ended up; incarcerated in a living hell for years and years and bearing the stigma for the rest of their lives. Nicholas had always had soft scented sheets to sleep on, freshly laundered clothes to wear and everything of the best quality. A nanny, servants, private schools – the list was endless.

'It has to be this way,' she said quietly.

'No, it doesn't.'

'I'm sorry.'

He nodded, his handsome features carved in granite. 'Then there is nothing left to say but goodbye.'

'Goodbye, Nicholas.' It was as though the kiss had never happened, she thought helplessly. He had gone from her. He might still be in the room but he had left her.

He made no attempt to touch her again, walking over to the door and opening it without glancing her way. He shut it quietly, so quietly she wasn't sure he had gone until she turned round and saw she was alone.

So alone.

PART FIVE

A Divided World

1939

Chapter Twenty

For the first few years after the final parting from Nicholas, Abby's life had, on the whole, run smoothly. She'd made up her mind within weeks after he had left that her career would have to be her life. A husband and children were now ruled out for her. She'd told family and friends that she was married to her job and her patients were the only dependants she wanted. No one knew the real reason she'd given up on a husband and family of her own, but when Nicholas had left the hospital that Christmas Day he'd taken her heart with him. It was as simple as that. She knew there could never be anyone else for her and having made that decision, Abby set out to be the best nurse she could possibly be.

By the time she took her finals at Hemingway's it was generally acknowledged that Nurse Kirby, was a cut above the other trainees. Her results were gratifyingly outstanding, and Abby rose swiftly through the ranks. When Pam finally married her Dr Ferry some years after their first night of unbridled passion, Abby was already the youngest sister that Hemingway's had had.

Most of the time Abby would have said she was, if not happy, then content with her lot. She was an auntie three times over now that Robin and Rachel had twin boys and a baby girl, and she enjoyed visits to the farm to see her grandfather and indulge her nephews and niece with armfuls of presents. She had gradually relaxed about going back home when the years had ticked by and there was still no sign of Joe McHaffie. Most folk were of the opinion that he had grown tired of living with his parents and the prospect of being their carer and provider in the future, and had taken the easy way out by skedaddling to pastures new while he was still young enough to make a different life for himself. It was typical of him, the farm folk murmured out of earshot of his parents. Joe always had been a moody and taciturn individual and selfish to the core. The only time people thought of him now was when they saw his mother standing at the cottage window. From the day he had gone, she had taken to watching for him for hours, and it was generally acknowledged that his going had sent her a bit funny in the head.

Abby would probably have continued working at Hemingway's indefinitely, but it was Matron Blackett, her fears about the future having gathered steam with Hitler gaining power in 1933 and launching Germany into wholesale rearmament, who first brought up the subject of Abby and several of her other nurses becoming military nurses. Matrons all over Britain were being encouraged by the government to apply pressure to trained nurses along this line, and Matron Blackett could see that in the event of war the army would need well-trained, capable and dedicated nurses, and who better than her girls from Hemingway's? Matron Blackett had watched as the worldwide depression had damaged ordinary people's faith in democracy and capitalism, helping to bring Hitler's National Socialists to power in Germany, and boosting Mussolini's imperial ambitions. It had distracted the world leaders' attention from Stalin's terror in the Soviet Union and stimulated the rise of new dictatorships. As she explained to Abby and some other nurses one morning in her sitting room, war was inevitable and their skills and devotion to duty would be needed as never before.

Abby needed little persuasion to put herself forward to become part of the Queen Alexandra's Imperial Military Nursing Service. She was patriotic and found herself hungry for adventure, and the QAs' uniform – a strikingly attractive combination of grey dress and scarlet-trimmed cape – was an added bonus. Once the matron had spoken to her, the thunderclouds of a Second World War became obvious and she wondered why she hadn't seen it before. In the Far East two of the world's ancient civilizations, China and Japan, had clashed in a war that looked as though it would engulf the whole of the Pacific; Europe's dictators were using a bloody civil war in Spain as a military exercise, and democracies were seeking to appease Hitler by sacrificing a free nation, Czechoslovakia, while Stalin's Russia was entering an unholy alliance with its bitterest enemy.

So it was, as Britain was forced to go from a policy of appeasement to declaring war on Germany when Hitler invaded Poland at the beginning of September, Abby and another nurse from Hemingway's found themselves on the way to a mobilizing unit some twenty-five miles south of Edinburgh. Kitty and four other nurses had joined up at the same time but had been allocated to a different unit, much to Abby and Kitty's disappointment. They had hoped to remain together.

In peacetime, the centre had been an imposing five-star hotel and it was set in glorious countryside. Now, however, the elegant tennis courts were covered in khaki tents. As Abby and Sybil climbed down from the bus that had transported them to the centre from the train station, the warm September air echoed to the despairing bellow of a sergeant major who was drilling a number of nurses in the distance.

The two women looked at each other. The September afternoon was beautiful, the sky so blue and the sun so hot it was like a July day, and the scents of summer hung in the gentle breeze. It seemed impossible they were actually at war. But here they were, and already, from the way the sergeant in charge of the bus had yelled at everyone, they felt they were in the army. At Hemingway's, their positions in the hierarchy of the hospital had earned them a well-deserved respect. Now Abby felt as nervous as when she had first arrived at Hemingway's as a trainee.

It was clear Sybil was feeling exactly the same, her murmur of, 'What on earth have we let ourselves in for?' bringing a rueful smile to both girls' lips. Not that they were given any time to reflect. After being shown their sleeping quarters, they were chivvied along to the army doctor for a full medical examination, after which their inoculations for typhus, typhoid and smallpox followed. Once that was over, and while their arms were still stinging, they were marched to a room for their initial 'welcome'.

The sergeant major who surveyed the new intake appeared distinctly unimpressed. He walked among them, hands clasped behind his back and chin up, shaking his head now and again. 'So you want to serve your country as army nurses?'

No one replied, surmising – correctly – that the question was rhetorical.

'Well, let me tell you, ladies, that you will need to be toughened up before you can be moulded into the army's idea of a nurse. Right? The purpose of this training unit is twofold. One, to train you physically and professionally for what lies ahead, and believe me, it won't be pretty. It is also to create a mobile hospital unit in which you will remain together, in different locations as needed, for the duration of the war. Your unit will comprise doctors, pharmacy and laboratory technicians, and army privates trained in first aid who are known as orderlies. Is that clear? Good.'

More pacing up and down.

'In the army you are not required to think, merely to obey,' he continued loudly. 'Rank is paramount. Everyone has their role to play, and there is no room for what you might call initiative. You are now QAs, and that means more than the new uniform you will be wearing.'

Much more followed, and by the time Abby and Sybil were dismissed and told to make their way to the mess room where their evening meal was waiting, Abby's head was spinning. Sybil felt the same, her mutter of, 'Come back, Matron Blackett, all is forgiven,' bringing a smile to Abby's face.

After their meal another lecture followed. This

one was regarding the list of endless forms that the nurses would be required to complete in a military hospital for even the most simple of procedures, after which each girl was given a photograph detailing the correct locker layout and told to memorize it. Inspections would take place each morning, and woe betide any nurse whose locker was less than perfectly arranged. Abby didn't dare look at Sybil for fear of laughing. The army was making Matron Blackett appear to be almost flexible.

In spite of being tired that night, it took Abby a long time to fall asleep, her mind so active she wished she could flick a switch and turn it off. She had gone home for a brief visit before she had left for the training centre in Scotland, and her grandfather hadn't been able to hide his distress when she'd told them she had enlisted as a QA.

Why couldn't she have been content to nurse the ill and needy here at home? he'd asked her more than once. She didn't have to put herself in danger to fulfil her vocation. Robin had said nothing, but it was clear he agreed with Wilbert by his very silence. It was only Rachel who had hugged her and said she had to follow her own star.

But it wasn't really the family she was thinking about as she tossed and turned in the narrow army bed. It was Nicholas. There hadn't been a day in the intervening years that she hadn't dissected their last meeting word for word, doubts about whether she'd done the right thing in sending him away paramount. And now, with Britain at war, she found herself even more uncertain.

Useless to tell herself it had been the only thing she could have done. Her head knew that; her heart was a different matter. The years had been a subtle torment at times, knowing he was out there living, laughing, perhaps even loving, and all without her.

She'd written him letters many times pouring out her regret but she had never sent one of them. It wouldn't have been fair because nothing could change.

Now it was worse, though. They were at war and although nothing much had happened yet, it would do. Everyone said so. Nicholas might be injured or killed and she wouldn't know. Of course that had always been the case – war or no war – but somehow it was more poignant now.

Eventually she drifted off into a troubled sleep, waking in the morning in a more positive frame of mind. It was the nights, when she was exhausted and her resistance was low, that doubts and regrets consumed her. Her days were always so busy she didn't have time to brood. And she soon found being in the army was even more exhausting than life at Hemingway's but that was welcome. It meant she fell asleep as soon as her head touched the pillow.

The nurses were certainly put through their paces physically and Abby often wondered how poor Kitty was coping. Her friend was two or three stone overweight, added to which Kitty hated any form of exercise. Now, at the training centre, Abby and the others were made to hike up and down the steep Scottish hills in battledress and tin hats with full packs on their backs, along with vaulting five-bar gates and learning self-defence. More crucially, they learned how the army dealt with casualties in the field and exactly what was expected of a nurse under fire. They mastered how to keep medical records in the field, how to purify water and the layout of a hospital under canvas. Abby became familiar with the progress of a patient from the time they were picked up by the stretcher bearers until they were evacuated by sea or air back to the United Kingdom, or – if sufficiently recovered – sent back for service with their company.

The lectures the women attended were no less challenging. They detailed the kind of injuries the battlefields inflicted on human flesh and bone, and the surgical officer describing the amputation of a cold and gangrenous limb took no account of the nurses' bleached faces. Neither did the army dental officer when his turn came. When lecturing on how to deal with a fractured jaw he spoke matter-of-factly and coldly, but the content was no less harrowing for that. 'Treat for shock first,' he said flatly, 'and then pick out any loose teeth and bits of bone before you put a stitch through the patient's tongue and tie it to a button on his jacket. Only then send him down the line on a stretcher for the surgeon.'

Abby glanced round the room at this point. More than one of her fellow, trainees were looking distinctly green about the gills, and she knew how they felt.

One of the things the centre placed a great deal of importance on was teaching the hitherto civilian nurses the necessity of becoming rank conscious, and to feel and behave like the army officers they were. Fraternizing with other ranks was a definite no-no. While undergoing their training, they were to mix socially only with other officers. Whenever they left the camp to go into Glasgow or Edinburgh, the sergeant major bellowed, as though they were hard of hearing, that full uniform must be worn, and they were always to be accompanied by other officers. Did they understand? *Always.*

Saluting was another aspect of training some of the nurses found difficult. As Sybil complained to Abby, 'When someone salutes me I'm always so surprised and flummoxed the last thing I think to do is to salute back. And then by the time I do remember it's too late, and I'm in trouble again. I mean, it's *embarrassing,* this saluting thing. I'm a nurse, for goodness' sake. Just a nurse.' It was a view shared by quite a few of the trainees and one that the army was determined to erase.

By the time Abby and Sybil had been at the training centre for a few weeks, it had become apparent to the powers that be that the first rush and scramble to ship nurses to join the British Expeditionary Force in France was somewhat unnecessary. The expected assault by Germany on Western Europe wasn't happening, and the thousand or so QAs who were residing in France by the end of the year were writing home that time dragged. Despite the dampening down of the initial panic, however, the rigid training at the centre continued, but at least the nurses gained more time to pull their full QA uniform together and become more accepting of what was required of them.

Christmas came and went, and Abby and Sybil, like everyone they spoke to, were finding the 'phoney war' tedious towards the end of their mobilization period. As the finish of training grew nearer, a certain tension mounted among the nurses. Speculation was rife as to when they would be leaving – and for where – but the war warning of 'Walls have ears' was the watchword, and the nurses were under strict orders not to discuss their movements with anyone. 'Chance would be a fine thing,' Abby complained to Sybil one evening in February when they had been at the centre for several months. 'We are never told anything at the best of times.'

Sybil nodded, adding in an undertone, 'But the writing's on the wall, sure enough. Why else have they started us pulling everything together today?'

A little shiver of excitement slid down Abby's spine. Sybil was right. A crucial task that had to be undertaken before a unit could embark for overseas service was packing up the equipment a mobile military hospital would need in the field. The laborious job took days as each piece of hospital equipment had to be wrapped, labelled and crated in meticulous order so that the whole lot could be reassembled with the minimum of delay in the field. Each surgical instrument had to be greased to prevent rust, wrapped in oiled paper, sewn in sacking and packed in the crates which were then stencilled with a number.

Abby looked down at her hands. Her fingers were already sore from sewing the coarse sacking, and her hair and skin stank with the smell of lubricating grease, but if it meant they were finally going to be on their way... Wherever their way was, of course.

The next day the QAs knew their departure date was imminent when the sergeant arranged for the purchasing of a kit that would provide them with warmth and shelter in any kind of terrain. The list comprised a tin trunk, a camp bed, a bedroll, a canvas wash bowl and tripod, a collapsible canvas bath that looked woefully inadequate, a canvas bucket and a tiny paraffin stove. This, they were told, along with their regular uniform and tropical kit, was to be packed in the way they had been taught to make the most of every inch of space.

The next days were ones of cleaning, painting, sewing and hammering as the finished crates grew in number and rumours abounded. But still no one knew anything for sure.

It was on the fifth day, as the nurses were finishing their evening meal in what the army insisted on calling the mess room, that Abby turned to Sybil and the others and said softly, 'We're going to hear something in the next twenty-four hours. I feel it in my bones. Perhaps even tonight.'

'Well, I'm ready.' Sybil glanced towards the window where a sleety snow was falling. 'And I hope it's anywhere but England. This winter seems to have gone on and on.'

It *had* been a vicious winter which hadn't exactly lifted the spirits of the common working man. In January the Thames had frozen over for the first time in decades and the worst storms of the century had swept a beleaguered UK. Two million nineteen- to twenty-seven-year-olds had been called up to add to their womenfolk's distress as food rationing had come into play; the rigid new rationing laws demanding the compulsory registration of every household with their local shops.

Yes, Abby thought, it had been a long, hard, cold winter but as yet the UK had been relatively untroubled by Hitler and the war. It couldn't continue and the warning signs were already trickling through the apathy which the 'phoney war' had caused. The Germans had gained ground in January in a fierce onslaught along a 120-mile front north of Paris, and the Luftwaffe had attacked British ships in a flare-up of the sea war. Just the week before, Hitler had ordered German U-boat commanders to attack all neutral shipping as well as Allied vessels in the Channel, declaring that all shipping was fair game.

The nationwide government anti-gossip campaign had gathered steam too, and posters were everywhere – in offices, barbers' shops, banks, docks, hotels and pubs. Hitler was depicted crouching under a bus seat, leaning on his elbow on a bar counter and even lying on a luggage rack. 'Walls have ears' and 'Keep it dark' were the new catchphrases, and when one of the nurses had giggled at a poster showing two old women gossiping on a train with Hitler and Himmler sitting behind them, remarking that one of the old ladies looked like her granny, their sergeant major had nearly burst a blood vessel. The poster had been stuck on the wall of the mess room in front of where they queued for their food, and he'd come up behind her and screamed so loudly in her ear that she had dropped her plate of stew all over his highly polished boots.

Abby glanced across the room to where the poster still hung. It *was* funny, she thought, and they shouldn't make it so comical if they didn't want folk to laugh. But then, the army didn't see the funny side of anything and she was sure their sergeant major didn't know *how* to smile.

As though her thoughts had drawn him, she watched in the next moment as he made his way over to them. 'Lecture room two in' – he consulted his watch – 'three and a half minutes.' His unforgiving gaze swept over the table. 'And for crying out loud, try to look more like army personnel in front of the major else he'll wonder what the hell I've been doing over the last months.'

'The major.' Abby looked at Sybil. 'We're going, they're going to tell us we're going...'

Chapter Twenty-One

Hong Kong, October, 1941

'It can't go on, you know.' Nicholas took a sip of his gin cocktail. 'We're sitting ducks here and the Japanese must know it.'

'Here he goes, the prophet of doom.'

'I mean it, John.' Nicholas looked at his friend who was a fellow army doctor, having joined up, like him, as soon as war was declared. The two of them were comfortably ensconced at their table in the officers' club. 'Look at how many Chinese refugees have fled here to escape the slaughter in their country in the last few years.'

'But that's a private fight between two age-old oriental enemies, Nick. You know that. I'm not saying the Japanese aren't brutal so-an'-sos, and the massacre of all those thousands of unarmed men, women and children in Nanking was horrendous, but the Japs won't target us here. Why would they? They'd be fools to take the colonies on.'

Nicholas shook his head. John was like many others here who genuinely believed that the British and Empire forces in the Far East, alongside the Americans, wielded enough military muscle to defeat the Japanese if they dared to attack. They forgot that Britain's Asian forces had been severely depleted by the need to send men and machines to Britain and the Middle East. The trouble was that John *wanted* to believe that life on this paradise island where everyone was busy having a good time would continue. The endless parties, squash, tennis, dancing and sailing that were part of colonial life were seductively dangerous. 'John, you know as well as I do that we're hopelessly unprotected here, both in equipment and men. Before the war Hong Kong might have been a key staging post of the British Empire but not any more. The RAF are still recovering from the Battle of Britain and our navy are stretched to the limit defending the homeland and maintaining our fragile lifeline across the Atlantic. Churchill's hung us out to dry. I'm sorry but that's the way I see it.'

John Baxter stared at the man he counted as a dear friend. He had a lot of time for Nick but he could be one hell of a killjoy. 'You don't think this might be because you've always felt guilty about being posted here, especially since the war's hotted up? Look, we were sent here, end of story. It could have been anywhere but it happened to be the exotic East where when the day's work's done, we're forced to sit on airy verandahs drinking Singapore slings and chatting up women. Not that you ever do any of the latter. It worried me for a time, you know, your lack of interest in the opposite sex. Especially with us sharing a room.'

Nicholas's head shot up. He was totally taken aback. 'What?'

'It's all right. I realized very quickly you weren't that way, even before you told me about her. The one who got away.'

'Look, John–'

'I know, I know. It's in the past.' John took a swallow of his drink. Only he didn't believe that for a moment. Whoever this girl was, she'd ruined him for other women. Male officers far outnumbered females, and yet he'd watched both civilian women and the QAs giving Nick the come-on on various occasions, some following up with a dedicated pursuit that always came to nothing because Nick simply didn't seem to notice them.

John sighed ruefully. If Nick wasn't such a good friend he'd punch him. Here was yours truly, not having had a roll in the hay for months, and there was Nick turning 'em down without batting an eyelid. Of course a good number of the men on the island took advantage of the dance halls where Hong Kong's thousands of prostitutes did business, but having learned they were dubbed the

311

'gonorrhoea racetrack' and having treated count-less men who bore evidence to this, he hadn't availed himself of this dubious pleasure.

'It is in the past. She is in the past.' Nicholas's voice was terse. 'And don't try and change the subject from the matter in hand. You know as well as I do that it was the height of stupidity for the great minds who are supposedly in charge to inflict us with a new general and a new governor last month, men who are totally unfamiliar with the island's terrain. It's asking for trouble and the Japanese are the ones who'll give it to us.'

'Nick, Nick, Nick...' John's eyes were half on his friend and half on a group of QAs who had just walked into the club.

'And yes, you might be right about me feeling guilty about being here when Britain's being bat-tered by the damn Luftwaffe and starved by food rationing and the rest of it.'

'I don't think they're actually starving–'

'We've had it easy. Most of the time since we've been here we've been treating casualties of the gonorrhoea racetrack alongside the usual tropical diseases, training accidents and routine surgery.'

'All necessary and requiring our attention.'

'But not what I joined up for.' Nicholas ran his hand through his hair. 'And who the hell are you looking at anyway?' Irritated, he turned to face the way his friend was staring.

Abby had had mixed feelings when she had learned her next posting was to Hong Kong. Her first posting to France had been a baptism of fire, it was true, but after Dunkirk when most of her

312

unit had been wiped out and she had suffered severe injuries, she supposed she ought to be grateful that she was being given a passport to paradise. That's what Sybil had called it, anyway, when she had visited her friend in the hospital where Sybil would remain for some long time.

Poor Sybil. Abby wasn't really seeing the inside of the officers' club that she and the other four QAs who had arrived in Hong Kong that morning had just entered. As her hand involuntarily touched the left side of her face where the scars were still pink and raised, she was remembering the look in Sybil's eyes when they had said their goodbyes. There had been a cage over the stumps that were all that was left of Sybil's legs after the bomb that had killed most of their unit and blasted Abby in the face and arm had scored a direct hit, but Sybil's eyes had spoken of her despair at being crippled. Sybil had shrapnel lodged in her chest and other injuries too. She was lucky in comparison, Abby thought. What were scars compared to losing limbs?

She had told herself this on the journey on the luxury liner from England – the ship having the protection of Royal Navy fighting ships – especially when she looked in a mirror. Some of the other QAs on the ship, revelling in the freedom of leaving a war-torn Britain, had had affairs right under the nose of the matron who had accompanied them from England. Fifty-five QA nurses had been on board, but only Abby and four others had disembarked at Hong Kong, leaving the other fifty to sail on to Singapore.

She had been told by the plastic surgeon who

313

had treated the injuries to her face and left arm that the scars would fade to barely noticeable silver lines in time, but right now she was still very conscious of her marred face when in company. But she had been fortunate not to lose her eye, and after two operations on her arm when the surgeon had dug and delved for pieces of shrapnel, he had announced there was no reason why her arm and hand shouldn't work as well as ever, as had since proved the case.

'I'm *dying* for a gin fizz.' Delia Cook, one of the QAs Abby had struck up a friendship with on the journey from England, slipped her arm through Abbys. 'And look at all these lovely officers. I adore the tropical uniform they wear, don't you? Who would have thought we'd end up in Hong Kong? We're so *lucky.*'

Abby smiled. Delia was a petite, vivacious brunette and she was determined to make the most of this posting. Newly qualified and leaving home for the first time, Delia had been transparently thrilled at what she saw as a dream destination. She had entered into a torrid affair with one of the officers on the liner the moment they had left England, saying goodbye to him when they had docked at Hong Kong with tears and promises to write. They both knew she wouldn't. Delia's officer was married for one thing, and for another Delia wasn't the type of girl to tie herself to one man. As she had said to Abby just before they had walked into the officers' club, 'Why have just one delicious chocolate when you can sample the whole box?'

Much as she liked Delia, Abby found the other

314

girl made her feel aeons old. Although there was only four years' difference in their ages, it could have been forty. Delia was happy and carefree and as bubbly as the gin fizzes she had a weakness for, but she was kind too, as her next words bore evidence to. 'You look beautiful,' she whispered to Abby. 'Really, you do. No one notices the scars when they look into your eyes.'

'Thank you.' Abby squeezed the arm in hers. She had confided how she felt to Delia on the boat, and ever since then the other girl had tried to boost her confidence in the sort of situation they were facing now. 'Let's get you a gin fizz before you *die,* as you put it.'

Abby hadn't shared Delia's enthusiasm for their posting. After Dunkirk, Hong Kong had seemed almost a cop-out in a way. True, nurses were still needed there for the garrison of a little over 12,000 men, but everyone knew it had been the life of pleasure the soldiers had enjoyed that had taken its toll on the health of the troops. Gossip among the nursing fraternity had it that a posting to Hong Kong was a 'safe' one and positively magical compared to most. Abby had done her homework and knew the colony of Hong Kong was composed of the island itself, with its capital Victoria overlooking the magnificent harbour and, across a narrow strait, a piece of mainland bordering China, the peninsula of Kowloon and various islands. This constituted the New Territories. Hong Kong's only airport was on the eastern edge of Kowloon.

She had briefly wondered, with China so close, if the Japanese posed any threat, but had been assured this was not the case. And such had been the determined optimism of the authorities that she, along with all the other QAs, believed them. As one of the QAs in England had said when she had learned of Abby's posting, 'You'll see out the war in one of the cushiest postings on earth, you lucky thing.'

'Don't look now but there are a couple of officers coming over,' Delia murmured in her ear in the next moment. 'And one is a walking dreamboat, I kid not. Yours isn't bad either.'

Of course Abby looked. And then froze. For a frantic moment she wanted to turn and run, away from the bright lights in the club to the kinder darkness outside. But it was too late. Nicholas was in front of her, taking her hands in his. His voice was just as she remembered it as he said softly, 'I can't believe it, after all this time. Abigail, is it really you?'

He had always called her Abigail. It was a silly thought to hit at such a moment. No one but Nicholas and her old headmaster, Mr Newton, had ever given her her full name. She was aware of Delia at the side of her, face agog, and that Nicholas had another man with him, but they were on the perimeter of her vision. Somehow she managed to form words, words that seemed so very ordinary in the circumstances: 'Hello, Nicholas. How are you?'

He didn't reply immediately, just staring into her eyes, but such was his expression that she felt herself begin to tremble deep inside. She wanted to turn the damaged side of her face away so that she appeared like the old Abigail but that was impossible, impossible and ridiculous because she couldn't hide for ever.

'I've missed you.' His voice was no more than a whisper and it could have been as though they had parted just days before.

Her voice was equally low. 'I've missed you too.'

It was Delia who moved in where angels fear to tread. Her voice fairly smouldering with curiosity and just a little peeved that the walking dream-boat had eyes for no one but Abby, she said brightly, 'So you two know each other?'

'We're old friends,' Nicholas answered without taking his gaze from Abby.

So this was her, the girl who had broken Nick's heart. John felt the very air was crackling between the two of them. And by the look of her face she'd had a hell of a time of it in the not-too-distant past, he thought grimly. His curiosity was every bit as avid as Delia's but John was a gentleman first and foremost, besides which, Delia was an extremely attractive female. Taking her arm, he said softly, 'While these two are catching up why don't we go and get the drinks in?' and he guided her away towards the bar before she had a chance to object.

Nicholas continued to look down at her for a moment more. His face had drained of colour when he noticed the left side of her face; he couldn't bear to think of what she had been through to have sustained such injuries, but she was still beautiful. Breathtakingly beautiful, his Abigail... 'Can we–' His voice caught in his throat and he had to clear it before he could say, 'Can we go for a walk and talk? The club gardens are lovely. Have you seen them?'

317

'We only arrived today.' Abby lowered her head; his gaze was hurting her. Not because of her scars – he hadn't seemed to notice them – but because he was looking at her in the same old way and she had forgotten how wonderful it was to be looked at like this.

'Come on.' He kept hold of one hand as he led her out of the club and into the tropical night that sounded and felt so different from England. She walked blindly, her head spinning, unable to think beyond the fact that Nicholas was here, here in Hong Kong and with her.

When they reached a small arbour heavily festooned with sweet-smelling flowers, he drew her down onto the slatted bench inside. The club gardens had lamps positioned in various spots but the arbour was in shadow and for this she was grateful. She knew it was vain and not worthy of people like Sybil who were so much worse off than her, but right at this moment she would have given everything she possessed to be as she had been before Dunkirk. She hadn't thought that she cared overmuch about her looks before that time, but since then she had often had the thought that she was glad Nicholas would always remember her as she had been. But now that comfort was gone.

When he took her hand again she let him, but her body had stiffened. Delia had called him a walking dreamboat and he was. What was he feeling for her now? Pity? Sympathy? He was a kind man, she had always known that. He could have any girl he wanted, he always had been able to. Perhaps he was married or engaged? Whatever, she wasn't the same and he – he was wonderful.

'You arrived today?' he said quietly. 'What hospital have you been assigned to?'

Please don't let it be his. Please, God, don't let me have to see him every day, love him every day... She must have opened her mouth and told him although she wasn't conscious of it through the pleading in her head, because he said, 'Me too.'

'You ... you've been here for a while?'

Nicholas didn't reply to this; what he did say, very, very gently was, 'Abigail, look at me.'

She raised her face and his eyes were waiting for her. 'You said in there you had missed me. Is that true?' She couldn't speak, and he said again, 'Is it true, Abigail?'

She closed her eyes, striving to be strong.

'Because I've missed you, every single day that we have been apart I have missed you, but missing you is too weak to express how I have felt. For a while after you sent me away I thought I could purge you from me by having other women. No, don't pull away, listen to me. I tried, Abigail. I really did. I'm not proud of it but I bedded quite a few before I realized the futility of it. I didn't want them and the sex was meaningless beyond a temporary relief. And so I stopped. I resigned myself to putting everything into my work. I worked the longest hours of anyone I knew and when I wasn't working I was reading textbooks, researching new ideas, learning all I could. I'm a damn good surgeon, Abigail, thanks partly to you.' His voice had been rueful and he paused, before going on, 'And I chose for my work to become my life, only it wasn't a choice. It was a necessity, if I was to keep my sanity. But I never stopped loving you.

Not for one minute, one second.'

'Don't...'

It was a whisper and he bent his head. 'What?'

'You loved me before–' She took a tortured breath. 'Before this...' She touched her cheek.

'Your face?' It was incredulous. 'You think that, or *anything*, could stop me loving you? The scars will fade but I'm sure you have been told that. My love won't fade. It hasn't over the last painfully long years, much as I've tried to make it so. Abigail' – he brought her hand to his lips for a second and she shuddered at the touch – 'your grandfather and brother, my father, all of that, does it still hold sway over any possibility of a future together? I know we have a hundred things to say to each other but I need to know that first. Does it?'

She had been so stupid. She gazed at him, at his dear handsome face. She had known long before Dunkirk that she had made the wrong decision when she had sent him away but she had clung to it, knowing it was far too late and it would have made a mockery of her life if she had admitted the truth. Through her own foolishness she had lost him. Rachel had said regarding her decision to enlist as a QA that she had to follow her own star; perhaps it had been that which had opened her eyes. And then Dunkirk with all its horror, the carnage and loss of life, had further strengthened the little inner voice deep inside that wouldn't be silenced, a voice that had said that her grandfather and Robin, Nicholas's father, society, weren't so important as the love she and Nicholas had shared. If her grandfather and brother and the farm folk had turned against her because she had fallen in love with someone they didn't approve of, then that would have been sad but it was Nicholas who mattered. But the belief had come too late, or so she had thought. Now she had been given a second chance. Against all the odds, she had been given a second chance.

Her voice breaking, she whispered, 'I love you. I've always loved you and there has never been anyone else. I was so wrong to let anything or anyone part us, I know that now and–'

Her words were lost as his arms, telling of his hunger, crushed her into him as his mouth took hers.

It was much later when John and a very tipsy Delia came in search of them and, having found them wrapped in each other's arms and oblivious to the world, tiptoed away again.

Chapter Twenty-Two

The next few weeks were the happiest of Abby's life despite knowing Nicholas was worried about a possible Japanese invasion. Nothing could dampen her joy, and like the other QAs she comforted herself with the fact that the powers that be didn't seem unduly concerned. In fact one officer, accused of spreading alarm and despondency by voicing the sort of views that Nicholas held, had been imprisoned for a term, his commanding officer declaring that invasion was not 'on the cards' as the man had stated. And the Geneva Convention would protect medical staff, the QA nurses said to each other umpteen times when the situation was discussed, along with any wounded and POWs. International law would be respected, everyone knew that.

Abby just lived for the time she spent with Nicholas when they were off duty, a time they spent alone together because every moment was too precious to share with anyone else. And when he was with her, for her sake Nicholas tried to hide his growing fear that they were living on borrowed time.

He wasn't alone now in believing that the Japanese were on the verge of hostilities; even John had come round to the idea. Churchill's pledge in the middle of November when he'd warned Japan that if she went to war with the US, a British declaration of war would follow within the hour, had further sealed Hong Kong's fate, the men felt. And it was clear that the island was chronically short of experienced soldiers and equipment, and any stand against the Japanese would be militarily unsustainable.

At the end of November, a rumour – believed to be true – swept round the officers' club. It was murmured that Major General Maltby, Hong Kong's commanding officer, had been told by Churchill that if an attack came, British prestige in Asia had to be maintained at all cost. This meant the garrison would be expected to fight to the death. It wasn't comforting, but it was believable.

It threw Nicholas into further torment. He didn't mind so much for himself, but the thought that Abby was in such danger and he couldn't protect her was unbearable.

In the first week of December, with US–Japan relations deteriorating further, Nicholas went to see the commanding officer he reported directly to. He had a special request that he knew the lieutenant colonel wouldn't look kindly on, but the two men had become friends when Nicholas had fought to save the lieutenant colonel's leg from being amputated when it had become infected after an accident the year before. The two men had a frank, off-the-record talk, at the end of which Nicholas felt his worst fears had been confirmed. But he had the piece of paper he had requested. He left the lieutenant colonel's office and found the military chaplain, and from there he went to find Abby.

She was just coming off duty, and her initial delight at seeing Nicholas waiting for her was immediately dampened by his grim face. 'What's the matter? What's happened?' she asked anxiously as he took her arm.

'Nothing's the matter.'

'Then why are you looking like that?'

'This is my doctor face,' he joked quickly, kicking himself for not preparing his expression before she caught sight of him. 'It doesn't do to go round grinning like a Cheshire cat. Come on, I want to talk to you.'

'Now? I need to get changed and–'

'Now,' he said firmly, keeping hold of her hand as he led her out of the hospital onto the wide verandah beyond, down the steps and then across the lawn to the shade of the trees surrounding the compound. It was sufficiently distant from the hustle of the hospital to be quiet, the only sound being of birdsong in the branches above their heads and the drone of an aircraft somewhere high in the deep-blue sky.

Abby was just about to ask him again what was the matter, when to her amazement Nicholas dropped down on one knee. 'Abigail, my darling, beautiful Abigail, will you do me the honour of marrying me?' he said throatily, his dark-brown eyes holding her wide grey-blue ones. 'Will you be my wife, my precious girl? Now, today?'

Her heart thundering, she stared down into his dear face, her astonishment robbing her of the power of speech.

'I would have liked to do this in the time-honoured fashion,' he murmured, still on one knee. 'I would have liked to court you and woo you, to have gone through an engagement and for you to have chosen a beautiful dress and all the trimmings you deserve; but I don't want to wait to make you mine. Do you? Do you need more time, my darling?'

She didn't have to think about her reply, sinking down beside him and into his arms so they both fell backwards onto the grass as she whispered, 'Yes, I will be your wife and no, I don't want to wait. I love you, I love you, I love you...' She would gladly have given herself to him without the legality of a wedding ring, but Nicholas had made it plain within the first few days of them finding each other again that he wanted to 'do things properly' as he had put it.

'You're different to all those others,' he had whispered one night when he had drawn back from their lovemaking, 'and I want our first time together to be different. I want to honour you with my body – I don't know how else to put it. I want it to be perfect, when we've stated our vows as man and wife and we're joined together in the sight of God and man. You'll be the mother of my children, my darling, my *wife*. I want to protect you and cherish you and adore you, do you understand?'

She had said she did, and she had, in a way, but with the war and the uncertainty that each day brought, she had just wanted to belong to him, heart, soul and body.

'The padre will be ready to marry us within a few minutes.' Nicholas sat up, positioning her on his lap. 'You find Delia and I'll find John for our witnesses.'

'How did you get permission?' Such unions were frowned on. And then, as a thought occurred, she said, 'It will mean we can't serve here together, won't it?'

'Perhaps, perhaps not.' He wasn't going to go into that. 'Darling, I want you to be my wife. That's all that matters.'

It was all that mattered to Abby too.

She got married in her QA uniform because she didn't have time to change. Delia insisted on stopping and picking one of the sweet-smelling white lilies that grew in profusion on the island though, carefully winding the stem of the lovely exotic flower in her friend's silver-blonde hair, and then plucking a few more for Abby's bouquet, before they hurried on their way to find Nicholas and John.

The padre, a young man for whom romance wasn't dead, was clearly delighted at his unexpected duty, performing the ceremony with relish as the young couple stood together, hands clasped tight and faces aglow. And at his, 'I now pronounce you man and wife,' John let out such a whoop that Delia jumped a mile. It was doubtful if Nicholas and Abby even heard him, wrapped in each other's arms as they made the most of their first kiss as a married couple.

'Congratulations, Captain Jefferson-Price, Mrs Jefferson-Price.' The padre smiled when Nicholas and Abby drew apart. 'May your life together be long and happy.'

Once the necessary papers had been signed, the four of them strolled over to the officers' club where Nicholas ordered a bottle of champagne and Abby kept glancing down at the inexpensive ring of some indeterminate metal that Nicholas had managed to procure from one of the native servants at the last moment. 'It will make your finger go green,' he whispered to Abby as he noticed her gaze, 'but I'll get you a beautiful engagement ring and wedding ring as soon as I can.'

'They won't be as precious as this one.' She smiled mistily at him, her eyes starry. She was his wife, his *wife*. Mrs Jefferson-Price. She could barely take it in.

They spent their first night as man and wife in a

tiny guest room at the officers' club. Abby had been worried that she wouldn't be able to please him like the women he'd had in the past, experienced and worldly-wise females who knew all the tricks to make a man happy. She needn't have worried. From the moment they were alone Nicholas set about proving she was the only woman in the world for him. Mindful of her innocence he didn't rush her. Once they were naked together in the small three-quarter-size bed the room held, he spent a long time caressing and kissing her, touching and tasting her until Abby was delirious with pleasure. And it was only then, when she was ready for him, that he took her, even then restraining his hunger until her tightness had eased and her moans were ones of pleasure.

When it was over they lay entwined as he gently stroked the hair from her flushed face, dropping little kisses where his fingers touched.

'I'll never be as happy in my life again as I am right at this minute,' Abby whispered dreamily.

He chuckled, deep in his throat. 'I hope you are. I want us to have many more nights like this until we're old and grey and wrinkled, and perhaps even then.'

'But tonight is special.'

'Yes, it is, my love. I grant you that. No regrets then?'

'Only that I was so blind and stupid in the past.'

'You were never that.' He raised himself on one elbow, his dark eyes suddenly serious. 'You tried to do what you thought was best for everyone concerned, I understood that.'

'How can I ever make it up to you? All the

wasted years?'

'Ah, now, let me think.' He winked lasciviously, making her giggle. 'Oh, yes, I've got it...'

They made love twice more that night, sleep the last thing on their minds as they loved and laughed and whispered until dawn broke, a beautiful tropical dawn that filled the sky with colour and brought a thousand birds singing.

Later that day, a peaceful Sunday, the Japanese bombed Pearl Harbor, 360 Japanese war planes making a massive surprise attack on the US Pacific Fleet in its home base in Hawaii. Japanese planes also attacked American bases in the Philippines and on Guam and Wake islands in the middle of the Pacific. Imperial headquarters in Tokyo announced that Japan was at war with the United States and Britain.

It had begun, and Nicholas was too late to do what he had agreed with the lieutenant colonel and have his new wife shipped home to the relative safety of the UK.

Events moved rapidly. The day after Pearl Harbor, the 38th Infantry Division of the Japanese Army launched a ferocious attack on the mainland with the prize of Hong Kong in their sights, while their planes totally destroyed the airport at Kowloon, and with it Nicholas's hopes that he might get Abby off the island by air. Whether Abby would have agreed to leave was a different matter, as she told him in no uncertain terms when he was foolish enough to reveal his thwarted plan to her. Her place was where it had always been, she said firmly, and that was as a QA nurse doing her duty.

And now she had an added incentive, to remain close to her husband, and he needn't think the Japanese would intimidate her into doing anything else.

The aerial bombs soon did a great deal of damage, and within hours medical teams were despatched to several makeshift hospitals set up across the island. Army ambulances began to stream backwards and forwards loaded up with wounded men. There was no time for the medical staff to get into cellars and basements during the bombardments as the ceaseless stream of stretcher bearers brought in fresh casualties. All the hospitals were quickly overwhelmed, and stretchers were left wherever there was space while fresh beds were made up.

Each night, grimy and exhausted, Abby and Nicholas would find each other and have something to eat, too tired to do more than sit close with her head on his shoulder. After an hour or two's rest, they would go their different ways back to tend the injured and dying. There had been several direct hits on the three-storey hospital and the two top floors had been evacuated, all the patients and equipment being squeezed into the ground-floor area. Nicholas was soon working in an emergency operating theatre in the basement of the building, doing what he could in difficult conditions.

In spite of the shelling and the constant line of exhausted stretcher bearers bringing in fresh casualties, the gruelling shifts, the terrible injuries she was dealing with and the fear, Abby found that the shortage of water was the hardest thing to come to terms with. The island's reservoir had been bombed in the first day or two of the attack, and water had been rationed to a pint a day per person for drinking and washing. Needless to say, no one washed and they were desperately thirsty all the time. Water became priceless. On more than one occasion Nicholas tried to persuade Abby to drink some of his ration, but she refused so hotly the last time he attempted it, he was forced to give up.

Filthy, exhausted beyond words, hungry and thirsty, medical teams all over the island battled to take care of the injured and dying, all sizeable buildings – schools, convents, hotels, even the local racetrack – being turned into emergency hospitals to care for the mounting casualties, each staffed by one or two doctors, two or three QAs and locally recruited volunteers and orderlies. The volunteer nurses who had joined the local Voluntary Aid Detachment when war had broken out had, for the most part, had the briefest of medical training, but Abby and the other QAs were full of admiration for these colonial housewives and young single women. As Nicholas remarked to Abby some days into the attack, each one was a heroine fighting for her country, her family and those around her – as were they all.

The merciless bombing continued twenty-four hours a day. The Japanese had complete air superiority over the colony, having quickly destroyed the small RAF contingent on the ground at Kai Tak airport on the first day of the conflict. Abby and the other nurses soon became accustomed to the different types of shells the enemy was using and whether they were going to strike close by.

The ones passing overhead were terrifying, roaring like express trains, but these burst beyond the hospital with a sound like boulders tumbling down a mountainside. Others, the really deadly ones, had a different tone and exploded in the garden area or scored a hit on the hospital itself, filling the air with red-hot gusts of metal. Everyone knew the Japanese would cross the bay sooner or later using small boats and barges they had taken on the main land; it was as inevitable as day following night.

A couple of days after the onslaught began, Abby and Nicholas managed to have a few hours together one night. Too weary and traumatized to do more than hold each other close, they slept for a while in spite of the noise from the shells screaming overhead and the explosions. The day before, Nicholas had continued without a break for nearly twenty-four hours, and it was only when his lieutenant colonel had ordered him to take some rest that he had capitulated. When they awoke, still in each other's arms, they came out of the layers of sleep slowly, and Abby's voice was still dazed with exhaustion when she whispered, 'How much longer can we hold out, do you think?'

'Not long.' Nicholas moved her more comfortably into his side, kissing the top of her head. 'It was always going to be a hopeless fight.' But it was what would happen after the garrison surrendered that worried him. He hoped the Japanese would observe the rules of war under the Geneva Convention, but the atrocities committed by marauding Imperial forces in the war against China were nagging at him constantly. Japanese soldiers had been permitted to terrorize the Chinese population in an orgy of sadism the world hadn't seen since the Mongols had first surged west, and it seemed women had often been deliberate targets of Japanese cruelty. Gang rape, torture, mutilation and murder had been commonplace and Chinese women had been raped in all locations at all hours, the soldiers never being punished for their crimes. He had shared his agony of mind with John the day before but his friend had been unwilling to even consider that such things could happen in Hong Kong.

'Look, Nick,' John had said quietly, 'I can understand you are worried sick for Abigail but what happened in China is not going to happen here. You know as well as I do that the Japanese have been taught to think of the Chinese as subhuman. It's one of those terrible culture things. That's why their soldiers treat all Chinese women as prostitutes and sexual playthings – it's been ingrained in them from birth. But white women, Europeans, are different. And nurses, well, I mean, they're respected everywhere.'

He hoped John was right. Nicholas kissed the top of Abby's head again. He would rather kill her himself, quickly and cleanly with a bullet in the head, than let her fall into the hands of murdering rapists. The fingers of his right hand felt for the revolver he now kept in his pocket at all times. The slightest suggestion that what had happened in China was going to be repeated here, and he would kill her and then himself, because he couldn't live without her. But perhaps

John was right and his love for Abigail had distorted how he was thinking, that and the exhaustion and lack of food and water. Nevertheless, as soon as they were invaded he would keep her close to him no matter what. She came first, even before his patients.

'I love you.' Abby snuggled closer into his side. Even with the whine of the shells and explosions that seemed to make the building shudder, she would rather be here, with him, going through this, than somewhere safe without him.

'And I love you, my sweet.'

'Do you ever think about when the war is over?'

'Since I married you, yes. Before ... well, I'm not sure I cared enough.'

'We haven't talked about children. Do you want them?'

Nicholas smiled to himself. Here they were, in the midst of mayhem where any moment could be their last, and she was talking about whether he wanted children. But that was his Abigail, and he loved her for it. 'Yes, I want children. Do you?'

'Of course.' She sounded almost indignant. 'A little boy first who looks like you, and then maybe two girls. After that we'll see.'

'Unless you've got a direct line to the Almighty that I don't know about, I think you have to take what you get.'

'That's all right too, I don't mind. I just want your babies, lots of them.'

'So the first three are just for starters?'

'Exactly.'

They talked on in the same vein for some minutes more – silly lovers' talk about a future that seemed as far away as heaven itself with the sounds of war vibrating in the distance, but it didn't matter. It made them both feel better by the time Nicholas stood up, pulling Abby up after him as he said, 'Time to do our duty, Mrs Jefferson-Price.'

'OK, Captain Jefferson-Price.'

They kissed, long and hard, and then walked hand in hand out of the room and back into the real world.

It was later that same day in the evening. Nicholas had left the operating theatre in the basement of the building after working non-stop for ten hours, and was making his way to the ground floor. He needed to breathe fresh air – or at least as fresh as the dust and smoke from numerous shells made it. The cloying sweet smell of blood was in his nostrils and anything was better than that. He felt he had been drenched in blood during the last little while; at times the floor underneath the operating table had been swamped with it. The shelling was causing slaughter on a mass scale, which of course was exactly what the damn Japanese intended. He ground his teeth as hatred and loathing of the enemy engulfed him briefly.

They had heard that there was serious rioting and looting in the coastal town of Kowloon across from Hong Kong island. One of the injured sailors who had been brought to the hospital earlier that day had reported that British sappers were getting ready to destroy anything in the town of military value, after which the oil depot would be set on fire. It was the same at the naval base, the sailor had whispered. They were preparing to scuttle ships in the near future, and dynamite, petrol and sledgehammers were already being gathered into one place so that when the time came, the soldiers and sailors would know exactly what to do and with what.

Nicholas knew there were three destroyers still at the base although the sailor had told the CO that two of these were making ready to sail very shortly. There were also a few gunboats and motor torpedo boats, and a handful of smaller vessels.

It seemed impossible that a month ago both the RAF and the navy, along with the rest of the military personnel on the island, had been going about their business oblivious to the approaching threat.

'There's none so blind as those who don't want to see.' Who had said that? he asked himself wearily. He couldn't remember but if ever a quote was apt, that one was for this situation. For a decade Japan had been carrying out raids in China and Manchuria; hadn't the writing been plainly on the wall for all to see?

He climbed the steps to the ground floor of the hospital, still in his theatre whites which were stained red. For a moment he wondered whether to change before searching out Abby, but decided not. He needed to see her, to know that she was all right. Medical staff were getting injured all the time and her safety was a constant worry at the back of his mind.

A shell impacted close to the building as he walked on, throwing up a great cloud of dirt and rock. The night sky was lit with far-off gun flashes, and for a moment Nicholas found himself wondering if the world would ever be quiet again. He had taken silence for granted before the last days, the luxury of peaceful, untroubled sleep. If he survived the war he would never do so again. There were lots of things, if it came to it, that he would never take for granted again...

He shook himself, willing the weariness that was causing his mind to wander, back under control. It was always the same when he took a break. While he was busy operating he could keep his mind focused on the matter in hand and the needs of the patient took priority, but as soon as he left the theatre exhaustion would hit.

He ran his hand through his hair, rotating his stiff neck a few times to ease aching muscles. Come on, Nick, he told himself silently. Stay with it, man.

Abby had been working in a ward at the far end of the building for the last couple of days and so he made for there. It wasn't easy. Every available inch of space had a bed or a piece of equipment wedged into it. Corridors had become makeshift wards, along with storage facilities, bathrooms and even the pharmacist's store. The hospital's gas and electricity supplies had failed and even the emergency water tanks had been holed by shrapnel. The building was without heating, and the sterilizers, kettles and X-ray machines would no longer work.

He was just in the process of easing his way round a number of beds situated in the corridor outside the ward where he believed Abby was, when he heard the whine of the bomb and he knew it was going to be close. He caught the terrified gaze of a young soldier who couldn't be more than eighteen years old, and who had clearly been badly injured. Instinctively Nicholas threw himself to the side of the young man's bed so he was lying partly over him on the window side of the corridor, in an effort to protect the lad from the worst of the impact.

The blast was deafening; shattered window glazing flew in all directions, along with plaster, chunks of masonry, bits of the wooden shutters that kept the corridors cool in the heat of the day and red-hot spears of shrapnel.

Screams and moans of the injured and dying filled the air but Nicholas knew nothing about it, still lying across the soldier as their blood turned the white sheets red...

Chapter Twenty-Three

In Abby's ward, any glass that remained in the windows had shattered, showering a few unfortunate patients with razor-sharp shards, but as she and some of the other nursing staff emerged into the corridor, a scene of utter carnage met their eyes. The bomb must have landed practically at the base of the wall of the building, and a gaping hole halfway along the corridor showed where the worst of the impact had been. Any patients in that immediate area had had no chance of survival. At either end of the corridor there was movement and men were crying out, but the dust was heavy in the air and this, combined with the deepening twilight, made it difficult to see clearly.

Abby saw the form of a doctor lying over a patient close to the ward door almost immediately, and winced as she took in the large piece of glass wedged in the man's back. It was like a huge icicle in shape and had been driven deep into the flesh, and both the doctor and patient were covered in other debris and thick powdery dirt. When she saw the patient try to move she called a VAD to help her, and together they lifted the doctor who they both presumed was dead such was the extent of his injuries, off the young soldier.

It was as the doctor's face came into view that Abby felt the world stop spinning. For a horrifying, chilling moment all she could do was to stare down at him.

'He was trying to help me.' The soldier was crying openly. 'He covered me with his own body. Is he dead?'

Nicholas. Oh, oh, Nicholas. She couldn't answer the patient such was her terror. Instead she felt for a pulse, and then, when there was the slightest of tremors beneath her fingers, her legs went weak. They were holding Nicholas half on and half off the bed, and as the VAD went to remove the glass, Abby stopped her with a sharp 'No!' adding more softly, 'Leave it, please. He's still alive and you might cause more injury trying to take it out.'

There was so much blood. Abby's mouth was dry. And after Nicholas, John was the best surgeon in the hospital but he and Delia, along with several other doctors and QAs, had been transferred to support smaller hospitals when the bombardment had begun. But regardless of that, Nicholas would have to be operated on immediately because her husband was dying in front of her eyes.

The next hours were ones of endless waiting for Abby.

In the last day or so and with great reluctance, a decision had been made that with no electricity, all operations would have to cease once darkness fell. The basement windows gave limited light as it was, but with the aid of oil lamps they got through during the day. Now, as Nicholas's colleagues fought to save him, they worked by the light of oil lamps and candles which tested the surgeon, in particular, to the limit. But he did his best, and his best meant Nicholas was still alive when dawn broke, although deeply unconscious.

It was later that morning when Abby saw Nicholas's lieutenant colonel walking towards her and immediately thought the worst. She knew the officer thought a great deal of Nicholas and assumed he had come to break bad news personally.

Seeing her white face, the lieutenant colonel said quickly, 'It's all right, m'dear, he's still alive, but I need to talk to you.' Drawing her away from the patient she had been dealing with, he led her to a quiet corner, clearing his throat before he spoke and obviously uncomfortable. 'The thing is,' he said softly, 'the doctor who operated has informed me there is no hope if your husband remains here. Dangerous though it would be to move him, the amount of shrapnel inside him means more operations are necessary and this would involve specialized care. Do you understand me?'

Abby nodded. Patients were dying every day, and the noise and dirt and overcrowding meant specialized care was impossible.

'The Japanese are going to be in Kowloon very soon, and after that any hope of getting him away will be gone.'

'Away?' Abby stared at the officer. 'Away where?'

'What I am proposing is risky, Mrs Jefferson-Price. Very risky, but it gives the captain a slim chance. There is a submarine waiting some way out of the harbour and a very important intelligence officer is to be taken to it tonight by means of a small boat. There is absolutely no guarantee that the boat won't be blown out of the water, the submarine too, come to that, but the documents in the officer's possession are considered vital enough to merit the risk. The journey home will be difficult and hazardous but there are, of course, medical personnel on board to attend to the captain.'

'But...' Abby was so taken aback she couldn't think. 'How ... how do you know they would agree to take Nicholas?'

'The intelligence officer in question is my son-in-law.'

'Oh.' Abby blinked. 'I see.'

'It would be strictly a passage for just two men, Mrs Jefferson-Price.'

He was telling her she wouldn't be able to accompany Nicholas, Abby thought, not that she had been thinking that far in her confusion anyway. She tried to clear her head.

'I'm sure I have no need to say this is in the strictest confidence, m'dear.'

Abby nodded. 'Of course, yes.' She took a deep breath. It was Nicholas's only hope. 'Thank you, sir. May ... may I see him before he leaves?'

'Of course.' The lieutenant colonel cleared his throat again. He was an army man through and through, and normally kept his soft centre well hidden; 'And well done, m'dear. Well done,' he said gruffly.

Abby wasn't quite sure what she was being complimented on but she said, 'Thank you, sir,' anyway, before following him out of the ward.

Nicholas was lying in a small anteroom off one of the wards. It was supposed to be for one bed, but had three crammed into the small space and each occupant was desperately sick. He hadn't regained consciousness but she hadn't expected him to. His face and lips were as white as the sheet covering his still form and again she put her fingers to his wrist to feel his pulse and see if he was still alive.

'Oh, my darling.' Desolation flooded her. He was too ill to be moved – in normal circumstances it would have been unheard of – but what other choice was there? They were running out of medical supplies, had little food and practically no water. Blood and dirt and dust was everywhere, and on top of that Nicholas would need further operations by a skilled surgeon in the future. She had to let him go. It was his only chance. But the thought of him dying alone, without her there...

She bent and kissed the cool white lips, her eyes streaming with tears. *He wouldn't die.* If there was any justice, any good left in this awful world, he wouldn't die. He had been injured trying to protect that young soldier, surely God would spare him because of that? He had to, He had to. She couldn't live without him. Oh, God, God, please help him. I'll do anything, put up with anything, but please don't let him die.

How long she stood there she didn't know, the tears blinding her as she held his limp hand and prayed as she had never prayed before. Eventually she left the ante-room and stood for a moment drying her face and trying to compose herself. Her anguish was such that it was almost as though he had died already, and it was this thought that brought her self-control to the fore. He was going to be all right, he *was*. She had to believe that and go on believing it or else she might as well lie down and give up right now, because she wouldn't want to go on without him.

Nicholas was spirited away that night. The lieutenant colonel came to see Abby the following morning and told her that as far as he was aware all had gone according to plan. Of course, nothing was certain, he added gently. Not in times such as these.

Abby nodded, thanked him and continued with her work, her heart breaking.

The following day the Japanese army reached Kowloon and five days after the attack on Pearl Harbor the Japanese flag flew over Kowloon hospital. The Japanese immediately hauled artillery batteries into position along the coast and opened a devastating fire on Hong Kong island's north shore as they prepared to make an amphibious assault crossing of the harbour. Within hours of the enemy reaching Kowloon, Abby and the other medical staff were told that from now on, owing to snipers, everyone would need to be especially vigilant.

Their particular hospital was built on a slope overlooking Victoria Harbour and was directly in the firing line as the Japanese pounded them from the mainland. The QAs were told to change into dark slacks and shirts with merely a Red Cross brassard to state they were nurses. Now the enemy were so close they were watching the nurses go about their business through binoculars, the CO warned, and the women's white uniforms made them easy targets. It was clear the Japanese were specifically targeting medics, ambulances and aid stations now in flagrant violation of the Rules of War, and not differentiating between combatants and non-combatants.

Abby and the other nurses looked at each other as the matron read out the CO's instructions, the stories they had heard about the Japanese atrocities towards the Chinese flashing through every woman's mind. Abby wished Delia was here with her. She had other friends among her colleagues, but Delia had many of Sybil's attributes and the two of them had got on so well. But there was no time for such thoughts, overwhelmed as they were by injured and dying patients.

The next morning, Abby, two other QAs and three orderlies were called to the matron's office and told that some of the other hospitals were calling out for more trained staff. They were being sent to assist where needed most. Casualties among the British, Indian and volunteer troops were increasingly heavy as the deadly accuracy of the Japanese shelling, bombing and sniper attacks forced them from their fixed positions.

To Abby's delight she discovered she was destined for a college on the south-east corner of the island. Originally built as a boys' school in the heyday of the Empire, it had been converted into a military hospital at the outbreak of war. It was where Delia and John were working.

When Abby reached the hospital after a hair-raising ride in an ambulance that was fired on several times, she discovered the physical conditions were appalling. Many already injured patients had suffered further wounds from flying glass, and so every ward was shuttered, plunging the interior into permanent gloom. Even the hurricane lamps the medical staff had been using initially had made them too conspicuous from the air, and so now they worked by the light of pocket torches.

Delia found her almost immediately, flinging her arms round Abby and hugging her as she said, 'Oh, am I pleased to see you. I've so missed you. We heard this morning we were getting some extra help and I prayed it'd be you although I knew the odds were against it, knowing how Nick likes to keep you with him. Is he all right?' And then, at the look on her friend's face, Delia's eyes widened. 'What have I said? What's wrong?'

Amazingly, Abby managed to fill Delia in on what had gone on without weeping, and after more hugs, Delia led her to a building in the grounds of the college that was the nurses' living quarters. Within half-an-hour Abby was back in the main building and at work, but feeling much better for being reunited with Delia. That evening John joined the two women and they ate together, each of them acutely aware of the missing member of their quartet. It was only as the three of them sat together talking that it dawned on Abby the matron had chosen her for this hospital knowing that Delia and John were good friends of her and Nicholas's, and she wished she had realized in time to thank the matron for her kindness before she had left.

The hospital was full to overflowing with wounded British and Canadian soldiers, and again, every inch of space was being used. Even so, over the coming days, as the Allied forces on the island put up a cohesive resistance against an enemy riding high on victory, more patients were admitted.

The inevitable happened ten days after the beginning of the air attack when the Japanese landed at night on the north-east corner of the island. It was three days before news filtered through to other areas where the enemy had not yet reached, due to the determined and stubborn defence being put up by young British, Indian, Canadian and Chinese men, and when it did, Abby and Delia and their colleagues found it hard to believe at first.

In Kowloon the behaviour of the Japanese towards medical personnel had been humane on the whole, according to the local radio station. This went off the air the day after the enemy landed on

Hong Kong island, but news of a massacre at the Salesian Mission religious buildings at Shau Kei Wan, an advanced dressing station, soon became known. The mission buildings were very isolated, but it seemed the Japanese had stormed into the area and, in defiance of international convention, had begun an orgy of killing. All the medical staff had been herded outside and the men had been made to strip naked. Doctors and surgeons were made to kneel on the grass and then a Japanese officer walked down the line shooting each man in the back of the head with his pistol. Then eight young Canadian soldiers and a number of men from the RAMC, similarly stripped and with their hands tied behind their backs, were decapitated by Japanese officers while ordinary Japanese soldiers cheered and applauded with glee. The nurses at the hospital had been forced to stand and watch this happen, and then observe the butchering of wounded patients.

Abby and Delia stared at each other, and it was Delia who whispered, 'The world has gone mad.'

They were standing with John and the rest of the hospital's medical staff just outside the front doors of the college, after the hospital's commanding officer had called them together to confirm the rumours that had reached them earlier that day. 'Let me make one thing clear.' The CO, a middle-aged man, gazed round at the white distressed faces in front of him. 'It seems the Japanese wanted some survivors to relay what occurred to cause collapse in morale. This will not happen.' His mild blue eyes swept over the assembled company. 'We will continue to do our job here to the

346

best of our ability and let God take care of tomorrow. Is that understood? Good. Back to work.'

That same day, to the delight of Delia, who hadn't had one of her gin fizzes since the shelling had begun, the nurses were told they were to be included in the daily tot of rum issued to the troops. Abby didn't like rum but, desperately thirsty due to the acute shortage of water and worried to death about Nicholas, she drank her allowance, as eagerly as the others. She found it was warming and comforting and did make a difference to morale.

Over the next two or three days it became impossible to do what they had done that afternoon and have a meeting outside the hospital. The surroundings were infested with snipers who made anything moving their target. And then, on the morning of Christmas Eve an hour or so after it had become light, a nurse ran into the ward where Abby was. The girl, a young VAD, called out in a trembling voice, 'The Japs are here!' and then burst into tears.

As the only QA present, Abby quickly took control. Leading the shaking teenager out of the ward after telling her VADs to carry on with their work, she took the girl to the area where her mother was working, also as a VAD, and left them together. On returning to her ward, Abby saw Japanese soldiers and Allied troops fighting on the lawn outside the hospital. The building had become the front line but the fight was a terribly uneven one and over within minutes, hordes of drunken Japanese soldiers bursting into the hospital shouting and screaming yells of victory.

It was the beginning of a nightmare that Abby was to remember for the rest of her life, each moment etched on her mind with terrible clarity.

Chapter Twenty-Four

'Wh-what are they going to do to us?'

The fifteen-year-old Chinese girl Abby was cradling in her arms lifted up her head, tears streaming down her dirty face. Abby tried to think of something reassuring to say and failed. The killing rampage by the Japanese soldiers that they had all witnessed had robbed the women of any hope that they would be spared simply because of their sex or profession. Now she just hugged the girl tighter, and glanced at Delia over the teenager's head. Delia looked as terrified as Abby felt.

They had watched as the CO and John had gone out to meet the Japanese and were dragged away, to who knew where, seconds before the dirty and dishevelled soldiers had flooded the building. What had followed had been pure carnage. The Japanese had begun bayoneting and shooting patients in their beds and stretchers, tearing the bandages off the wounded men and stabbing them repeatedly as they shrieked and lunged, laughing and shouting. Herding doctors and male members of the St John Ambulance Brigade into a room they had slaughtered them all in an orgy of killing, before marching any patients who could walk and the rest of the male medical staff away up the stairs, along with Abby and the twelve other women and girls at the hospital, eight of whom were nurses. On reaching the first floor, the soldiers separated the women from the men, forcing the male patients and staff into what had once been a lecture room, and the women into a storage facility that was little more than a large cupboard with a window.

Every so often the women heard blood-curdling screams coming from the corridor outside. It seemed the guards were torturing unarmed prisoners of war for sport.

It was hot in their small room and the thirst that had been a torment for days increased as the hours ticked by. Abby's scars were irritating her, especially on her face as her skin dried out, and although she tried not to scratch them she couldn't help herself now and again, only stopping when she saw blood on her fingers. They had no idea what time it was; the Japanese soldiers had robbed them of their watches and also taken the wedding rings of five of the VADs and two of the Chinese women who were married to British soldiers. The soldier who had taken Abby's watch had looked with disgust at her cheap wedding ring, spitting on the ground as he had knocked her hand away in contempt. Abby didn't mind; it meant she still had Nicholas's ring.

By midday a couple of the women had been reduced to relieving themselves in a corner of the room. They didn't dare to knock on the door and ask their captors if they could use the bathroom, not wanting to draw attention to themselves. One of the Chinese women had described what the

Japanese had done to women and young girls in her country and it had been chilling. Abby had tried to reassure a couple of the younger unmarried girls that the rape and murder the woman had described wouldn't happen here, but she hadn't believed it herself and her words had carried no conviction.

It was early afternoon when the door to their tiny prison was suddenly flung open. A group of grubby, sweaty Japanese soldiers stood there looking at the women with toothy grins. Screaming at the women and girls to stand up, the spokesman of the motley bunch told them they had to bow whenever a soldier of the Imperial Army was in front of them, his broken English making him hard to understand.

It wasn't worth antagonizing their captors unnecessarily and they all did as they were told as the guards jabbered amongst themselves. Then the soldier who had spoken before pointed at Saffron, the Chinese girl whom Abby had been comforting. 'Come now.' He pointed to two of the younger women, both Chinese, and repeated the order. 'Come now or kill all.'

Fearing the worst, Abby thrust Saffron behind her and stepped forward. 'These women are nurses, leave them alone.'

The little man didn't hesitate as he lifted his arm and slapped Abby so hard across the face that she fell backwards, hitting her head against the wall and landing on the floor as she blacked out. When she came round, her head was in Delia's lap and her friend was sobbing. Forcing her eyes open, Abby murmured weakly, 'Where's Saffron?'

'They took them. No, don't try and sit up, lie still. You've been unconscious for ages.'

A little while later Saffron and the others were returned to the room. All were crying; Saffron could barely walk and her legs were bloody. After thrusting them forwards the soldiers banged the door and locked it, but it was only a few minutes before it was opened once again. Four different soldiers stood there, and this time, as the women stood up and bowed, one of them slowly came forward and scrutinized each of them, stopping at Abby who was virtually holding Saffron up such was the state of the young girl. 'You come.' As he spoke, Abby turned fully to face him and it was then he saw the left side of her face where a couple of the scars were bleeding and the whole area was red and raw looking. Stepping back with a look of distaste, he said, 'You stay. You' – he pointed at Delia and then another European, the very attractive young wife of a British officer – 'you come now or kill all.'

'Abby...' Delia clutched at her but the guards drew their bayonets and the soldier who had spoken grabbed Delia by her hair forcing her from the room, along with Geraldine Henderson, the officer's wife. Still dazed from her head injury Abby could do nothing but watch as the women were manhandled away.

One of the Chinese women, her face still streaked with tears, came and sat by Abby when the door had closed. 'You can do nothing for your friend,' she said softly, 'and if you resist them they will kill you. They have us in their power and they enjoy torture and sadism as my country knows only too well.'

This woman was married to a British soldier and when they had first been imprisoned in the room, she had told the women that when he had brought her out of China and married her some years ago, she had told him stories about the Japanese that he hadn't believed at first.

'He thought I was ex-exa...'

'Exaggerating?' someone had said.

'Yes, exaggerating.' The woman had nodded her head. 'But I did not exaggerate. Expect no mercy because they will give none. They do not understand the concept. Nor that of surrender. From infants the Japanese are conditioned to believe it is better to die with honour than surrender to their enemy, and they do not understand the European ways. Courage means fighting to the death and that is that. A white prisoner has chosen humiliation and disgrace by not killing himself and therefore is to be utterly despised, that is the way they think. Therefore torture and atrocities are what they deserve, they are less than nothing. Less than an insect.' She had shrugged. 'It is the Japanese way.'

And now Delia had been dragged away to endure the torments of hell. Abby looked at the Chinese woman. 'What did they do to you, to Saffron?' She had to know, to prepare herself for when Delia came back.

Even in her distress the Chinese woman was very beautiful with a fragile purity about her that her brutalization hadn't dimmed. Now she spoke almost dispassionately. 'They took us to a room where other soldiers were waiting. They made us take off all our clothes and lie down, and then each soldier removed his trousers before raping us. I asked them to spare Saffron because she hadn't known a man but that only made her more attractive to them. Each of them, ten in all, had her first, and then several moved on to us. They wanted to hurt us. When Saffron cried out it made them laugh and be even more rough with her.'

And Delia was in the hands of these fiends. Abby felt nausea rise in her throat and swallowed hard. 'But if they care so much about honour as you say, where is the honour in raping and murdering women and children?' She glanced across at Saffron who had curled herself into a ball since her return and would accept no comfort from anyone, crying constantly in pain and badly injured as her bloodstained clothes bore evidence to.

The woman looked at her almost pityingly. 'We are the spoils of war. Playthings, that is all. My sister was at a Bible training school and thirty soldiers raped her to death in the seminary compound.'

Words failed Abby. She, like many white Europeans, had had no idea of the savagery of Japan's war against China. Now they were all paying the price for ignoring the gathering stormclouds of war that appeasement towards the Japanese had, in part, encouraged. 'But we're nurses,' she whispered. 'Surely that means something, even to them?'

The woman didn't answer but her silence did.

Delia and Geraldine Henderson were returned

to the room as darkness fell, but even in the dim light from the small window it was clear the two women were in a terrible state. Their clothes were badly torn, their hair in disarray and their eyes were blank and staring. Both were in evident pain, and when Abby went to Delia it was almost as if her friend didn't recognize her at first. And when she did, she became hysterical for some minutes.

Geraldine was in a similar condition and it was clear they had been repeatedly raped.

The thirteen women and girls sat huddled together for warmth and comfort as the sky outside the window became black. Saffron was calmer, falling asleep with her head on the shoulder of one of the women who had been taken out with her earlier.

Spine-chilling screams still echoed from outside the room now and again, and every time they heard footsteps in the corridor everyone tensed. At some time in the early hours of Christmas morning the door was opened again. As the women struggled to their feet, Saffron and the two Chinese women and Delia and Geraldine were pushed to the back of the group by the others who knew all five were in a state of collapse and would find it devastating to endure another gang rape.

This time a Japanese officer stood with two guards in the doorway and he looked at the prisoners dispassionately. 'Come with me, please.' His English was nigh-on perfect.

Again it was Abby who spoke as the other women shrank back. 'What are you going to do with us?'

As they had been forced to use a corner of the small space as a toilet, the smell in the room was now pungent, and the officer wrinkled his nose when he said, 'You are being taken downstairs and then to a room where blankets will be provided. You will follow me now.'

They had no other choice but to do as he said, although each of them suspected the worst as they filed out into the corridor. Saffron was in a bad way and was being half-carried by the young VAD who had burst into Abby's ward earlier and her mother. Abby's head was aching and she felt dizzy and sick and knew she had concussion, but she tried to show no weakness as they followed the officer, the two guards making up the rear.

True to his word, the officer led the women down the stairs and into a classroom on the ground floor of the building that had been a ward for the badly injured. Not one soldier remained in the room and Abby didn't like to think what had gone on in there. The floor and walls were stained with blood and strewn with feathers from the destruction of scores of pillows. Some mattresses were left on the narrow iron beds; others were lying haphazardly here and there and all of them were bloodstained.

The officer pointed to a table where a few tins of bully beef stood already open and several pitchers of milk. 'You will eat and drink. I will return in one hour and inform you of your duties.' He motioned to one of the guards to step inside the room before he and the other guard left. The soldier who remained was short and bandy legged and he regarded them impassively, his gun held across his chest.

Abby and the others had to persuade their five companions who had been attacked to eat and drink. 'Come on, Delia,' Abby whispered as Delia sank down onto one of the beds with a mattress still on it and put her head in her hands. 'You need to eat.' It was the first food and drink they'd had since the Japanese had stormed the hospital.

'Why?' Delia looked at her with desperate eyes. 'They are going to rape and kill us anyway.'

'They won't kill us.' Abby fetched some of the beef and a glass of milk, standing over Delia while she ate and drank and then pouring herself a glass of milk. 'I think that officer has restored some sort of order to his men. Why would they bother to feed us if they were going to kill us, and look, there are a heap of blankets over there. And this guard is behaving himself.'

Delia looked over to the soldier and shuddered convulsively. 'I hate them,' she whispered.

'We all do.' Abby was glad Delia was speaking at last.

For some time after she had returned to the room following the rapes she had said nothing coherent.

Some time later the officer returned. He had four guards with him carrying buckets of water and scrubbing brushes which they placed in front of the women. 'You will clean this ground floor, each room and the corridors,' he said shortly. 'Begin here now.'

Abby looked into the hard bullet eyes and then turned and pointed at Saffron who was sitting swaying backwards and forwards on the edge of one of the beds, her eyes closed. 'Your soldiers have hurt her so badly she cannot work.'

The man's jaw clenched. 'All will work. *Now.*'

By the evening the ground floor was clean. Any orderlies who had survived had carried the bodies of the dead out of the hospital onto the lawn outside and the Japanese had set fire to them with kerosene. The stench of burning flesh was horrific.

Inside, the thirteen women had worked all day under the merciless eyes of the guards. At one point a soldier had roughly grabbed one of the VADs and tried to drag her into a classroom but an officer had appeared in answer to the girl's screams and the women's shouts and the guard had immediately let the girl go.

That night more food and drink was brought into the room where the women were held, and Abby asked the officer who again accompanied the guards for medicine for Saffron. She was running a temperature and was very unwell. He refused point blank and the women were left to comfort the young girl as best they could. The guard who remained in the room all night sitting on a chair near the door made no attempt to talk to them or molest them which was something.

Early on the morning of Boxing Day the colony at last surrendered to an enemy who had total control of the air and seas, and more officers appeared to impose discipline on their troops. That day the women were marched out to attend to the wounded who had survived the massacre, and there they learned the fate of the CO and John, who had both been beheaded. Abby was able to get some medicine and ointment for Saffron through the course of the day, but by now the young girl was vomiting and unable to keep anything down. It was only on further questioning of one of the women who had been taken with the girl that Abby learned Saffron had been dragged into another room at one point during the attack, and piercing screams had ensued. It appeared the men abusing her had thought it highly amusing to force all kinds of objects into her childish body through her vagina.

Delia forgot her own troubles and stayed awake with Saffron during that night, only catching some sleep herself when Abby relieved her at four in the morning. By the time the guards came with their breakfast of more tins of beef and milk, it was clear Saffron was dying, and Abby, aware that Delia was still weak and ill from her own ordeal, asked if her friend could stay and sit with the little Chinese girl that day and be spared having to work. After a moment's deliberation the officer agreed.

Of the patients who had already been in the hospital when the Japanese stormed it, only half remained alive. A good number of the medical staff had been murdered, including all the doctors and the male members of the St John Ambulance Brigade. It made the job of Abby and the other women impossible at times as they fought to save patients who needed surgery. All that day as Abby toiled on only one thought sustained her – Nicholas hadn't had to endure being tortured and killed. If his submarine was torpedoed or if he died en route to England, at least he wouldn't have tasted the horrors that had been enacted on the island. She tried to picture him in her mind as she worked but his face wouldn't materialize; nevertheless the ring on the third finger of her left hand was a solid link that was infinitely precious. If they survived this war she knew she would never want another to replace it, despite the fact that it constantly left a green stain on her skin.

When the nurses and other women returned to their quarters that evening Saffron had sunk into a coma and a terrible odour emanated from between her legs, accompanied by a sickening trickle of pus and other bodily fluids. It was some comfort to them that the girl was unconscious and out of pain as the twelve women stood round the bed crying and praying, but they were heartbroken that her life was ending in such a way. Saffron was little more than a child and small and underdeveloped for her years; it was monstrous she had been used in such a way.

Abby summed up what they were all thinking when later that night as the women settled down, she prayed, 'God, take her to be with You quickly out of this horrible world. Let her enter into heaven whole and restored and happy, where she will know only peace and love and joy.'

At one o'clock in the morning, as Abby and Delia sat either side of Saffron's bed holding her limp little hands, Abby's prayer was answered.

Chapter Twenty-Five

During the month of January, life at the hospital settled into a kind of routine for a while. Abby and the other nurses were allowed to tend to their patients with relatively little interference from their captors, although Delia and the other women who had been raped found the constant bowing to the guards especially hard. None of them could recognize the individual soldiers who had hurt them but they knew they were among the guards, and having to bow to their attackers was humiliating and degrading.

Water supplies had been re-established, but there was no fresh food of any kind, only tins of beef and stew and vegetables. The Japanese supplied sacks of rice when they felt like it, which wasn't often, and no one knew how long each sack was expected to last. Inevitably as the days progressed the store of tins began to dwindle, along with any medical supplies that had been salvaged.

Abby found her role as a nurse was changing as time went on. All of the women nursed their patients to the best of their ability, but whereas in the past they would have been expected to keep a professional detachment to some extent, now their relationship with the men had become much more pastoral. Abby and the others spent a lot of their time listening to the problems and anxieties and fears of the men they were caring for, things the men found too embarrassing or 'unmanly' to share with their own sex. Some of them were suffering badly from shell shock and could be unhinged at the slightest loud noise, and these patients Abby spent the longest with. She thought about her father often, with a deep and aching regret that she'd been too young to help him, but every fevered brow she wiped and every tortured soul she comforted brought him nearer.

Some of the soldiers, young men of eighteen or nineteen, could be incredibly childlike in their dependence and trust in the nurses. As Abby remarked to Delia one day, they had become more mothers than nurses, especially to the seriously wounded and the dying. Abby didn't know how the other women who had been raped felt, but she knew the work Delia did among the injured men was helping her friend to carry on from day to day.

Any patients who recovered sufficiently to leave the hospital were given fresh clothes and two army blankets and taken to Sham Shui Po, the men's POW camp on the main land at Kowloon. The Japanese didn't recognize mental trauma, only physical injuries, and Abby was fearful of what would meet some of her 'boys' with shell shock when they entered the camp. At great risk to herself she kept their physical improvement secret from the guards as long as she could, knowing that she could be beaten within an inch of her life if the Japanese caught on to what she was doing.

Over the last days and weeks they had all – nurses and patients alike – learned the hard way that resistance of any kind to orders, or to the constant bowing and scraping the Japanese demanded, only fed the obsession their captors had for 'face' and 'respect'. For any slight, imagined or otherwise, punishments could range from a vicious slap across the face to a serious and prolonged beating with a rifle butt, pickaxe handle, shovel, riding crop, or in the case of the Japanese officers, a sword scabbard.

In spite of the severe rationing of food by their captors which meant Abby was always hungry, the exhausting days on the wards with the injured and dying, and the constant threat of beatings, it was the nights that were the worst time. Tired in body and soul, Abby would fall asleep to the sound of Delia quietly weeping in the bed next to her, something her friend had done every night since the rapes. And then the nightmares would begin, terrible nightmares in which Nicholas would be kneeling on the ground as Japanese soldiers hacked and hacked at his neck. Sometimes his face would change and become that of her grandfather or Robin, and she would shout and tell them that they should have stayed at home on the farm where they were safe. Another time she and Nicholas would be running, hand in hand, from a deadly dark force that was pursuing them, but her legs would be like lead and every step was harder and harder and she knew they were being overtaken. And then, still in the dream, she would wake up back at her grandfather's cottage and look around her bedroom and be so glad it was just a nightmare; she would open the bedroom door and go downstairs to begin cooking the breakfast but instead of the ground floor of the cottage there would be a vast expanse of dead and mutilated bodies, piled high, with wide staring eyes and open mouths. Sometimes she felt she was more tired when she woke up than when she had gone to sleep, unable to work out what was real and what was not.

She had told Delia about the nightmares, asking her if she thought she was going mad, and for a brief moment her friend had seemed more like her old self. 'Going mad?' Delia had given a snort of disgust. 'Don't be so daft. If you're going mad then there's no hope for the rest of us because you're the sanest amongst us all. You're dead tired, Abby, as well as being half starved, but barmy you're not.'

Dear Delia. Abby glanced at her friend now in the dim morning light. Everyone was still asleep but she hadn't been able to drop off again after a particularly horrific nightmare had woken her up an hour ago. It was the monsoon season and the rain and wind lashing at the building hadn't helped. Delia would deny it with typical British stiff-upper-lip fortitude, but she had been so brave and sacrificial in how she had carried on after her ordeal. Tending to the wounded, giving a word of encouragement where needed and showing compassion and unfailing gentleness to the patients under her care as well as her fellow nurses, she was a remarkable woman. And on top of what she had personally gone through, Abby knew Delia was mourning the loss of John. The two of them had become a couple within twenty-four hours of meeting, and Delia had confided that John had asked her to marry him the evening

363

before the hospital had been captured.

Lying quietly in the early morning, Abby admitted to herself that she had been guilty of misjudging her friend initially. She had thought her to be a lot more frothy and empty-headed for a start, probably because of Delia's behaviour on the ship that had brought them from England to Hong Kong.

But who was she to be judge and jury? Abby twisted uncomfortably. She had done the same with Rachel; there was no excuse. When would she learn?

Abby berated herself for a few minutes before reason asserted itself and told her to stop. She wasn't perfect, heaven knows she wasn't perfect, but she had always been there for Delia and that was something in her favour. And at least Nicholas loved her. Abby smiled wryly to herself before the worry and longing that always came with thoughts of her husband invaded.

'Please let him be safe, God,' she whispered in the silence. 'Let him live. I can put up with anything if You let him live. I promise I won't judge anyone else and I'll be everything You want me to be if You just let Nicholas live and have a good life, even if it's without me.'

After the first few days, the guard had been removed from their sleeping quarters which was a huge relief to everyone. The women assumed that the Japanese had come to understand that they would not try and escape and desert their patients; not that there was anywhere to escape to. They were on an island, after all. Every morning one of the soldiers banged on the door of their room when it was time to rise, but this morning instead of just knocking, the door was opened and one of the officers strode in.

Half-asleep and bleary-eyed, the women struggled to their feet and gave the customary bow as the bristling little man paraded importantly back and forth, his hands behind his back. It was clear he had something to say, but when he spoke it was quite a bombshell. 'You will leave here in one hour.' It was the same officer who had dealt with them on more than one occasion and who had given permission for Delia to remain with Saffron when the Chinese girl was dying. He now stopped in front of Abby. 'This hospital is closing and you will be moved to a building on the main land. The Japanese Imperial Army will allow you to take any supplies and equipment you need with you.'

He paused – obviously this was a concession in his opinion and one that required thanks. Abby didn't take the hint. 'We've only got an hour to get everything together?'

'This is sufficient.'

'But some of the patients are too ill to be moved.'

He regarded her impassively. 'One hour.'

The next sixty minutes were chaotic as they worked against the clock, but the male orderlies were terrific, loading patients onto the trucks the Japanese had waiting while the nurses took care of the mattresses, blankets, linen and medical supplies.

In the midst of the organized mayhem it dawned on Abby that it might be a trick and they were all going to be killed but she had no time to dwell on that. It was every hand to the plough if the hospital was to be cleared in time. It was, but the orderlies reported that some of the seriously injured were in a bad way after being moved and might not make the journey to the main land.

With several guards escorting them, Abby and the others were herded out of the hospital and into a truck which deposited them at the harbour. They crossed over to the main land in an open-topped boat getting wetter by the minute, and once they had reached Kowloon they were put in a large wire cage with other POWs. Again there was no shelter from the torrential rain and wind as they huddled together for hours, chilled to the bone. Since the rapes all Delia's confidence and boldness had vanished, and now she shrank into Abby whenever one of the Japanese guards came to inspect the prisoners through the wire, terrified the same thing would happen again. Nothing Abby said could reassure her. One guard in particular seemed to enjoy tormenting the women, eyeing them up and down and making obscene gestures.

It was after one of these episodes that Delia whispered to Abby, her teeth chattering, 'I won't let them take me again, Abby. I'll kill myself first.' She brought a scalpel out of the pocket of the battledress all the nurses had taken to wearing since the capture of the island. The traditional ladylike uniform was all very well but with the realities of modern warfare the more practical khaki was far more serviceable. 'See?'

Abby stared at her friend, aghast. 'Delia, if they see you with that it will be taken as a threat, that you're planning to kill one of them. Get rid of it.'

'I won't let them see it and if they do, at least I can slit my throat quickly and cleanly before they can touch me.'

Abby didn't know what to say. One of the orderlies had told them that the Kempeitai, the Japanese military police officers, were devils incarnate. It would be to these fiends Delia would be handed if they found her with a weapon. According to the orderly who had been chatting to one of the Chinese truck drivers who delivered the sacks of rice, the Kempeitai were greatly feared in his country for their obsession in rooting out 'anti-Japanese' elements and 'spies', among prisoners and civilians alike. They delighted in gruesome medieval tortures on men and women to extract confessions and didn't know the meaning of the word mercy.

Swallowing hard, she tried again. 'Look, you know the officers have got their troops under control now. All right, the guards might be brutal and vicious but there's been none of the behaviour of those first few days. Please, Delia, get rid of the knife. What if they grab you before you can do what you've planned? They won't believe you were only going to kill yourself and not one of them.'

'I'd like to kill one of them. I'd like to kill *all* of them. They're not fit to draw breath.'

Delia was trembling, whether from the rain and wind lashing them or the intensity of her hate, Abby wasn't sure. Gently, she reached for the scalpel and drew it out of Delia's cold fingers. The guards had retired to the hut from which they periodically emerged to do their rounds, and now Abby walked across to the edge of the concrete floor of the pen and knelt down as though to tie up her boot. Surreptitiously she put the scalpel through the wire and into the muddy ground on the other side of the cage, working it down into the soft dirt until it had completely disappeared.

Walking back to Delia, she took her friend in her arms. 'I won't let anyone hurt you again, I promise. Trust me.'

It was an impossible promise to make and they both knew it, but Delia smiled wanly in spite of herself. 'Amazon Abby,' she said wryly, sniffing hard.

'You'd better believe it.' Abby hugged her tight, 'We're going to stick together like glue and watch each other's backs and make it through this war. All right?'

Delia nodded. 'All right.'

It was dark by the time the transport arrived to take them to their new quarters. After a short journey they found themselves entering the grounds of an old hotel. One of the guards led the women to an annexe at the back of the main building which must once have been used by the resident staff of the hotel, and which had its own entrance from outside. Weary, cold and hungry, they filed through the door and straight into what had been a sitting room at one time but which now had a number of the mattresses they had packed on the trucks that morning spread on the floor, along with two blankets apiece.

As they entered, a young British nurse came to meet them. 'We heard you were coming earlier. The Japanese dumped your mattresses and the blankets in the rain this morning, but we got them in as quick as we could and they're only a bit damp. There's no food I'm afraid but I can offer you hot water with a touch of cocoa powder,' she said cheerfully.

While they drank their weak cocoa the VAD filled them in on the situation. Apparently the Japanese had ordered the closure of the smaller outlying hospitals, hence the move. They were busy establishing POW camps and, the VAD said bitterly, badly injured and dying patients didn't matter a jot to them. She was one of several nurses who had been brought to the hotel the day before. Their matron, Matron Fraser, had been summoned to a meeting with the Japanese director of medical services a short while ago. He had told her that the hotel had been given over to them as an exclusive POW hospital, and they would be caring for existing patients who had been here since the surrender as well as those men who had been transferred from Hong Kong island.

'What this means,' the VAD said, her blue eyes filled with fury, 'is that the Japanese army doctors and dentists and pharmacists keep all the medical supplies for their wounded, and release next to nothing for our boys. When we got here we found all the existing patients in a terrible state. They're starving and so emaciated they've got nothing to fight with. The lack of medicine and basic supplies means even those who would have had a chance of survival are dying. It's horrible, just horrible. Dysentery is rife and we've got nothing to treat it with. There's no nourishing food' – she paused – 'what am I saying? There's no food, full stop. Just a starvation diet of rice, and sometimes we get a sack of turnips to make a kind of soup with. Our matron told this director that he needs to release sufficient drugs and so on or else he is guilty of war crimes against the men, and he apparently just looked at her as though she was an insect he'd seen crawl out from under a stone.'

Abby thought she liked the sound of Matron Fraser. It took a strong woman to take the Japanese to task, knowing what it might mean to them personally.

'So...' The VAD shrugged. 'Welcome.'

It was tongue in cheek, and Abby and Delia smiled. The enemy might have taken away their liberty, brutalized some of them and imposed a regime intended to crush their spirits, but the Japanese would never understand the British sense of humour which rose to the fore even more when the chips were down. Somehow that was immensely comforting.

Once they'd drunk their cocoa they fell onto the mattresses just as they were, wearily pulling the slightly damp blankets over them and falling into the sleep of the mentally and physically exhausted.

Tomorrow was another day, and if one thing in life was certain, it was that it would bring a whole host of heartbreaking challenges and misery with it.

PART SIX

When All That's Left is Hope

1944

Chapter Twenty-Six

'For crying out loud, Nicholas, face facts. Even if this girl survives the POW camp what state is she going to be in when she comes out? You read the papers and listen to the news, you know what those brutes are like. If she hasn't lost her mind it'll be a miracle, and she'll be in no state to give you children, m'boy. Have you thought of that? Far better to cut your losses and move on.'

Nicholas hadn't thought he could hate his father any more than he did, but if he had had a pistol to hand he would have used it. *'Get out. I mean it, get out.'*

'No need to take that tack. I'm only stating the truth because no one else will. You're not in particularly good shape yourself, man. You need a wife who will look after you, not the other way round. A wife who can provide children to carry on our name–'

'I said get out, Father.' Nicholas rose from behind his desk, his eyes fiery. 'You came uninvited and I don't want you here again.'

'Damn it, man! What is the attraction this girl holds for you anyway? You could have any number of high-born women and yet you persist in holding a candle for this farm girl. One of our ancestors had a taste for gutter flesh but at least he had the sense to marry well and keep his appetite fed on the quiet.'

Gerald Jefferson-Price had walked to the door as he spoke; now he turned on the threshold to survey the livid face of his son. 'Start using your head instead of concentrating on another part of your anatomy, Nicholas, because I swear this is the last warning I'm giving you. I'll cut you out of my will and you won't get a penny.'

'Damn you and your money, and for the record this "girl" you keep referring to is my wife, *my wife*. Mrs Jefferson-Price, legally and in the eyes of God, and there isn't a thing you can do about that.'

'I've had enough of this.' Gerald had made a promise to his wife that he wouldn't lose his temper but no one could make him so blazingly angry as Nicholas. 'Who got the best medical minds dealing with your case when you were shipped back to England more dead than alive? If it wasn't for me, you wouldn't be here now.'

'Funny, but I thought it was the surgeons who saved my life.'

'Don't try and be clever. You know damn well what I mean. You were like a colander, and you'd have lost your leg when the osteomyelitis kicked in if I hadn't brought that surgeon over from Switzerland.'

'And I've thanked you. A hundred times I've thanked you. But we both know if you'd had another son and heir available you wouldn't have gone to so much trouble to keep this one alive, don't we? All you really care about is Brookwell and the estate and a son – any son – to keep it going. Well, I've told you before and I'll tell you again, I've no intention of doing that. And unless

I have a son who takes after you – and frankly I'd rather strangle him at birth than have that happen – but unless it does, and you last long enough to pass Brookwell and the rest of it on to him, you're up the creek without a paddle.'

'You think I'd give the lairdship to the flyblow of a farm girl?'

'Not a flyblow, Father, not that. Oh, no. She is my wife, and any children we have won't be bastards, but I pray to God they'll inherit nothing of you in their genes.'

'Children!' Gerald snorted contemptuously. 'Do you seriously think you will ever see this farm girl again? I think not. And I tell you this, boy. I pray every night she's long since dead and gone. You haven't heard for a while, have you? Well, think on.'

White to his lips, Nicholas stared at the tall military figure standing across the room. *This was the end.* He had thought it was the end on several other occasions over the last two and a half years when his father had been particularly obnoxious, but his father had never expressed his thoughts about Abigail quite so openly before or with such venom.

The mad rage, that had him wanting to leap across the room and smash his fist into the cold handsome face and keep on smashing it until it was a bloody pulp, drained away. His voice quiet and flat, he said, 'From this moment on I have no father and you have no son. I never want to see or hear from you again, is that clear?'

'Spare me the histrionics.' Gerald's voice was scornful. 'And shouldn't it be me who is saying that? I'm the one who has been wronged.'

Nicholas shook his head slowly. 'You actually really believe that, don't you? You have gone through life throwing your weight about and expecting everyone to dance to your tune, and on the whole they have. This war, the devastation it has caused in people's lives and the sacrifices so many have made haven't touched you in the slightest. You're still encapsulated in your own little world where you are lord of the manor. I find it incredible that a soldier, as you have emphasized to me so many times you are, can have so limited a perspective.'

'How dare you.' Gerald had been hit on the raw. If there was one thing he was proud of it was his military background. 'You didn't fire a shot in this war so don't come the hero, not with me, boy.'

'I've never pretended to be a hero, just a doctor doing the job he was trained for. I'm not a soldier, I've never wanted in the slightest to be a soldier as you know full well.'

'Oh, I know it, and as you say, only too well. Making excuses for you at the club when they enquired when you would be following in my footsteps–'

'And there we have it,' Nicholas interrupted bitterly. 'It's all about you again. Following in *your* footsteps, doing what *you* decree. Well, I'm done with that, Father, for good or ill. I'm done with it all. I pray Abigail will come back to me but whether she does or she doesn't, this is the parting of the ways. You can call it histrionics or anything else you choose, but I want nothing more to do with you.'

'And does that include your mother?'

If Gerald had thought he'd played an ace card he had another think coming as Nicholas's next words said only too clearly. 'Mother made her decision about what she wanted in life and what was important to her a long time ago. If she wants to see me she knows where she can find me. If not' – he shrugged – 'then so be it.'

'You would turn your back on your own flesh and blood for this ... this...'

'I think the word you are looking for is my "wife", Father.'

For a moment the two men stood staring at each other, a mutual enmity so strong each could taste it, and then Gerald flung open the door and was gone, his footsteps sounding on the tiled floor in the hall outside before the front door opened and then crashed to.

Nicholas sank down into his chair, his stomach churning. It had always been going to happen. This confrontation, it had been on the cards for years. He just hadn't been expecting it today. But then that was his father all over. Catch the enemy when he was off his guard.

Nicholas ran a hand over his face as he began to sweat and shake. His teeth clenched and his eyes closed, he fought the wave of darkness that he knew would consume him if he didn't master it. Take a deep breath. Slowly now, slowly. That's right. His medical expertise kicked in as though he was talking to a patient, which he supposed he was, in a way. He hadn't had one of these episodes for some months, but then again he hadn't seen his father for a while. Strange that, but even when he'd first been back in England and enduring one operation after another he had been able to cope with it all, except when his father paid a visit. One of the doctors, an intense young chap who some of the more uncooperative men on the ward scornfully labelled a headshrinker but who was, in fact, an extremely gifted and compassionate psychiatrist, had told him that it was shell shock exacerbated by stress that caused the attacks.

'We're beginning to understand that shell shock can manifest itself in a hundred different ways,' Dr Reynold had explained earnestly. 'We're wonderfully and fearfully made, Captain, and the human mind and body were never meant to experience the horrors that this war has thrown at it. There's no disgrace in being ill in the mind any more than there is in being sick in the body. Get that clear in your head and you're on the way to dealing with how you feel.'

The good doctor had stopped Gerald from visiting for some months, which had gone down like a lead balloon, Nicholas thought now as the roaring darkness retreated. He'd been a doctor after his own heart, had Dr Reynold. Utterly focused on his patients and to hell with pandering to the likes of Gerald Jefferson-Price.

Still breathing slowly and deeply, the way Dr Reynold had taught him, Nicholas swung his chair round from his desk to look out of the window.

It was late June, and the sky was as blue as cornflowers with not a whisper of a cloud marring its beauty. Outside, the essence of summer was everywhere. Clusters of creamy-white blooms prominently decorating dogwood and elder, and the white clover's heads of clustered flowers and patches of forget-me-nots painting meadows and stream banks with intense patches of colour. It was in town and village gardens where the reality of war had intruded; instead of lupins and hollyhocks and wallflowers there were stretches of vegetables in neat rows. No plot was so small that it hadn't been turned into a 'victory' garden, and even flat-dwellers had been encouraged to utilize window-boxes and grow radishes, lettuce and dwarf beans, and sunny windowsills all over Britain boasted tomato plants in flowerpots and seedboxes containing mustard and cress.

Nicholas's housekeeper, an elderly, rosy-cheeked widow of seventy-odd years who had more energy than a woman half her age, had taken the minister of food's declaration that housewives were war workers to heart from the outset. 'Potatoes and onions are munitions of war as surely as shells and bullets,' she had told Nicholas on several occasions, and even the Anderson shelter in the garden had lettuce, beetroot and marrows growing on top of it while inside they shared the cramped space with buckets of rhubarb and mushrooms.

It was this little powerhouse of a woman who now knocked on the door of Nicholas's study before entering with a cup of tea and a slice of her eggless sponge cake which actually tasted surprisingly good. 'I gather you sent Lord Muck away with a flea in his ear,' she said, without any preamble.

From her first run-in with Gerald Jefferson-Price, shortly after Nicholas had arrived to take over the position of doctor in a small market town to the south of Durham – the previous doctor, who had been well advanced in years, having dropped down dead whilst digging up potatoes for Sunday lunch – she had referred to him in this way. Nicholas didn't mind; in fact, he agreed with his housekeeper's summing-up of his father.

'Left in a right old tizz-wazz,' she added with considerable satisfaction, placing the cup of tea and plate on Nicholas's desk. 'If we had a dog, he would have kicked it.'

In spite of himself, Nicholas smiled. Mrs Wood often had this effect, and he thanked God for it, and her. Swinging round to face her, he shook his head wearily. 'He's a devil of a man, Mrs Wood, and I've had enough. I've told him not to show his face here again.'

'And not before time.' Gracie Wood didn't let on that she had been listening at the keyhole and had heard what had transpired between the two men. As uppity and full of himself as the doctor's father was, she could scarcely believe the evil old beggar had wished the lad's young wife dead, and her a nurse taken captive while doing her job to help folk as well.

From the moment Nicholas had come to the practice twelve months ago, just a short while after his final discharge from the hospital where he had been incarcerated for well over a year, Gracie had labelled him a lad in her mind. It didn't matter he was a grown man of forty and more; to Gracie he was and always would be a lad. He had arrived one weekend looking like death warmed up, as she had termed it to herself, and had made most of their patients appear positively glowing with health in comparison. From that day, never having been blessed with children herself, Gracie had assumed the role of fussy mother hen to her one damaged chick, and had been fierce in her determination to make sure Nicholas ate properly and took enough rest. Unbeknown to Nicholas, he had taken the place of the son she had never had and she loved him dearly.

Nicholas reached for his cup of tea and was irritated to find his hand was shaking, causing the cup to rattle in the saucer. One of the many operations he'd gone through to remove the shrapnel peppering his body had resulted in nerve damage in his right shoulder; sometimes his right hand was as steady as a rock, but when he became tired or upset the shaking could occur. This had effectively ended his career as a surgeon. Barely discernible to most people, such a handicap could be potentially disastrous whilst operating on a patient. The osteomyelitis that had ravaged his leg had left him with a pronounced limp, but that was of little concern. It had been the knowledge that he would never use a scalpel with minute precision again, never bring a patient back from certain death purely by his skill and expertise, that had been hard to take. But none of that could compare with the anguish and guilt and grinding torment about Abigail.

When he had woken up in an English hospital, having no memory of how he had got there and being amazed to find some weeks had passed, he had nearly gone out of his mind with worry and remorse that he had left her unprotected and alone. Dr Reynold and others had spent hours trying to convince him that the decision hadn't been his, that their parting and separation had been taken out of his hands, but it had made no difference to the self-condemnation and shame. He had vowed to cherish her and what had he done? Abandoned her into the hands of those murdering vermin. For a time his thoughts had unhinged him, his only respite being when he was pumped full of drugs to combat the pain of his lacerated body and render him unconscious for an hour or so.

For a long while after he'd arrived back in England it was as though Abigail and the rest of the Hong Kong-based nurses had disappeared off the face of the earth. No one could establish any information regarding their fate following the fall of the island, but then chilling rumours and snippets of news about rape, torture and murder of women prisoners of the Japanese in the Far East began to filter through. Enduring his own kind of captivity in the hospital and unable to find out anything definite about his wife, Nicholas had not been the best of patients.

It was only at the beginning of 1943 that he had received notification, as Abigail's husband and next of kin, that she was one of a number of army, navy and Canadian nurses being held captive in a POW camp on Hong Kong island. The relief of knowing that she was alive had immediately been followed by torment about what was happening to her. He had written to her at once, and had also seen to it that her grandfather and brother were informed that she was a POW. How long it took for his letter to reach her he wasn't sure, but it was a long time – nearly twelve months – before he received a reply written on a postcard of twenty-five words, all the prisoners in the camp were allowed.

She had sounded delirious with joy that he had survived and that had broken him afresh. She'd written that she would come home to him one day and that she was well, but had made no mention of the conditions in the camp. She had told him Delia was with her and that had been of some comfort to him.

To his great surprise, shortly after he had written to Abigail's grandfather, the old man and her brother had come to see him at the hospital. He hadn't been expecting a reply, let alone a visit, and when they had walked into the ward he had thought he was in for a difficult time. They had been the main reason she had refused to marry him all those years ago, after all, and as far as they were concerned, nothing had changed. He was still the hated laird's son, one of the gentry, a spoiled and privileged man who wasn't worth his weight in washers. That was the way they would think and he couldn't say he blamed them. And now Abigail was his wife. It couldn't have gone down well.

Wilbert and Robin had walked slowly to his bedside and none of them had spoken for a moment. Then the old man had said in a tone that could only be described as gentle, 'By, lad, you don't look too good if you don't mind me saying.'

He had smiled, he couldn't help it. 'I've felt better, I must admit.'

'They told us' – Wilbert inclined his head towards one of the nurses – 'you're lucky to be alive. Miracle, they called it. Said you've been through the mill, lad.'

Nicholas shrugged, and then winced as the movement disturbed his recently operated-on shoulder. 'I can't complain. I can see and hear and I've still got two arms and two legs. There's plenty worse off than me. I just hope' – he swallowed hard – 'Abigail is being treated well. You hear things...'

'Don't think that way, lad, else you'll go stark, staring barmy. And our Abby's a survivor, she's had to be. So, you two being married came like a bolt out of the blue, I don't mind saying. How come Abby never told us?'

Nicholas looked at the old man and then at Abigail's brother. They didn't seem hostile, just the opposite in fact, but then knowing that she was a POW would have moderated their attitude to him. He decided to tell them the whole story, starting from when they had first met and her reasons for refusing to continue their association, and then their meeting up in Hong Kong and their sudden wedding on the eve of the Japanese invasion.

By the time he had finished talking, Wilbert seemed happier. 'I thought it was strange my girl didn't tell us she'd got wed but I can see how it happened now. And frankly, lad, she was right about the other thing – me and our Robin not wanting her to get mixed up with the laird's son – but this war has changed everything, hasn't it. Made you think about what's really important, I

384

suppose, and a blind man could see you're not like your father. I can't see that old blighter wanting to help his fellow man by becoming a doctor, not him.'

Robin had nodded his agreement, and now Nicholas looked at them both as he said quietly, 'Thank you for giving me a chance. I promise you I love Abigail more than life itself. I always have. All I want is for her to get out of that hell-hole – nothing else matters.'

'No, you're right there.'

'Will you write to her and tell her everything's all right between me and you two? I know it would mean the absolute world to her.'

'Aye, I'll do that, lad. I'm not much of a letter writer but I'll pen her a few words and our Robin can put in his two penn'orth an' all. Rachel's the letter writer, she'll fill the lass in on everything that's going on at home an' the like.'

'Thank you.' Nicholas had suddenly felt exhausted, much the way he was feeling now after the confrontation with his father although for polar opposite reasons.

'There's a full waiting room out there.' Gracie's voice was disapproving. She believed half the patients only came to natter with each other, the main topic being the D-Day landings at the beginning of the month. She'd got so she was sick of hearing about it. She was also annoyed that patients who could dose themselves at home for things like a bad cough or the belly ache troubled the doctor. But there, she told herself, it was the lovely manner he had with him that drew them to the surgery half the time. Nicholas had told her on

385

more than one occasion that some of his patients who had received one of the dreaded telegrams, telling them that a loved one would never be coming home, just needed to sit and talk to someone outside their family. Most folk knew his wife was a POW too, which immediately made him seem more approachable. And then there were the young women – brazen, some of them were – who clearly had fallen for the deliciously handsome doctor who had been wounded doing his bit for King and country. She always made sure she popped into his study at least once or twice during their visits, the young madams. Girls were so much more forward these days, not like when she was a lassie.

'Right.' Nicholas stretched his shoulders and rotated his neck for a few moments. His body had been so hammered by the effects of the explosion that he was always full of aches and pains, but since he knew Abigail was alive he was just thankful he had made it. 'Let's get the first one in then, shall we, Mrs Wood?'

'Right you are, but you drink your tea and eat your cake first, Doctor.' It was an order, and Nicholas recognized it as such, especially because he knew Mrs Wood would stand over him until he obeyed. She did exactly that, talking about the weather and how her precious vegetables were doing – never anything about the war. She had once said to him that she wouldn't give Hitler the satisfaction of thinking that he had made her life revolve around the war, and although Nicholas didn't think the leader of the German people cared overly much about what a little old lady in a small market town near Durham did or didn't think, he admired the sentiment.

The tea drunk and the cake eaten, Gracie picked up the cup and saucer and plate. Fixing him with an eagle eye, she said, 'I've got a nice bit of brisket for tonight's meal, Doctor, and it's been pot-roasting slowly all day, just the way you like it. I shall expect you to clear your plate this evening, Lord Muck or no Lord Muck. All right?'

'All right, Mrs Wood.' Nicholas grinned. She'd made it her life's mission to try and get him as fat as a pig and would allow no upset to get in the way of that. He didn't know how she had come by the brisket because he was sure they'd already had more than their meat ration on the table this week, but there were certain things you didn't ask of Mrs Wood.

He watched the little figure as she bustled out of the room, shutting the door behind her, and not for the first time wondered how he would have coped over the last twelve months without her devotion and support. He had never really been mothered before and he found he liked it, he liked it very much indeed. And then, as invariably happened if he reflected on how fortunate his present circumstances were; the thought came that Abigail was probably enduring hell on earth while he took it easy as a country doctor. The gnawing ache in his heart that accompanied thoughts of her made him inwardly groan, and he was glad when the first patient knocked on his door, even if it was old Mr Davidson expecting him to lance the boil on his ancient sagging bottom...

Chapter Twenty-Seven

Abby and Delia sat either side of the bed of one of their fellow nurses who had succumbed to a bad attack of diarrhoea a few days before. Anyone who became sick in the camp had to trust to luck to get them better, and Hilda was no exception. She had reminded Abby of Kitty when she had first met her, having the same plump, heavy build and bright red hair, but now, after two years in the camp on Hong Kong island on starvation rations, Hilda was nothing but skin and bone like the rest of them. None of the women in the camp saw evidence of their monthly cycle any more – malnutrition had long since stopped them menstruating – and they all looked like walking scarecrows. Abby had just given Hilda a drink the women made from pine needles they collected and made into an infusion. It contained vitamin C which was missing from their diet of tiny amounts of boiled rice and a watery vegetable stew. Occasionally they were given a few cubes of meat or fish, but the daily ration of food to internees was kept deliberately low, causing starvation and encouraging the spread of tropical diseases.

The matron at the camp, a formidable career army nurse, had had battles with the Japanese over the prisoners' health from the first day. Their captors callously allowed large numbers of internees to sicken and die, even though their own medical personnel had huge quantities of the very drugs the prisoners needed. Apart from a small supply of Javgel septicide powder and a topical antiseptic, the nurses at the camp had nothing to work with, which was terribly frustrating.

The camp was a mixed-nationality one for both men and women, along with a number of children, and the sexes were allowed to mix freely. It comprised the whole of the peninsula and added up to several acres. Abby and Delia and the rest of the women from the hospital in the hotel on the mainland had been taken there after they had been working at the hospital for nearly eight months. It had been a blisteringly hot day in August and the Japanese had made them stand for hours in the compound when they had first arrived, counting them over and over again and coming up with a different number every time. It had been a relief for everyone concerned when at last the numbers tallied. As Delia had whispered to Abby, it was clear counting wasn't one of the guards' attributes.

This August was equally hot, and now Abby leaned forward and guided the cup holding cooled boiled water and the infusion of pine needles to Hilda's cracked lips as she said, 'Come on, finish it all. You've got dehydrated and you know you need to keep your fluids up.'

That said, it was becoming increasingly hard to swallow enough liquid in the last months as food rations had been cut still further and water had become more scarce. Prisoners made a little water go a long way when it came to washing and so on. There was no soap, but the male POWs made a substance called lye from wood ash and used it to wash their clothes with some success. They often distributed it to the women in exchange for them mending their shirts and trousers which were becoming increasingly ragged and thin. The seamstresses among the female POWs made threads for sewing by drawing them out of bed sheets.

Delia had struck up a romantic friendship with a Norwegian POW after she had nursed him back to health. Hans had nearly died from beriberi and had been at death's door for days, and was convinced it was only Delia's devotion that had saved him. He had made both women a pair of wooden clogs after their shoes wore out, the tarmac in the compound where the Japanese insisted on holding their relentless and unending roll calls being too hot to endure in the summer for bare feet.

Abby was glad Delia had found Hans. The love the two shared and which had come about gradually in the last months had healed something in her friend. Delia had told Hans about what had happened to her when the Japanese had invaded, and she said he had held her close while she had cried for a long, long time. Delia had been more at peace with herself since, and had regained some of her old bounce and optimism.

Abby gently took the cup from Hilda who had drifted off to sleep, and she and Delia crept out of the tiny room the three of them slept in, shutting the door behind them. Hilda was past the worst, thank goodness, but in the tropics a patient could go downhill rapidly just when it appeared they were making progress.

It had been stifling inside, but as the two women stepped out into the blazing sun it was beyond hot. Abby was always amazed at the fierceness of the heat. It was like stepping into an oven. In pre-war days, when the Europeans on the island had lived in light airy houses with fans and wide verandahs and umpteen servants to attend to their needs, the heat had probably been nothing more than a minor inconvenience most of the time. Now it was quite literally a killer.

Hans had been waiting outside for Delia and he smiled at the two women. Tall at six foot three inches, he weighed less than nine stone, but it was the same for them all. No one in the camp had an ounce of fat on them except for the Japanese.

As Hans and Delia wandered off hand in hand, walking with the slow steps of the malnourished, Abby made her way to the shade of a rubber tree and sat down on the sparse grass beneath it. The rainy season which began in May through to late July had finished a little while ago and the heat and humidity were unbearable. On top of this, the lack of food meant she was constantly tired, the ulcers in her mouth and the dry cracking skin all over her body meant infection was a worry, and her eyes were sore most of the time. She leaned back against the trunk of the tree and closed them against the fierce white light.

Out in the world beyond the camp, Nicholas was alive and breathing, she thought dreamily. The thrill of finding out he'd made it to England hadn't left her since the day she had got his letter. She'd been sobbing and incoherent as she'd read it, and everyone had gathered round her thinking she'd had bad news. She had been nearly as euphoric when she had read her grandfather's letter and known everything was all right between them all.

Since that time, her priority had been to keep as fit and well as she could. No easy task. A few of the POWs had Chinese friends or relatives still at liberty in Hong Kong, and they received a food parcel now and again. They were the lucky ones. In the last two years, the Japanese had allowed only a couple of Red Cross parcels into the camp, making a song and dance about their benevolence in the process. The parcels had contained tinned food, which was welcome, and sanitary towels which, due to the effects of malnutrition, were not needed.

Abby and other POWs grew their own crops in little plots in a corner of the camp using urine as a fertilizer. These included a form of runner bean, pumpkins and sweet potatoes, but the harvest was always tiny and never enough.

Abby opened her eyes and looked up into the blue sky. Nicholas might be looking up into an English sky right at this moment; she couldn't remember if it would be night or day in England but that didn't matter. A blue summer sky or a night one filled with stars, it was all the same. She just had to survive until the war was over and one day it had to end. If she could keep from getting sick, she would make it. She willed it every day.

Unlike some of the POW camps, the fact that this one was mixed had proved a blessing, because the men did more than their fair share of the heavy work like cutting the grass to create fuel so they could cook the rice they lived on. There had been no rapes or molestation of women within the camp either; the horrific massacres, torture and murders that had occurred when the Japanese had invaded the island were in the past. As long as the POWs paid due respect to the guards, bowing to them and obeying orders without question, they were left pretty much alone.

None the less, Abby reflected, for every prisoner at the camp the anguish of not knowing when – or if – they would be set free was the same. The memory of those terrible first days was at the back of everyone's minds, and who knew what the Japanese might do to them if the Allies won the war? Their captors were quite capable of slaughtering them all in an orgy of retribution for the Japanese people having lost 'face', before then committing suicide themselves – an 'honourable' death, in their opinion. Some of the guards took great delight in taunting them that the war would last at least another ten years. If it did, it was unlikely there would be any POWs left to either slaughter or set free if the rate at which men and women died here was anything to go by. The young VAD and her mother who had been working at Abby's hospital when the Japanese had invaded the island had both come to a sad end. After the mother had died a long and agonizing death due to a wound on one of her legs becoming gangrenous, her daughter had lost her mind. She had screamed and cried incessantly for weeks, and although Abby and the others had tried to hide her condition from the guards, it was inevitable they would eventually cotton on. When the disturbances became continuous they had taken her away to somewhere on the mainland, or so they said. Some of the POWs were doubtful if she ever left the island and instead was buried in an unmarked grave outside the camp.

Shutting her eyes again, Abby forced her mind away from thoughts of poor Constance and her mother. It was something she had learned to do in the last years; focus her mind on the positive and physical survival and feed her spirit with thoughts of Nicholas and life on the farm and England's green and pleasant land. It didn't always work, but this was encouraged wholeheartedly by the matron who often gave the nurses in the camp pep talks, pointing out it was noticeable that when POWs became ill, it was those who believed they would get better who were more likely to recover. And in spite of their constant exhaustion and wasted bodies, Abby and Delia and many others found that keeping busy helped. Apart from growing crops in their little plots, the POWs put lectures and concerts and plays on to entertain each other. Those with a gift for storytelling had evenings when they spoke for two hours or more. The fact that the camp had been a boys' school before the war had meant certain things could be utilized by the POWs, and the piano in the hall was in excellent working order. They had a professional pianist among the POWs and he had organized musical soirées to rival any in high society. Even some of the guards had been known to form part of the audience.

Because of the tropical heat and humidity, it had been found that any exertion in the day soon took its toll on bodies ill from recurrent malaria, fatigue and other problems. Entertainments were therefore put on at night, but then the mosquitoes and other insects were out in number. Diphtheria and tuberculosis were feared everywhere, but nowhere more than in the tropics where the diseases progressed with lightning rapidity. Heat and humidity acted as incubators for disease and infection, and although Abby and the other nurses were forever encouraging the POWs to stay as active and bright as they could, they also warned them that sufficient rest and hydration were essential. The first was easier to come by than the second, Abby thought now, licking her dry lips and thinking longingly of what it would be like to swallow icy cold water again. Any water they had was always tepid. So many things she had taken for granted before the war...

Abby stretched her aching legs, hoping the vicious muscle cramps that were a part of daily life due to the lack of salt in their meagre diet wouldn't make themselves known. Sometimes they were so severe she would be writhing in agony for long painful minutes, and cramp was a regular cause of fainting among the POWs when the pain became too much for their feeble bodies.

The next moment she was aware of someone sitting down beside her and opened her eyes to see one of Hans's pals, a young, good-looking Norwegian man who had made it plain in the early days of their meeting that he would like their relationship to go further than friendship. When she had explained she was married and more than that, very much in love with her husband, he had accepted the rebuff good-naturedly and settled for friendship after all. Bright blue eyes smiled at her from a face that was still handsome in spite of its skeletal thinness.

Abby smiled back. There was something very endearing about Kurt, not least his determined optimism that the Allies would soon win the war, their captors would set them free unharmed and they'd all be home within a month or two. The fact that he had been saying the same thing for the whole time Abby had known him in no way detracted from the lift in her spirit she always felt when she was in his company.

'Heard the latest?' Kurt raked back his thick mop of blond hair as he spoke. 'US bombers have reached the Japanese mainland. Peter told me.' Peter was a British journalist who had married a Chinese woman and had been living in Hong Kong when it was invaded. He could speak fluent Japanese as well as a number of other languages, and was one of the fortunate POWs who had close Chinese friends still at liberty on the island who provided him with regular food parcels and Japanese newspapers. 'Won't be long before it's all over now, you'll see.'

Ignoring what he'd said, Abby looked more closely at her friend. His voice was hoarse and he appeared unwell to her trained eye. 'What's the matter? You're feeling ill, aren't you, I can tell.'

'I'm going down with a cold, that's all, funny throat and bad head. Did you hear what I said, Abby? About the bombers? We're taking the fight to them now for the first time and you can bet the swines won't like that. And the Germans are being driven out of Normandy at last. The tide is turning and fast.'

'When did you first start to feel off colour?'

'Abby, stop being a nurse for two minutes and listen to what I'm saying.'

'Kurt, answer me. When did you begin to feel ill?'

He shrugged. 'I'm not sure but don't worry about it, it'll pass.' He coughed, and then wiped his nose with a piece of rag from his pocket. 'It's just a cold.'

'Yes, you said.' She reached out and felt his forehead; he was burning up. 'Can you swallow OK?'

'I've told you, my throat's sore.'

'So that's a no.'

She put her hands either side of his neck and he grinned at her. 'Hey, not out here in the open. If you want to get cosy we can go back to my place for a glass of champagne.'

This was no joking matter; his lymph nodes were enlarged and if she wasn't mistaken he was already beginning to show signs of a swollen neck due to diphtheria. Of course it could be an upper-respiratory infection but somehow she thought not. She had always trusted her sixth sense where patients were concerned, and now she said, 'Kurt, you're sick, really sick. We need to get you over to the hospital.'

'For a cold? Come on, Abby, I'll be a laughing stock.'

'It's not a cold. At the very least it's a severe respiratory infection but I'm not going to argue with you. You are coming with me now.'

She stood up, holding out her hand, and after a

moment he took it, letting her pull him up. He swayed slightly, muttering, 'Damn heat,' but she was very much afraid it wasn't the heat or humidity causing him to feel weak.

He wouldn't let her assist him as they walked to the camp hospital but by the time she had him inside his breathing was laboured. She wasn't due to start her shift for a couple of hours, but she went straight to the matron and told her of her fears, requesting that Kurt be put in the nearest thing to isolation they could manage with their limited space and resources. Matron Fraser didn't waste time asking questions but with Abby on her heels went to inspect the patient herself. After a thorough examination, Kurt was whipped into a side room that had been harbouring a patient dying of kidney failure who was unceremoniously moved onto the main ward.

'You are right, Nurse.' The matron took a deep breath. A diphtheria epidemic in prison-camp conditions, with no drugs to treat it and only the most primitive disinfecting facilities, could be a major catastrophe. In the past, she had seen doctors perform tracheotomies more than once, but that had been in the sterile confines of a theatre and under anaesthetic. Even then it was a risky procedure, but if diphtheria hit with a vengeance it was certain a number of patients would suffocate to death if a passage wasn't opened into their windpipe, and that was besides heart and kidney damage leading to death if the toxin was absorbed into the bloodstream. 'We need to make masks for ourselves whilst dealing with this patient. See to it, would you? I'm going to see

Major Fushida to ask him to release the antitoxin we need. I know the Japanese have a plentiful supply of it locked away for their use.'

The matron wasn't away long and she merely shook her head at Abby as she walked back into the ward.

In an effort to stop the disease sweeping through their numbers, the matron asked the rest of the members of Kurt's hut, along with anyone he had been in close contact with, to come into the hospital whereupon they were put in a separate section from the other patients. It wasn't ideal, but it was the best they could do.

By the next day, Kurt was gasping for each breath as the thick grey coating from dead tissue caused by the toxin that is produced by the bacteria built up over the nasal tissues, tonsils, voice box and throat.

The matron went to see Major Fushida once more, asking that a doctor be brought in from the officers' camp and, again, that the antitoxin be released. The doctor was brought to the camp two days later by which time Kurt was beyond his help. The request for the antitoxin was refused.

Abby had insisted on sitting with Kurt in his last hours. She talked to him of his home in Norway that he had told her so much about in the past, of the clean pure air, the mountains, the deep valleys and the sparkling fjords that worked their way between high cliffs and were as blue and clear as the sky above. She spoke of the sister he adored and his three young nephews, reminding him of the funny things they had said and done. She held his hand tight as he fought for breath, feeling her heart break at his frantic eyes and contorted face that was black with the effort of getting air past the mass of tissue constricting his throat. And in her mind she cursed the war, Hitler, the Japanese and men's quest for power.

Delia came to relieve her several times but Abby wouldn't leave Kurt, knowing he wanted her there, and Delia was beside herself as it was, worried to death that Hans would fall victim to the disease next. All the nurses knew that patients who were fit and healthy before they caught diphtheria could still lose the fight against the toxins that did such vicious harm to the body, and the POWs were anything but that. And they feared for the smallest and most cherished group of prisoners, the children. Surprisingly, the children in the camp were very resilient on the whole, partly because they were encased in a protective and altruistic network by male and female POWs alike. It was an unspoken rule that children ate first, even if it meant the adults going without, and it mattered not a jot if the POWs were related to the little ones.

Kurt died early in the morning three days after Abby had brought him to the hospital. Abby forever remembered it as one of the worst experiences of her life. After it was over, she stroked his brow, whispering, 'You're home now, and if there is any justice, heaven will be full of those mountains and fjords, and you're in the midst of them right now, my brave boy. You're out of here, just like you said you would be...'

Within the week all the members of Kurt's hut,

including Delia's Hans, were fighting the disease, but with their weak immune systems and skeletal bodies it wasn't much of a fight. Delia was frantic; she had lost John and now it seemed she was going to lose Hans too. The doctor conducted several traumatic tracheotomies without anaesthetic and without the guards' knowledge, bringing the required instruments into the hospital hidden in his socks. It was a grim time. A number of the POWs died. Four lived, one of whom was Hans, but they were terribly frail and each day the nurses feared they would develop complications that would finish them off. But it seemed as though the quick response of isolating Kurt and then his close friends had paid off, because there were no new cases for five days. And then on the evening of the fifth day a distraught mother brought her young child to the hospital. She was a Norwegian woman who had been married to a British businessman, and they had had a sumptuous house on the island before the invasion. Her husband had been killed when a shell had wrecked their home but she and her little girl had escaped unhurt.

Abby was on duty when Janna and her child came in, and on questioning the woman she discovered Kurt and some of the other Norwegian POWs had looked out for them, slipping them extra rations whenever they could, whittling little wooden dolls for the child and playing with her on occasion. And now she was sick and it bore all the signs of diphtheria. Little Kristine was running a fever and floppy in her mother's arms, and the five-year-old's neck was swollen. The child, quite naturally, played with other children in the camp, and owing to the highly infectious character of the disease would almost certainly have passed it on to other little ones.

After getting Kristine settled in bed with her mother sitting beside her, Abby stood for some minutes wondering what to do. They needed the antitoxin medication more than ever. Matron Fraser had gone to see the major every day but he wouldn't budge, added to which the matron was currently ill herself and confined to bed. But they needed to get the medication into Kristine *now*, tonight, if the child was going to have any chance at all, along with any of her friends or their families who were beginning to show symptoms. It would be against camp procedure for a lowly nurse to ask to see the major, and she would be risking punishment, but that couldn't be helped.

Her mind made up, Abby went and found Delia who was sitting by Hans's bed holding his hand, and whispered what she was going to do. Then, her heart in her mouth, she left the hospital.

Five minutes later she was standing in front of Major Fushida. Abby knew this officer was not as bad as some of the other camp commandants. They had heard vile and gruesome stories from some of the POWs who had been transferred here of what they'd endured elsewhere, but nevertheless Major Fushida was every inch a Japanese officer with a mindset as different from the Europeans as chalk from cheese. But the Japanese did like children. This had become apparent early on in the camp's life, and many POWs suspected it was because the camp contained little ones that they were, on the whole, treated less harshly. As Abby looked into the flat hard face in front of her she sincerely hoped that was true.

She had bowed nearly to the floor when she had first entered the room, hoping to get off on the right foot, and now she began with a lie as she said, 'The matron sends her apologies for not coming herself but she is ill and confined to bed, Major Fushida. Do I have your permission to proceed further?'

It was overtly servile and ingratiating, but if it saved children's lives, it was worth it.

Major Fushida looked at the woman in front of him intently. He had noticed her before on more than one occasion when he had inspected the camp hospital, not just because she was beautiful but because of the silvery scars on one side of face. Lifting his hand to his own face, he said, 'How did it happen?'

Taken aback, Abby found herself flushing. 'I was nursing the troops at Dunkirk when I was injured myself,' she said shortly, before quickly adding, 'sir.'

The major nodded slowly. 'And this did not prevent you coming to Hong Kong?'

'Of course not. I'm a Queen Alexandra nurse, Major Fushida, I go where I am needed.'

Again the major nodded. 'Like your famous Florence Nightingale, the Lady with the Lamp. You see, I know of your country's history even though you know little of mine. The Japanese are an educated and cultured people.'

Abby didn't think it wise to point out that

403

Florence Nightingale was not a QA, but then there was no doubt that this formidable woman's intellect, energy and vision had given existence to the QAIMNS at the beginning of the century, so she supposed the major was right in a way. She couldn't think of an answer to give and so she bowed deeply again.

'I attended one of your universities in my youth. Does that surprise you?'

'Not at all, Major Fushida,' Abby lied. But it did explain his command of the English language.

'It was a pleasant time, but one which convinced me that the Western nations have no sense of honour or pride.'

He stared at her, obviously expecting a reply, and this time Abby neither spoke nor bowed.

'You disagree with me?'

'I do not presume to venture an opinion, Major Fushida.'

The officer settled back in his chair. 'This is a good reply. An intelligent reply. The "Onna Daigaku: The Whole Duty of Women" is a guide for all Japanese men – have you heard of this?'

'No, I have not.'

'It is as I say, you know little of my country or our ancient traditions. You English are an arrogant people, believing only that the Japanese nation is inferior. Oh, yes, I know this personally myself from the time I spent in your country. But we have shown you otherwise and this is a good thing.' He paused. 'The guide teaches why all Japanese men are superior to women. Women have five fundamental character flaws that beset their minds – those of indocility, discontent, slander, jealousy and silliness. Without doubt, the guide teaches, these faults exist in seven or eight out of every ten women, and it is from these that stems the inferiority of the female sex.'

Again Abby wondered what on earth he expected her reply to be. She had no wish to be handed over to the dreaded Kempeitai who every POW knew were the equivalent of the German Gestapo, but did he really think she could agree with him? Carefully she said, 'And what of men, Major Fushida? Does the guide list their character flaws?'

The bullet eyes looked hard at her. The major was clearly trying to work out if she was being insolent. Then he seemed to make up his mind to take her words at face value. 'Men have no character flaws. Their destiny, without exception, is that of being loyal subjects of the Emperor. Emperor Hirohito is a direct descendant of the sun goddess Amaterasu who created the Japanese islands in all their beauty and magnificence. There is no greater honour than dying for the Emperor. It is the ultimate glory and highest expression of worship. Male children from the age of six are taught the ways of a warrior, and experience the greatest joy and satisfaction in following the commands of their Emperor. In Japanese society, male and female children grow up knowing their rightful place.'

Seizing the opportunity Abby bowed again in acknowledgement of the major, before straightening and saying, 'It is about children, the children under your care and command in the camp, that I wish to speak to you, Major Fushida.'

'Then speak.'

'As you know we have had a diphtheria outbreak which we hoped had been contained. Un-
fortunately in the last hour a child has been
brought in suffering the first stages of the disease.'

'You are saying you failed in your duty?'

Warning herself not to let the slightest inflection
of her anger colour her voice, Abby said calmly,
'Diphtheria is a communicable bacterial disease,
Major Fushida, and most commonly spread when
someone ingests or inhales the cough or sneeze
droplets from an infected person. Symptoms can
occur as late as ten days following infection so
there was always a high chance the outbreak
could not be controlled as we would have liked.'

The flat face was impassive. 'You give me excuses.'

'I give you the facts, sir.'

He had leaned back in his chair as he sat surveying her; now he straightened, his eyes narrowing.
'My Japanese nurses would not try and justify
their shortcomings.'

'Forgive me, Major Fushida, but your Japanese
nurses would not need to – they would have
antitoxin to administer to their patients.'

'Ah...' He slapped his small hands on the desk
in front of him. 'Now we have it. You have come
with yet another request for what I have already
denied.'

'You denied it for men and women, Major
Fushida. I am asking that this outbreak be treated
and stopped for the sake of the children in the
camp. The little girl I spoke about has friends that
she has played with and almost certainly will be

406

infected. We can get a list of those concerned and anyone who has had close contact with them and again, try and contain the disease, but without the antitoxin the children will die. It is as simple as that. And if the disease begins to spread, who knows where it will end? I am asking for the children, Major, little ones who have been caught up in a conflict not of their making.'

'The children of enemies of our glorious Emperor.'

'But still children.' She was getting nowhere; she could see in his face he was about to tell her to get out. Throwing caution to the wind, she spoke from the heart. 'Have you got children, Major Fushida? Little ones that thrilled your heart when they were born and for whom you would sacrifice your life if it was necessary? If the position was reversed and it was *your* children being held captive in a POW camp, wouldn't you want them to be treated with tenderness and compassion? Wouldn't you expect it as their right? Please, I'm begging you. You have the ability to stop this outbreak before it becomes an epidemic simply by releasing the medication we need.'

She stopped as he jumped to his feet, one hand on the pistol in his belt. For what seemed an endless time they stared at each other. Expecting each moment to be her last, or for him to bark orders to the guard stationed at the door behind her to take her away and see to it she was transported to the Kempeitai, she felt her knees nearly give way when instead he removed his hand from the gun and sat down once more. A long silence followed. The last days had taken every ounce of her strength and now she felt herself swaying with a mixture of exhaustion and despair.

Why had she even tried to appeal to his better side? she asked herself wearily. He didn't have one. None of them did. They were without normal feelings and emotions. But the children, little Kristine and the others. What were they going to do? She couldn't bear seeing children die the way Kurt had.

She was so lost in misery she visibly jumped when Major Fushida stood up again, walking round his desk. 'Follow me.' He spoke an order to the guard in his native tongue and the man sprang to open the door for his commanding officer, standing aside for the major and Abby to leave the room whereupon he shut the door and followed behind them.

Abby had no idea where the major was leading her as they crossed the compound, wondering if she was going to disappear, like the poor young VAD who had lost her mind. It was only as they approached a building some distance away that hope flared.

The guard outside the medical store bowed and then stood aside as the major barked some words in Japanese. The major unlocked the door with a key from the bunch he had brought with him and flung it open, marching inside. Abby followed hesitantly, not knowing if she should or not.

'It is fortunate for the children of the camp that you are one of the two out of every ten women that the Onna Daigaku speaks of,' Major Fushida said drily, handing Abby a box containing a supply of the precious antitoxin.

Trying to hide her amazement, Abby bowed and took the box in her arms, stuttering her thanks. For a moment, just a moment, she thought she saw a gleam of amusement in the oriental eyes, and then the major brushed past her.

Once outside, he locked the door again and strode off into the night, the guard at his heels, and Abby followed slowly, unable to believe he had given her what she had asked for. For a moment she paused, staring up at the immense beauty of the tropical sky as she murmured, 'Thank you, thank you, God.' Blackout conditions prevented the usual light pollution and the stars were radiant in their clearly marked constellations. Best of all, there was no barbed wire or bamboo fencing in the sky, just a God-given magnificence that took her breath away.

She knew this moment couldn't last. By the time she got back to the hospital and the enormity of the task in front of them overwhelmed her she would be in the thick of it once more, but just for a second or two she felt as free as a bird flying in the heavens and it was food to her soul.

Chapter Twenty-Eight

It was a full ten months since the diphtheria outbreak, which had been mostly contained thanks to the antitoxin. However, since that time conditions in the camp had got radically worse. Abby wouldn't have imagined the Japanese could cut the food rations further, but cut them they had, along with the water allowance. Besides the constant thirst and dehydration, the feeling that they could never get themselves clean was a trial to most of the women and deeply demoralizing.

Malnutrition was a killer, along with beriberi, dysentery, malaria and other tropical diseases and more and more prisoners were dying every day. Poor sewerage was another cause of disease, and many of the POWs had open sores on their ankles and legs from infected cuts, and the bacteria they housed caused great skin ulcers. Abby and her colleagues did their best to relieve their patients' suffering, washing out the ulcers with the precious supply of water and limited disinfectant the Japanese gave them, and then bandaging the raw flesh with strips of linen taken from bed sheets, but they knew they were fighting a losing battle. Without the proper medicines to treat the sick, survival rates were very low. And the nurses themselves were often ill now and very weak from continuing with their work despite their physical frailty.

Since before Christmas, the Japanese had suddenly clamped down to prevent any communication at all with the world beyond the camp. None of the POWs' Chinese friends from the main land were allowed to bring food parcels, newspapers or approach the camp, and the penalty for disobedience was the dreaded Kempeitai. Abby and the others hoped this was due to the fact that the Allies were winning the war and the Japanese were getting worried, but that in itself was a scary prospect. No one knew how their captors would react if Japan was forced to surrender, but with the Japanese obsession for 'face' they feared the worst.

Certainly the guards' callous indifference to the POWs' pain and misery was relentless, and all the men and women in the camp viewed their captors as inhuman, although the Japanese were slightly more lenient to the children. Even with the little ones, however, the necessary medicines were not forthcoming and many times Abby reflected on the miracle that had occurred when Major Fushida had released the diphtheria antitoxin. Matron Fraser still continued without success to ask him for a portion of the medical supplies that were stored for Japanese use, and now, with the POWs having become walking skeletons, beriberi was the worst killer.

There were two types of the disease, dry and wet. With the dry, Abby's patients just shrivelled up and wasted away, but it was the wet kind that was more deadly. The male POWs succumbed to the wet type more than the women because they needed more protein, and sometimes Abby had seen a man admitted to the hospital one day looking as normal as anyone could look given the conditions, and then the next day the same individual could be bloated like a puffer fish, his face, hands and legs several times their normal size. Such patients died quickly with heart failure.

But maybe they were the lucky ones, Abby reflected, as she walked into the camp hospital for her shift, making for the bed where Hilda was lying. Contrary to what they had hoped, their fellow nurse had never really recovered from the severe bout of diarrhoea that had had her bedridden the year before. It had weakened her severely, and Hilda had been battling beriberi for some time. Her legs had become so swollen from oedema that she could no longer walk. Like most of the nursing staff, Hilda hadn't submitted gracefully to becoming a patient, even though she had had no choice in the matter. Every few hours, Abby or one of the other nurses had to turn their friend over by gripping her by her hip bone. Hilda was so thin and malnourished that there was no flesh beneath her skin and bed sores were a real problem. It was fairly easy to turn her – she was so emaciated and underweight that it was only her legs that were heavy, and her hip bones were like handles sticking up underneath the thin layer of skin covering them. Every time Abby handled Hilda she inwardly raged against the cruelty of their captors. By rights Hilda was a big buxom lass like Kitty, and instead she was a caricature of a woman.

But then they all were, Abby thought, forcing a smile as she reached her friend's bedside. Every one of the medical staff now shuffled slowly like old women as they nursed their patients, and when she bent over to see to someone's needs it was all she could do to straighten up again for the grinding ache and pains in her back.

Abby was pleased to see Hilda looking brighter than when she had left her friend the day before, and the reason for this became apparent when Hilda whispered, 'Have you heard the latest rumour, Abby? They are saying Germany has surrendered. Hitler's lost the war.'

Abby had heard such a story, but then there was

always some rumour or other doing the rounds in the camp. Since Major Fushida had forbidden any contact with those outside the camp the stories had got more extreme too. Nevertheless, Abby and the medical staff as a whole encouraged such gossip. They had watched the death rate of the POWs double in the last months, and sometimes the only difference between those patients who died and those who lived was their mental resilience and optimism. The patients who gave up in spirit invariably lost the will to fight to get better – it was as simple as that – and so anything that gave them a glimmer of hope was welcome. It didn't really matter if it was bona fide or not.

Pulling back the thin, threadbare sheet covering Hilda, Abby carefully manipulated her friend on to her other side as she said, 'I've heard it, yes. It would be wonderful if it's true, wouldn't it.'

'I think this time it might be. You know that old Chinese man who delivers the rice to the camp? He managed to slip a note to one of the POWs which was incredibly brave of him, all things considered. Anyway, Geraldine Henderson was admitted last night with chronic malaria, and you know she can speak and read Chinese? Well, she told Delia who was on duty that she saw and read the note herself when it was passed round, so this is first-hand, if you know what I mean.'

Abby stared at Hilda as a surge of hope and excitement raced through her. After their ordeal at the hands of the Japanese soldiers, Delia and Geraldine had become good friends and as a consequence Abby had got to know Geraldine well too. The young British woman was not the

413

sort to exaggerate or make up stories. If she said she had read the note, she had.

'Geraldine said the note was very specific. The Germans surrendered in May and Hitler is dead. And the Allies are stepping up the attacks on Japan itself. You know that Peter can speak Japanese and he eavesdrops on the guards when he can? Well, he's saying the guards are getting worried amongst themselves. Their officers keep them in the dark, apparently, and they're expected to just unquestionably follow orders, but they've heard rumours too.'

Abby nodded. The normally inscrutable and impassive guards had been edgy recently, everyone had noticed, which had further fed the talk about the war not going well for Japan.

'The thing is, Abby' – Hilda beckoned for her to bend down closer as she whispered – 'you know what the Japanese are like. Even if they're beaten, they'll never surrender, will they? This bushido code of conduct they all believe in says it's better for them to commit hara-kiri than to suffer the shame of defeat, so where does that leave us? If they're going to kill themselves they'll kill us first, won't they? It's obvious.'

Abby thought exactly the same but Hilda was a patient first and fellow nurse second, so she said, 'Not necessarily. The officers might think of themselves as warriors and follow bushido, but from what I can see most of the guards are just ordinary Japanese men who became soldiers when war broke out. They might delight in lording it over us because they've got this inferiority thing about Europeans looking down on them,

414

but as for actually killing themselves, I'm not so sure. And even the most stupid of the guards know that if Japan does surrender and then the Allies find out they've executed all the POWs in the camp, their lives will be forfeit.'

Hilda sank back on the bed; just the effort of talking had exhausted her. 'I hope you're right.'

So did Abby, but she wouldn't have placed money on it. The trouble was, the Japanese mind-set was so fundamentally different, and so extreme in certain areas, that she didn't know which way things would go.

She straightened up, the muscles in her back threatening to tear apart, smiling as she said softly, 'Of course I'm right – I'm a QA, aren't I? Now have a nap and I'll bring you something to eat shortly.'

And that was right, she *was* a QA, she told herself as she glanced round the ward. She couldn't predict or change what the guards would do in the event of Japan being defeated; all she could do was the job she was trained for and moreover good at, and that was caring for her patients to the best of her ability and with the limited resources at hand. Worrying about whether she would ever see Nicholas again, or how she would die if the Japanese decided to butcher all of them was weakening, and she couldn't afford such an indulgence.

She and Delia and the rest of the medical staff had to be a solid, strong unit for the sake of the weak and ill and vulnerable; it wasn't bravery or heroism, it was simply what was expected. Especially with the patients dearest to her heart, those that were called 'battle fatigue' cases. There were a couple of men in the hospital at the moment suffering with this owing to a massive explosion they'd all heard somewhere outside the camp when a plane had crashed, whether one of theirs or an enemy plane no one was sure. The men's pals had brought the two to the hospital, explaining that when the explosion had occurred the men had started digging desperately at the ground with their hands, for all the world like animals looking for shelter underground. The patients' friends were worried the guards would incarcerate them in one of the 'sweat boxes' – little huts where prisoners were kept without food or water after misdemeanours – if they came across them like this, as the men would be oblivious to orders or threats by their captors when they were gripped by what their pals called 'the horrors'.

And they were the horrors all right, Abby thought, a mental picture of her father's face on that Christmas Eve so long ago flashing onto the screen of her mind. Shattered nerves were every bit as horrific as shattered bodies.

She breathed deeply, willing away the memory along with her exhaustion and aches and pains. She had a job to do and she needed to get on with it…

Chapter Twenty-Nine

Nicholas sat listening to the wireless, hardly able to believe what he was hearing. Gracie, standing at his shoulder, was transfixed too. For the second time, only three days after an atomic bomb had vaporized the Japanese city of Hiroshima, another bomb had fallen on Nagasaki, the shipbuilding centre on the Japanese island of Kyushu. Smoke and dust clouds completely covered the town, it was reported, and rose five miles high in a giant mushroom-shaped cloud. Both raids were carried out by the US Army Air Forces' Superfortress aircraft, and President Truman had delivered a fresh warning in the wake of them that if Japan did not surrender, atomic bombs would be dropped on her war industries. He had already threatened a 'rain of ruin from the air, the like of which has never been seen on this earth'.

'By, lad, you can't take it in, can you.' Gracie plonked herself down in the armchair opposite Nicholas. 'All them folk gone in the blink of an eye.'

Nicholas nodded but didn't speak. In truth he didn't know how he felt, but if this new wonder weapon created by British and American scientists could end the war with Japan, then he was for it. Not the death of women and children, not that, but it had been increasingly clear in recent months that Japan would never surrender and Allied

417

POWs would never be coming home unless something extreme was done. But this? It was beyond comprehension, and he, for one, thanked God that he hadn't been asked to make the sort of decision Churchill and Truman had faced.

'Do you think this second bomb will do it? Do you think this Emperor fella will give in now? He must know he's beaten, mustn't he?'

'I hope so.' In July the Allies had told Japan to surrender or face 'prompt and utter destruction' but that had been ignored, Nicholas thought, along with other calls for the end of the war. But this, this was different. The Allies had made it clear they would show as little mercy as the Japanese, and with action rather than words. Now that the bombs had been dropped, more facts were coming into the public domain. It appeared the secret project, which had involved 100,000 workers, had taken years to bring to completion. How the Americans had kept the whole enterprise under wraps, Nicholas couldn't imagine, but although it had involved three new cities being built with factories covering several square miles, the vast majority of the workers hadn't known what they were making.

Nicholas shook his head to himself as Gracie bustled off to make a pot of tea, her panacea for any event, great or small. What would those workers think now? And then he answered the question. If any of them had loved ones who were prisoners of the Japanese they'd consider it a job well done, as did he.

The newsreader talked on, and as Nicholas listened he became more amazed that there had been no leak of information to the enemy, while the 'Manhattan Project' had been ongoing. It had cost two billion dollars, a sum of money Nicholas couldn't imagine, and central to the undertaking had been the new city of Los Alamos in the New Mexico desert. It was here the international team of scientists had carried out their research, and designed and built the most devastating weapon of all time. In addition, two gigantic factories, one in Tennessee and one in Washington, had produced materials for the bomb. The scientists were not prepared to reveal their exact nature, but it was known uranium was involved.

Nicholas leaned forward and switched off the wireless, his head spinning from both the content of what he had heard and what it might mean for Abby. Relieved though he had been in May when peace had come to a battered Europe at last, he had been unable to celebrate with Abby still in the hands of the Japanese. The blaze of multi-coloured flags, fireworks and floodlights, the wild joy that most of the nation had felt that had expressed itself in kissing and hugging strangers, dancing, blowing whistles, throwing confetti and forming impromptu parades, had left him cold. He had tried to join in, contributing to the victory tea that the women had organized in his particular street and putting in an appearance for a while, but after the bairns had had their meal and the dancing had begun, with 'hokey-cokey' and other exuberant expressions of unrestrained gaity, he had quietly slipped away.

Gracie had understood and he dared say others did too, but whether they did or they didn't, he didn't really care. He had heard nothing from Abby for over eighteen months. He didn't know if she was dead or alive, and if it was the latter, what sort of a state she would be in. They had heard such terrible, wicked, unbelievable things, things that were beyond the comprehension of the average Englishman. QAs were military nurses, and yet they had been raped, murdered, tortured, starved, shot at and shipwrecked in the Far East where the enemy had made no allowance for their officer status.

He ran a hand over his face; thinking about what she might have gone through always made him feel ill. These bombs were fearsome things but if it prevented the deaths of tens of thousands of Allied troops and POWs at the hands of the Japanese, then so be it. He was a doctor and he believed in the sanctity of life one hundred per cent, but this war had to end. Whether Emperor Hirohito genuinely believed himself to be a god like the Japanese people did, Nicholas didn't know, but one thing was for sure. He had as inflated an idea of his own importance and supremacy as Hitler had had. He had sanctioned atrocities in both China and the Far East as a whole, beyond the comprehension of the normal mind, just like Hitler and the Nazis. The world had already been numbed by the horrors of the German death camps, but it was rumoured that equal cruelty had been shown by Japanese captors to Allied prisoners of war. And Abby was one of them. And John and Delia and the rest of his friends and colleagues – those who had survived, at least.

The August day was a hot one but it wasn't the

weather that caused the perspiration to bead on his brow and top lip. He dug a handkerchief out of his pocket and was mopping his face when Gracie came in with a cup of tea. She took one look at Nicholas and came immediately to his side. 'Drink this.' She put the cup in his hand and pretended not to notice how it was shaking. 'Come on, drink up. This is the end of it, lad, you mark my words. Even them devils will give up now. And I tell you something else, your lass will be coming home, I feel it in me water, I do straight. She's all right and she'll be coming home.'

'I hope so, Mrs Wood.' He was cursing himself for letting the weakness come over him again. He wanted to be strong in mind and body, a proper man, and he didn't feel like that a lot of the time.

He forced himself to drink the hot sweet tea and found it did help. The tremors under control, he looked up into the anxious little face staring down at him. 'I'm all right, Mrs Wood,' he said softly. 'Really.'

He was far from all right, and Gracie feared that if this wife of his didn't come home then he never would fully recover from what ailed him. Hiding her thoughts with a cheerful bob of her head, she said, 'That's the ticket, lad. Now I've got a nice bit of fish for our tea with a baked jam roll to follow, so don't you let the evening surgery go on too long. I saw old Mr Davidson is here again and there's nowt wrong with him now.'

Very gently, Nicholas said, 'He's grieving, Mrs Wood.' Elias Davidson had lost all his three sons in the war and his wife hadn't been able to cope with the loss. She had just faded away, leaving

421

Elias on his own with a houseful of memories of happier times and a broken heart. It was true that the boils that afflicted the old man now and again had cleared for the time being, but even when they had been at their worst it hadn't been that which had brought Elias to the surgery. It was being able to chat to Nicholas and pour out his heart in a way Elias would never have dreamed of doing with any of his neighbours or pals, for fear of being talked about. But he trusted the young 'fellow me lad' as he called Nicholas, trusted and liked him, and he knew anything he said to his GP would be treated with the strictest confidence.

Gracie sniffed. She felt sorry for Elias but not when the old man hogged more time than he should and made Nicholas late for his tea; a regular occurrence. Glancing at the small watch pinned on the lapel of her crisp white blouse, she said, 'I'll show your first patient in in five minutes, and mind you eat them two biscuits in your saucer. You didn't finish your midday meal and you're as thin as a lath as it is. You don't want to be poorly for when your wife comes home, now, do you?'

So saying she bustled out of the room, leaving the faint scent of the lavender water she favoured behind her.

He prayed to God Abby *would* be coming home. However ill, however frail, however broken, he wanted her home where he could take care of her and make her well. And he *would* make her well; he would devote his life to it.

He glanced at the newspaper on his desk that he

422

had been reading earlier that day. How many other husbands and wives and relations had thought that about their loved ones who had been murdered in the German concentration camps? There was an article in the paper reporting that German civilians were being taken on forced visits to the Nazi death camps, to view for themselves the hideous evidence of mass extermination which many apparently were refusing to accept ever took place.

Coachloads were being taken daily to the former camps to see the gas chambers, which the SS guards, with cruel euphemism, had called 'bath houses', and the ovens, in which hundreds of thousands of victims were cremated, many of them while they were still alive. And the Japanese camps would be no better, perhaps worse.

He had wanted to stop reading the report at that point. Just as he wanted to turn off the wireless when the newsreader spoke of things he found it hard to listen to, because he always related such horrors to Abby and what she might be suffering; but it was as though some inner force drove him on to torture himself. The article had described how grim-faced Allied soldiers had pointed out monstrous heaps of human ashes, unburned bones, hair shorn from women prisoners and toys taken from children before they were herded to their deaths. It related the details of the torture equipment the sadistic SS guards had used on their helpless captives, and the 'sound machine' which had been built to hide the noise of human screams.

And all the time, with many of those who had been so horribly murdered, there had been loved ones thinking they would come home, or at least hoping for the best, just as he was doing. But those men, women and children, babies some of them, *wouldn't* return. Some of them had been dead for a long time. And while he had been here in England, drinking his nice cups of tea and eating three meals a day and sleeping in a soft bed, Abby might have died and he didn't know. Damn it, he didn't know. He had left her, his darling, his beloved, his precious wife whom he'd promised before God to cherish and protect, he had left her in the hands of those inhuman fiends. Hell, he couldn't bear it.

Rising to his feet, he flung open the window and gulped in great gasps of the fresh air. Birds were singing in the trees bordering the garden, the sky was as blue as cornflowers and the sun was hot, but none of it registered on his senses for a few moments.

What would he do if she didn't come home? Lose his mind, most likely. Descend into a spiral of darkness that would draw him for ever down, sucking all the life and will out of him.

He opened his eyes, which had been shut, as the tweet-tweet of a bird penetrated the blackness. Two baby robins, still small and speckled and clearly just out of the nest, were dancing round one of their parents who was standing with a worm dangling out of its mouth. The wide-open gapes of the fledglings as they vied with each other for the meal, and the determination in their tiny feathered bodies, brought a reluctant smile to Nicholas's mouth. Life was going on. In spite of the last six years and the unimaginable death and destruction that had resulted when madmen had tried to take over the world, life was going on. He had to do exactly what he told his patients to do, and take each day one at a time, minute by minute, hour by hour. Those birds had got it right. It was the only way to survive.

He left the window on the latch, where a warm breeze sent the scents of summer into the room, and sat down at his desk again. Finishing the tea, he ate the two biscuits and mentally composed himself for the couple of hours ahead, with his list of patients and their varying complaints.

One day at a time. It really was the only way.

Chapter Thirty

'What on earth's that hullabaloo?' Hilda struggled to sit up in bed, her face turning white as the ruckus from outside the building filtered into the hospital.

'I don't know.' Abby had only just come on duty and had been helping Hilda get more comfortable. The heat and humidity always seemed more unbearable in August after the rainy season had finished.

For some days now, the guards had seemed visibly upset. The POW grapevine, via good old faithful Peter, had gleefully reported that their captors had been talking amongst themselves about a very big bomb or bombs having been dropped by the Allies somewhere in Japan itself. The fact that the Japanese were seriously disturbed lent more credibility to the rumour that things were hotting up for the enemy. Many planes had been seen and heard in the vicinity and there was a different atmosphere in the camp. The guards were jumpy, very jumpy, and the POWs didn't know how they were going to react from one day to the next. If it was true that the Japanese were close to losing the war, no one doubted that they were quite capable of lining everyone up and shooting them, or worse.

Wondering if the executions had begun, Abby went to the door of the hospital with her heart in her mouth, fearing what she would find. None of the POWs wanted to die – they had fought so hard for the last torturous years to live – but to be butchered rather than liberated would be the final twist in their uncertain existence.

As Abby stood in the doorway, one of the colonial administrators' wives called to her. 'The Japs are releasing Red Cross food parcels from storage. There's tea and sugar and powdered milk and loads more. Come and see.'

Abby stared at the woman. 'Did the guards say why?'

'I don't think so, but it's got to mean the war is over, surely?'

Abby hoped so, but there had been so many cruelties, so many times that the Japanese, not content with breaking the POWs' bodies through starvation and disease, attempted to break their spirits too with mind games.

Her heart thumping fit to burst, she went back into the hospital where all the patients who could sit up in bed were doing so. 'It's all right,' she tried to reassure the anxious sea of faces. 'Apparently the guards are distributing Red Cross parcels to us, that's what all the noise is about.'

Almost as she finished speaking, Matron Fraser walked into the ward. For a moment the matron stood surveying the scene in front of her. Although the hospital was called that by name, in reality it had been a place where most people came so that the nurses could make their last days as comfortable as they could. With no medicine or equipment, it had been a mockery of what it should have been. She looked at her nurses, their unhealthy, pasty and malnourished skin no better than that of the patients in the beds, their clothes hanging off their gaunt frames. Her girls, as she thought of her nurses, had carried on with their duties even on the days when they were feeling so ill themselves they could barely drag themselves from bed to bed. She was proud of every one of them.

Swallowing against the lump in her throat, the matron took a deep breath. 'The war is over and Japan has surrendered,' she said, and to the chorus of questions that followed she held up her hand. When it was quiet, she spoke again, purposely keeping her voice level and controlled. Control was very important to the matron. 'It appears the Allies dropped two bombs on the Japanese, the like of which has never been seen before. The second bomb tipped the balance and Emperor Hirohito called an end to the war. I understand from Major Fushida that the gist of the Emperor's address was that he had decided to end the conflict and that the Japanese would have to endure the unendurable and submit to the Allies.' The matron's voice hardened. 'Apparently the word "surrender" was never used in the Emperor's speech and the major made it clear to me that such a word is not in the Japanese psyche. 'Whether it is or it isn't, that is what they have done.'

The matron did not add here that the major had also said that there had been orders from his superiors – apparently coming from the Emperor himself – that all POWs were to be killed in the event of Japan losing the war. Major Fushida had looked her straight in the eye as he had said in his clipped and formal way, 'This will not happen in my camp. In my camp the prisoners are treated with kindness and respect.' She had wanted to shout at him, 'Kindness and respect? You've starved many of us to death and mistreated us in a hundred different ways, and you talk about kindness and respect?' But she hadn't. She had merely nodded, and left his presence without the customary bow.

'The major has assured me that medicines, bandages and mosquito nets will be brought here by one of the guards shortly. In addition we are being given soap and other supplies. I think this is a blatant attempt to gloss over the maltreatment we've all suffered at the hands of the Japanese, but I was not about to refuse any provisions.' She smiled. 'We will be going home, that's the main thing.'

Abby stared at the matron. So many times she had dreamed of this moment and imagined how she would feel if it actually happened. But the wild joy and excitement weren't there. In fact, she felt numb. The memory of those patients she had nursed in the camp and who had lost their struggle to survive was strong. Kurt, in particular. The transformation of an optimistic, brave and cheeky young man into a pathetic, tortured soul fighting for every breath would always remain with her, and she hated the Japanese. She did, she hated them, she told herself fiercely, and she would die hating them. And it wasn't just the few at present in the hospital who were suffering and desperately ill either. All over the camp men, women and even a number of the little ones were in terrible shape, suffering from severe malnutrition and deeply traumatized by what they had been through. Because of the lack of protein and roughage in their diet, they all had varying degrees of colitis and other bowel trouble, and Abby knew there were those who would have to go through the indignity of colostomies in the future, Hilda for one. If Hilda made it home, that was, which was doubtful.

She glanced round the room which was strangely quiet in view of the news Matron Fraser had brought, and the same kind of numbness she was feeling was reflected in other faces. They had been through so much and now it was over, how could they pick up the pieces again? The effects of their captivity, both physical and mental, would go with them into freedom; the enemy was still winning. They would go on winning.

And then the door opened again and Delia rushed in, an armful of toilet rolls held against her chest. 'Look!' She grinned at them all, her face alight with laughter. 'Look what the guards are dishing out! Victory rolls.' And as everyone stared at her, she giggled. 'That's what everyone's calling them, victory rolls. Every time we wipe our backsides it signifies the Japs have lost. How appropriate is that?'

Abby looked at her friend. Delia had suffered so much and still had problems internally because of the savage brutality with which she had been repeatedly raped. Delia was a shadow of her former self physically – they all were – and looked at least twenty years older than her actual age, but the Japanese hadn't been able to crush her spirit.

As others in the ward began to smile and nod and then laugh, Abby felt a release of something deep inside bubble up. She had been wrong. The Japanese weren't still winning, not when there were women like Delia around. Truth and justice, love and compassion, mercy and tenderness were qualities the enemy knew nothing about, but she had seen them enacted between her fellow POWs hundreds of times in the last years. Men and women making sure the children – and not just their own children – were fed even if it meant their gnawing hunger would drive them mad with pain for hours; individuals stepping up to take a beating in place of a friend because they knew the person concerned wouldn't survive such treatment; her fellow nurses, racked with pain sometimes and bent over like old women, going about tending to their patients with a smile and a kind word and a gentle hand, and most of all humour. A humour the Japanese didn't understand and could never understand, but which had provided strength and comfort on a thousand different occasions, like now.

Even the matron was laughing, her head thrown back and tears of amusement streaming down her weathered face, and for a moment Abby felt such a surge of love for her fellow POWs that it overwhelmed her. Hilda was in stitches, clutching her sides and chuckling helplessly, and Abby knew she had been wrong to let herself assume the worst. Perhaps Hilda would get better but whether she did or she didn't, she'd endure her lot with the fortitude and guts of a true Englishwoman.

As Abby met Delia's eyes that were still full of glee, she sent up a silent prayer of thanks for her friend, and for other friends too. They had done it, they'd survived the war, supporting each other and loving each other to the end. And now she would go home to Nicholas. Not today, not tomorrow, but she would be going home. The Japanese might have taken years of her life but she wouldn't let them take a moment more by dwelling on her hate and bitterness. One day she would deal with how she felt but for now it was too raw and consuming, and so she would consign it to the future. Package away the enmity and loathing into a place at the back of her mind. It probably wasn't a healthy thing to do; she was sure the psychiatrists would say she needed to bring her feelings out into the open and deal with them, but she couldn't. And so she would do the next best thing and bury them.

She walked across to Delia and flung her arms round her friend. Her voice thick with emotion, she murmured, 'We're going home, Delia. We're going home.'

'I know.' Delia hugged her back, adding, 'Some of the guards are drunk, Abby, and apparently we only had about eight days to live as the POWs were becoming a liability as far as the Japanese were concerned. We were going to be killed in groups of thirty.'

Abby recoiled. 'Even the children?'

'I suppose so.'

'So why didn't it happen when they knew they were defeated?'

Delia shrugged. 'Major Fushida didn't give the order, I should think.'

Abby nodded slowly. 'I don't know if he would ever have given it. He likes children.'

Delia looked at her sceptically. 'He would have given it. If the war had dragged on, he would have given it. They're not human, Abby. That's what we have to remember.'

'He released the antitoxin that time, though. And that was for the sake of the children.'

Delia shook her head. 'I know you think that and you might be right, who knows, but I think it was because he didn't want the diphtheria to spread and infect his guards.'

'But they had the medication to protect themselves.'

A closed look came over Delia's face. 'He didn't do it for the children, Abby. They're not capable of thinking like that. They're demons from hell, all of them.'

The matron's voice penetrated the silence that had briefly fallen between them, ordering her nurses to resume their normal duties and telling the patients that their food quota would be increased slowly so that their shrunken stomachs could accommodate it. Freedom or no freedom, the work of the hospital carried on.

Later in the day, the news spread like wildfire. Major Fushida had committed hara-kiri and fallen on his sword. The guards, intent only on saving their own skins, were attempting to melt away across the harbour and onto the mainland.

The war really was over.

Chapter Thirty-One

Abby stood hand in hand with Delia as the ship that had brought them home sailed into South-ampton at the beginning of November. The quay-side was packed and it was impossible to see individual faces in the throng, but even so Abby searched the crowds, hoping for a glimpse of Nicholas.

The two women stood on the deck of the ship which held mostly Allied troops and a few nurses like them, breathing in the cold damp air and the smell of England. It couldn't have been more dif-ferent from the tropical heat they had endured for so long and it was unbelievably welcome. They were home. Against all the odds, they were home.

They had been taken from Hong Kong on a hospital ship, a large old-fashioned vessel that was one of many such ships which had performed heroic tasks throughout the war, taking wounded men from various destinations and conveying them to base hospitals behind the lines. Originally a passenger ship in its heyday, the vessel had three tall grey funnels and vivid red crosses painted down both sides of her hull, and Abby had been amazed at the size of her. The ship had had five hundred and six beds divided into six wards on three decks, with a team of doctors, a matron and nurses to care for the sick. And to Abby's surprise, she had been one of them. After struggling along for so long, the day after the matron had told them the war was over, Abby had gone down with a severe attack of beriberi that had threatened her life.

She had been so sick she had drifted in and out of consciousness for some time and could remember little of the departure from the camp or her arrival on the ship. It was only after some days that the medication she'd received began to pull her back from the brink, that and the amount of fluids and puréed food she was fed in tiny quantities every so often. Once she began to improve, Abby became aware of the number of former prisoners who were too weak and ill to survive the journey to India where they were to be nursed back to health before going home. There were many burials at sea, when the captain would stop the ship and prayers would be said, before the body was respectfully and slowly lowered over the side of the ship.

Hilda had been in the next bed thanks to Delia, who had asked that the two women be kept together, and she had told Abby that they had been brought to the dock by ambulance and loaded onto the ship, whereupon the seriously ill were separated from those POWs who were still fairly mobile, although suffering the effects of malnutrition, tuberculosis and other problems.

Delia came to see them regularly, and through her they learned the stories of some of the men on board and what they had endured. The more Delia told them, the more Abby realized that Major Fushida had perhaps been one of the better camp commanders, cruel and unfeeling although he had seemed most of the time. In talking to the ship's nurses, Delia had heard tales of torture and ill-treatment in other camps in the Far East that beggared belief. Indian prisoners, who had been segregated from other POWs in special Asians-only camps by the Japanese, had been repeatedly tortured in an endeavour to force them to join the Japanese-sponsored Indian National Army, raised in Singapore.

'Apparently they were terribly brave and endured untold pain,' Delia had murmured to her two friends, tears in her eyes. 'The Gurkhas resisted to a man. But the awful thing is many of them had become unhinged by the time they were rescued. It's made me realize that what I went through isn't the worst that can happen. At least I'm in my right mind.' Then she had smiled wanly. 'Whatever that is.'

Abby had taken her friend's hand and squeezed it. Hans had tried to persuade Delia to marry him immediately and let the ship's captain perform the ceremony, but she had decided to wait for a while. She wanted to give him and herself, too, time to adjust to being free before they took such an emotive step, but Hans couldn't see her point of view at all. Privately Delia had confided to Abby that she needed to know Hans was marrying her for the right reasons, and not just because of their relationship in the camp. He was a very good-looking man, and had been wealthy in his own country before the war. There had been a childhood sweetheart somewhere in the background too, although they hadn't been engaged, let alone married, when Hans had gone away. 'If he writes, if he comes to see me when we're both in our own homes, and if he still feels the same after some months of being apart, then I'll marry him,' Delia had told her. 'But I want him to be sure. And I want to be sure too, after John. I still think of him, you know.'

'Of course you do, and you'll always remember him in a secret part of your heart. He was a lovely man,' Abby had reassured her. 'But that's not to say you won't be happy with Hans, or someone else if that's what you decide.'

Delia had wrinkled her nose. 'Who would want me looking the way I do now? I mean, we all look pretty poor, let's face it. My skin's ruined, my hair's thin and patchy and I look as old as my grandmother, let alone my mother. They're not exactly going to be queueing up in droves, are they?'

Abby thought of her friend's words now as the ship began to dock. Admittedly, thanks to the intensive nursing the POWs had had, along with food in abundance and all manner of tonics and creams and potions for their bodies and skin and hair, she and Delia and others did look much better than they had, but what they'd been through was still apparent.

What would Nicholas think when he saw her? She knew he loved her, but would he still find her desirable?

The thought wasn't a new one by any means. Abby knew she had changed, not just physically but in herself too. It wouldn't be too extreme to say that she was a different woman from the one Nicholas had known before they had been parted. The things that had happened, the atrocities she had seen and the last years as a POW had taken their toll in various ways, and she didn't think anyone who hadn't been a prisoner of the Japanese could possibly understand. Would it drive a wedge between her and Nicholas?

For all her joy that the war was over, she almost felt that a further battle was in front of her now. A battle to readjust to civilian life, normal life if you like. Because the last years had been far from normal. It had been wonderful over the last weeks to sleep on a real mattress, to have a proper bath with sweet-smelling soap and then dress in clean new clothes, to eat until she was full, to have no more humiliating bowing and roll calls, but it hadn't seemed right somehow. Not with so many of her friends and colleagues having died. The appalling brutality and cruelty she'd lived under for so long was no more, and liberation had certainly freed her body to a large extent and put her on the road to physical recovery, but she didn't feel liberation had freed her mind. It was a strange thing, and but for the fact that she knew Delia and Hilda

437

and many others felt exactly the same, she would have felt she was going mad.

'Look at all the Union Jacks,' said Delia at her, side, returning the waves of the crowds on the dock. 'It looks like the whole world's turned out to welcome us home.'

Abby smiled but said nothing. She hoped the ships returning some of the families who had been in the POW camps and who had young children, wouldn't be met by such a fanfare. Some of the little ones had been fascinated and excited by seeing shops and parks and ornate buildings in their recuperation period in India, but others had been much more timid. Scared of every aircraft flying over, speaking politely but only in whispers, and utterly terrified of anything remotely approaching violence, even just among the children playing together. If a crust of bread had been left, or if crumbs had fallen from the table where they were eating, these were the children who would scrabble about to eat them or put them in their pockets to save for later, even though they were no longer hungry. It had broken Abby's heart.

They had heard that the war had cost fifty-five million lives, lives that could never be recaptured, but there were others who still lived, men, women and children, whose painful and frightening memories would shape their lives in the years ahead. Abby prayed every night for the children, that their deep psychological damage would be healed, and every time she did so she thanked God she'd had no children who might have been caught up in the atrocities. But she did want children in the future, she thought now, and to date she had seen no sign of her monthlies returning, even though her weight had increased from a mere five and a half stone when she'd come out of the camp to just under seven. She hadn't been able to tolerate food as well as some of the other POWs at first, probably because she was still weak, and ill from the beriberi, and even now there were days when her stomach complained after a meal, and she felt nauseous and unwell. What if she couldn't have children because of the privations her body had gone through? Nicholas wanted a family as much as she did, and it would be a huge blow. Nicholas would stand by her – he was that type of person – but she didn't want him cheated of becoming a father because of her.

'I hope Hilda experiences this, Abby.' Delia's voice was soft and had lost some of its excitement. 'She has to get better. I can't bear the thought of her not making it.' Hilda had still been too ill to make the journey home with them.

'I know.' The two women looked at each other and then hugged tightly. Their bond had been forged in fire and they understood each other perfectly. Abby knew she would never have another friend who would mean as much to her as Delia did.

'Come on, let's get ready to disembark.' Delia giggled, her mood changing. 'Hark at me, "disembark". I sound positively nautical, don't I.'

As Abby followed Delia to the cabin they shared with two other nurses, she gave herself a mental rap over the knuckles. She had to stop crossing her bridges before she came to them. She knew it was one of the worst things she could do and it never helped her state of mind. Of course the future was full of 'what ifs' and 'maybes' – it was the same for everyone, and she couldn't deal with all the potential problems now. The first thing, the most important thing, was seeing Nicholas again. After that, for better or for worse, everything else would fall into place.

He hadn't expected there to be so many people at the dock in Southampton, which perhaps was naive in hindsight, especially because the first port of call by the hospital ships months ago had been Hong Kong. The trip had been recorded by cinema newsreels, when images of the emaciated human cargo had been broadcast to a horrified world.

Nicholas shook his head at the memory. He would never understand what had driven the Japanese. He'd been glad Gracie had been at his side that night, because he'd been beside himself with shock and rage, and shame, too, that he hadn't protected Abby.

They'd filmed the ship entering Hong Kong harbour, a destroyer in front of it and mine-sweepers either side because the seas were mined, and then had cut to the ambulances bringing the POWs from the camps. He hadn't been prepared for the sight that had met his eyes. Men, women and children who had seemed horribly deformed due to malnutrition and tropical diseases. He'd gazed in disbelief at their legs – the two little bones, the tibia and the fibula, hanging onto the huge patella with just a fragile coating of skin over them. It had been a scene of utter misery and he had wept openly, not knowing at that point if Abby was alive or dead. And later, when he'd received word that she was fighting for her life, he'd nearly gone mad with worry.

But now she had come home. Nicholas gazed up at the massive ship as it slowly manoeuvred into position at the quayside.

He knew Abby would still be suffering the effects of long-term malnutrition, and that she would be fragile and vulnerable to illness, but he felt that if he could just get her home under his care he could make her well. He would devote the rest of his life to making sure she was healed in mind and body, if she would allow him to.

He had written to her in India during her recuperation there, and the letter he had received back had been loving and had emphasized that he mustn't worry about her. She was getting better, she'd written, and soon the doctors would let her home, but somehow it hadn't sounded like Abby. It had been restrained, that was the only way he could describe it to himself, and of course after everything she had gone through that was natural enough.

He bit down on his lip, his eyes on the huge ship, as the doubts and fears that had tormented him since he'd read her letter came to the surface once more. Abby had told him that Delia had met someone in the camp, a Norwegian man, and that they had fallen in love. Had Abby met someone too? Was that the reason for the change in her? Someone who had supported her and been there for her through the last years, when he, himself, had been having it cushy at home? Did she resent that he had left her with no protection at a time when she had never needed it more? He knew now that John had been murdered, and he had grieved for his friend, but at least John had died an honourable death, whereas he had been shipped out of the mayhem like a lily-livered coward.

His hands had clenched into fists at his side and he forced himself to relax his fingers, one by one. He had never really had a faith as such, but he had prayed every night after her letter that she would forgive him.

It was beginning to rain, but he didn't even think about the umbrella that Gracie had made sure was in the car before he had left to drive down the day before. He had booked into a little hotel overnight, and reserved a room there for Abby's first night in England too. She was going to be exhausted after the journey and the excitement of being home, and they could make the drive to the north-east tomorrow.

He thought about the huge bunch of flowers in the hotel room and the champagne he'd arranged to be brought up directly they returned, and again his heart somersaulted. He would know when he looked into Abby's eyes whether she still felt the same about him. Her eyes had always been a window to her soul. This night would either be one of talking and sharing and laughing and crying as they began their new life together, or...

He straightened his shoulders, resolve bringing his head up. No, he wouldn't accept the 'or'. He would *make* her love him again.

'It will be fine, you know.' Delia had sensed something of what Abby was feeling and the reasons for it, and now she took her friend's arm as they began to walk down the gangplank. 'Nicholas loves you to distraction – everyone used to talk about it. He literally had eyes for no one else.'

Abby smiled and patted the arm in hers. She was so worked up now she couldn't talk about it. She just wanted to see Nicholas and look into his face. Then she would know. For better or for worse, then she would know.

There were reporters on the dock and cameras flashing and such a babble of noise that Abby's head was spinning. Delia's parents appeared, Mrs Cook elbowing other folk out of her way as she made towards her daughter. Delia had confided in Abby that her mother – much as she loved her – was one of the reasons she had wanted to get away from England when she had joined the QAs, and just seeing her now Abby could understand why. She wondered how the weeks and months ahead would be for Delia because her friend had told her she didn't intend to live in her parents' home for long. 'I couldn't go back to that, I just couldn't, Abby. Mother has to have everything done her way and runs the house on such a rigid timetable that you'd be in fear of your life if you were so much as a minute or two late down for breakfast or something. And that's fine, it's her house and she's entitled to do what she wants in it, but I couldn't put up with it now. Not like I used to.'

Abby found herself pushed aside by Mrs Cook when she reached them who, after kissing her daughter, moved Delia to arm's length and said.

in a voice similar to that of a sergeant major, 'Good grief, girl. You're as thin as a rake and wherever did you get this coat from? Green never did suit you.'

Just before Delia was enfolded in an embrace from her father who had stood meekly by – something Abby dared bet he was used to doing – her eyes met Abby's, and the rueful grimace she made said, 'I told you so. I can't put up with this for long.'

The two girls had exchanged addresses and knew they would be keeping in touch, but now, as Mrs Cook went to drag her daughter off, Delia shrugged away her mother's arm and said, 'I'll stay with you until you find Nicholas.'

'No, it's all right, you go.' Abby meant it. Much as she loved Delia like a sister, she wanted to be on her own when she first saw Nicholas. The QAs had been told that the matron-in-chief and other staff from the Queen Alexandra's Imperial Military Nursing Service would be at the quayside, but again, Abby didn't want to talk to anyone until she had seen Nicholas.

The two women hugged goodbye and Delia was escorted off by her mother, for all the world as though she was a prisoner being led from the dock of the Old Bailey. Abby gazed after her friend, not knowing if she wanted to laugh or cry. Poor Delia. Oh, she did so hope that Hans came through for her.

And then she turned her head and there Nicholas was. As tall and handsome as she remembered but looking so much older. For a breathtaking moment the world stopped spinning and everything else, the noise, the clamour, the push-ing and shoving, faded into insignificance. He was still fighting his way through the throng but his eyes didn't leave hers as he pushed forward, and then he was right in front of her.

She dropped the little overnight bag that she was holding and practically leapt into his arms, and then they were kissing as they had never kissed before, not even in the midst of wild passion. 'My darling, my darling, my darling...' His words were punctured by more kisses until they were both breathless and gasping, but she had seen what was in his eyes when he had first caught sight of her and nothing else mattered...

Chapter Thirty-Two

Christmas Eve, 1948

Abby held tight to Nicholas's hand, her body straining with the contractions that were en-deavouring to bring their child into the world. Outside the house it was bitterly cold, the snow thick and more falling in a Christmas-card land-scape, but inside the bedroom a coal fire in the small grate made it as warm as toast.

Abby had been in labour for fifteen hours and she was exhausted, but even before the midwife had told her she could begin to push, she'd sensed a change in her body. The knowledge that they'd soon see their baby had given her fresh

445

strength, that and Nicholas's encouragement. He had remained with her throughout the whole labour, whispering words of love, and not even grimacing when she'd crushed his fingers again and again.

The buxom midwife had been aghast that her patient's husband intended to stay throughout the birth, even if he was a doctor. The fact that Abby had said she wanted Gracie to be with her was fair enough; Mrs Wood was a woman, after all, and the midwife had been led to understand that she was much more than a housekeeper to the doctor and his wife and quite one of the family. But Dr Jefferson-Price attending his own wife? It wasn't decent. By rights, he should be pacing the floor downstairs and drinking whisky; that's what fathers did, doctors or not.

Gracie, who had heard exactly what the midwife thought when that good lady had come down to the kitchen earlier in the day for a bite to eat, would normally have agreed with the sentiment. But not on this occasion. This was different, as she had tried to explain although the midwife was having none of it. Nicholas and Abby were as one, in a way she certainly had never seen before, and it would have been unthinkable to both of them for Nicholas to be shut out of the birth of this longed-for child.

The midwife had shook her head and pursed her lips but had said no more, and Gracie had given up trying to explain. The midwife was old school, added to which, how *did* you describe the sort of love her lad and his wife shared? Gracie had to admit she had been a bit concerned, when Abby

446

had first come home, that everything would change and that Abby might – if not exactly resent her being around – want her kept at arm's length. But she needn't have worried, she thought fondly. As the old saying went, she hadn't lost a son but gained a daughter. And she loved the pair of them to the depths of her soul. And now their little family would increase to four, and oh, she prayed everything would be all right with the babby. The lass had been so poorly in the first year after she was home, and even when she'd got more on an even keel, she hadn't fallen for the child she'd wanted so much and had got herself into a right state about it.

Gracie was sitting on the other side of the bed from Nicholas and now she smoothed the hair from Abby's hot forehead and wiped it with a cool flannel.

Month after month Abby had cried on her shoulder when she had known yet again there was no babby, saying she was failing Nicholas, and although she'd tried to tell the lass that was nonsense, she knew it hadn't got through. Something had been needed to break the cycle of anxiety and stress, she'd seen that, and so she had gone out of her own accord and brought home a puppy for the lass shortly after the New Year, a dear little thing that Abby had instantly fallen in love with. And what do you know, within a month or two Abby was in the family way.

Gracie smiled to herself. She might be getting on in years but she still knew a thing or two, and Bailey had certainly proved himself to be a blessing. Daft as a brush half the time, mind you, and

447

the garden would never be the same again after the holes he'd dug, but a sweeter-natured animal you couldn't wish for and with a zest for life that was infectious. And by concentrating on the new 'babby' the lass had relaxed, and hey presto, here they were.

Abby let out a long deep groan, and as the midwife who was perched at the foot of the bed said, 'Aye, that's it, m'dear, go on, that's it, the head's coming,' Gracie leaned over Abby and murmured, 'That's me bairn, that's me bairn,' which was exactly how she thought of Nicholas's wife.

Abby was scarcely aware of her surroundings any more, but tired and spent as she was, Nicholas and Gracie's love was like a warm, reassuring balm. She could do this. Hadn't she been waiting and longing for this moment for the last three years, if not all her life? She gave everything with the final push, and as she felt the baby slide out of her body, the next moment was filled with the joyous sound of new life wailing its displeasure at being expelled from the nice comfortable place where it had been so happy for the last nine months.

Weakly, Abby gasped, 'Is it all right? Is everything all right?'

The midwife, not one for sentiment, pretended not to notice that the new father was crying unashamedly as she cut the cord and wrapped the baby in a blanket. 'All right? By, I should say so, lass. You've got a bonny daughter and she's got a good pair of lungs on her.'

'A daughter,' Abby murmured contentedly. Nicholas had so wanted a daughter, insisting that a miniature Abby whom he could love and protect and indulge would be the icing on the cake.

'Aye, and she's a beauty, lass. You can be right proud of her.' The midwife placed the small cocoon in Abby's arms. 'What are you going to call her?'

Abby looked into the tiny face in wonder. She *was* beautiful, with a shock of black hair just like Nicholas's. And her daughter looked back at her, showing small pink gums as she yawned widely and then shutting her eyes as though satisfied now she was in her mother's arms.

Abby looked at Nicholas who was bent over them, the tears still running down his face. And it was he who said throatily, 'Molly. It was always going to be Molly for a girl. Molly Grace, if that's all right with you, Gracie?'

They had dropped the 'Mrs Wood' and 'Doctor' shortly after Abby had come home. Abby had insisted it was far too formal and rather ridiculous with Gracie being one of the family.

Gracie nodded – it was all she could do as she was crying too now – but she hugged Abby and kissed her before gently stroking the baby's downy head.

'Well, she got here at last,' the midwife said cheerfully as she began to gather the dirty towels together. 'And she's a nice size, m'dear. She knew what she was doing in hanging about for a bit. She might have been a bit small if she'd come when we thought.'

The baby had been due well over two weeks ago by Abby's calculations, but as the time had come and gone without a sign of the impending birth,

Abby had begun to wonder if she was going to be pregnant for ever. For the last little while she had been hugely uncomfortable, and her worry that something was wrong, that her years as a POW had somehow affected the baby, had been strong. But here she was. Abby smiled down at her daughter. And she was so worth waiting for.

The midwife and Gracie made short work of changing the bed and tidying Abby up while Nicholas held his daughter, cooing and murmuring sweet nothings as though there was no one else in the room. It was magic to Abby's ears. He would be a wonderful father. He was a wonderful man altogether. And a great doctor. She'd been sorry at first that Nicholas's war injuries had meant he had been forced to give up the career he loved as a surgeon, but after a while she'd realized that as a GP he had a very special gift for dealing with people.

Once Abby was well enough, she had worked with him as the practice nurse and seen first hand how Nicholas's patients adored him. The practice had grown rapidly, and now Nicholas employed three more doctors along with a nurse, who had taken Abby's place once she had become pregnant, and a receptionist and office girl.

They had moved out of the old premises so that it could be converted to accommodate the expanding practice, and had bought a pretty little house on the outskirts of the town with a huge garden overlooking rolling countryside. Gracie had moved with them, of course, and was enjoying her twilight years fussing over Abby and Nicholas and Bailey. And now she had the baby too, and was going to thoroughly enjoy her role as honorary grandma.

Nicholas, at Abby's prompting, had written to his parents shortly after she had returned home. She had hated the idea that he was estranged from them because of her, and had urged him to let bygones be bygones, if only for the sake of any children they might have in the future who would miss out on having a grandmother and grandfather. They had received a curt and offensive letter in return, which had sealed the future as far as Nicholas was concerned. Gerald had written that he had made a new will, and a distant cousin was now his heir. If, in the future, Nicholas came to his senses and realized where his true loyalties lay, the will could be revoked, but only, of course, on the dissolution of Nicholas's disastrous marriage.

They had shown the letter to Wilbert when he and Robin and Rachel and the children had paid one of their visits, and her grandfather had summed up what they were all thinking in his own inimitable way. Handing the letter back to Nicholas, he had patted the younger man on the arm. 'Lad, I wouldn't give that beggar the drippings from me nose and you're better off without him. You've given him every chance as far as I can see, and you'll find he'll want you afore you want him. Wipe the dust off your feet and put it behind you now. You can lay your head on the pillow at night with a clear conscience, which is more than that evil old blighter can do.'

Nicholas had nodded. He hadn't wanted to write to his father in the first place and had only succumbed because Abby had become distressed about the whole thing, but the letter had convinced her that nothing more could be done so perhaps that was a good thing. Abby's family was his family, and Robin the brother he'd never had. He was content with that. More than content.

It was Abby who now murmured as she looked up at her husband, 'Will you write and let your parents know they have a granddaughter?'

Very gently, his voice soft, he said, 'No, my darling, I will not. Not even for you. I have drawn a line under my past life, and you and Molly are the present and the future. Please be with me in this, my sweet.' He had never told her what Gerald had said the last time he had come to the house, the year before the war had finished, but the word his father had used about any children he and Abby might have had severed something deep inside concerning his parents. 'Flyblow'. It was a word intended as a deep insult, much worse than 'bastard' or other such terms, suggesting something horribly tainted and defiled. Nicholas looked at his daughter's infinitely sweet and innocent face, the perfection and sheer beauty of her making him want to weep anew. He didn't want his parents within a hundred miles of his family.

Abby reached out and took his hand, his other arm cradling their daughter. 'I had to ask,' she whispered, 'but I'm glad you feel that way. I don't know if it's right to be glad, but I'm glad anyway.'

'It's right.' He bent and kissed her, his heart in his lips.

She reached up her arm and held him close for a few moments, knowing she was the most blessed

452

woman in the world. They kissed again, and when he had straightened, she said, 'Would you send Delia up? I know she would love to see Molly.' Delia had married her Hans eighteen months after she and Abby had returned to England, but the downside of this, to the two women, was that Delia had gone to live in Norway. Hans's family had extensive business interests there, and it wouldn't have made sense for them to make their home anywhere else. Nonetheless, Abby and Delia hated the fact that so many miles were between them, but due to Hans's wealth, which had been breathtakingly more than either woman could have envisaged, Delia and Hans had been able to come over to England several times since the wedding. Expecting that the baby would be born in the first week or so of December, Abby and Nicholas had invited the couple to come and stay over Christmas.

'Of course.' The midwife and Gracie were already bustling out of the bedroom, presumably to give them a few moments alone, and Nicholas tenderly placed the baby back into her mother's arms. Delia and Hans had been asked to be godparents, and were thrilled at the prospect. 'I love you more than words can say,' he murmured. 'Thank you for our daughter.'

'And I love you so much. We're so lucky, aren't we.' There was a catch in her voice.

'We are.' He didn't want to leave them, his wife and his daughter, but Delia had earned her place in sharing this time with Abby.

It was only a minute or so before Delia opened

the door and tiptoed into the bedroom. Abby couldn't help but smile at her friend's stance. 'It's all right, you don't have to walk on eggshells. I've had a baby, that's all.'

'Oh, Abby, she's gorgeous.' Delia was all misty-eyed and emotional, the more so because shortly before they had come over to England she had found out she was expecting their first child. 'And doesn't she look like Nicholas?'

'I know. There was him expecting a little girl would look like me and she's the spitting image of him. I haven't pointed that out to him yet.'

'He'd love her whatever she looks like. He's over the moon. He's just poured two *huge* whiskies to celebrate for him and Hans. Honestly, Abby, he's going to be pie-eyed.'

Abby giggled. She was feeling light-headed with happiness.

'But that midwife! She's a bit of a dragon, isn't she? When I said I'd bring a whisky up for us two she looked at me as though I was something the cat had dragged in. "It wouldn't be good for baby," she said. "Mother can have a glass of stout to help with the milk, but that's all." I mean, stout!' Delia wrinkled her nose in disgust. 'That's what old men drink. When I said that she went even more uppity. It appears she's been drinking it for years.'

Abby was rocking with laughter now and so was Delia.

It was a few minutes later, when they had oohed and aahed some more over Molly and Delia had had a hold of her goddaughter, that Delia murmured softly, 'New life, Abby. Despite all that has happened, new life has come into the world. There were lots of times in the worst of it that I didn't think life *would* go on, but it has. I just wish Hilda and John and the others could be here to see it.'

'I know.' The two of them looked at each other with perfect understanding.

Hilda had never recovered from her weakened state and had died in India, despite all that the medical team there had done for her. And so many more of their friends and colleagues had made the ultimate sacrifice. When she'd arrived home from the Far East, Abby had found out that Sybil had died from complications with her injuries, and dear Kitty had been killed while nursing the troops in North Africa.

Together, they looked down at little Molly, who was back in her mother's arms, as Abby said softly, 'I pray this war *was* the war to end all wars. That lessons have been learned. Ordinary men and women don't want to fight each other, do they? Not really. Most of the people I know just want to live together in peace, enjoying family life and bringing up their children the best they can.'

Delia was sitting at the head of the bed and now she put her arm round Abby's shoulders, and the two leaned against each other for a while, a host of memories flooding their minds.

In the grate the fire spat and crackled as it sent blue-red flames shooting up the chimney in a shower of sparks, and the wintry afternoon outside the window made the inside more cosy. Downstairs the faint refrain of Christmas carols being played on the wireless filtered through, and the two women heard Bailey barking joyfully in the garden, no doubt racing around crazily in the snow as he was apt to do.

After a bit, Delia stood up reluctantly. 'I'd better go and help Gracie with the evening meal and leave you to have a little nap. You must be exhausted.'

Funnily enough, now that Molly was here and all was well, Abby didn't feel as tired as she expected, but she did want a few moments alone.

Once Delia had gone downstairs, Abby slid out of bed, still with Molly in her arms. Walking over to the window, she looked out into the snowy afternoon, her mind skimming back over the years to that Christmas Eve that had changed her life for ever. She pictured her mother's face in her mind as she whispered, 'You've got a granddaughter, Mam. A little girl named Molly and she's beautiful, like you. I miss you, I miss you so much but I shall see to it she hears about the wonderful grandma she'll never meet. And her granda too. I know he loved you, Mam, and I hope you're together, wherever you are, and happy.'

Sinking down in the big old armchair set at an angle to the window and with Molly cradled in her arms, she gazed at the huge fat feathery flakes falling from a laden sky, and began to hum softly, and as she did so she could hear her mother's voice singing the lullaby that was part of her:

'There's snowflakes in the wind, my bonny babby,
Snowflakes in the wind, my little lamb,
But don't you fret, don't you cry,
The sun will come out by and by,

And till then I'll keep you warm, my bonny babby.'

'I love you, Mam. I always will.' Abby shut her eyes, a tear stealing down her cheek, and for a moment, just a moment, she felt the touch of a soft hand against her face and could smell the scent of the Pears soap her mother had favoured. She didn't open her eyes for fear the moment would evaporate, but a sense of peace that was from outside herself flooded her innermost being.

Her mam was still with her, she saw that now. She would always be with her because love was the most powerful force on earth. It hadn't been a final parting that long-ago Christmas Eve. She would see her mother again one day, she knew it now, in a place where death was just a memory and tears were no more.

She looked up as Nicholas entered the room, and such was the expression on her face that he came swiftly to her side, saying, 'What is it? What's happened?'

Abby had been unaware of the tears on her cheeks but her voice was trembling with emotion when she murmured, 'Nothing really, it's just that I see something I should have known a long time ago.'

As he bent down and lifted her and the baby out of the chair and carried Abby over to the bed, scolding her gently for getting up, she leaned her head against his breast and let the solid reassuring bulk of him envelop her. Just like her mother before her she had chosen her own path, and look at the special place it had led her to.

She let Nicholas take Molly and place her in

457

the crib next to the bed, whereupon the baby gave another huge yawn and then went promptly to sleep. They smiled at each other. 'She's had a busy day,' Nicholas said huskily, 'and so have you, my sweet. Now snuggle down and have a nap before Gracie brings your tray up.' He tucked her up in bed for all the world as though she was a little girl, and then kissed the tip of her nose. 'Sleep,' he ordered firmly. 'All right?'

'All right.' He had his hand on the door handle when she spoke again. 'Nicholas?'

'Yes?' He turned to see her smiling a smile so radiant it took his breath away.

'This is the most wonderful Christmas.'

'The start of many, my love. The start of many.' He shut the door behind him, leaving her alone with their daughter.

The room was bathed in deep winter twilight, and from the little fireplace the glow of the coals and the small flames licking round their base sent flickering shadows over the walls. The softly falling snow outside the window, the little grunts and snuffles the baby was making in her crib, and the comforting warmth of the bed were lulling Abby to sleep, but she fought it. She wanted to remember every moment of this day for ever and it was too precious to be wasted.

Drowsily, more asleep than awake, she began to sing gently: 'There's snowflakes in the wind, my bonny babby, snowflakes in the wind, my little lamb,' before whispering, 'I love you, Mam.'

She fell asleep with the words on her lips and a blissful smile on her face...

Epilogue

1949

The spring day was raw, but the hard, relentless snowstorms that had battered the north-east over the previous months was over, and a weak April sun peeped hesitantly from a grey-blue sky.

The building site some distance along the road from the Hemingway hospital in Galashiels was unusually quiet for eleven o'clock in the morning. The area was being cleared so that work could begin on the new housing estate scheduled to be built there. Some of the surrounding villages had protested about the ancient woodland and forest area being bulldozed, but their objections had not been upheld. With Hitler's bombs having caused an acute housing shortage by devastating large parts of the country, added to which no one had ventured into the dense woodland for decades as it was impossible to fight your way through the tangle of briars, brambles and other hazards, what was the loss of habitat for a few badgers and foxes and the like, compared to homes for men, women and children? it was argued. Reluctantly, the locals had accepted defeat.

But the objections had delayed the work from beginning when it should have done the previous year, much to the fury of the owner of the building firm, and by the time all the i's had been dotted and the t's crossed, winter had set in. This had meant a serious delay on the projected time-scale, something that was very much to the forefront of the owner's mind as he now stood talking to his foreman at the site.

Josiah Howard was a tough, hard-bitten and ruthless individual. He had dragged himself up by his bootlaces – as he liked to inform folk at the drop of a hat. He was immensely proud of having risen out of the slums of Edinburgh to the exalted position of town councillor, with a splendid detached residence in the suburbs and each of his four children at private school.

Josiah had a reputation, justly earned, of letting nothing and no one get in his way. In that regard, he was as formidable as the savage-looking bulldozer standing some yards away.

His steely-blue eyes narrowed, he stared at his foreman. 'You say it was only Barney Croft who saw this?'

'Aye, I told you, Mr Howard. Barney came to find me straight away and I told him to keep his mouth shut and say nowt to no one until I'd had a word with you. I sent the rest of the lads off for an early lunch. They'll all be in the Frog and Fiddler wetting their whistles.'

'Good, good. And you think this lad, Barney, will keep it to himself?'

'Oh aye, for sure, Mr Howard. He's a good lad, is Barney. Besides which, I made it plain if he opens his gob to the others he'll find himself out of a job. And no one pays better round here than you, Mr Howard,' the foreman added ingratiatingly. This had the added advantage of being true. Josiah had learned early in his rise up the ladder that loyalty could be bought. 'Barney's got a young family,' the foreman went on, 'and his wife had another bairn only the other week. He knows which side his bread is buttered, sure enough.'

'I hope so, Doug.' Josiah's voice was grim. 'I don't want any more delays on this damn project – it's turned into a white elephant as it is. If we'd managed to get the shells up before the winter we could have had the men fitting 'em out and what have you, rather than sitting round on their backsides on half-pay for weeks on end. I could wring the necks of those beggars who twittered on about wildlife and rare flowers and the rest of it. Half sharp, the lot of them.'

Douglas Banks nodded. He hadn't got to where he was today without being a yes man, and no one ever argued with the boss. There were rumours that the one or two who had tried it in the past had been made to regret it. 'So how do you want to handle this, Mr Howard?'

Josiah looked down at the bones. There was no doubt it was the remains of a human skeleton; there were even the remnants of what had been clothing still visible. And the skull was more or less intact and a few other bones were still there, but plenty of others must have been carried off by wild animals. He glanced at the leather belt still hanging from a branch of the tree under which the bones were scattered. 'Damn funny that, an old belt being stuck up there.'

'Perhaps–' Doug hesitated. He had learned over the years not to say too much. His boss could be a funny blighter.

'Aye?'

'Do you think he might have done himself in, if it was a man, that is?'

Josiah looked hard at his foreman. It was the

obvious conclusion but not one he was prepared to tolerate. A suicide would mean it was highly likely someone in the surrounding area had been reported missing at some time or other. The police might have to be involved, who knows? Not only that, but the law would put an embargo on the houses going ahead until they were satisfied they'd got all their damn clues or whatever they looked for. There'd be an investigation at the very least taking time, time he couldn't afford. Time was money.

'It's obvious what's happened here, Doug. Some old tramp thought it was a good spot to rest, and he likely died from cold or something similar. It happens. All the time. Right?'

'Right, Mr Howard.'

'There won't be a soul who will miss him or who cared about him when he was alive, or it wouldn't have ended like this. Right?'

'Right, Mr Howard.'

'And even if there was someone out there, what's the point in upsetting them now after all this time? Whoever he was, he's been dead umpteen years. Let sleeping dogs lie. No good comes of raking up the past, no good at all. Now you shin up that tree and unhook the belt – I dare say some animal took it up there – and we'll put these bits and pieces in the back of my car. You'll find some bags in there that the wife uses when she goes shopping. And then we'll get the men back to carry on working because nowt's happened here of any importance. Right?'

'Right, Mr Howard. What ... what will you do with the–'

'Don't worry about it, Doug.' It wasn't said in an arm-round-the-shoulder way, and the fore-man was quick to respond.

'No, no, of course, Mr Howard. I ... I'll get the ... the belt down then, shall I?'

'You do that, Doug. And tell Barney Croft there'll be an extra pound or two in his wage packet, all right? Josiah Howard looks after his own.'

As Josiah watched his foreman lever himself up the tree to unhook the decaying belt, he didn't question the decision he'd made. Whoever this bloke had been, he was nowt to him. And he dared say he was nowt to anyone else either. You reaped what you sowed in this life, and he wasn't going to let a few old bones spoil what he was about to reap in the way of this housing estate. When all was said and done, you had to look out for number one. It was what made the world go round, now, wasn't it...

The publishers hope that this book has given you enjoyable reading. Large Print Books are especially designed to be as easy to see and hold as possible. If you wish a complete list of our books please ask at your local library or write directly to:

Magna Large Print Books
Magna House, Long Preston,
Skipton, North Yorkshire.
BD23 4ND

This Large Print Book for the partially sighted, who cannot read normal print, is published under the auspices of

THE ULVERSCROFT FOUNDATION